Legacy

The Satellite Trilogy   Part III

L e e
D a v i d s o n

For Mom and Dad.
Your belief in me has opened more doors
than I could have ever imagined.
I love you.

Contents

Grant → Engaged to (Tate) → Elliott / becomes Satellite (older brother)
↘ Fischer (younger brother)

assignments → Ryder - Willow's son / Engaged to Hannah
↘ Meggie - lost children & Mom / Married to Brody

Friends in Progression:
Willow - Grant's Mentor / retired Elite / Married to Troy
Rigby - "toothpick guy" / dating Whitfield
Anna - Grant thinks of as little sis ⎫ dating
Owen - "bulldog" / LOVES being a Satellite ⎬
Liam - British accent / Satellite to Tate
Clara - crushes on Grant / artist

✻

✱ Elites ✱
Lawson - "chocolate Hulk" / works w/ Grant on Meggie's assignment
Billy - Giant / dislikes Grant / competitive
Reed - close w/ Willow / Gives advice re: Grant's coding issues
Evelynn - wants Grant ... badly! / Wears very little
Trina - hooks up w/ Grant briefly
Jackson - talks a lot / good natured
Morgan - newbie Elite / replaces Trina
✱

Leaders in Progression
Jonathan · Landon · Wynn

✱

In secret we met —
In silence I grieve,
That thy heart could forget,
Thy spirit deceive.
If I should meet thee
After long years,
How should I greet thee? —
With silence and tears.
—George Gordon Byron, When We Two Parted

Prologue

Jonathan Clement looks up from his desk at the sound of the squealing cart. "Good morning, Beaman."

"Morning. Today's shaping up to be another busy one." Beaman scans the lofty stacks of books on Jonathan's desk. The pop of his knuckles is concealed by the crackling fire. "That's probably a good thing, now that the Elites have become Legacies."

"Indeed."

Beaman stretches his arms before shifting his attention to the purpose of his visit. Having done this hundreds of times before, transferring the books from Jonathan's sturdy mahogany desk to his rolling cart takes less than two minutes, even though the middle stack is well above five feet tall.

When Beaman's finished, he rubs his hands together like he's removing dirt from them and bends close to Jonathan. "There've been rumors circulating about a rebellion of sorts brewing." He lowers his voice to a whisper. "People are saying Grant Bradley wants to go up against the Schedulers."

Jonathan's focus stays on the open book as his feather pen waves through the air with each written word.

"Are the rumors true?" Beaman, asks when Jonathan doesn't reply.

The feather pen stops dancing and stills completely when placed in the black ink bottle. Jonathan entwines his fingers while his eyes move along the books lining the walls of the ceiling-less, octagonal room. "I do not comment on rumors, friend." After offering Beaman an amiable smile, he says, "I'll see you tomorrow."

Beaman nods in acceptance of the not-so-subtle cue to exit and pushes his cart out the door.

When the squealing wheels can no longer be heard, Jonathan whispers, "Time will tell," to the empty room.

1. Still have that great sense of humor

My door flings open and in comes Willow. After enduring these typical entrances from her, I don't even spill my coffee.

Her ratty, brown bag thuds against the floor. "What's up, kid?"

As she makes her way toward me in the kitchen, the metal charms in her dreadlocks clink together. Willow, along with everything she owns, is loud.

I move over as she helps herself to a mug from the cabinet over the sink.

Her eyes scan me up and down, certainly in effort to gauge my well-being. She's such a mom sometimes. "You look decent, considering the Legacy news."

"Wow, no sarcasm. What's got you in such a great mood?"

She shrugs. "Troy and I just finished watching the baseball game."

I almost choke on my coffee. "Baseball?"

"It was a great game," she says like this shouldn't be such a stretch to believe she's into sports. "I'm becoming rather fond of the Red Sox."

"You've always had poor taste, so I guess that makes

sense."

The knock on my door interrupts before she can shoot back a reply. By her feisty expression, I'm sure it would have been a good one.

"Come in," I say over my cup.

A second later, Jonathan is stepping over Willow's bag. "Willow, Grant, very nice to see you both."

Willow's mood sinks, along with her shoulders. "Jonathan."

He reacts to Willow's sour tone with a tired smile. "Grant, I need you to begin your reading as soon as possible. It's imperative that we get you into Programming right away."

"What's the point?" Willow mumbles.

Oh, this should be interesting.

Jonathan raises his eyebrow. "Pardon?"

Willow balances the empty seashell coffee cup handle on her finger, making the mug sway back and forth like a clock pendulum. "What's. The. Point?"

Jonathan's voice remains calm. "The very same reason you went through Programming, of course. To recover memories."

"No Jonathan, the reason is different, or have you forgotten? Grant isn't reuniting with family. He, along with the other Elites, is only doing this because of what you made us do."

"Let's be clear: I did not force your hand, Willow." Jonathan uses a kinder tone than I would choose if I were being so blatantly challenged. I want to interject and remind them both that this mess is all my fault, but Willow's already running her mouth.

"Are you telling me if I would have said no, your little experiment would have never happened? Cut the crap, we both know if I had refused, you would have found someone to take my place."

As if Willow hasn't even spoken, Jonathan says, "Grant, please begin your reading as soon as possible." He turns to Willow and nods once. "Goodbye, Willow. Please send my best to Troy."

"Mmm Hmm." Willow's tone is flat, but her volume increases. "You must be pretty special, kid. Usually you'd just get a note to begin your reading," she says before the door clicks closed.

"Way to go. You ran him off before I could talk to him about Meggie again. Every time I tell him how much Meggie's kids were helping her, he ignores me. Why won't he listen—"

"What's he expect you to get out of Programming? More importantly, what the heck are you supposed to do with your time once you've completed the process?" She reaches over me and fills her cup with coffee.

Sometimes I wonder if Willow and I are even in the same room. "You should get over your beef with Jonathan. We could use his help right now."

The bottom of Willow's mug clinks against the counter and fresh coffee spills over the top. "I'd think you, of all people, would have the bigger problem with the guy. He's the reason the Elites are all in this mess."

"Him or me?" I mumble.

Willow squeezes my forearm. "You can't really believe this is your fault?"

I hop myself up on the counter. "Billy would disagree."

"The Elites are understandably upset. But if you're going to say this is your fault, you could just as easily say it is my fault. We all went along with Jonathan's plan." Willow grabs her cup and slurps her first sip. "He should have never asked that of us. He put us all in a rotten position."

"Look, I'm about as happy as everyone else with what's happening, but to continue your wrath against Jonathan—I mean, come on, do you think he knew it would turn out like this? It's Jonathan we're talking about."

"Exactly my point." Willow stares back at me for a second before rolling her eyes.

"Stop pouting. You're just looking for someone to blame. Use that energy to help me. Blame the Schedulers! We can fight them. Wouldn't you love to see Ryder again?"

"Of course I want to see my son!" Willow barks back. She sucks in a deep breath and lowers her cup to the counter.

"So help me. We've got Elliot, Liam, and Clara."

"Clara still wants you, so she doesn't count," Willow interrupts.

"That's not true. We're just friends."

Willow's narrow, doubting eyes force me to change the subject. "I think Anna's got Owen talked into it. Plus all the Elites are in, even Billy."

"Yeah, and what about your buddy Rigby? Why isn't he as enthusiastic as the others to join your futile scheme?"

I hide how much the blow about Rigby affects me.

Despite our misunderstandings about my feelings for Clara (or lack thereof) and how I knew his now-girlfriend, Whitfield, from sharing an assignment, Rigby was my first friend in Progression. I thought he'd have my back. "He says he has his reasons."

"Reasons like, *this isn't going to work.* I can see how you swayed the Elites. Without their blocking abilities, their futures as Satellites are over."

She may as well punch me in the face like she did when we first met. The sting would be the same.

"Sorry, I didn't mean..." Willow's words trail off.

I pull away from her when she tries to rub my arm. "No. You're right. I'm not a Satellite anymore. I get it. That's not why I'm fighting for this, though."

Willow's expression remains sympathetic. "You're a Legacy now. You're still an integral part of this program. Being a Satellite is forever, kid." Willow's grin is forced. "Certainly I've shared this with you before."

I shake my head. "Not when your ability is gone. I can't even perform maintenance. At least you still have that."

Willow turns away from me, using a coffee refill as an excuse despite her cup being three quarters full. "Maintenance doesn't require blocking. Listen, what you're proposing is career suicide for an active Satellite. Rigby's not an idiot. He knows that."

"So, you think our other friends are idiots for joining me?"

"No." She turns back to me with her full cup. "But I think they'll regret their decision."

I glare at Willow and she mimics my expression. After a minute, she softens, but I hop off the counter and step away when she tries to hug me.

"I get why you're doing this, I really do, kid. It won't work, though. This program, the whole establishment, it's bigger than you and me." Her voice raises as my proximity to the sofa grows closer. "You can't change something that has been working for centuries. It's impossible."

"Nothing's impossible." I can't believe I just said that. When have I ever been the glass-half-full guy? It's this horrid sofa. I know it. Not only is the thing too darn comfortable to part with, but now it's turning me into Willow.

"I respect your passion and even applaud you for it, but listen, kid, you're setting yourself up for failure and it pains me to watch. I love you, I really do, and if you were asking anything else of me, I'd stand by you with guns blazing."

If she's waiting for me to turn around, she's wasting her time. I have zero plans of unlocking my eyes from the bookcase.

"But this—kid, you've got to give up on this." Willow pauses. "You're putting the others in a bad position. You're messing up their careers. Please think of them. I know the Elites are done, but the others don't have to be. They still have their ability to block. They have futures ahead of them, Tragedies whose lives are dependent on them, destinies they have yet to fulfill."

"I have no intentions of ruining anyone's future, but I disagree with you. There are other options for Tragedies, other options for us. We would all love to see our loved ones, to visit them after our deaths, to help them heal." OK, fine, she wins. I'm only turning around to plead my case, though. "Willow, please, having you on board would mean everything. You know so many Satellites. People would listen to you."

Willow belts out a long, dramatic sigh. "We'll have to agree to disagree on this one."

I stare at the seashells on her mug, wishing she would change her mind, but knowing she won't.

"You'd better start your reading. You wouldn't want to make Jonathan mad."

"You don't have to go," I say, wanting more time to plead my case.

Cut the crap, Grant, you just like having her around, my brain argues.

"I should get back to Troy." She lifts her mug. "I'm stealing this, by the way. Actually, never mind, it was mine to begin with, so I'm just taking possession of what I already owned."

Her shoes make the funny flip-flop noise when she comes towards me. "Please think this through, kid. If for no other reason than to consider how this will negatively affect the others."

"Send my condolences to Troy," is my reply when she leans down and hugs me.

Willow pulls back and smacks my head.

I can only force half a grin because I want her to join us so badly.

She returns my expression with a full-on smirk. "Still

have that great sense of humor."

"Oh, that wasn't a joke."

She flip-flops herself to the door and scoops up her dilapidated bag. "Please think about what I said. Thanks for the coffee." She lifts her cup in a *cheers* motion before pulling the strap of the ratty bag over her head.

"Anytime," I mumble as she's closing the door.

I chew on the inside of my lip, missing her already. I settle deeper into the green cushion, wishing I had a diversion other than the black book staring back at me.

Is this really it, the end of my short-lived career? I spent most of my first assignment fighting against being a Satellite, and now I don't want the work to end.

This isn't the way things should be, the louder voice of truth says in my head, drowning out the other until every molecule inside me joins in. Just because we're dead, even if there is a bigger purpose for ourselves or our loved ones, we shouldn't be kept away from the people in our lives, the people we love who have made us who we are. We shouldn't have our memories stolen from us. No one deserves that.

I put my focus on the book. Sitting there on the trunk, the thing looks innocent enough, yet reaching for it, my fingers retract like the black binding will bite me. I realize I don't want to know what's in those pages. I don't want to know what the future holds for another Satellite—or what my future holds, for that matter.

The most disturbing reality yet hits me: someone is about to die, and someone's family is about to suffer. A lot.

Breathe, Grant, breathe.

I scoot to the edge of the sofa cushion and lean my elbows on my knees. Still staring at the book, I bite my thumb knuckle. Why is this so difficult?

A minute later, I'm up and pacing. Instead of allowing visions of what the unfortunate future holds for an unnamed family, I tune in to the movie reels of my short Satellite career: meeting Willow, training, learning to block, protecting Ryder, becoming an Elite, fighting against other people's blocks, helping Meggie, losing my blocking ability as a result of a supposed fiancée I don't even remember—

I snap the book up from the trunk.

Why can't I remember my life?

The word *Legacy* shines, holding my eyes there the same way I'm holding my breath. I want to remember my life.

Shouldn't I be happy? I'm about to go through Programming. I *will* remember my life soon.

Nerves make my stomach muscles clench. A minute later, my anxiety mixes with anger and the book is skating across the hardwood floor. After a light thud, the book stills at the base of the bookshelf.

What is wrong with me? This is good news. I'll complete this Legacy thing and be free to lead a rebellion against the Schedulers.

Yes. I'll complete this Legacy thing.

A coffee run to the kitchen and a few deep breaths later, I return to the living room where the book has magically returned to the trunk. Figures. Like my regular assignment books, the gold text is bracketed by wings. Line one: *Grant*

Bradley, line two: *Legacy*.

    Legacy.

    Legacy.

    Legacy.

    I reach for the book—still half-expecting the thing to bite me—and will my fingers to work. I manage to flip to the first page, which, like the cover, states my name above the word that is sounding more terrible by the second. Not because of what it means to me, but what it means to whoever is in this book. They will lose their memories and be separated from their family the way I was.

    I swallow and turn the page, which displays a handwritten letter from Jonathan.

Dear Grant,

    With enormous gratitude for your service as a Satellite and an Elite, I welcome you to the Legacy program. You have proven to be exceptional in your abilities. I trust you will continue performing increasingly amazing feats.

    I am hopeful you have found the Satellite program to be a rewarding experience. The coming weeks will be challenging. Like many others before you, I realize the task of letting go of this life may be met with a touch of resistance. Let me assure you that your future will hold abundant happiness, and that this closing chapter marks the beginning of a life filled with exceptional possibilities. If you should need assistance at any time, please do not hesitate to contact me.

All My Best,
Jonathan Clement

I look up at the ceiling. This is really happening, not just for me but for all the Elites. My teammates are facing this emotionally grueling task right alongside me, and I'm the reason why. Billy's initial reasons for wanting to kill me when I became an Elite were unwarranted, but now the guy actually has a decent motive. If I were him, I'd want to rip myself in half also.

Thinking about Billy, along with Lawson, Reed, Jackson, and Evelynn—yes, even Evelynn—having to give up the only life they know, I slam the book closed and send the thing back on the familiar course across the room.

⸺⸺⸺

After an hour of fighting the sick feeling that whatever is about to happen cannot be undone, progress—at least where Jonathan is concerned—is about to be made. Staring at the instructions to *place hand here,* I swallow.

On the page titled *The Present,* I reluctantly place my hand inside the outlined, perfect-fitting glove.

A gentle tug fools me into relaxing because a second later, my arm is all but ripped from the socket. My stomach churns as I twist through the tight, black space of needles that was just a book moments ago. The painful pressure, combined with the thought that this may well be my last trip into a book, makes my gut feel worse.

When the yanking finally halts, I'm not in the stone well of doors. Instead, a five by five circle of thick, frosted glass imprisons me. A lone, glass door is my only escape. Even if the door was clear and showed a landscape as magnificent as the courtyard, I'd still rather be locked in this small space for eternity than face what—or rather, who— awaits on the other side.

"Welcome, Grant. Please hold while I configure your settings," GPS Jeanette's voice pipes into the room. "Locating Satellite Christopher Timothy Baxter." After a short pause, three clicks like turning deadbolts echo in the glass room. "Please proceed through the door ahead."

Not caring that my fingerprints are going to mar the clean, glass knob, I also leave a large handprint on the door when I push through. As soon as my foot is over the threshold, I'm propelled out of the glass room at a speed that makes my stomach tighten. My eyes lock closed until the sick feeling subsides and my body stills.

A gasoline odor assaults me, so strong that it takes a few seconds to register the bad sound system. The low bass vibrates the plastic dashboard of the dated car. Alone, I dart around to look out the back window, but my attention quickly shifts when the driver's door creaks open.

A lanky teenager falls into the seat and the air rushes out of my lungs. He's so young, much too young.

I can't get my breathing under control.

Staring at him while he grips the steering wheel with

one hand and turns the key with the other does nothing to help diminish my panic being fueled by adrenaline. My focus turns to the gas pump to my right in hopes of getting my emotions in check. The rattling music cuts off, but begins again with the start of the engine.

Slowly, when my breathing has dialed down a notch, I turn back to the kid. Yes, kid. He hardly looks old enough to drive. He has his whole life ahead of him. Or should anyway. His shiny, dark fingernails match his black V-neck tee and leather pants. When he rummages through the center console, his black-lined eyes hold my attention. My hand goes to my chest and I rub circles into my breast bone to relieve the tightening. Overlooking his makeup and clothing, I mull over the much larger problem I'm facing: this kid's life is about to end.

We drive away from the gas station with him drumming on the steering wheel and bouncing his head along with the noise. The bass is not helping my nerves. Thinking of Willow, I remind myself not to judge anyone by appearance. She turned out to be pretty great, after all. Still, the word *punk* won't stop bouncing through my head. Punk or not, this kid doesn't deserve to die.

I force myself to look away from him while we drive through a town that feels both quaint and isolating. The majority of the license plates on the cars parked along the street are from Illinois. Turns out Chris and I were practically neighbors when I was still alive, though I don't recognize this part of the state or the narrow river we've just crossed. Rows of historic brick buildings house a few gift stores, a coffee shop, a pizza place, three bars, and a mix of homes.

About a mile out of the small town, an emptiness slides through my stomach. I want to grab a fishing pole and check out the river. I want to spend more time in a little town like this. Much to my disbelief, I'm homesick, I realize.

We turn into a neighborhood with mid-sized, well-kept houses, bringing me back to the mission at hand. Wouldn't it figure? The nice, middle-class family gets stuck with the rebellious guy who blatantly refuses to wear color. Oh, and he's about to die. To ice the cake of this unfortunate family, a hundred bucks says he hates his parents. Everything about him, from his eyeliner to his loud music, screams attitude.

Stop it, I scold in my head as a reminder to stop judging him.

I mimic his steps up the sidewalk and pause at the door, dumbfounded when he knocks instead of letting himself in. Guess this isn't his house after all.

A woman wearing a haphazardly wrapped bun of brown hair answers a minute later. Her smock is covered in a rainbow of paint smudges. "Hi there, Chris. Come on in."

"Hi, Mrs. Mackerly."

She opens the door wider so he can pass through, but closes it before I'm all the way in. I shake out my arms to rid myself of the uncomfortable feeling. We're greeted by a bright yellow foyer flaunting an eclectic collection of abstract paintings as bright as the walls. My eyes follow up the open staircase to the second floor above us.

"How was work?" the woman asks.

"Oh, you, know the usual. Saving the world one dish at a time."

I don't understand the comment, but Mrs. Mackerly's laugh says she does.

"Is Liv upstairs?"

The woman nods and unties her painting apron. "Go on up."

"Thanks. My parents said to tell you hello."

"Please tell them the same for me. How's your dad feeling?"

Chris pauses his game of two-at-a-time step hopping and turns to the woman. "A little better. They say he's about over the infection."

"I'm glad to hear that. He's had bad luck this year."

"His kidneys just can't keep up with him." Chris's voice is humorously cheerful when paired with his death-inspired threads.

Mrs. Mackerly nods at his light comment. "Well, if your family ever needs anything at all, Liv and I are happy to help."

"Thanks," Chris says and bounds up the rest of the steps.

Where is all the emotionally tortured talk to match his clothing, I wonder as I follow him up the stairs.

Chris lets himself into the first door on the right. "Hey beautiful," he says to the girl who must be Liv.

"Hey yourself. How is Benghazi Grill's employee of the month, and more importantly, my favorite dish washer?" From her relaxed position on the bed, her too-sweet voice doesn't match her look, which has come straight out of a Tim Burton film. Like her boyfriend, she's clad in all black with the exception of her tights, which include thick white stripes circling her thin legs. The red yarn holding her two black braids in place below her shoulders is the only other piece of color she wears. Even her fingernails, eyeliner, and lipstick are the same coal hue. I'd probably find her attractive if I could see her face, and if she changed clothes.

Needing a distraction while they kiss—because by the looks of them, they won't be stopping any time soon—I survey the room. The music choice isn't my cup, but at least the female voice coming through the speakers is singing more than she's screaming, and in a lower volume than Chris prefers.

When Chris and Liv conclude their greeting, Liv plops down on the pink bean bag chair. The pop of color seems out of place amidst the dark curtains, bedding, and posters adorning the room. I step closer to the dresser when Chris walks towards me. He stops at the bookcase and thumbs through the paperbacks.

Liv stands and straightens her extra-long, black T-shirt. "My dad called today."

Chris's finger stops on one of the worn books and he clears his throat. "What did he say?"

"How sorry he is that he's been away so long, he misses me and wants to see me. You know, all the usual things."

Unbeknownst to Liv, Chris makes a decent effort in putting away his sour face before he turns. "Yeah? What did you say?"

"Pretty much the same as I always do, that I'm really busy with school and my music. Seriously, what does the man expect out of me? He calls, what, every six months after avoiding my voicemails and then wants to be my best friend?" Liv's voice picks up in pace and volume. "I wish he'd just go away forever. Doesn't he realize popping in and out of my life only makes our relationship worse? Besides, he only sees me out of guilt anyway."

Chris slides a switch on the radio and the music stops. He plops down beside Liv on the overstuffed bean bag, looking funny against the bright pink vinyl. "He's missing out on more than he'll ever know."

She leans into him. "I'll never understand how he could replace Mom with a girl who, by all rights, could be my sister. Oh, and get this: he asked if Jess could take me shopping! Can you believe that? I'm surprised she didn't want to go clubbing." Liv pauses and her anger morphs to sadness. "I just wished he loved me, you know?

"Liv, he loves you." Chris plays with one of her braids until she smiles.

I shove my hands in my pockets and look at the strange jewelry on her dresser to avoid watching another lip-lock marathon. Not understanding who would wear a giant eyeball ring, I turn to the picture frame showcasing her and Chris. Liv's laughter from the fish face Chris is making is so genuine the photograph seems animated. I find myself softening to the guy even more.

And then I can't breathe. The horror sets in once again that he's dying and this poor girl will be alone.

"I love you," I hear Liv whisper through my panic.

"I love you, too," Chris replies.

After an hour of Liv and Chris talking about an art class she's taking and their concert plans next week, I've calmed down from my panic attack. Chris announces that he has to get home and my stomach does an uncomfortable somersault. If I wasn't a ghost and he could actually hear me, I'd tell him to stay and spend as much time as possible with Liv. My pro-love stance proves I'm becoming soft. I don't waste my breath telling him to stay, and instead, it's off we go.

Before we make it out of the house, Chris stops and talks to Liv's mom, who's traded her painting smock for a wine festival T-shirt. She invites Chris to stay for dinner. He graciously declines, explaining he ate during his work break and his family is expecting him home. There's no arguing that the guy is polite.

Flying behind Chris's beat-up car on a clear afternoon like this would be my preferred method of travel to escape the rattling bass, but the smelly, white smoke from the muffler changes my mind.

After the ten-minute ride, we're walking into another well-kept home, though this one is older and larger.

Chris slumps his shoulders and swings his arms until his backpack slides down his long body. The bag then greets the counter with a heavy thud. "Hey, Mom."

"Hi, hun," is the reply from the next room as Chris is

nearly mauled by an excited, medium-sized, tan mutt.

As I follow Chris into a dining room taken over by piles of green fabric spread across the table, the dog's interest has moved from Chris to me. The dog barks and it's cropped, wagging tail makes the animal's entire back side a moving pendulum.

"Rex! That's enough!" Chris says over the barking and then grabs Rex's collar and pulls him away from me.

The dog pulls against Chris in effort to get to me. He can see me!

I step towards Rex in hopes that he will settle down. Chris releases his collar and the dog goes to my jeans and frantically sniffs my knees. I try to push him away, but my hand ghosts through his floppy ears.

Thankfully, Chris overlooks the animal's odd behavior and directs his attention to his mom. "You're sewing." His tone is one that says this hobby signifies something unpleasant. "How's Dad?"

The dark-haired woman's eyes are red when she lowers her glasses and looks up from the machine. "He has to begin dialysis." When she fails at offering a sincere happy face, she turns her attention back to the sewing machine. "If you don't mind, dinner looks like it's going to be a free-for-all tonight. I'm not feeling up to eating. There's cereal and soup in the pantry if you're hungry. Your dad's quite worn out from the doctor visit, but you should say goodnight."

After a long sigh, Chris nods and kisses his mom on the cheek. "No worries about dinner. I ate at Benghazi's. Let me know if your appetite comes back and I'll make you something. Love you."

"Love you, too, hun and thank you."

I follow Chris up the steps with Rex's oversized paws thundering behind us. Chris pauses before opening the door at the end of the hall. He looks older than he did a minute ago.

Chris, Rex, and I parade into the dark room. The blackout curtains are doing an impressive job at concealing the late afternoon sun.

"Hey, Dad." How the heck does the kid muster such a cheerful tone? I'll admit, his acting is award worthy.

The man under the covers squints against the hallway light cutting through the darkness.

Chris lowers his voice to a whisper. "I'm sorry, did I wake you?"

When the man tries to sit up, Chris hurries to help him.

"My water," the man's low voice croaks in the darkness.

Chris holds the glass while his father takes slow sips from the straw.

"Thank you," the frail man whispers when he's done and reaches for the lamp on the bedside table.

Chris beats him to it and clicks the light on. "Mom told me," is all Chris says.

The dog follows me to the foot of the bed and sits beside my leg. When I move to the left because his tan fluff is ghosting through my calf, Rex scoots closer.

Chris's dad takes a labored breath. "Doctor Graff says the dialysis can be quite effective in some cases."

The conversation stops when a tall girl, maybe a year or two older than Chris, joins us. The dog leaves my side to greet her. She's pretty with clear skin and defined cheekbones. The resemblance to Chris is strong, despite the fact that she wears less makeup and her clothes are earth-toned.

"I thought I heard you two in here." The girl reaches down and scratches the dog behind it's ears, prompting the dog to stand. The canine's backside, once again, becomes a swinging pendulum.

"Hi Sweetie. Come in." The pain of speaking is apparent in the man's pale face.

"Need some water?" The girl crosses to the table beside Chris and reaches for the glass, but her dad declines by raising his hand.

The dog thunks to the ground beside me with his extra-long tongue hanging out of the side of his mouth. He looks up happily and acts as if everyone else in the room can see me, too.

"You two better get your homework done. School night, you know."

The girl leans down to give her dad a kiss and then switches off the bedside lamp. "You know we never have homework on Sunday," she whispers in a humored tone like this is an old joke. "Night Dad. I love you." She disappears into the rectangle of light and her footsteps quickly fade down the hall.

Chris follows the path of his sister. "See you in the morning."

"Son?"

Chris's silhouette in the doorway becomes motionless. "Yeah?"

"How's Liv?"

His dark form instantly changes from a stiff posture to a more relaxed stance. "She's good. She said to tell you hello."

"I hope she'll visit soon."

"I'll bring her by tomorrow."

"Treat her well, son."

Chris's posture morphs back to rigid, probably because the order sounded an awful lot like a last request. "I promise I will." Chris reaches for the doorknob. "I love you."

A strange pulling sensation grabs me. In half a second, my vision blurs as I go through Chris's body and the bedroom door. Through the sounds of the whooshing air, I swear I could hear Rex barking behind me.

When my boots feel braced on solid ground, I right myself and look around the glass room.

"Please return after break," GPS Jeanette announces through an invisible speaker.

All too familiar with the next bit, I'm braced for the ride this time. I'm sucked out of the room and into needle-scrapping darkness with quick jerk. When the pressure releases, I'm flung out of the book, which hits the floor and flops closed.

After falling into the sofa cushion, I run my hands along the top of my thighs. My mind gets stuck on futile thoughts, like how Chris will die. He's too young. Much too young.

The distraction of my calimeter is welcomed, forcing my mind off Chris, or rather, the awful scenarios playing through my head of what will become of his family.

2. The last time I broke a rule, you nearly burned to death

I try to open my fists on the way down the hall. Why am I even bothering to code? Relaxation is meaningless without any Tragedies to protect. Then again, forgetting about Chris for a short time is a decent idea. With each step, though, my mind repeats the bad word in my head: Legacy. Yes, coding is probably a good decision.

Legacy.

Damn.

Legacy.

I think I'm going to be sick.

Catching my breath, I sit on the black mat in the coding room and stare at the mirrored wall. I expect to look older because it feels like my life is about to end. My jawline is sharper than usual from my clenched teeth and my dark hair sprouts in all directions. I don't bother with my hair, but try my best to relax my jaw. Since I'm not being reunited with someone, I can't help but wonder what the heck I'm going to do with myself.

Breathe, Grant, breathe.

I close my eyes and am grateful when I'm pulled into

my happy place in under a minute. My tired muscles unwind until they feel like goo. Despite being mid-summer, here in my make-believe world, the autumn air is crisp and cool. My lungs fill over and over and I sink more comfortably in the metal seat of my tree stand. A few minutes after the monster buck enters the field, I blink my eyes hard to send myself back to the coding room.

Legacy.

The word crowbars itself back into my head and my body tenses. So much for the glorious muscle state I was enjoying moments ago.

After changing clothes and pouring a cup of coffee, I head down to Benson, hoping I'll have time to eat and catch a few words with some of the Elites. I wonder what they're making of this mess.

The image of one Elite in particular swirls in my mind. Billy never liked me to begin with, which he continued to prove during our Elite training sessions. He was awful to all the Elites, I remind myself and push away the image of me twirling like a ballerina under his blocking spell. His distaste for me was apparent during my first week as an Elite and that was before he had any real ammunition to hate me. Now he's going to want to detach my head and punt it like a football, no doubt.

My feet move fast as I walk into Benson and glance at my usual table in the back. Owen and Anna are about to sit with their food trays. Seeing Anna calms me. I'd much rather reminisce about my first meeting with her when we were both newbies in Progression than to think about Billy. Owen destroys my calm moment as usual when he leans down to kiss sweet, olive-skinned Anna. He's always been like a bulldog, but why he insists on displaying their love in public like she's his favorite rawhide is beyond anything I'll ever understand. I look away for fear that their clothes will fall off. I don't need the image of a naked Owen burned into my retinas for all eternity.

Halfway through the room, I stop and look around, confused by the low murmurs that have now cut to silence.

Dead, pin-drop silence.

My heart rate quickens from the stares cutting through me.

Elliott's eyes meet mine as he pulls a chair out beside Anna. He shrugs his shoulders in a sympathetic gesture. This makes me feel bad for saying I didn't care that his sister was a Rebellion. Still, I doubt I'll ever believe the girl could have been my fiancée. Me engaged? The thought is absurd, though I'm unsure why this makes my gut so queasy. Certainly the feeling has to do with the unwanted attention that has settled on me.

I force myself forward, and in effort to ignore the gawks and whispers, I count the eighty three strides it takes to the buffet entrance. When *Legacy* is hissed by a few people, I can feel the blood drain from my face.

Because I really want steak, I'm nearly jogging through the doorway that opens to the best buffet in the world. Thankfully, the volume in this room is heightened well beyond what was happening on the other side of the entryway.

I push my way around three girls who freeze when I say excuse me.

Oh, come on.

"I guess you've all heard the news?" *What am I doing?* "You're probably aware of the rumors, as well, then?" Yep. They are no doubt aware. Their open-mouths say so. I consider making a getaway, but decide since I've already confirmed my insanity, I may as well go all out. "The rumors are true. I'm a Legacy. So are the other Elites. We're going to confront the Schedulers." I almost laugh at the dubious expression shared among the surrounding Satellites. "If we have more numbers, they're more likely to listen to us. Things can be different. What if you could watch over your own family? Wouldn't that be better than being a Satellite?"

Crickets…

Crickets…

Crickets…

"Told you, kid."

I turn toward Willow's voice while the crowd morphs back to life and keeps a cautious distance from us.

"They act like I asked them to go on a puppy-killing spree," I whisper to Willow.

"They love this life," she replies at a normal volume.

Grabbing a plate, I stalk past the vegetables, breads, and pastas to the meat section. My hand strains under the weight of the six thick slabs I've piled on my plate.

"If you're going to use the old 'told you so' act, don't bother," I say because I can feel Willow behind me.

"I'm just trying to be helpful."

I set my plate on the narrow counter in front of a pan of mashed potatoes and turn to Willow. "Helpful?"

"Yes, helpful. And honest. There's no way you're going to talk a Satellite into career suicide."

"Is that so?" Feeling the challenge, my mind scrambles for a way to prove her wrong. An idea surfaces, an extremely embarrassing idea, and my mind races for something—anything—instead. It's not like the idea would even work.

"Told you so," Willow says after a minute of silence.

Needing to wipe the smirk off her face, I step around her and pace across the room, certain the desert table is far enough away for anyone to have heard my failed entrance speech minutes ago.

"Excuse me?"

The spiky-haired girl doesn't answer, but her fingers freeze over the tray of brownies, proving she's heard me.

Before she comes to her senses, I reach over the table and grab her hand. "I'm Grant."

Her limp arm shakes like a noodle as I pump it up and down. "Vanessa."

"Would you be willing to talk with me for a second?"

Vanessa turns to grin at a group of girls by the cake table.

"I'm trying to get some people together for a...uh... meeting." I can't believe I'm doing this. "Could you help me?"

Just when I'm accepting the reality that Willow is right as usual, Vanessa nods.

"Really?" *Pipe down, you sound like an idiot,* my brain says. "Great. I mean, thanks. We're going to meet over our next break. Do you think you could bring some friends with you?"

"Sure." She becomes more animated. "Grant."

OK, weird. "Cool. Bring as many people as you can. Oh, ah, let's meet in the back corner of Benson." I point my thumb over my right shoulder to clarify which side of Benson I'm referring to.

"Around where you usually sit?"

Now we've gone beyond weird and both she and I know it. "Same general area, yeah, but maybe a little further back so we have some privacy."

She nods in a spacey way that makes her look drunk. I back away, knowing the forced smile on my face would be better paired with a straight jacket.

Willow smacks the back of my head and follows me back to the steak table. "What in Grace's name are you doing?"

I grab my tray. "Who's Grace?"

"Stop with the jokes! What just happened there?"

"I just recruited someone." I can't hide my enthusiasm, and for good reason. Since becoming a Legacy, nothing has gone as I've planned. "And possibly a few of her friends."

Willow follows me back to the table, ranting. "You flirted your way in. That's cheating!"

"Whatever," I argue. "I don't even know how to flirt."

"Like Hades! That was flirting at its best. And now that poor girl is going to run to all her friends and gather up a bunch of Grant groupies."

I'm glad she's behind me so she can't see my face,

heated from embarrassment. "I just asked for help. If we stand any chance of being heard by the Schedulers, we're going to need more people."

"Not *we*. You."

I stop beside a vacant table for three. "Fine. Me. Why are you so against this?"

Willow sets her tray on the table and puts her hands on her hips. "Listen, kid, I think you may have swan-dived off the reality cliff here. You're talking about the Schedulers. The odds of them listening to you are about as great as an earthquake hitting this place, even if you have hundreds of others backing you. I don't want to see you get yourself, or anyone else for that matter, in trouble."

"Haven't you ever done something a little crazy?" I look at the colorful inked design on her toned, upper arm "Never mind. Come on, Willow, live a little. Break a rule or two. Stand up for what's right."

"The last time I broke a rule, you nearly burned to death." Her eyes dart around the room. Before I can question what she's talking about, she lowers her voice. "Rules are set up for our protection. This establishment is put in place for the well-being of others. It may seem unfair to us, but the bigger picture is more important."

My tray joins Willow's on the vacant table. "Meggie's kids helped her. If you could have seen them, you'd understand. You and me, the Satellites, we are all strangers to our Tragedies. They can't feel us there."

"We have the advantage of blocking. How will Meggie's kids help her if she needs to be pointed back on track? They don't have her book. They know nothing about her future."

"They don't need to block. They have a connection and they have common sense. They can actually speak and be heard, unlike us. We have to force ourselves in." I use a calmer voice. "I get what you're saying, I really do, but if you saw how Josh saved Meggie—Willow, I was useless. Meggie would have required multiple blocks throughout the day. Not just that day, either, but for the months ahead. I'm certain of that. Josh shows up, tells her he's there, and she calms down, just like that. How can you stand here and tell me that's not better?"

"How do you know it will always be that easy?" Willow fires back. "What if it doesn't work that way for everyone? What if being with Meggie has negative effects on Josh?"

"On Josh? Willow, wait!" I say to her back as she jogs towards the lobby.

I decide against going after her because arguing with Willow is like bottling air. Instead, I shoot a nasty look at the tray she left behind, grab my own, and walk to the table.

"What's with Willow?" Owen asks when I slump into my chair. Smoothing his hand over his head is an unnecessary gesture. His oil-black hair undoubtably shares the same molecular make-up as plastic.

When I don't answer, Owen, Anna, Clara, and Elliott take the hint that I'm not feeling overly chatty and return to their game of Sats. I'm grateful for friends who know me well enough to let me sulk. I prod one of the steaks on my plate, thinking of Meggie.

Elliott throws his remaining cards down when Anna

wins. "When are we going to go to the Schedulers?"

The foursome look my way for an answer.

"Soon, I hope. Without more people, I doubt they'll take us seriously, but I think I may have a few others on board."

"I've talked to some people, too," Elliott says.

"Any interest?"

Elliott shrugs and we all stay quiet for a couple minutes.

I push my tray forward and stand. "Have you seen any of the Elites?"

"They were in the lobby earlier." Clara twists the tab of her soda can and straightens her back. Her pink sweater hugs the curves of her supermodel body and her blond hair falls over her shoulder, making me wonder why I'm not interested in being more than friends.

I glance at Elliott. Could his sister have anything to do with my lack of feelings for Clara? My brain assures me of the impossibility. Even if I forgot my life, I'd have remembered being engaged. Willow remembered her husband and daughter, after all, just not much about them.

A twinge of doubt enters my head recalling that Willow didn't remember her son, Ryder. That's different, I convince myself. Willow died during Ryder's birth, so she didn't know him well anyway. If I loved someone enough to marry her, there'd be traces. There'd have to be.

I ignore the uneasy feeling in my gut and we all agree to meet in the back corner of Benson at next break. I ask if someone will tell Rigby our meeting place if they see him.

Only when I catch Owen staring at my hand do I realize my fingers are rubbing circles into the scar on my chest. I pull my hand away just as quickly as his eyes dart to the table. "Sure, but I doubt he'll show."

I hate that Owen's right. "Why is he so against this idea?"

"He likes his life here." Owen's lowered volume is unusual for him.

"He'll still have a life here," I argue.

Hugging herself, Anna pulls at her red T-shirt sleeve and shoots Owen a sideways glance. "Maybe."

"Instead of going to an assignment, we'd be helping our own families. Nothing else has to change."

Clara appears to be trying awfully hard not to open her mouth.

"Do you disagree?" I ask when she turns her focus to her soda can.

Clara keeps her eyes lowered, showing the sparkles in her silver eyeshadow. "I hate to argue, but you can't be certain of that. I mean, what if the Schedulers decide to relocate us."

I shake my head. "Why would they do that?"

Clara bites into her glossy lip. "Well, for one thing, we wouldn't need to be close to the courtyard for training. We wouldn't necessarily need our mentors anymore, either. Who's to say they wouldn't house us somewhere differently, apart from one another?"

"That's your argument for going against what we all know is the right thing to do?"

Clara pushes further back into her seat, making me

regret my harsh tone. "Rigby has settled into a nice life here with Whitfield. Maybe he's afraid he'll lose that. I don't know. I'm just saying there are a lot of uncertainties with this plan."

Feeling slighted sours my attitude. "No one said you had to join us."

Clara's chair screeches across the floor. "That's not what I meant!" she yells after me, but I'm already stalking out of Benson. Maybe she's right. We have no idea what changes this could prompt. Still, it's the right decision. If I'm the only one who can see that, then I guess I'll be challenging the Schedulers on my own.

I head out to the lobby on a mission to find at least one of the Elites. The volume mutes at each table I walk past. I consider trying to recruit more people, but already feel uncomfortable being the focus in the large crowd. Maybe Rigby and Willow are right, maybe this is a bad idea. Or an idiotic one, anyway. How are we going to get to the Schedulers? I remember the way through the maze of hallways about as well as I remember Astronomy.

I force this detail from my brain when I see Jackson talking to Evelynn, Billy, and Lawson. Surrounded by the threesome, he could pass as a child. Size-wise anyway.

"Oh, hi, Grant. Good to see you. Are you OK? You look kind of pale," Jackson says in a speed only he can deliver when I park myself on the floor beside him. "I was just telling these guys that I think I have a few people interested in joining us. Well, maybe not entirely interested. They want to know more. That's a start, right? If we can get people to listen, I think they'll be in. It's a really great idea—"

"For those who can no longer block," Billy says, cutting Jackson off in a demeaning way.

Jackson's mouth pops closed and his face turns as red as his plaid, flannel shirt.

Evelynn flips her shoe on and off of her right foot, causing the thin, five inch heel to click against the marble floor. "No offense, Jackson, but Billy's right. Why would anyone do this if they still have their ability?"

"Would you?" I ask her.

"No way," she says without hesitating.

I try not to let this deflate my tone. "I think I have a few others interested. We're going to meet in the back corner of Benson at break. Does that work for you guys?"

Evelynn pouts. "Seeing as training is out, what else do I have to do?"

I hit the face of my calimeter, wishing I had more time to talk with them.

Billy cracks his knuckles. "This blows."

Thinking of having to visit my Satellite, Chris, again, I couldn't agree more. At least Billy didn't try to maul me. Yay for small victories.

We separate into our own hallways after agreeing to meet back up later. Once I'm off the elevator and GPS Jeanette has bid me farewell, I trudge through the empty corridor to my room.

On the sofa with the book in my lap, I stare at my gold name on the cover before talking myself into opening it.

"Like a glove," I mumble when I finally work up the courage to place my hand within the bold outline. When the discomfort I've come to know and loathe is gone, I stand upright in the five-by-five room.

"Welcome back, Grant. Please hold while I configure your settings," GPS Jeanette's voice seems to bounce off the frosted glass. "Locating Satellite, Christopher Timothy Baxter."

Ding.

"Please proceed through the door at this time."

After three deadbolt-sounding clicks, I turn the glass knob and my body is sucked over the threshold like before.

Though my body has stilled, I'm slow to open my eyes as if this will help me stay invisible to Rex, who has entered full on postal mode. Why I feel anxious is beyond me. It's not like anyone, other than the dog anyway, will ever see me here on Earth.

"Rex, that's enough!" Chris yells, pulling the dog by the collar to back him away from my leg.

"What's with him?" Chris's sister asks while she stirs something in a pot on the stove.

"He's been acting weird since I got home." Chris's voice is labored from trying to subdue the focused dog, and eventually he gives in. "Fine! Go!"

Rex bolts to me and the dog's entire backend shakes from excitement while he sniffs my shoes.

"Crazy mutt," Chris grumbles and steals a cracker from his sister's plate.

"Want some soup?" the girl asks.

Chris leans over his sister's shoulder to look inside the pot and then appears less than humored. "Funny."

"I thought Tomato soup was your favorite?" she sneers.

Chris slides one of the closet doors open and rummages through the shelves until he retrieves a box of corn flakes. "Still not hungry, Mom?" he hollers into the next room.

The hum of the sewing machine stops. "No thanks, hun," his mom's voice replies before the machine kicks back to life.

After a stop at one of the cabinets, a drawer adjacent to the sink, and the fridge, Chris is sitting at the island with his sister. "What do you think she's making now?" he asks through a mouthful of his cereal.

"Maybe she's replacing the living room curtains she made last week. That'll be what…six swap-outs so far?"

"I can hear you!" their mom's voice says. I can't help but smile from her amused tone.

Neither Chris nor his sister mention anything about their dad throughout the informal meal. They talk about a couple mutual friends at school and their plans for the week. His sister asks how work is going. He thanks her for getting him the job. Their kindness towards one another makes my heart hurt worse. Chris's death is going to devastate this family.

After eating, Chris says goodnight to his mom and sister. In his room, he puts in earbuds and lounges on his bed, flipping through a Rolling Stone magazine. After searching for a place to sit amidst the scattered black clothing and who knows what else, the best I can find is a small area in the middle of the floor.

When Chris gets bored with the magazine, he grabs The Great Gatsby from his nightstand and finishes the last third of the book. Then he spends an hour texting—probably Liv, though I don't eavesdrop—and the lights are out. Chris is asleep in under five minutes.

In the dark room, Chris's shallow, rhythmic breathing is accompanied by the hum of the ceiling fan.

I rest my chin on my knees and give more thought to approaching the Schedulers. How many people will it take to make an impact on them? Should we get Jonathan involved or will he continue to ignore us when we broach the subject? What's Plan B if the Schedulers tell us to get lost?

After an hour of mulling my questions over without resolution, the door creaks open. Rex's square snout is the first to enter, sniffing at the air. When I'm discovered, the dog's backside turns into the usual pendulum and his barks pierce through the still house.

"Shhhh!" I hiss.

Surprisingly, this demand does the trick, but not before Chris shifts in bed. I freeze, forgetting for a second that he can't see me. The lump under the covers stills and the breathing becomes heavy and rhythmic again.

Seated on the floor, Rex's nose nearly touches mine. Since I can't pet the animal, I hold my palm out to offer a focal point that's not my face. Happy enough to oblige, the dog backs up a step. After a few seconds, Rex does a quick spin and then lays so close to me that his fluffy, front paw ghosts through my outstretched leg. When I move an inch, the paw follows. It seems I've made a friend.

When Chris's alarm clock buzzes, I jump and reach for my calimeter out of instinct. The night passed quicker than I expected. My new friend on the floor lifts his head and sighs. Before resuming his prior position, the dog inches impossibly closer to me.

Chris responds to the relentless noise with a groan. After the lump of blankets shifts, his hand appears from under the covers and hits the clock on the table beside him to mute the buzzing. Ten minutes later, this motion is repeated. Thirty minutes after that, the little game is still going on. I wish he would get up already.

I lift my head from my knees at the sound of footsteps in the hallway. Rex mimics me, lifting his head from his tan, oversized paws.

"Honey, you've got to get moving or you're going to be late for school. There you are, Rex. Come on, let's go out."

The dog hops up and trots to Chris's mom. Chris groans and pulls the blanket tighter over his head.

Mom yanks the covers off him. "Get moving!"

Chris mutters something incoherent and grabs at the air four times before making contact with the corner of his blue bedspread. Upon successfully locating what he was searching for, Chris transforms from human form back to a mere lump.

Chris's mom flips on the light and wins the tug-of-war game, pulling the cover onto the floor and out of Chris's reach. Smart woman.

After mumbling his displeasure, Chris raises from his

bed like a zombie.

Five minutes later, the faucet squeaks on and the shower water drones into the hallway where I've made my new home.

The door opens after forty minutes and it's back to Chris's room we go. It must be true that black is slimming because in only a towel Chris is not as scrawny as I originally thought.

"Oh Jeez!" I say out loud after he drops the only piece of fabric that was concealing his goods. Seeing more of Chris than I ever wanted to keeps my eyes focused on my boots until I'm sure he's fully clothed.

He spends the majority of his time putting on all of his jewelry, finishing with the spiked dog collar even Rex wouldn't touch, and then it's down the steps we go. At the kitchen table, Chris slings a messenger bag over his shoulder in the same way Willow does. His bag, however, is in much better shape. He grabs a banana off the counter, gives his mom a fast kiss on the cheek, and we're out.

"Tell Dad I said 'bye,'" Chris says before the door slams behind him.

"'Kay, honey. Have a good day."

Our next destination is the small Honda parked on the street. Rex interrupts before we get there, running at me instead of Chris. Chris eyes the dog up like he doesn't believe what he's seeing. I can't blame the guy. It's not everyday someone observes an animal jumping happily at nothing but the air.

Rex seems to find enjoyment in the fact that my legs

don't stop his front paws like they should. He continues with the game, leaping at me and then ghosting through my knees, adding a few barks in the mix.

I jog to the car, but Rex follows me.

"Rex!" Chris yells. "Back in the yard!"

Rex ignores Chris and, though I've made it into the passenger seat, the dog continues barking at the car door. Chris walks around the car and grabs Rex by the collar, pulling him back into the grass. The dog is relentless, so Chris ends up dragging him all the way inside. By the time Chris is back in the car, he's out of breath.

"Crazy dog," he mutters and turns the key that brings the Honda, and the shoddy stereo system, rumbling to life.

We head out on a different road than the one we took yesterday. This one is much more winding, but seems to be no match for Chris. The Honda hugs the corners of the blacktop without the help of the brake. I'd probably be sick from the combination of gas fumes, sharp turns, and loud music if I wasn't so accustomed to Satellite travel. This kid doesn't even flinch. No question, he'll acclimate to his new life more easily than I did, physically anyway.

Coasting around one of the sharp corners, he reaches for the banana in the messy console. He glances down for just a second, but the short diversion is enough. The garbage truck is stopped two driveways ahead.

"Haze!" I yell out of habit.

*Brake, brake, brake, brake, brake…*I repeat over and over, waiting for the jolt of electricity that never comes. Instead, the Honda crashes head on into the unforgiving compactor of the truck.

The sick, crunching noise is louder than his radio, which dies a second later, leaving behind an overwhelming, eerie silence. My body doesn't jolt from the impact, but the passenger seat is no longer a seat at all and I'm awkwardly ghosting through the crunched bowels of the vehicle.

I jump out of the car that now appears less like a vehicle and more like a crushed aluminum can. Adrenaline pulses through my veins. "Chris!"

I can't make out where the driver's side should even be. Broken glass has flown more than twenty feet and the contorted metal is covered with red spray. I focus my energy, trying desperately to unfold the metal. Even though my head screams with the impossibility of my undertaking, I continue to try. The driver of the garbage truck joins me, sweating and cursing through clenched teeth from his lack of success.

I barely hear the wailing sirens, but I can't ignore the unnatural feeling when the police officer runs through me.

The garbage truck driver begins yelling, "The car came out of nowhere! I don't know how many people are in there! Everything happened so fast, I don't know..." he goes on and on, reminding me of a panicked Jackson.

The officer runs to his cruiser and returns with a crowbar, jamming it into what may or may not be the driver's door.

"Sir, please calm down. Are you injured?" the officer asks through labored breaths while he uses all his weight to will the anchored crowbar to move.

Standing in the middle of the road, dumb and frozen, I

don't hear the man's answer. My shock washes away and the sick truth hits me like a baseball bat to the gut: Chris is dead.

I knew this was coming; I mean, the guy is becoming a Satellite after all, but I hadn't expected things to happen so quickly.

I sit on the narrow strip of gravel bordering the blacktop road and pop my knuckles, wondering what happens next for Chris and me, mostly so I won't think of his surviving family.

Newcomers join the scene that would be more fitting in a horror flick. They bring with them a flutter of activity. The total count is five police officers, four medics, and a whole lot of firefighters. Eventually, they graduate from the crowbar to a loud saw.

I rest my forehead on my knees. The scream of the saw makes me think of my dad, which turns to thoughts of my mom. Then I think of Chris's parents, which leads to nausea.

When the workers finally pull what's left of the door from the frame, Chris's body is bent and contorted in the remains of the vehicle. I flinch away from the sight of his disfigured face.

"He's still breathing," one of the medics yells.

What?!

No!

Oh God, please put this kid out of his misery! *Please!*

"Got a wallet here," another medic's voice muffles. "We need to get him to the hospital right away. He's an organ donor."

Oh hell.

⸻

Chris flatlines in the operating room twice. The paddles fail at resurrecting him the third time. In a matter of minutes, the doctors' purpose shift from keeping him alive—which, from one look at the poor guy, was an obvious long shot—to harvesting his organs. I'm sucked out of the scene and the strong force hinders any chance of recovering from my nausea.

When my feet finally hit the ground, my mind feels like it's been sent through a blender.

"Thank you, Grant. Phase One is complete," a morphed voice says.

The floor, along with my boots, won't stop spinning, though this is likely happening only in my head.

"Following break, please allow your Satellite to attempt coding and then proceed to Programing. Directions to Programming can be found in your Legacy book." The voice of GPS Jeanette becomes more normal just a second before she decides to shut up.

I'm yanked upward until I'm eventually thrown from the book. The black binding thunks against the floor and the book closes.

I struggle to lift my wrist, and then immediately wish I hadn't bothered. Even worse than the unpleasant mode of travel, my calimeter shows break is still a ways off.

After spending a good twenty minutes on the sofa trying to calm myself, I decide a drink is needed. Wishing for something stronger, I opt for the only thing available and fill the largest mug in the cabinet with black coffee, straight-up.

I want the image of Chris's mashed face out of my head. I've seen enough to know death is not always pretty, but knowing the guy was kept alive merely to harvest his organs hurts my stomach. Those Schedulers are dangerously clever and efficient. Progression gets a new Satellite. Chris's dad gets a new kidney or two and his life back.

I scowl, knowing Chris's dad would argue that life was better with Chris alive.

Five quick knocks interrupt my coffee time. I set my cup on the counter and kick my backpack out of the way to open the door.

Here stands Chris, looking a couple years older and sporting more muscles and less blood.

I spring forward and throw my arms tightly around him, despite the fact that he's fighting against my embrace. He may have more muscle than before, but I prove to be the stronger one. When I pull away, I touch his cheek, relieved to see a recognizable face in place of the mangled, bloody mess that I saw mere minutes ago.

Hello, Grant, what the hell are you doing? my mind questions.

I immediately take two steps back and straighten my shoulders, trying my best to reclaim my man card. "Sorry," I mumble after clearing my throat.

He's still covered, head-to-toe, in the unfortunate black clothing, which helps get my emotions in check, especially when I narrow in on his dog collar.

"Are you Grant?" Chris asks in a quiet voice when I say

nothing.

"That's me."

"Uh, hi."

"Hi," I respond.

My staring seems to be making him uncomfortable so I swing the door all the way open. "May as well come in."

Needing my coffee now more than ever, I head back for my mug.

The click of the door closing and the waves of my gulping seem to scream in the still room. My throat is burning, but I refill my mug anyway. Before I start on my second cup, I turn to be sure Chris didn't get lost along the way.

"I won't bite," I try to joke because he looks downright terrified. I can't blame the guy considering he just witnessed my biggest emotional lapse of all time. I'm feeling a bit frightened by the blunder myself. Or, more likely, he's still in shock that he's dead. I remember that feeling as well.

After standing, frozen, just inside the door, he finally moves a few feet toward me. His expression changes when he gets an eyeful of my glorious sofa.

"Trust me, I know. The thing's a hand-me-down."

He almost smirks.

"You want a drink?"

He shrugs.

"I've got coffee."

"Sure," he mumbles.

I pretend to be a good host by forcing a smile and bringing him a full cup. "So, tell me what you know so far."

3. Well, don't just stand there

Getting the kid to talk is like trying to get Meggie to smile. At least he's moved from the door to the sofa. The tension remains high, magnified by the fact that he says nothing the entire time we, or rather, I, go through the Satellite Basics handbook, or what I like to refer to as the *Satellite Handbook for Dummies*.

I explain as much as I can remember Willow telling me when I arrived. When I'm finished, he says nothing. The quiet game is beginning to bother me.

"Aren't you even a little concerned about Liv?" When the question falls from my mouth, I wonder why I would ask such a thing. A more proper question would be to ask why he prefers wearing a dog collar.

And just like that, Sparky speaks. "How do you know about her?"

"I saw you. In life, I mean. With her."

His eyes narrow on me. "*With* her?"

"Well, not *with* her. I saw the two of you together the night before your death."

"What were you, like, spying or something?"

"No. Trust me." Keeping surveillance on two black-clothed bodies making out is not high on my list of favorite things to do, but I keep this to myself. "Just part of the jubilant job of being your Legacy." I wish Willow were here to witness how well I'm doing. I'm using big words and everything.

"Do Legacies always spy on their subjects?"

"Dunno." I get up to pour more coffee. "And to be clear, I wasn't spying. Here's a bit of helpful information about this Satellite/Legacy pairing process. You're linked with your complete opposite." I slide the pot back into the coffee maker and wonder if I'm explaining this for his benefit or mine. "That way you can focus all your attention on training instead of getting sidetracked by your common interests."

He watches me plod back to the sofa. His eyes scan from my faded T-shirt down to my cracked leather work boots. "Well, that makes sense."

Looking at his dog collar, I have to bite my tongue.

"Hungry?" I ask with zero enthusiasm, even though I'm metaphorically throwing my fist in the air because my calimeter has finally chimed.

"No." At least he's making impressive vocal progress.

"Cool. Let's go."

Across the room, I sling my bag over my shoulder. After a sip of coffee, I throw the new edition, a black messenger bag, at Chris. The kid's got fast reflexes, I'll give him that. Curiosity paints his face, but he asks nothing about the magical appearance of his bag and follows me silently to the elevator.

On the way down, I hold out my wrist. "This is a calimeter. It works like a watch. The notches line up to signal break. A built-in alarm will tell you when break's over so you can go back to your assignment. It also signals on Earth so you know when to return here. You're the only person who will hear your calimeter's alarm. To turn off the alarm, push on the face."

There. I gave him more than Willow ever shared with me. My good deed for the day is done. "You'll get your own once you're cleared from training. They're tailored to each person's taste, so yours will probably have spikes." This last bit slips out before I can stop myself. Too bad, I was doing so well.

The elevator's golden doors slide open in unison with the familiar voice. "Have a fabulous day."

"GPS Jeanette," I say in introduction.

Chris continues pretending to be deaf and follows me across the expanse of the marble lobby into Benson Hall. In a hurry to dump him and get to the meeting, I walk fast. He keeps up easily. The place is about half full, but the crowd is growing. In an effort to ignore all of the glances in my direction, I pretend to drink my coffee. At least this hides half my face.

I lower my mug after a dozen paces and, instead of saying, *Speak, boy, speak,* I decide to use my manners. "Oh come on! You have to admit this place is amazing."

He maintains his role as a professional mute. That's fine. I have ways to retaliate.

Stopping at a table for five, occupied by only four, I say, "Hey guys, this is Chris. He's new here. Mind if he joins you?"

The foursome, dressed in identical suits with the

exception of their tie color, get an eyeful of Chris and his all-black getup. My forwardness appears to shock them as much as it shocks Chris.

"I'll grab you after break," I say to Chris when no one answers. My smirk widens even more when I say, "Have fun."

I jog to the back of Benson before Chris can argue. When I am on the other side of the fireplace, the tempo of my stride lessens. Where did all these people come from? Certainly they're not here for me. I'm only expecting a handful of people aside from the Satellites I already know are on board, and that's if I'm lucky.

I ditch my coffee cup on one of the tables and push through the bodies, mumbling my apologies along the way. If I actually succeed in shoehorning myself through this crowd, I'll be convinced that anything is possible. About halfway through, I pause, still stunned by the number of people blocking my way.

I stretch my neck to see over the heads. "Clara?" I yell in hopes that she may be back there. It occurs to me that, after our earlier dispute in Benson, there's a possibility that she may have changed her mind about coming. The thought turns my stomach. If I can't win Clara over, how will I ever get anyone else on board?

"Grant?" a voice hollers back.

Then, the weirdest thing happens: the Satellites begin to move in unison, pushing out until a pathway is cleared between the tables. My shock must be evident because my boots stay frozen in place.

"Well, don't just stand there!"

My focus turns from the staring Satellites to the newly formed path that leads to Clara. I force my feet to move, in spite of the stares that make me want to turn the other way and run like hell.

When I finally reach Clara, I lean down and whisper, "I'm really happy you're here, and I'm sorry about earlier."

Clara's lips are extra glossy and her eyeshadow, now pink instead of silver, matches her dress. In the silence, she returns my whisper with a soft voice. "Me, too. The right thing to do is often the hardest." She looks away from me. "This is the right thing to do, and apparently, recruitment is up."

We both gaze forward at more than one hundred Satellites looking back at us.

Clara leans up to whisper in my ear, even though we both know the people closest to us, along with some further away can hear every word we're saying. "They look kind of antsy. I think you'd better start talking."

"Me?" I hiss back.

"Well, yeah. This was all your idea, remember?"

I give Clara a look that hopefully says "thanks for throwing me under the bus," even though I know she's right.

"Um, hello."

Billy's laughter roars over the silent crowd and many of the Satellites turn in the general direction of his chortling.

I do my best to level my shaky voice. "Thanks for coming." I swallow, hoping to keep my nerves in check when the realization hits that these people may not even know why they're here. "Have any of you heard what we are proposing?"

A few Satellites nod, but the majority of them remain still.

"OK. Well, at the very least, I'm sure you've heard about the Elites. The rumors are true. Aside from the newest Elite addition, our team has lost our blocking ability and has been forced to become Legacies."

A few whispers hiss through the crowd.

"How'd you lose your ability?" a male voice somewhere in the middle of the crowd hollers.

"That's...um..." my eyes shoot to Clara, certain she can detect my pleading.

"That part is a bit complicated. We'll be happy to explain, but at another time. There's a more pressing issue we need to discuss first." Clara squeezes my arm and nods in encouragement for me to keep going.

I swallow again and take a deep breath, hoping to settle my anxiety. "My last Tragedy was a woman named Meggie. She lost her three children and her mother in a fire. While I was on her assignment, her kids showed up on Earth. Lawson was there and can back me on this."

"It's true," Lawson's low voice rumbles somewhere from my right.

"Meggie's kids helped her more than I ever could."

"Probably because you suck!"

I ignore Billy's heckling and continue. "In the months I was on Meggie's assignment, I never saw her so at peace as when her kids were with her." I look down at my fidgeting hands. "Their presence alone helped her. Meggie's kids talked to her. She didn't seem able to hear or see them, yet in a strange way, she could sense them. I've tried to tell Jonathan, but he won't listen to me, so I'm proposing we go to the next level."

I prepare myself for the fallout before saying the words.

"I'm proposing we go to the Schedulers."

I have to raise my voice to Willow-volume to project over the noisy chatter. "They need to know how much Meggie's children helped her!"

"It's true? You're actually proposing we give up our jobs?" a guy's voice yells over the escalating volume of the others.

"No!" I holler back. "I mean, in a sense, I guess. But wouldn't you rather—"

"You can't block, so you want to bring us down with you?" an angered voice yells.

"No! That's not what—"

Not only is the volume of the crowd intensifying, the tension is as well. I look down at Clara, but she appears too nervous to offer any help.

"You're mental!"

"I don't care who he is, there's no way—"

"I can already tell you how this will play out—"

"Wonder what Jonathan thinks—"

"That's enough!"

I startle, along with half of the other Satellites, and we all turn to Billy as he pushes through the bodies and steps in front of me. "Move it, pansy," he grumbles to me and then turns to the crowd. "No one is making you do this. You all came here to listen to Grant's plan. I personally hate the guy, but he may be on to something here."

"You can't block either!" a voice yells.

When Billy's posture morphs from keeping his cool to wanting to tear someone in half, Lawson steps forward.

"Neither can I!" Lawson's deep voice growls. "But I saw what Grant has explained firsthand."

"You expect us to believe someone's dead kids just showed up?"

"That's exactly what I expect. Grant may be a lot of things, but he's not a liar. I watched my own Tragedy benefit from his kids' presence more than he ever did from my blocks. I care about my Tragedies enough to want them to get better as quickly as possible. Don't you?"

"Maybe you just weren't any good at blocking either!"

Whoa!

Silence follows, while everyone looks in the general direction of where the slam came from. My muscles tighten because I can tell Lawson, usually the most cool-headed of our group, is unraveling quickly.

Clara steps in front of Lawson and me, putting her hand on my chest and then Lawson's, indicating for us to calm down.

"I can still block," she says when she turns to the crowd, "I'm just like the rest of you. I remember very little from my life, but I'd like to. I'd like the opportunity to watch over my parents instead of having one of you do it. I know each of you are capable, but I still believe I'd be a better choice for my own family. All we are asking is that you consider the bigger picture. Yes, some may call this career suicide," she pauses and straightens her shoulders, "but I look at it as more of a career change. Think of your families. If you don't remember them, think of your Tragedies. Your own parents, spouses, siblings, and in some cases, even your children, have experienced your death. No doubt, they have reacted to your loss much like your own Tragedies have reacted to theirs. If you could make a greater difference to your loved ones than a random Satellite placed on their assignment, wouldn't you want to? Wouldn't you want that for your family?"

The crowd remains silent. Some look at their feet, some at Clara, and a few at me.

Clara lowers her voice. "I want that for my family. I may not remember everything about them, but I love them. I see them in every Tragedy I protect. Even if nothing changes here, I know I'll feel this way until the day I'm reunited with them."

Clara's speech silences the crowd for almost a full minute. I step forward and give her hand a squeeze in gratitude.

"The more people we have, the more likely it is that the Schedulers will listen to what we're proposing," I say. "We're only asking that you stand with us. As Clara urged, think about the bigger picture. Lawson and I were witnesses to how different things could be. And Billy—well, I hate the guy as much as he hates me, but he was a damn good Elite. It's true we lost our blocking ability, and I realize you all have more at stake than we do, but please consider standing beside us."

Evelynn's blue dress stands out in the crowd, sparkling

from the floating lights overhead when she shifts her weight. I'm glad she's in, but I wish she had the choice.

The large crowd remains silent and their expressions are hard to read. Even if we've won them over, what will we say to plead our case? Will the Schedulers even take us seriously?

Before I finish my game of twenty torturous questions in my head, an approaching throat clears, followed by a demanding and firm, "Excuse me."

Knowing the voice all too well, Jonathan weaves easily between the pathway that has been cleared for him. He appears more casual than normal in his plain red ball cap, but his hands on his hips prove his clothing is not a proper indication of his mood. "Everyone," he says in greeting, and then, "Grant, where is Chris?"

"Oh…um…."

"I'm right here!" Chris answers and pushes through the crowd towards us. I owe him big.

Jonathan looks from Chris to me, clearly unconvinced that I knew of Chris's whereabouts thirty seconds ago. "As his mentor, your utmost responsibility at this time is Chris." He uses a direct voice that keeps me from spewing any excuses. Jonathan looks back at the crowd. "If any of you are considering joining Grant on his mission to the Schedulers, please heed my advice to choose otherwise. This meeting is over."

The Satellites move out like ants whose hill has just been smashed. Understandable, considering Jonathan's statement sounded an awful lot like a warning. In under a minute, all traces that there even was a meeting have vanished. Only Chris, my usual tables mates minus Rigby, and the powerless Elites remain.

"I will see you in Programming after you teach Chris to code." Jonathan says to me and then looks around at the others. "I believe a few of you have your own Satellites that require mentoring to as well. I suggest doing so."

"But—" I start to say, which doesn't matter because Jonathan is already headed towards the exit.

"Our recruitment might be down, but I think Clara pleaded a bloody good case," Liam says to break the silence.

I nod. "Thank you for that."

Clara busies herself with straightening her pink dress. "You act as though this is your battle. We all want this." She pauses. "Maybe we always have and just never knew how to go about it."

We agree to reconvene back here at next break despite Jonathan's opposition, but my mood has depleted. Based on Jonathan's unwillingness to consider our proposal, the odds of convincing the Schedulers are probably about as good as a tsunami hitting Progression.

Chris and I follow Evelynn and Lawson silently through Benson's mosaic corridor. I hit the face of my calimeter along the way to silent the droning buzz.

"Sorry about leaving you with the suits," I mumble to Chris when we reach the B Hall.

He ignores my apology, making me feel like a hypocrite. How can I expect anyone to join this fight if I can't even show my own student respect and compassion?

"Will I really forget my life?" Chris's voice is low on our way to the elevator.

I feel true empathy for what he's about to lose: his memories of his relationship with Liv and his family, possibly never knowing what happens with his dad's health, maybe even not remembering what was wrong with his dad in the first place. If Chris's dad successfully receives the kidney transplant, I know his old man will fare much better in recovery if he could somehow feel Chris's presence instead of some random stranger blocking him.

I nod in answer to Chris's question. "I really am sorry. About all this. I wish we had choices in our destinies."

Chris and I ride the elevator up to my room. *Soon-to-be his room,* I think. I love my place, even the horrendous sofa, but I'd willingly give it up. I'd give up my entire future— whatever it may hold— if I could change Progression.

I drop my bag at the door. Chris does the same, but his bag makes less noise because the only content is the *Satellite Handbook for Dummies.* As he follows me down the hall, I like that he keeps any other questions he may have to himself. My mind is too flooded to add more disappointment to his life.

And then there were two, I note and sit on the extra black mat that was not there yesterday. Watching him in the mirror, I motion for him to sit on the other mat.

This is likely going to be a one-way conversation, so I jump right in. "Coding is similar to meditating and we do it because our assignments are stressful. We don't sleep, so this is what helps our bodies cope with the tension."

Crickets.

All righty, then.

"Close your eyes and relax. You can visualize anything you want. Something or someplace peaceful usually helps. Counting down in your head can be helpful, too."

He closes his eyes, but then opens them.

"Are you really trying to change this program?"

My concern for Chris spikes for fear of pulling him into this mess. As much as I'd love an additional body to stand with us before the Schedulers, Chris should not have to carry the burden of my decisions, nor be judged for them. I nod, but then explain, "This whole thing is turning into a bigger mess than I thought."

"I only ask because I wonder what the point of all this *training,*" he mocks quotations with his hands, "is for if things are going to change around here."

I sigh. "I wish I could say things were going to change, but honestly, I'm not feeling overly optimistic about the outcome. There's a good chance things will continue as they always have." Saying this out loud makes my mood deplete even further.

Chris nods. "I guess we'd better get on with it, then."

I appreciate that he doesn't press for more.

Chris's first couple attempts are interrupted by his laughter, making me respect the guy even more.

"I was as skeptical as you were about this, which made my own mentor, Willow, insane." I grin, thinking back to how difficult I was. "Coding is actually pretty decent once you get it, though."

Chris agrees to give it a real shot, and within a few minutes, his shoulders slump. He seems to be in a full trance. I can't deny I'm impressed by his quick learning ability.

He's not a bad looking kid, aside from the makeup and clothing. Unlike my shorter brown hair that tends to go all over the place, his shoulder-length, black hair is slick against his head and tucked behind his ears. My eyes stop on his black fingernails, and instead of bothering me like I figure they should, a lonely feeling tugs at my insides.

I close my eyes and suddenly feel sick. My mouth waters in warning that I'm about to hurl. I jump from the mat and sprint towards the door with my hand clamped against my face. Barely to the kitchen sink, my dinner from two days ago reemerges. And reemerges. And reemerges. Good grief, how much did I eat?

With my lungs still in overdrive, my head raises and I wipe my mouth with the back of my hand. I splash water on my face over the red sink, noting that the vomit, of course, has already vanished.

"What's wrong with you?"

I look up at Chris's voice.

"Seriously, are you all right?"

"Probably just a bug," I lie. I have no idea what's wrong with me.

"That's some bug."

I close my eyes and concentrate on breathing for a minute.

"A person can actually get a bug here in Pleasantville?"

I pinch the bridge of my nose.

"Maybe you should get checked out by someone."

"Maybe."

After a few seconds, he asks, "Are you going to?"

"Probably not."

"But—"

I open my eyes and cut him off. "I can't believe I'm actually going to say this, but would you please shut up for a minute?" My tone is light enough that he doesn't appear to be offended.

I close my eyes and concentrate on my breathing. After a couple minutes, I trust my balance enough to release my grip from the countertop.

Chris has gotten over his staring fit and has made friends with my oh-so-comfortable atrocity of a sofa. From the kitchen, his head looks like a black balloon floating over the puke green cushions.

"It's ugly, but you have to admit the thing is comfortable," I finally say.

He replies with silence.

"Listen, I'm sorry if I'm being a jerk. Things have gotten complicated around here. Becoming a Legacy…well, it feels like this all got thrown on me. I'm still trying to adjust."

He turns and watches me over the back of the sofa while I drum my fingers on the counter.

"I've got to head out for a while. You can hang out here or make some friends in Benson. I'll walk you down there if you want."

"I'd like to sit here for a while if that's OK."

"Sure. I'll catch up with you later."

"What does it feel like to lose your memories?"

I pause at the door and pull down on my backpack straps. "It's not painful, if that's what you're worried about."

He shakes his head.

"I'm sorry." I wish I could offer him more than these two words.

4. The kid's proving to be difficult again

In the elevator, I memorize the blueprinted maze of hallways on page eight of my Legacy book. The task is complex enough to take my mind off my vomiting stint. I shove the book into my bag when I reach the lobby, and I'm glad my stomach feels more stable now.

My pace quickens as I cross the lobby; so does my heartbeat when I pass the courtyard doors and move through the first maze of hallways. I haven't given any thought to Programming. How will I feel when my memories are back, especially when I'm not being reunited with anyone?

"Hey," I say when the last hall opens into a modest seating area. Modest for Progression, that is. The arrangement of six over-stuffed leather chairs, three sofas, and a dozen small tables wouldn't fit in Ryder's entire lower level.

"Hey, yourself" Evelynn says from the leather chair.

"What are you doing?"

She half smiles. "Stalling."

Understandable. "Want to walk with me?"

She pushes her feet into her sparkly shoes. Her heels make her almost my height when she stands. As instructed in my Legacy book, I twist the third candlestick clockwise forty-five degrees. A wood panel on the right wall reacts and slides open to expose a hidden hallway.

Evelynn looks at the doorway like the space beyond is her enemy, but she takes a step forward. Her pace is slow when we walk together into the golden metallic room to face three hallways. These ceilingless rooms always feel less constricting. As we move into the left hallway, I wish they were ceilingless as well. At least the ornate, heavy trim work gives my eyes a focal point. Evelynn's outfits can be blinding if a person's not careful.

"You know, casual clothes look just as good on you." Typically, I wouldn't broach the subject of fashion. Evelynn is clearly nervous, though. I get it. So am I. Maybe a bit of small talk will help us both. Plus, there's no way the turquoise dress could be comfortable. A vacuum-wrapped freezer bag has more breathing room than her outfit of choice.

"I'm serious," I say to her dubious expression. "I thought the T-shirt and pants you had on the other day were nice."

I'm fairly certain she's not interested in the ceiling when her eyes move in that direction, even though the glowing balls of light floating above us are impressive. The next twenty paces are silent, with the exception of Evelynn's clicking heels.

"All I'm saying is you have a lot more to offer someone. When you dress…" my mind searches for the least insulting word choice, "in such a revealing way—"

"I do not!"

Good thing I didn't use my first choice. She would have undoubtedly opposed being compared to a call girl. "You're serious?" I bite my lip, but still my grin escapes.

"Of course I'm serious!"

My eyes move from her dark blue eyelids down to her high heels. "I didn't mean to offend you, but seriously, your dress code is a tad," deep breath, "brazen."

"If you're accompanying me just so you can spew out your criticisms, I'd prefer to walk alone."

"That's not what I'm trying to do." It really isn't. "All I'm saying is, you have a lot more to offer someone than just your body. I've seen how the guys in Benson look at you."

She crosses her arms. "Oh, I get it now. You're jealous."

So much for my small talk idea. I shake my head. "They only want your body. And I get it."

Her eyebrow raises.

"Evelynn, you're a beautiful woman. You know that. Sometimes, though, leaving a little more to the imagination isn't such a bad thing. You don't have to flaunt your body to get a guy. The attention you're drawing isn't from guys looking for a relationship, it's from the ones looking for a good time."

"That's not true."

I slow my pace and she does the same. "I'm a guy. I know how our minds work. After all the mess I've caused you and the other Elites, I just want you to be happy. Portraying yourself as an object won't bring you any long-term gratification."

"I don't portray myself as an object, and I'm perfectly happy, thank you very much!"

I'm not sure if she can see the sadness in my eyes, but I nod and drop the subject.

Snaking through the halls, distant voices grow louder as we continue deeper into the maze.

Focused on what sounds like the echo a basketball makes when it hits a gymnasium floor, I turn left and almost smack Willow in the face with my chest.

Willow is not humored by my "whoops" expression.

"Watch it, kid."

"Well hello, Willow. How are you?" I ask in a falsely chipper voice.

This makes her smile, yet her forehead creases like she's worried about something. "Hey Evelynn. I saw Milo down the hall a few minutes ago."

Evelynn brushes past the three guys congregating around the leather sofa that's been haphazardly pushed into the hall. All three guys stop their conversation to watch Evelynn as her heels click in the direction Willow pointed.

Willow blows out a breath and shakes her head. "That girl."

I keep my voice low. "I wish she had more respect for herself."

Willow eyes me as if what I've just said is deplorable, then tells me to follow her.

Our destination just around the corner is similar to the stone well where I first met my Tragedies. This space, though, is larger, and flaunts a dozen much fancier doors and a dark hardwood floor instead of dirt. Since I didn't think my assumption moments ago could actually be accurate, I mentally high-five myself for guessing correctly as I watch the one-on-one basketball game in progress.

"We're this way." Willow is smart to maneuver along the curved wall to skirt the two guys because they've turned their game into a full contact sport. They're too focused on stealing the ball from each other to notice us.

I take her cue and follow, staying close to the wall myself even though these guys would do much less damage to me than they would to Willow. The ball and squeaky rubber soles echo in the circular room, while the guys trash talk to each other on the makeshift court.

Willow opens the fourth ornate door and motions for me to go in.

I can't keep my laugh contained. "Your room, I'm guessing?"

She nods and bounces across a faded rug to an orange sofa. She pats her hand for me to join her. I half expect dust to float from the velvet cushion.

The thing is as comfortable as mine. Figures.

"You honestly can't be surprised by my décor choice?"

I shake my head while my eyes continue to scan the room. "I thought you'd be living with Troy."

"Oh, I do. This is where I stayed during my transition in Programming. Guess who's the receiver of this phenomenal space now?"

Searching for the silver lining, I eye the coffee maker, identical to the one I'm leaving behind. Also promising is her reassurance that I won't have to sacrifice a comfortable sofa. Progression has had quite the effect on me. I'm almost feeling like a glass-half-full guy.

"How are things going with Chris?"

Strike that last thought.

I look up at the cloud-spotted sky where the ceiling should be and rub my hands on my thighs. "Not great. Wait until you meet him. We couldn't be more opposite."

Willow's lips purse together. She can't keep her placid charade hidden for more than a few seconds. Her body reacts to her laughter, folding in half like a lawn chair.

"What's so funny?"

"Trust me, I get it," she manages to say.

"I was nothing like this kid. He wears a frigging dog collar!" I add to solidify my point.

She proves she can laugh even harder. "I love it!"

"You would."

When she's back in a normal sitting position—normal for her, meaning her legs and bare feet are underneath her—she sucks in a few long, deep breaths. "I love seeing everything come full circle. If you had any idea how annoying you were when I met you, you'd apologize every time you see me."

"Please. You had it good."

She wraps a rubber band around her dreads. "Have some patience. He'll grow on you. Even you aren't half bad anymore." She ruffles my hair and then bounces up, skipping over to the coffee maker on the small counter across the room. The fun-sized ball of energy needs caffeine about as much as I need another pair of boots in my closet.

She returns with two full cups, giving her flip flops a kick to move them out of her path, and resumes her position beside me. "Try not to worry. I felt the same way. Not just about you, but about the new life that was awaiting me. I had no idea what I would do with myself without my assignments keeping my busy, let alone what life would be like with Troy."

"I remember."

A grin freezes between her dimples and she stares at me while I sip my coffee.

Feeling like a subject change is needed, my eyes point to the orange sofa arm. "Where did you find this thing, anyway?"

Willow rubs her hand along the velvet cushion. "It was my grandmother's."

"Huh. Well, that explains the age and the prehistoric color."

"I have really good memories of this sofa and the one from your room. That's why they're here. I was convinced they were replicas because I hadn't seen either of them for years before my death. Every wear and tear mark is exactly the same, though, so I think they're both originals." She puts on her drama face. "Oh, kid, you should've seen Julia's face when she found out I was the reason the green sofa appeared in her room. Becoming my Legacy was a bad enough blow to her, and then that thing showed up with me. Her expression was awesomesauce!"

My eyes skim over the orange sofa arm. "I can only imagine."

"You can't deny their comfy-coziness." She settles deeper into the cushion and closes her eyes.

"Why didn't you take the green one with you?"

"I knew you'd fallen in love with it."

"Please tell me you're kidding."

With her eyes still closed, she shakes her head.

"I guess it's grown on me a little." I'd never admit that the constant reminder of her is comforting.

She opens her eyes and watches the Scarlet Tanagers flying overhead. "I'm leaving this one to you as well since I expect you'll leave its sister with Chris. No sense hoarding all this great stuff to myself. You're lucky, by the way. Most Legacies don't get rooms nearly as fabulous as this one."

Arguing about receiving another one of Willow's hand-me-downs is a waste of energy, so I keep my mouth shut.

After two full minutes of silence, my mind forces my mouth to say what it's thinking. "Won't you at least consider joining us?"

Willow turns her head to me, but she stays quiet for a long time. "I'm sorry."

I figured this would be her answer, but it was worth a shot.

Willow looks up at the birds. "How do you plan on getting to the Schedulers?"

When I don't answer she says, "That's your plan, right? To see them and plead your case?"

"You make it sound simpler than it is."

"I may be able to help get you there."

"Really?"

She sighs. "I've been there. With you, as a matter of fact, just after Elliott died."

I open my mouth, but she keeps going.

"Of course, you don't remember, but you threw a

serious fit. Oscar-worthy, even. Jonathan let me accompany you to see the Schedulers. They gave you a slap on the wrist for your little rant. I'm not sure why, maybe my nerves needed something to occupy themselves with, but I memorized the way. I can still run the pattern in my head: first left, third right, second right, fifth left—"

I want to dispute the fact that she couldn't have gone there with me. Instead, "This is great, Willow!" comes out of my mouth.

She puts her hand over mine. "I'll meet up with you at break and take you there. This is all I can offer you. I'm still not in. You need to understand that."

I really do love her. So much so that I decide against pursuing more information about Elliott and her made up story. Jonathan never took the two of us to see the Schedulers, but the fact that Willow can get us there is excellent news. I almost spill my true feelings about her right here on the sofa.

"Ready for some Programming?" she says before I have the chance to get sappy.

"Why not?"

"There's that zeal I've come to expect from you." She grabs my cup, pulls me up by my arm, and pours us both a refill before we leave. I wrap my arm around her in an effort to show her my gratitude.

She grins at my gesture. "You're welcome, kid."

The abandoned basketball court has been transformed back into a seating area and the hallways are silent when Willow leads me through another maze of corridors. Taking a pointer from her, I try to memorize the way, but lose the game after our seventh turn. We end our journey in a light blue circular room much like the six other rooms we've just passed. Liam and Jordan are both in gaming chairs, wearing atrocious goggles, and rocking back and forth. Liam's mud-colored hair is spiked in all directions around the head strap like he's been electrocuted.

Willow clears her throat. "What's up, guys?"

"Hey, Will, how's it going?" Jordan says without pausing his movements for the virtual game.

Liam lifts the binoculars to his forehead and stares at me before saying, "It's time?"

Willow's eyes narrow. "You two just happened to pick this place, on this day, to play a game?"

Jordan looks like he's been caught with the neighbor's wife when he pulls off his goggles. Liam keeps his head gear on his forehead and shrugs.

Willow lets out a long breath and then scans the ten doors. "Rooms are busy today, huh?"

Jordan nods and then pulls the binoculars back on, covering his close-set eyes.

Willow approaches the only door with a green light glowing over the frame. She punches a code into a number pad to the left of the door.

Willow pulls me through the doorway with her. Along the way, I glance back at Liam. His goggles are in his hand and I'm not especially fond of the worried look on his face.

Willow releases my forearm as the door closes behind us. She leaves me standing in the darkened environment. While my eyes adjust, she skips down the winding path into the shadowy forest like Dorothy leading Toto into the woods.

Figuring I have no choice, I follow without a word. As we move down the slight incline, trees and darkness grow thicker around the path. So does my uneasiness.

I almost run into Willow when she stops. My breath catches from the strange, translucent-red filter blocking our way.

"It's cool, kid, relax. This is the first of many steps in reviving your memory."

My eyes move from the slow pulsing filter to her, and then back.

"Go ahead," Willow urges.

"Go ahead and what?" I ask.

"Touch it."

"Will it hurt?"

Willow answers my question by laughing.

My reservations make my feet feel heavy when I step closer. Something solid stops my extended hand like a piece of glass. I press harder, but the wall doesn't budge. Instead, the road block curves like a ball around me, enclosing me in the center. I look back at Willow for help, feeling claustrophobic inside the red bubble.

The opaque red changes to solid black and Willow disappears. In the silent darkness, my heartbeat thuds like a bass drum in my ears. A television-like screen blinks a few times and then the image sticks, filling the space with artificial light. I slowly turn to absorb the three hundred sixty degree view of a busy park.

"Grant! Grant, where are you?" a deep voice yells over

a slew of squealing voices.

Is it really—? No, couldn't be.

Yep, definitely is.

A much younger version of my dad—wearing cutoff jeans so short they should be banned, a tight yellow T-shirt, and double-striped socks pulled up to his knees—yells my name again and scans the playground.

"Daddy!" A dark-haired boy leaps off the bottom of the slide and runs to my father.

I take a step back and almost tumble into the backside of the curved movie screen. The little boy is me—and my socks match my dad's.

"Stop running off like that. You're going to give your daddy a heart attack."

Daddy? Who the heck is Daddy?

My throat tightens. The old man actually knew how to hug?

Little-me pulls away from my dad's arms and takes off towards the swings. My dad wipes his forehead with a red handkerchief while his eyes stay locked on little-me. Then the image fades to opaque red.

Willow is visible again and the filter morphs into red smoke. A gust of wind kicks up, pushing the misty smoke down the stone path until it fades into the trees.

"Remember that?" Willow asks from behind me.

My head feels strange and dizzy. In my gut, I know the memory is real.

Willow passes me. "You okay?"

I nod and she leads us further down the shadowy

path.

When she stops, my front hits her back, and because of her lacking height, I almost walk over her. "Could you give me a little notice before you do that?"

She ignores me. "The screen is touch sensored, activated by only your handprint. Wild, huh?"

When Willow moves aside, I step towards the next opaque scarlet wall. Like before, when I place my hand against the glass-like barrier, the red encloses me in a giant hamster ball and turns black. This time, the image that arrives is a soccer field.

"Run, Grant! Faster!" My dad yells from the sideline.

My mom, dressed much like my dad, claps and jumps beside him. Oh, those socks! I can't help but laugh.

The focused expression on little-me's face is also comical when I kick the ball towards the opposing goal. My parents cheer and the image fades. The wind, again, carries the red mist down the path.

"That one?"

"Yeah," I answer Willow, now remembering that day as well. My heart even races with the excitement I felt from scoring a goal.

"Want to move on?"

I take a breath to put my adrenaline in check before nodding.

"Pay attention to your head, kid. You may think you feel fine now, but these exercises are going to exhaust your brain. Years' worth of memories are being injected in a very short time."

"I feel decent."

"All righty," she sings. "Let's proceed."

The next memory, according to the banner hanging over the long table, is from my seventh birthday party. A giant mouse mascot poses for pictures, waving beside little-me and my small friends like he's a rock star.

When little-me runs away with a group of boys, I turn to watch the portion of the screen behind me. The boys kick off their shoes and climb through a netted opening into a colorful ball pit.

What feels like a vice tightens around my chest and doesn't let go. When I realize the one screaming now is me, my knuckles shove into my mouth and I bite down hard enough to taste blood.

"Wake up!"

My eyes open to a sight I never want to see.

"What's wrong? Talk to me!" Willow shouts an inch from my nose. Why does she always have to be so close in moments like this? Her panic certainly isn't helping alleviate mine.

I prop myself up and the bumpy stone path digs into my elbow. "My chest," I say, pushing my hand against my breastbone.

Willow clutches my shirt and rips the green collar in half.

I try to push her away with as little force as possible to avoid hurting her. "What the heck are you doing?"

Her eyes stay on what's now my bare chest. "Where's the pain?"

I swore we just clarified that. "My chest."

"Where on your chest?" she demands.

"I don't know, my heart, I guess."

She backs up and drops into a sitting position beside me. Exhaling, she says, "Thank goodness." Her tone shortens. "We're done for the day."

I decide against arguing and force myself to stand. The ache in my chest lessons around the time Willow and I begin up the path. She was right about one thing, memory recovery really is exhausting.

The top of the path dead ends at an odd door with only a frame, no support walls. Willow grabs my arm when I reach for the handle.

"What happened in there?"

I shrug. "I felt like I was having a heart attack."

"Can't you just do anything normal?" Willow seems annoyed, like my body's reaction is my fault.

While I stand frozen in confusion, Willow side steps around me and disappears through the door.

"You're a bloody mess," Liam says as soon I'm in the round room.

I pull the edges of my collar together to cover my chest. Leave it to Willow to ruin a perfectly good shirt. At least I have a couple dozen more just like it. "Be nice. She doesn't look that bad."

Willow stretches to smack my head, but I duck away before her hand makes contact.

"I wouldn't have pegged you as the kind to have a tough childhood," Liam says.

"My childhood was fine." My reply probably comes across as a tad too defensive.

"What Liam means is that you look like trash and you've only just started. The first memories are always the easiest." Willow pauses. "The kid's proving to be difficult again," she says to Liam.

"Bloody hell. You should've known," Liam responds like he understands her nonsense.

"I know."

"Hel-lo! I'm right here. If you're going to talk about me, at least have the courtesy to fill me in." My heart rate increases with worry.

Willow rolls her eyes. "You remember the way back?"

Is she kidding? "No."

She points her eyes at my backpack "There's a map in your book. We'll see you at break."

"What are you two talking—"

"Bye, Grant," Willow says waving her hand in front of my face.

I huff, knowing Willow won't budge despite how hard I push.

Looking down at my calimeter while I walk away, I force myself to breathe easier. Break isn't too far off, at least, and then I'll have another chance to prod Tweedledee and Tweedledum to find out what they are talking about.

Remembering Willow's promise to be my tour guide during break, my uneasiness about their secret conversation morphs into panic. How I'm going to convince the Schedulers to let us protect our own loved ones?

5. Playing the martyr again, I see

After getting lost twice, I finally make it back to my room. I drop my torn shirt in the hallway and take advantage of Chris being M.I.A. by sneaking in a quick coding session.

I'm glad I decided to code. Walking to the closet for a change of clothes, my muscles are loose when I swing my arms over my head. In addition to feeling great, my chest no longer hurts.

In the kitchen, instead of my usual choice of coffee, I grab a Coke from the fridge and take a long swig.

Yowch, brain freeze!

The Coke's not even that cold, but the ache doesn't lessen. I press my palm against my forehead in effort to dull the pain.

An extension of the scenes I witnessed earlier in Programming plays out in my head. The before and after have been added to the park scene. On the playground, I remember my dad telling me to stay close. Instead, I ran to the far side of the playground to try out the slide. After the park, my old man went as far as prying open his wallet and splurging on the neighborhood ice cream truck. If it didn't feel like a real memory, I would have never believed it.

My head continues to throb while a memory of

watching my parents from the back seat of the family fun-mobile fills my mind. How could I have forgotten that green vinyl seat? It nearly took the skin of the back of my thighs every time I got out of the car in the summertime. My parents talked about my soccer game and the goal I scored. My school's upcoming science fair was discussed next, prompting the memory of my dad helping me build a rocket out of a soda bottle to surface.

My mind then refocuses on my birthday party and my dad helping with the decorations beforehand. I can't believe how involved he was with my life. Video games and cassette tapes were the hot gift item that year. In the years that followed, fishing and hunting gear topped the list. Now, I can even remember a couple hunting trips with my dad. How strange that these memories felt non-existent just minutes ago. Both my parents tucked me in the night of my seventh birthday. The image is so clear it could have happened yesterday.

After the throbbing in my head dulls to an ache, I step around the sofa and sink into the cushion. When my calimeter beckons fifteen minutes later, my head feels decent. I'm anxious to get to the meeting, but figure that failing to retrieve Chris will earn me another visit from Jonathan, so I hurry to Benson to find him first.

Chris is leaning against the wall just outside the elevator in the B Hall when GPS Jeanette bids me farewell. Finally, some luck on my side.

"Hey, man."

No answer.

I wave my hand in front of his face.

He doesn't flinch or show even a hint of a smile.

I mock pride when I look on either side of him. "Looks like you made a lot of friends in my absence."

No answer.

In a desperate move because I'm in a hurry, I apologize and ask as nicely as I can muster if he'll come with me. He's reluctant to follow, but gives in, staying a few paces behind me.

"You really do need to make some friends. Who knows, maybe you'll find someone with a passion for leather and whips."

When Chris doesn't react, I glance backward. The guy doesn't look completely miserable, so I use the opportunity to sharpen my mentoring skills. "How old are you?"

"Twenty-three." The shock on his face that follows is expected.

While we walk across the lobby, I talk over my shoulder and impress myself by explaining the age thing with zero sarcasm. When Chris learns he's taken his best physical form, he seems happy about being twenty-three instead of seventeen. He really isn't so bad.

My eyes catch the spikes of his dog collar and that thought drops right through the floor of Progression like a Satellite displacing.

"Do you really think you'll be able to save our memories?" Ah ha! The reason behind Chris's silence has surfaced.

"It's not a matter of saving your memories." Chris

increases his pace so we're walking side by side through Benson's corridor as I talk. "You'll get those back eventually. It's a matter of keeping what's rightfully yours and protecting your own family."

"Same thing."

"How do you know about all this, anyway?"

Chris shrugs. "Everyone's been talking about your plan. Those same people like to point out that I've been paired the most insane Legacy in this place."

"Well, let me assure you, that's a false statement. *I* was paired with the most insane Legacy in this place."

Chris raises an eyebrow.

My grin melts away when I spot the size of the group waiting for me. My football team had more players than this. Huh. Another new memory. This recovery process is certainly interesting. "You're right," I mumble. "I've got Willow beat."

We approach the Satellites who have agreed to join me on my path to the asylum.

"Good thing you're so arrogant. Most people would take offense to a statement like that," Chris says, a full pace ahead now because my feet have suddenly refused to move faster.

"I'm not arrogant."

"I hope you're kidding," he counters.

"Have you been talking to Willow?"

"Talking to me about what?" Willow steps between Billy and Lawson and grins up at me from my right.

Seeing her raises my mood a little. Despite my amped

up nerves, I turn to face my friends: the Satellites and Elites who are willing to risk their futures for a plan that most likely won't work.

Clara steps beside me and gives my arm an encouraging squeeze. I wish Rigby were here. Whitfield would also be helpful, but I accept that she's standing by her man, as one of my mom's favorite songs says. Another memory I didn't have before. This process is interesting indeed.

"Sorry I missed the last meeting," Morgan steps closer and bites into her red lip. "I hope I didn't miss too much. I wanted to be here, but I had to be in training. They've brought in replacements." She looks at Willow and then takes an interest in the marble floor when she lowers her voice. "The new team is," she pauses, "curious." Not saying the word Elite is a smart choice, seeing as she holds the current title that I'm sure six others in our company still covet very much.

"How so?" Willow asks.

"In the past, the team has always seemed more balanced. I mean, I know looks can be deceiving…" Morgan plays with the ends of her brown hair and shoots a quick glance in Evelynn's direction. Unfortunately, it's not quick enough.

I'm afraid Evelynn is going to pounce on Morgan. I'm even more fearful that if the beauty queen does pounce, her shimmery dress will split in two.

"They all look like him," Morgan blurts out and turns her focus to Billy, likely in hopes of saving her pretty face from Evelynn's soured mood.

"Well that certainly seems unbalanced," Willow mumbles to herself.

Poor Morgan isn't making friends very easily. By all rights, she should be our peer and teammate, but I can't blame the others for being upset.

"I'm sorry. I only meant—the new Elites are..."

"She didn't mean anything by it," I say in Morgan's defense. "It's not her fault we can't block. It's mine, remember?"

"Playing the martyr again, I see." Willow's voice sings behind me. "Hi Chris, I'm Willow. It's a pleasure to meet you. I'm sure Grant's told you all about me, but just in case he forgot, I'm his mentor. Please except my sincere apologies for having to deal with this one. I tried to teach him manners, but you know what they say about old dogs."

Everyone chuckles at Miss Popular. I expect people to react to Willow with laughter, but because she's an adult woman wearing a rainbow and unicorn T-shirt, not because what she says is humorous.

"Hello!" Am I invisible today? "What was going on between you and Liam earlier?"

"We have more important matters at hand, don't we, kid? I believe there's somewhere you'd like me to take you?"

"Yes. Right."

"Have you caught Chris up on things?" Clara asks.

I nod. "He's heard the gist."

Clara smiles at the only two new additions to our group, aside from Chris and Morgan. The two girls stand stiffly beside Billy and Evelynn. "Have you been filled in?" Clara asks them, using a pleasant voice that I hope will put them more at ease.

In opposite responses, the compact, sporty girl beside Evelynn nods while the tiny, reserved brunette next to Billy shakes her head. The rules for the Legacy/Satellite pairing process is obvious among these four.

Clara pulls her silver purse strap higher up her shoulder and adjusts her skirt, clearly annoyed that Billy didn't fill his Satellite in on our plan. "For time's sake, I'll give you girls the Cliffs Notes version. Our memories have been taken from us against our will. You're probably aware that our loved ones are hidden away from us until their death. This is an injustice not only to us, but to our families as well. We're going to talk to the Schedulers, the ones that run this place, and try to convince them to change the way things are done around here."

"Will it work?" the brunette girl asks while she knots her fingers together.

Willow gets my attention by clearing her throat. I hate when she looks at me like my cancer is back. "Probably not," she says as she loops her arm around my elbow, "but I'm true to my word. Shall we?"

Anna twirls her ponytail around her index finger. "Shall we what?"

Willow stays quiet, as if the answer is obvious.

Anna's eyes light up before she hisses, "Now?"

Willow nods.

"We…I…what will we say? We don't even have a plan."

Anna's stammering prompts Owen to grab her hand.

"Better get one figured out. Everyone ready?" Willow tugs me along when she begins toward the lobby.

"Do you really know how to get there?" Clara asks, keeping pace close behind us.

"As luck would have it, I do," Willow answers.

"You have no idea how huge this is," Clara is explaining to Chris. "No one gets to see the Schedulers. Well, except for Grant and Willow, but that guy is always breaking the rules. Willow was lucky enough to be along for the ride last time."

"And lucky enough to have memorized the way," Willow adds.

How does Clara know about Willow's made-up story? Despite what Chris thinks, I'm sane enough to know Willow was not with me when the Schedulers reprimanded my behavior on Meggie's assignment. I stand behind the fact that my actions saved that woman's life. Better keep that to myself when we see them. No need to get Landon's panties in more than one knot.

My legs move fast to keep up with Willow, who's now almost sprinting across the lobby. Clara's words keep running through my head. If Willow and I had seen the Schedulers, as the others seem to believe, I would remember such a thing. Wouldn't I? I glance over my shoulder at the Satellites and Elites keeping pace behind us.

Willow leads us down the Orders hall and then knocks on the golden desktop three times. The chime of a bell fills the hallway with each hit. After the third chime has silenced, a panel of marble recesses back and slides to the left, creating a doorway.

Willow pauses and sucks in a breath. "Huh, I wasn't sure if that would really work. Well, in we go."

I follow her into a tiny lobby with the others piling up behind us. Willow leads the group through the candlelit, but bright passages. After turning down three different hallways, I lean forward and whisper, "Are you sure you know where you're going?"

"*Shh!* You're messing up my mojo, kid." Willow looks up at the ceiling and mouths, "Left, right, right, left. Yeah, left," she says louder at the end of the hall. "Now keep quiet, would you?"

I do as she says and the others do the same. If it wasn't for the footsteps and claustrophobic feeling from glancing behind me, I wouldn't know anyone was following. The corridors get narrower the deeper we go, or maybe this is an illusion. Either way, I'm not sure how we will ever find our way out of here.

One of the hallways finally opens into a larger room, though the size of our group fills the space. Willow approaches the two doors on the far wall and pushes on one. The giant, seeded-glass door doesn't budge. Willow grabs the curved handle and pulls.

To avoid getting swiped by the massive door, I stumble into Chris before he has a chance to step back and we both almost fall over. Chris regains his balance and grabs my arm to steady me.

I have to press against Chris, Clara, and Liam to make enough room for the door to completely swing open.

"I'll wait here for you." Willow slips her hands in the pockets of her baggy camouflage pants. "Good luck, kid. You're going to need it."

Panic sets in, making my muscles tense. I rub my hands on my jeans to dry the sweat. "But we don't even have a plan!" I hiss to Willow.

"This is your gig, not mine." Willow whispers back. "Try some spontaneity. Some of the best ideas are born from it."

Ugh.

I walk past Willow slowly, though I'm not sure whether this is out of caution or because of the grandeur of the space. The last time I was here, I was so ramped up about getting in trouble for saving Meggie's pretty face from getting bludgeoned with a liquor bottle, l missed a lot of the details, like the craftsmanship in the carved columns.

It takes a few minutes for us all to file into the area between the double-tiered desk structure surrounding the perimeter.

"Now what?" Clara whispers beside me while we all survey the immense space.

Using the only idea I have, I yell, "Hello?"

Billy laughs after the echo of my voice has silenced.

I straighten my shoulders. "You got something better?"

"Hello!" Billy's voice thunders in the room. "Anyone home?"

He has the nerve to laugh at my idea, but then uses the same one himself?

My eyes circle around the freestanding marble

columns, joined together by arches. I stare past the columns to the overgrown, grassy field and the angular mountains far in the distance.

A tanager flies from one of the arches and disappears into the distance forest.

"Now what, mate?" Liam's accent is easy to recognize among the other Satellites.

I walk away from the group to a column and rub my hand along the smooth, cool marble. What a strange structure to have in the room. It's aesthetically appealing, but other than that, I don't see the point.

"Got any ideas in that pretty head of yours?" Owen asks Liam.

The volume in the room begins to rise as the Satellites voice their opinions about possible options. I overhear Billy grumble that this is a waste of time.

Three columns down, the archway shifts.

"Hey, guys!" Morgan's voice yells out.

I look in the direction of her pointing finger and stare at the dark paneled hallway that has replaced the grassy landscape in between two of the columns.

I'm the first to move through the now quiet space.

"Do you think that's a good idea?" Anna's voice says, but I'm already into the hallway.

Clara catches up and by the sounds of the footsteps, she has company.

I trace my finger on the paneling while I walk. "Where do you think this leads?"

"Looks like we're about to find out." Clara stands

beside me, staring at the closed door the has become our dead end. Together we fill the narrow corridor. Glancing back, Lawson and Evelynn stop behind me. The rest of the group inches closer together, squeezing into the narrow hallway like a cork in a wine bottle.

I grip the brass doorknob, hoping no one notices my shaking hand. This is important to me. I don't want to fail myself, the Tragedies, or my Satellite peers. I think of Meggie holding that knife to her wrist. Too much is at stake.

The knob is cold and heavy under my hand, requiring more force than I expect to make it turn.

When the door squeaks open, I am as surprised as Clara, but I keep my gasp to myself.

Jonathan stands from behind a desk and marches over to us. Yes, he marches. And he's not exactly happy.

"Is there something I can help you with?" he asks sternly, seeming to purposely block the view by placing his hand on the doorframe.

"We came to see the Schedulers." My unsteady voice betrays my feigned confidence.

He looks from me to Clara, then over her to the crowd behind us. He stays quiet. Not good.

"We have to talk to them about Meggie's kids and how much they have helped her."

Jonathan's glare is back on me. "I was under the impression that this topic had been closed."

My nerves evaporate and my temper flares like a sparkler dipped in gasoline. "The topic was never opened! You're supposed to be the good guy around here, the one who helps us out when we need it!"

Jonathan looks down at my wrist and I can't help but wonder if he summoned the buzzing of my calimeter. I push on the watch face without dropping my stare.

"Then, by all means, let me be of assistance." Jonathan looks over Clara's head at the others. "I am ordering everyone back to their assignments promptly. If you refuse, I will find a replacement. Understood?"

The Satellites behind me remain silent. Then, one-by-one, beginning with Owen, they mutter the magic word and drop through the floor.

"Sorry, Grant." Clara gives me the pitying look I hate so much before she follows the other still-employed Satellites through the floor.

When only the Elites, Chris, the two new girls, Morgan, and I remain in the narrow hallway, Jonathan says, "This topic is to be dropped immediately."

Lawson steps forward, forcing Chris to move back a few steps. "But—"

"I said immediately! I believe most of you are expected in Programming. Morgan, you have some reading to contend with." With that, Jonathan steps back and slams the door.

"Should you need anything at all," I mock in a sour tone when I turn, "don't hesitate to ask. Yeah, right."

———

I would have never found our way back to the lobby without Willow. That girl's got one heck of a memory.

Thankfully she spared me the *I told you so's,* keeping the walk back mostly quiet once we all finished our rag session about seeing—or more appropriately, not seeing—the Schedulers. I'm surprised by the Elites' enthusiasm, which seems to now extend beyond not having their abilities as if they truly believe we are fighting for the right thing. With the exception of Billy, that is, but I figured as much from him.

"Walk Chris to Benson and meet me by the courtyard doors. We'll head to Programming together," Willow says.

I want to argue with her that Chris can walk himself, but I know walking him will take less energy than fighting with Willow, so I oblige.

Nearly empty, Benson hosts only a few Legacies and some new Satellites. Chris mopes behind me, stopping five feet short when I reach the sofa by the fireplace.

"Hi. I'm Grant," I say to the curly-haired blonde perched on the arm of the sofa. The knitting needles in her hands stop moving and she looks up from the ball of orange yarn.

"I know who you are. Is it true that you're going to take on the Schedulers?"

I'd like to, but the odds aren't working in my favor. "Something like that, I guess. And you are?"

"Daniella, but just Dani is fine."

I turn to motion Chris closer, but empathy tugs at my gut. "I'm sorry for interrupting you," I say to Dani.

Chris gives me a funny look when I put my hand on his shoulder. "Will you be alright here by yourself for awhile?"

Chris nods.

I hope my apologetic expression comes off as sincere. "I'll be in Programing. I'm not sure how long it will take, but you can hang out in my room later if you want." I catch my mistake of claiming the room as my own. It's his now, or will be in the near future. My stomach tightens because I feel like a territorial dog. Good thing I no longer have a need to urinate.

"Wow. Grant Bradley is really your Legacy?" I hear Dani ask Chris as I'm walking away.

I look over my shoulder and bite into my lip, surprised to see Chris conversing with Dani. He doesn't even look miserable.

When I arrive at the courtyard doors, Willow is waiting.

"Well, your mood's certainly lifted from a few minutes ago." She pushes off the marble wall to stand up straight and then slides her feet back into her flip flops. "You're that stoked about Programming, huh?"

"No. Not that. I just get a kick out of Chris."

Willow shakes her head. "You're more like me than you'll ever admit."

"Hardly."

She doesn't buy my rebuttal.

I slow my pace to stay beside her when we walk through the maze of hallways to the Programming room. She snaps her fingers and hums, but there's no music playing. She's likely singing along with the voices in her head.

She stops snapping but keeps her pace. "You got a plan

B in that thick skull of yours yet?"

Willow's flipping shoes are the only noise for the next few steps until I answer the only way I can, which is admitting that I've got zero ideas.

"You're not one to give up, so I'm sure you'll think of something."

"Any ideas on what that something might be?"

"This is your gig, not mine, kid."

"See. Right there. That's why I love you. You're always so eager to help."

She snickers. "Are you ready for Programming?"

"Will today be like yesterday?"

"Pretty much exactly the same, headache and all. New memories are the only difference. How is your head, by the way? Aside from the obvious."

I ignore her jab. "Fine."

Willow stops and raises her arms over her head when we reach the round room of doors, curving her body to the right in a stretch. "Did more memories return?"

"Yeah."

She stretches to the left. "Stellar. I initially had to go through twice before my memories returned."

"Makes sense."

Willow puts her hands on her hips. "What's that suppose to mean?"

"I don't know how anything can penetrate through all that hair."

She thinks I'm joking. "The headaches are hangover city, aren't they?"

I nod. "Thanks for the heads up about all that."

"Oh. Oops," is all she says.

The two gaming binoculars on the sofa remind me about my last visit here. "Are you going to tell me what was up with you and Liam earlier?"

"Nope." Willow drops her arms to her side. A second later, she punches a code into the keypad and the door opens.

"I'm not going to drop it."

She stays silent as I follow her along the stone path through the dark forest.

My hands squeeze into tight fists. "Do you have any idea how infuriating you can be?"

Willow seems pleased by my comment and leads me further down the path than before. She stops before I even notice the slight red filter ahead. Either she has X-ray vision or she's somehow being prompted to stop. Either is plausible in this place.

When we're side by side, I ask, "Do you think there's even a remote chance the Schedulers will listen to what I have to say?"

Willow's shoulders slump. "Look, maybe it's not such a good idea. It sounds like Jonathan was pretty direct about keeping you away from them."

"Maybe he thinks we have a good chance. I don't know why he is so against this, but it feels right, Willow."

She sighs. "I know you believe in this, and I respect you for that. I'm afraid if you push this, though, the others are going to get in trouble. Anna, Owen, Clara, Liam, and Elliott, they all still have their abilities. And Morgan, she has the most at stake. She's risking her future as an Elite. Most people would give their right arm to be in her position."

"Have you considered the possibility that their memories and their families are more important than their careers?"

Willow doesn't answer.

"Is remembering your family more important than your career?" I pry.

"How dare you ask me such a thing!" Willow, popped back to life, is her fiery self again. "Of course my family is more important!"

"So you can see my point," I say calmly.

Willow does not look pleased by my comment. "It's time to proceed."

"You can't stand being proven wrong!"

"That has nothing to do with it. I have a job to do here and you're making things difficult, as usual."

"Oh, that's right, the important job of getting my memories back. So, you're admitting that having our memories is important?"

"Of course it's important!"

"Then why are they taken away to begin with?"

"Because it's necessary for our job! You know that!"

"You sound like Jonathan, and I don't mean that as a compliment." I walk past her and place my hand on the red-tinted wall, thankful when the bubble forms around me and turns black to block Willow out.

The images begin on the futuristic television screen.

Moving day. My parents walk around me carrying boxes into the empty house I will live in until my death. Little-me, extra tall and lanky in my preteens, enters what is to be my bedroom and begins unpacking baseball cards while my dad yells at my mom for putting something in the wrong place. There's the old man I know so well.

The image fades and the translucent red bubble around me turns to red smoke and blows down the stone path. I press forward, repeating the steps again and again, ignoring the unusually silent Willow as she leads the way: two years later at a job site with my dad for the first time, a year after that at my Grandpa's funeral.

Next, an even taller, more awkward me is in a closet with a girl named Holly. My cheeks burn in embarrassment as I watch myself. Not just because of the way my jeans are rolled tightly around my ankles or that my shirt resembles something Charlie Brown would wear, but because my clumsiness proves this must be my first kiss. I hope so anyway. Twenty grit sandpaper is smoother than my moves.

"That's probably enough for today," Willow says from behind when the smoke has vanished.

Turning and looking beyond her up the path, I see we've traveled far enough that the door is no longer visible. After a quick inventory to determine that I'm feeling all right, I turn and continue down the hill.

"The more you take in, the more pain you'll endure later," Willow says behind me.

I keep walking.

"It's your head." Her voice is casual. I'm certain it was

paired with a shrug.

Without Willow leading the way, I smack into the next wall with my face. Willow's laugh is snuffed out when the bubble forms around me. I'm even taller now, but still string bean thin. I'm trying to please my dad while we build the shed, but he curses at me for bringing him the wrong hammer. I struggle with the four-by-eight plywood sheet that's too big for me to grip while the old man vomits obscenities to no one in particular.

Because I'm too proud to ask Willow to lead me to the next screen, I hold my hands in front of me on my way down the path. I probably look like a zombie, but at this point, I don't care. As my vision sharpens, the red tint becomes clear before I make contact.

My next memory takes me to a school dance. Though I can tell I'm less lanky by the broadness of my shoulders, the roomy blue suit doesn't do much to show this. Four different girls approach me to dance, Holly included, and I deny all of them. At least I am nice when I say no. Still, watching the girls' disappointment from the outside makes me feel like a jerk.

When the image vanishes, Willow says, "I'm calling it. If I have to drag you up the hill myself, I will. I don't care how you feel right now, you'll be paying the price later."

I consider arguing, but chances are she's right. I keep my mouth shut while we walk up the long, stone pathway. When we reach the top, Willow holds the door open for me.

A red light turns green above one of the doors across the room and Evelynn comes through the doorway with a short guy trailing behind her. I wonder if I look as bad as she does.

"Can I have a second?" Evelynn asks the guy. When he nods, she says to Willow, "Do you mind if I talk to Grant for a minute?"

Willow looks speculative, but agrees.

I walk with Evelynn around the corner. Her heels click against the marble floor. My work boots, on the other hand, are silent.

Two guys pass by, talking about some new game. When they've passed, Evelynn leans closer to me. "When you mentioned my clothing choice earlier…turns out, I was raised thinking my self worth came from my looks."

This is not the conversation I was expecting. I was hoping maybe she had devised the perfect plan of attack against the schedulers. No such luck.

"My mom was like me in the whole clothing department. Or, I guess I'm like her." Evelynn glances down and pulls on the hem of her short dress. "You were right. There are people out there who are only interested in one thing. More than a dozen men paraded in and out of our lives. They either left my mom for a younger woman, or they wanted to be more than my father."

No wonder she looks so beaten up. I shake my head. "I'm sorry."

She smiles, but a doleful look remains in her eyes. "I didn't realize why I am the way I am until now. I thought I had things all figured out. Anyway, I just thought I should say thanks."

"Evelynn, don't—"

"No. Thank you. You're the only person that has ever called me out about my appearance, at least in a way that felt sincere. What burns me the most is that I couldn't see it myself. I thought everyone was jealous of me. That probably sounds pretty shallow, huh?"

"I'm really sorry," I repeat because I have no idea what else to say.

"We have to win this, Grant. If I had kept my memories, I think I would've been a different person here. One of the few memories I had from my life was of my mom curling my hair and doing my makeup. It's like she wanted me to look like her. I guess I missed her enough that I wanted the same thing." Evelynn catches me off guard by laughing. "Would you believe I didn't use to dress this way?"

"Everything all right?" Willow's voice interrupts.

"Yeah, fine." Evelynn leans into me and her breath tickles my ear. "Thank you for caring."

I nod.

"I'll see you later." Evelynn steps back and pivots around Willow. "See ya, Willow. Oh, by the way, I like your shirt."

Willow gapes at Evelynn as she strides in the opposite direction like a runway model. Then she glances down at her tee. "What's with her?"

I shrug. "I guess she likes unicorns."

"Huh," is the best Willow can come up with.

6. You're not the only one around here with an opinion

As we walk, the gears in my mind spin in search of a solution to this memory loss mess. "Seriously, what am I going to do about the Schedulers?"

Willow looks too tired to answer.

"There has to be a way to see them," I urge.

"Maybe if you get in trouble—" She stops herself.

"What?"

"Nothing. Listen, kid, you're right. Our memories and our families are important. What you're proposing does feel like the right thing. I wish it could have been like that with my own kids, but the plausibility of actually making that happen is slim."

"I can't give up."

"Unless you get Jonathan on board—"

"There's no way that will happen."

Willow rubs my arm for a second. "Keep thinking, OK?" She pauses. "I'm sorry about before. I don't think you should give up."

Sometimes it's hard to believe there was a time when Willow wasn't one of my favorite people.

"After break, take Chris to get his first assignment in the Orders hall and then to training. Come back here after that."

Training. Sigh. I don't even bothering hiding my deflated tone when I say, "Later."

Willow and I go our separate ways. When I reach the quiet lobby, it's clear break has not arrived yet. I head to the B hall, hoping that Chris isn't in my room.

His room.

Screw it, I'll call it my room if I want to.

I mentally throw my fist in the air when I find—oh, this is getting confusing—our room lacking Chris's company. I walk down the hall to code, figuring after the memory injection thing, I could use a little relaxation.

I go under with little effort and come out feeling refreshed. My calimeter buzzes on my way to the kitchen. After a quick cup of coffee, I decide a wardrobe change couldn't hurt. I grab a fresh T-shirt, but keep the jeans. It's a silly thing, really, that Satellites ever bother to change clothes. I'll take this inconvenience over the funny looks the girls give me when I've been in the same shirt for a week, though.

When I make it into Benson, I spot Chris on the sofa where I left him. His head is resting on the cushion. Instead of acknowledging the noisy Satellites weaving through the furniture, he looks entranced by the floating lanterns.

"Let me guess, you scared her off," I joke.

He remains focused on the overhead lights as if he didn't hear me.

"How long did that take?"

He continues ignoring me.

"All right." I clap my hands together. "Good talk. I'll be over at the table with my friends. You can join me if you want, or I can meet you after break to get your assignment book."

Ta-da! Chris bounces back to life.

"Assignment book?" he questions, but I've already started walking away.

"Hey!" he shouts behind me. "What do you mean, my assignment book?"

Empathy grabs at my gut because I was just like him when I got here. Wearing less black, of course, and no makeup. Still, I can remember the same panic that has his face contorted. This causes my feet to stop moving until Chris catches up.

I fall into a chair at the table to join Clara, Owen, Anna, Rigby, and Whitfield. Chris grabs the other available seat across the table between Owen and Clara. I can't help but feel a tinge of resentment at Rigby's unwillingness to join my fight, but force myself not to show it. "Chris, here, just found out he's getting his assignment book."

Clara shows more sympathy than I ever got around here, squeezing Chris's arm. "Don't worry, you won't actually begin your assignment until you're ready."

"Put your eyes back in your head before you hurt yourself. What Clara means is, you won't be released into the wild until you're properly trained."

By her expression, it seems Clara doesn't approve of my teaching method. "I'm sure Grant has told you all about training."

Chris glares at me through his eyeliner.

"You haven't told him?" Clara accuses.

"I've been busy!"

Rigby and Owen's laughter only rattle Clara more.

"Grant! You were upset when Willow did that to you!"

Rigby and Owen try their best to pipe down.

I sit up straight, elbows off the table, and mock professionalism. "We'll be picking up your assignment book after break. You won't actually begin your assignment until you've passed training. In training, you'll learn to block. Rigby, want to tell Chris about blocking?"

"It's mind control, man! Wait until you see it! You'll have to practice with this guy, though. That sucks for you; he's a decent blocker."

Rigby stops talking. Everyone but Chris understands why and, therefore, avoids eye contact with me. Yes, my blocking was so good, I apparently stole everyone else's ability away.

"Not decent," I correct. "Not even close."

Anna is the first to look up. "You're being modest. You're probably the best this place has ever seen."

"I doubt that!" Chris's attempt at a joke could have been funny if the atmosphere hadn't depleted. Instead, you could ice an invisible cake with the thick air settled on the table.

"You're right," I say to Chris. "It's not true. Even if it were, it wouldn't matter. I lost my blocking ability."

I commend Chris for being the only one with the balls to break the silence, especially after his last comment bombed. "Lost it? I mean, I don't know what 'it' is, but I'm guessing it's important."

"Important enough around here that without it, they make you a Legacy." The thought occurs to me for the first time: how am I even supposed to train the guy?

"How do you lose something you've learned?"

"That's a good question. Anyone want to enlighten Chris about why I can no longer block?"

Not surprisingly, there's no taker so the job is mine. "I guess you could say it was an experiment gone awry. The best I can figure is something inside of me—my cells or chromosomes maybe—got permanently altered."

I've lost Chris and no one else seems anxious to jump in, so I continue. "The ability to block is genetic. You're here because your chromosomes set you apart from the majority of people. We're all here because of that; a defect, if you will."

"I'm defective?"

My eyes scan over Chris's collar.

Clara clears her throat, obviously in effort to change my focus. "No. You're not defective," she assures.

I muster enough self-control to go on without making a joke. "This defect allows us to get into people's heads. We can plant thoughts that would not have been there otherwise. Jonathan will tell you that we can assist people in emotional distress. You'll train until you've learned to hone in on this ability. Sadly, we can only do half the job that someone's family member could do for them without blocking."

By his expression, Chris took another detour without directions. "Then why are we here?"

"That seems to be the question, doesn't it?"

Rigby decides to talk. "There's no proof that someone, family member or not, can do a better job than we can."

My chair falls over when I stand. "Are you calling me a liar?"

Rigby stands to face me, bringing silence to our table and the tables around us.

"You're not the only one around here with an opinion," he says, his face dangerously close to mine.

"I never said I was."

"That's enough!" Whitfield wedges herself between us.

Rigby pulls at the bottom of his T-shirt, making his defined chest puff out through the thin material. He looks down at Whitfield, and then turns and stomps away. Whitfield gives me an apologetic look and runs after him.

I right my chair, sit, and try to will my adrenaline to evaporate.

"But if you lost your blocking ability—I don't understand," Chris says.

I look down at the table. "Neither do I."

The friction among us lingers during the remainder of break, even as the others do their best to divert their attention to a game of Sats. Chris, like me, gets food, but I only pick at mine.

When my calimeter finally buzzes, I mimic the others around the table by pushing the face to silence the alarm.

Chris can't hear a single one.

Clara tucks a few stray blond hairs behind her ear as she stands. "Good luck today." Although she should be saying this to Chris, her statement is directed at me.

The rustling of the Satellites digging for tockets and securing book bags and purses to their bodies has Chris's attention. I can tell he hasn't been brought up to speed about displacing, though he witnessed it during our field trip to see the Schedulers when Jonathan sentenced everyone back to their assignments. I should probably spend more time teaching him, but I feel so distracted.

As he and I make our way out of Benson, Chris stays focused on the surrounding Satellites as they drop through the floor.

"It's how we travel to our assignments on Earth. You enjoy a good adrenaline rush?"

He nods.

"You'll love displacing, then."

He says nothing and follows me to the end of the long line of Satellites in the Orders hall.

Five minutes later, we're at the front of the line. Bubblegum-girl, who gave me my first assignment, is at it again. Her school girl uniform is unusual, mostly because I've never seen a plaid skirt in such bright pink hues. Her eyes scan from my feet to my head and she appears amused. Smacking her gum, she shifts her attention to Chris. Upon asking his name, she accepts that Chris 's name is fitting for him and then she spins into the floor.

Staring at the place Bubble-gum girl just stood, Chris can't hide his confusion.

She reappears from the floor, smacks her gum, and holds out Chris's first assignment. Chris looks at the red book like it may bite him and then pulls on his collar as if he's being strangled.

"Here," Bubble-gum girl says after a few seconds.

Still reluctant, Chris finally accepts the book.

When we reach the courtyard, I swing one of the doors open and keep my back against the carved wood to watch Chris. In the bright sunlight, surrounded by vivid greenery and colorful flowers draping over car-sized planters, Chris could pass as a mere shadow in his all black getup.

His reaction to the place doesn't disappoint.

"Even I'll admit it's impressive."

He nods and his eyes stay large when I pass by him. I have to slow down twice on the curved path to let him catch up.

Chris follows me to an open space on the bleachers between Lawson and the girl he was talking to in Benson earlier. Dani, the girl from Benson, adjusts her knitted hat and crosses her legs in effort to take up less space. One row down in front of Dani, Billy's shoulders are so broad, the arm seams of his red shirt could split at any moment.

"Why are we here?" I whisper to my left. "We can't even block."

Lawson turns and opens his mouth to answer just as Jonathan clears his throat. The rustling in the bleachers settles and Lawson faces forward.

"Welcome, everyone. It is a pleasure to see you all again. Due to some scheduling conflicts, I haven't yet been given the chance to speak with your Legacies regarding your progress, but I expect you are all doing well. I am hopeful you have found your accommodations agreeable. Today is your first day of training, which always proves to be exhilarating."

Jonathan pushes up his sleeves and continues with the same spiel I remember. He wraps up *Introduction to Training* and asks for volunteers.

I chew on my lip and think about Willow volunteering, and how furious that made me. Then I stare at Chris's black-lined eyes. I wish I could block for so many reasons. Seeing the guy's face if I could volunteer is one of them.

How am I going to train him? Worry creeps back into my skull.

We watch with everyone else as Jonathan gives his first demonstration. Not from a volunteer, of course. Willow is the only person loony enough to do that.

Chris is puzzled, but also in awe after witnessing a block firsthand. "Jonathan will give another demonstration. Things will make more sense," I whisper into his pierced ear.

The next pair does the same drill and he looks less confused. By the time Jonathan wraps up the session with three more examples, Chris, like all the other newbies, is impressed.

Jonathan asks us all to join him after break tomorrow and we're dismissed.

"How are we supposed to teach something we can't do ourselves?" I say to Lawson while the bleachers clear.

Billy steps closer. "Just because you can't do it, doesn't mean you can't teach it."

Who is this guy, and what did he do with the jackass I used to know?

Lawson slides his hands into his jean pockets and leans forward to keep his voice low. "Are you still interested in seeing the Schedulers?"

"Sure, but I'm out of ideas on how to make that happen."

"Let's walk," Lawson says to Billy and me.

I jump down the bleachers behind him. Chris follows us, walking with the girls that Billy and Lawson are mentoring.

"I know when they're meeting."

Billy is as shocked as I am by this news. "How?"

We wait for the last few Satellites to go through the door, including our trainees. "That's not important."

I match Lawson's whisper. "OK. Then when?"

"Next break."

"Do you think we could get everyone together in such short notice?" I ask.

A grin plays under Billy's pointy nose. "Only one way to find out."

"Hey! Try to keep it on the DL!" Lawson yells after Billy, who is already through the door.

"What's got him so enthusiastic?" I ask Lawson.

When Lawson shrugs, his army-style shirt moves stiffly like it's been starched. "Who knows."

"So, seriously, man, who's your source?" I ask Lawson.

He shakes his head. "I wish I could spill, but I don't want to get in trouble."

"You can't tell me you're honestly worried about getting in trouble at this point."

Lawson chuckles. "Well, no. I don't want my source to go down for this, though. She doesn't deserve that."

"She, huh?"

"Forget I said that."

"Fine. Forgotten." I'm just glad he got the information. "Do you think the Schedulers will listen to us?"

"Based on Jonathan's reaction to the idea, probably not. I'm going to go catch up with Billy before half of Progression knows what we're up to and it gets back to Jonathan. I'll take care of getting the Elites together. Can you collect the other Satellites when they return from their assignments?"

"I can try. I'm going to see Willow in a few minutes so I'll let her know, too. Where should we meet?'

"Orders hall?"

"Sounds good. Thanks, man. I really appreciate this."

"It's the right thing to do," Lawson says over his shoulder as he jogs into the lobby.

I cross the hall to Chris. "I've got to head to Programming. You want to come with us to see the Schedulers?"

"Definitely."

"You don't have to, you know. Just because I'm your Legacy doesn't mean you have to risk getting in trouble."

Chris spins his leather bracelet until the buckle sits on the top of his wrist. "I don't know much about this place yet, but the funny thing is, I don't really mind being dead. I hate that my family and my girlfriend are beginning to feel really distant, though, and not in the same way as when I was alive."

"What do you mean?"

"When I went away last summer, the longer I was gone, the more I missed them. But here, it's the opposite." He shrugs. "It's like they're losing their place inside me. I don't like it." He cracks his knuckles. "It doesn't make sense why I can't be the one to help them."

I can't deny the guy is growing on me. Maybe like an unwanted mold, but growing on me all the same. "Where'd you go last summer?"

His blank expression shifts to dismal, making me regret asking the question. My curiosity about where Chris currently falls in the memory loss process wasn't worth depleting his mood.

"I wish everyone felt the way you do. Thanks for helping." My attempt at an emotional rebound works, but I pull for more. "I didn't get a chance to tell you before, but you did really well coding."

He rubs the back of his neck. "You did all right explaining it."

All right, enough with the niceties. "I'd better go." I smack his shoulder hard enough that he steps to the left to catch his balance. He doesn't seem to mind, though, probably because we both want the conversation to end. "I'll find you when I'm done."

Chris straightens his bag on his shoulder and his shoes squeak on the marble floor when he turns and walks toward Benson.

On my trek to Programming, I think of the best way to approach the Schedulers. Maybe Lawson's right about the Schedulers unlikeliness to listen to us. Why would they?

It's in the best interest of the Tragedies, that's why. Certainly they will consider that.

When I'm past the seating area and into the third hallway, the pain in my head starts, dull at first like before. I lean against the wall when the pounding blurs my vision. With my eyes squeeze closed, the memories come.

———

"Grant!"

Willow's voice is far away. I pull my face from the crook of my elbow and open my eyes. When I focus, Willow's running toward me, her ponytailed dreads so tall they almost hit the ceiling. For someone who's five foot nothing in a hallway with ten foot ceilings, that's saying something.

When she reaches me, I stand from my squatting position to stretch my aching knees. "I'm fine."

"Did your memories come back?"

I answer with a single nod, feeling overwhelmed by the flood of new information.

"Bringing the seventies back, huh?" I mumble, glancing at her tie-dyed tank and extra wide bell-bottom jeans.

Willow ignores me. Her bag rattles as it hits the marble floor and she's sitting cross-legged beside it a few seconds later. "Take some time to let your memories sink in. Wanna talk about them?"

I mimic Willow's position and tell her about meeting my neighbor, Nick, the day we moved into our new house.

We were instantly best friends, inseparable until he moved to Arizona my sophomore year. I tell her about my Grandfather's funeral and about how sad my mom was; she shut down like my father for a long time after that, driving a deeper wedge between her and my dad. I share the next memory, where I was on the job site with my dad. The old man taught me all about the basic tools and their purposes. I remember practicing saw cuts for my dad when I became a little older. I also remember him yelling a lot when the cuts were imperfect.

I purposely neglect to tell Willow about Holly, the girl that chased me all through high school and asked me to every formal dance. Maybe I'm old fashioned, but the guy should be the one to ask such things. She was cute and personable, but not my type. Thinking back, no girl in high school was really my type.

I force myself up off the floor and offer Willow my hand. She accepts and bounces to her feet. I swear the girl's teal flip flops are spring-loaded.

"Round three, here we come," she says and winks at me.

We walk side-by-side to the round room.

"Oh, hey, good news. Lawson found out the Schedulers are going to be together during next break. Think that big mouth of yours can help plead our case?"

Willow's happy-go-lucky attitude dials down half a notch. "You're off your rocker, kid."

"We're going to meet in the Orders hall," I sing in a worthless effort to persuade her.

"You're gonna need to come up with something wicked persuasive. If Jonathan's not buying it, they surely won't either."

"Will you at least be our escort again?"

Willow punches a code into the number pad by one of the six doors sporting a green light instead of red over the door frame. "Fine, but that's all I can do." Her feigned annoyance is comical.

I thank her and agree that getting us there is more than enough.

On the stone path, her steps are not bouncy and she's wringing her hands. What's got her dreads in a knot?

"You won't get in trouble, if that's what you're worried about. You can wait in another hallway when we go see them."

Her feet stop. "See who?"

My eyes narrow at her odd behavior. "The Schedulers."

She resumes her sluggish pace. "Oh, right."

"Is everything OK?"

Her shoulders raise when she inhales. I'm not sure, but there may have been a nod in there.

Instead of bulldozing her with questions, I accept her nonverbal cue to stop pressing. This turns out to be tough because I don't like seeing her look so worried, but I remain mute through the dense, green forest.

Based on the distance we travel down the path, I must be making decent progress. When Willow stops, I pass her and push my hand on the tinted red filter.

When the screen circles around me and the blackness

clears, a sweaty, post-puberty me is sitting in a *Bradley Construction* company truck with the window down. I look similar to what I look like now, minus some extra muscle definition. It's strange to watch.

My white truck moves out of the contractor's bay and becomes blocked by a guy transferring bags of mulch to his vehicle. Post-puberty me has clearly left his patience inside the home improvement store.

A Jeep backs up from an adjacent parking space. Watching the event feels like seeing a movie in slow motion. By the Jeep's path, there is no questions it's going to—

Crash!

Yep, that was an easy call. The Jeep's bumper won the fight against the company truck's fender. Watching post-puberty me, I realize I inherited some of my father's temper. Poor steering wheel.

Forget about the steering wheel, the girl who gets out of the Jeep is the one I really feel bad for. I cringe at post-puberty self's reaction. What a jerk! I don't recognize the guy that rips the paper from her hands and slams the door so hard her curls blow around her face.

The image fades and the red smoke blows away.

"You all right?" Willow asks.

When I don't answer, she says, "You remember that one?"

After a minute of slow breathing, I look up at Willow and shake my head. That was me in the movie, but nothing about it sticks in my head like the previous memories did.

Willow is acting even more strangely now. Mrs. Happy

Hippy bounces down the stone path like she's on a pogo stick. "Come on, kid!" For someone suddenly feeling upbeat, I can't help but wonder why her voice is shaky.

Frozen in place and staring at her, I blink to pull myself out of my stupor.

I'm still attempting to recall the memory presented in the last movie reel when I pass Willow. While I'm pushing against the next glass-like filter, I see Willow drop her facade an instant before the black screen encloses me. Her distress is unsettling enough to raise bumps on my arms.

Before my stomach calms, the screen pops to life, declaring another injection is on the way.

What is Crash doing back? And why is post-puberty me checking out the back of her pink gym shorts as she climbs from a rocky dirt path onto a large rock?

"It's beautiful!" Crash says from the top.

"You're beautiful." Post-puberty climbs the rock with much less effort and grabs her hand.

She tries to keep her windblown curls away from her face. "Do you believe in fate?"

The wind pushes Post-puberty's T-shirt against his chest. The worn cotton is almost see-through, revealing the defined lines between his abs. "No."

I didn't believe in fate, huh? What an idiot I was.

"Don't tell me you do." Yep, total idiot.

Crash bites her lip, and leans against post-puberty me. The kiss is much smoother than the one shared with Holly in the closet.

"Still all right?" Willow says from behind me.

Any shot of having a real memory of the event is carried off with the red smoke. My heartbeat skips faster and I try to keep my voice level. "Uh huh."

Afraid of Willow seeing my face, or maybe afraid to see hers, I push forward to the next memory in hopes that this one will stick. When the black screen vanishes, post-puberty me is in a blue kitchen kneeling in front of Crash. The couple's wardrobe is opposite from the last scene. Crash is wearing a black dress that could possibly turn a gay man straight and post-puberty me is in khaki pants, a dark red button up shirt, and a striped tie. Good thing that outfit didn't travel to my closet here.

Crash is gaping down, probably because Post-puberty looks an awful lot like a car salesman.

"Tate," he says. "You could do so much better. Every day I wonder why you're with me. Even though I'll never be able to give you the life you deserve, as long as any part of me exists I will love you. So much more than you'll ever know."

Tate?

My eyes stay frozen on the screen. The diamond catches the light and the white flash blinds me, making me feel even more discombobulated. The gears in my head spring apart from being in hyperdrive.

I turn away from Crash and car salesman me to regain my vision. Across the table from the small boy in the Captain America shirt is...*Elliott?*

When the image fades, I'm certain I'm going to vomit.

"You still okay?" Even in my state, the concern in Willow's voice is hard to miss.

Unable to speak, I push ahead. Someone's screwing with me. This has to be one of Willow's demented jokes. The girl, Tate, isn't even real. I'd remember her if she was, just like I remember my parents and my best friend. I'm waiting for Willow to say something like *gotcha* when I touch the next wall.

She doesn't.

This time, post-puberty me is sitting in the bed of the company pickup truck. The tailgate is open to face the lake and the wooded area across the water. The moon shines on Post-puberty like a spotlight, making his wet hair shine.

"Oh, come on!" the real me yells, taking a step back when Crash pops her head up from the truck bed.

Kneeling beside Post-puberty, she pulls a yellow child-sized T-shirt over her plaid bikini top.

Post-puberty disappears when he lays back in the truck bed. Crash falls forward, becoming invisible as well, and her laugher halts the crickets for a brief moment.

"I love you," Crash says.

"I love you more." I dislike hearing my own voice because it's so different than the one in my head. I especially don't like hearing my voice ramble these words specifically.

"It's not too late to run away to Vegas and get hitched," she says.

"Fat chance, woman. You're walking down that aisle so everyone can see how beautiful my future wife is." My twin's voice lowers. "And so everyone will know you're taken."

I take another step away from them and my heel hits the curved movie screen behind me.

"I love it when you flatter me," she says.

"Tate Bradley. You have to admit, the name has quite a ring to it."

I gasp and the image fades.

"Think you're up for one more?" Willow asks when the wind carries the lie away.

I ignore her and continue ahead.

The next fabrication rolls. Tubes from my nose and wrist connect almost-dead-me to various machines. Seeing myself with cancer, I have to swallow back vomit. Crash comes into the hospital room. She hands almost-dead-me a picture frame. The same frame, in fact, that currently houses a photograph of Willow and me. Guess that answers the question of where the frame came from. But it couldn't be, this isn't real.

"You forgot this," Crash whispers.

I think Crash is speaking to the real me until almost-dead me shows off his gray smile. His papery skin crinkles around his eyes. Putting the frame on the bedside table, he uses a lot of energy to move his body to the far side of the hospital bed. Crash, strangely, is not repulsed by him (that or she's an Oscar-worthy actress). She curls into his side and traces circles around the monitors on his bare chest. In the photo, he looks—*I look*—alive and healthy. Here in person, though, the pretend-me looks like a corpse beside her. At least her face has a bit of color, even if it is just the red around her puffy eyes.

I'm hunched over and looking at my boots when the red haze blows away. My head feels as heavy as a sandbag.

Lifting it, I almost scrape my nose on a brick wall.

"We've reached the end." Willow, now at my side, squeezes my hand. "You will have another killer headache, but the good news is, over a short time the spaces in your head will fill with loads more memories without being accompanied by pain. The headaches are just a result from the initial kick-start." Her optimism sounds fake.

After verifying that the wall extends deep into the woods in both directions, I look down at Willow and pull my hand from hers.

"What's wrong with you?" I demand.

"What?" She actually has the nerve to look hurt.

I never thought she would play so dirty, making up these scenes to back her and Liam's stories.

"Grant, wait!" Willow yells behind me, but I'm already halfway up the path.

"Grant!"

"Screw you, Willow!"

7. She's as real as you and me

Willow's small size makes her fast. Within a minute, she grabs my wrist and yanks me hard enough that I'm forced to change directions on the stone path of this memory hell.

"Oh my Gosh. You don't remember any of it, do you?" She pauses. "You're going through the memory replays again!"

"No, I'm not."

"You have to, it's the only way." She stops and loosens her grip. "Remember when I told you I had trouble with my memories?"

I stay quiet.

"I know it can be confusing—horrifying even—when you watch yourself and real recollection never comes. I get it. You're convinced what you're seeing is fake. I had to go through parts of the memory process twice. Jonathan says it's uncommon, but all of the Legacies are trained to take their Satellites through again if needed." Willow fidgets with the hem of her tie-dyed shirt and her voice lowers to almost a whisper. "Give it another shot. Please."

I weigh my options. What if Tate is real? Wouldn't I want to remember her? Why would I be so afraid of this part of my life? It's just that, though: that Tate actually could be real. Then what? It's not like I can have a life with her. Heck, with the way this place runs, I couldn't even visit her.

Willow's pleading look makes me soften. I've come to respect and love her so much that I don't want to disappoint her.

So, with reluctance, I finally agree.

Willow's grateful expression takes away some of the sting I feel from uncertainty. She instructs me to stay where I am, jogs up the hill, and opens the door. The top half of her body disappears into the round room.

"What are you doing?" I yell.

Her head reappears in the doorway. "Reconfiguring your settings."

Willow is down the path a couple minutes later and we proceed, side-by-side, to the red screen. I watch all five movies play out again. When I'm finished, I'm even more frustrated.

A part of me secretly hoped I would remember. At least then, maybe I wouldn't feel so disturbed by the images. Watching my cancer-ridden self act out the unfamiliar scene is like watching someone steal my life by pretending to be me.

"So?" Willow's voice is almost a whisper.

I shake my head.

Willow squeezes her hips like she's kneading dough. "Well, frick."

That's the worst she can come up with?

I start up the path, deciding with finality what I

watched wasn't real. It couldn't have been.

"Grant, listen, we need—"

"I don't want to talk about it."

"Do you remember her at all?" Willow asks, breathing heavy behind me. "Grant, you have to believe me. She's as real as you and me." She's a good actress. Maybe even better than Oscar-worthy Crash from the movies.

"I've never lied to you."

Feeling my anger expand like a balloon in my chest, I push the door open with more force than necessary. "I hope you're kidding."

"No, I'm not kidding! I may have forgotten to tell you a few things now and then—"

I spin around, stopping her when she's a few steps inside the room of doors. "A few?"

Even through her panting, she looks wounded. "Okay, maybe slightly more than that. I've never lied to you, though. You honestly don't remember anything about Tate?"

"Of course not! She's not real!"

Willow's eyes begin to water. She takes a slow step back, followed by another. Her pant legs sway with each step, earning their bell-bottom name.

She slides down the curved wall between two of the doors.

"Are we done here?" I ask in a rough voice.

She pulls her hands away from her face and stares at the floor.

Willow flinches when my fist pounds into the wall before my departure out of this hell. Why is this happening to me?

Unsure of what I'm supposed to do to kill time until break, I pace in the last hallway of Programming before exiting. If I go back to my room or Benson, Chris may be there, and I don't have the patience for him right now.

Forcing the made-up girl from my head, my thoughts shift to Meggie because she's actually real. I wonder how she's dealing with the incomprehensible hurt from the loss of her kids and her mom. She feels so far away. I hope her kids are with her.

If only Jonathan or the Schedulers could see firsthand how Josh and the twins have helped Meggie, they would understand; they'd have to understand. How will I and a few other Satellites convince the Schedulers? My attempt at persuading Jonathan has been futile.

I try to devise a plan, but my thoughts keep returning to the three movie reels.

Darn it! Why can't I just let this go?

I snake my way back through the hallways I traveled just minutes ago.

Willow is still in the same place and position she was in when I left her, but now her face is hidden in her knees and her shoulders are bouncing up and down.

"Hey, freak."

When she looks up, my heart becomes weighted, sinking below my ribs. Uncomfortable around crying girls, I try to lighten the mood. "Know where a guy can get some coffee around this place?"

Willow wipes her cheeks with her fingers. When she's pushed herself up from the floor, I put my arm around her and we walk silently back to her room.

Once there, I get Willow to the orange sofa and then go to work pouring coffee. A minute later, I'm crossing the room with two full cups, black, straight up.

I hand Willow the mug that's painted like a candy cane. "I need to talk to you about my memories."

"What if what we did broke your connection to Tate permanently?"

I decide to entertain the theory that what Willow says is true, that Tate is real. The idea is difficult to grasp, though, no matter how hard I try to believe it. "So, what if it did?"

"We would be responsible for—my God, what if we've messed up your entire future? I mean, I realize we kind of already have, with the blocking issue, but this is bigger than that. What if you're damaged mentally as well?"

"Seeing as you've always thought that about me, I guess you'd be right again." My effort to elevate her mood is wasted.

Willow places her coffee on the end table without taking a drink. "How do you feel about all this?"

"What kind of question is that?"

"A valid one. Are you mad? Do you believe me about Tate being real? Do you forgive me?" she adds quieter.

"Is that what this is about? You're looking for forgiveness?"

She weaves her fingers together. "No. Yes. I don't know. I feel like this is all my fault."

"A lot of Satellites had a part in this, including me,

apparently."

"I'm your Legacy. I'm supposed to protect you."

Chris's face pops in my head, black eyeliner and all. "You're supposed to teach me, not protect me."

"That's not the way I work. You won't either once you get to know Chris." Willow hugs her arms around herself. "I'm so afraid that what I've done has permanently broken your connection."

"What would be so wrong about that?" I try my best to sound convincing.

Willow pushes on the face of her timepiece a second after mine buzzes. "We'd better get going." She lacks her usual pep when she stands. I like her better when her attitude matches her colorful shirts.

Break's here already? Oh no. "We have to meet the others!"

"Lucky for you, I know a shortcut. You're gonna love it, kid."

"I hate the sound of it already."

Willow forces a smile.

I follow Willow out of the room and through the circular common area, happy that her pace has quickened. After a couple of turns, she leads the way down one of the more narrow hallways, and my breath hitches.

Larger-than-life photographs of Ryder and Meggie look back at me from the walls. The vibrant images flow together like a collage at different stages of my Tragedies lives. My eyes stop at a much younger Meggie. She was so beautiful, so happy, before her life was stolen from her.

Willow stares at the wall with me, no doubt focusing on Ryder's photos. After a few seconds, she yanks on my arm. My eyes continue to scan the photographs while she pulls me through the corridor. We dead-end at a golden door.

"Put your hand here," she directs, pointing to a rectangular, glass insert on the wall by the door.

Willow's ideas usually scare the crap out of me. I'd rather hang out here in the photo gallery for a while, but I know there's no time for that. We have to collect the others and get to the Schedulers before break ends.

Willow doesn't give me a chance to lift my hand. Instead, she grips my wrist and forces my hand against the cool glass. A blue light glows around my palm, prompting a wall panel showing Ryder's photo to descend into the floor. Expecting the golden door in front of me to open instead, I look to Willow for an explanation.

"Go ahead," she urges.

I lean over the edge and look into the darkness. "I'm not going down that! It's an elevator shaft!" *Minus the elevator!*

"May want to hold on to your bag, kid."

Willow pushes against my spine hard enough that I stumble into the narrow hole of the unknown.

"I'll meet you down there," Willow's voice echoes after me. I'd swear she's laughing.

Brightness blurs around me, but the space constricts tighter as I'm sucked down. I'm shocked that my arms aren't scraping against the sides. My feet hit a hard surface where an illuminated golden wall awaits three inches from my nose.

"Have a fabulous day," GPS Jeanette says and the wall slides upward.

I look up, half-expecting to see Willow plummeting after me, but the elevator shaft is now dark and seemingly empty. Shaking my head, I step out.

"So, what'd ya think?"

Willow's voice makes me jump back and my body hits the black marble wall. There's zero trace of the opening I exited from two seconds ago.

"Quick, right?"

"Uh huh. Quick," I reply.

Willow grabs my hand and pulls me through the crowded lobby in silence. As I turn towards Benson, Willow tugs me in the opposite direction.

"What are you doing? We have to meet the others!"

"This is more important."

I try to pull away, but Willow's grip tightens. She jerks me along and for a few minutes, I'm unsure if I could get free of her grasp even if I tried.

"Willow, we have to meet the others. What about the Schedulers? You said you'd take us!"

She says nothing and drags me through the courtyard door and down the stone path.

"Finally we get bone," she mumbles, leading us straight to Jonathan, who is observing the handful of Satellites on the field.

As we get closer, I realize it's not just a handful. It's seven, to be exact.

I lean down to Willow as we jog. "The new Elites?"

"Based on how Morgan described the team, I would assume so."

I hadn't considered we would be replaced so soon, although, how could we not? There are still jobs to do, Tragedies to save. I scan the faces and can't help but feel a pinch of jealousy.

"I thought there would be an even number of girls and guys," I mumble.

Willow doesn't reply, but trusts me enough not to flee because she's released my arm.

Aside from Morgan, the only other female Elite is in the distance, and the new girl looks nothing like Morgan. Amidst the field of would-be professional body builders, poor Morgan looks out of place not only physically, but socially as well. Literally the odd girl out, she's playing Watcher a.k.a. referee while the others practice blocking drills. All six Elites are either constipated, or so focused on their training they've forgotten that it's all right to relax their facial muscles.

Morgan takes her attention off two of the guys and throws Willow and me a quick wave. I wonder if anyone was able to get the message to her about our next attempt to see the Schedulers. I consider saying something now, but Jonathan would probably be curious if I just walked over to her and began chatting.

"Willow, we need to get going," I hiss quietly because Jonathan is within earshot.

Willow reaches Jonathan and is all attitude with her hands on her hips. "We have a problem."

Jonathan keeps his eyes on the working Elites for a few

seconds before acknowledging us. "Willow, Grant, what a surprise." If Jonathan is annoyed by Willow's rudeness, his pleasant expression and tone hide his true feelings. "Grant, would you be so kind to excuse us for a moment?"

Before I can answer, Jonathan leads a very unhappy Willow to the corner of the field. I do my best to not be the weird eavesdropper by turning my attention to the practicing Elites.

My nerves are in overdrive as I tick away the minutes we are losing. We should already be in Benson with the others. As I watch the Elites perform blocks, it's clear no one is playing dirty like we did in training. Amazing how things change when Billy is pulled from the picture.

"What you made us do was wrong!"

Willow's volume doesn't only catch my attention; the Elites have stopped working and have shifted their focus as well.

Jonathan's hand is on Willow's upper arm, but she jerks out of his grasp. "He's not right! We ruined him!"

That's as good a cue as any to join the conversation.

"…take him through again," Jonathan is saying.

"I already have! He's gone through twice!"

Jonathan's creased forehead fills my gut with nausea. I force the extra saliva down my throat. "What's going on?"

"Everything's fine. Please allow us another moment," Jonathan says lightly, all evidence of his concern gone. He even has the nerve to smile.

Willow's eyes are so narrow I doubt she can see. "No, stay. Everything is definitely *not* fine."

"Willow—" Jonathan starts.

"He doesn't remember her. Not at all. Do you hear me? Nothing, Jonathan!"

Jonathan turns and takes a few steps on the field. "Elites, please continue with training. I will send Wynn to release you." He pace is brisk when he walks past Willow. "Come with me."

"Earth to Grant," Willow says over her back and motions me to hurry up.

After four paces, I catch her and we follow Jonathan up the path and out of the courtyard.

The three of us are silent as we move down the hall, away from the noise in the lobby. I turn to glance in the direction of Benson and my stomach feels sour. I have to meet the others.

"Come on, kid!"

Willow's voice snaps me back to her direction. She's almost running to keep up with Jonathan. A return to Programming seems to be his plan of action, whatever the heck that entails, but when we enter the maze of hallways, his route is different than the one I have used in the past.

When we reach a long hallway of identical, gilded doors, a woman who I remember filling in on one of my training sessions approaches. "Jonathan, what an unexpected surprise. I'm just on my way to a meeting."

"Wynn, my apologies for the interruption, but I have an urgent matter and would be grateful for your assistance. Do you think the Schedulers can make due with your absence for a bit?"

"The Schedulers?" I blurt out.

Jonathan takes Wynn by the arm, redirecting her attention off me and to the golden door on the right that Jonathan has already opened.

"Allow me a brief moment," Jonathan says and, with that, they both disappear into the room.

Willow leans against the wall as if this is no big deal.

"Willow, we're wasting time! We have to get to the Schedulers. Maybe Wynn can help us. This may be our only chance."

"I'm sorry, but this is more important."

"Come on!" My patience is barely intact. "It's just a few memories!"

Willow spits a chip of orange fingernail polish on the marble floor. "It's more than that. You don't realize what this means and what it can change. You have to remember. There are no other options."

The door opens before I can argue.

Wynn extends her hand and shakes Willow's. "It's been far too long. Are you enjoying your time with Troy?"

Willow's eyes move in my direction for a second. "I was."

I wish Wynn wouldn't laugh. Lord knows the queen of sarcasm doesn't need to be provoked.

Wynn becomes somber and uses both hands to steal one of mine. With a firm squeeze, she says, "How are you holding up, dear?"

That's a strange question. "Uh, fine, I guess."

"Good, good. Listen, best of luck today." She looks at

Jonathan, keeping my hands between hers. "Everything will be fine. I'm optimistic that this confusion will be straightened out by this afternoon."

I look over at Willow, hoping she'll help translate whatever Wynn is talking about, but she offers nothing.

That's my Willow, always leaving me in the dark.

"I appreciate you relieving me and, again, offer my sincere apologies for not allowing you more notice," Jonathan says to Wynn after she's released my hand. "I do hope you are right."

Wynn splits off from us at the end of the hallway, her long ponytail swinging side to side when she walks. Jonathan, Willow, and I quickly move in the opposite direction.

After winding through twelve vacant hallways, we are at the round room I have come to loathe. "Please tell me we're not doing this again?" I say under my breath.

Jonathan is busy working the keypad with Willow on silent standby. After he opens the door, he steps to the side and extends his hand for Willow and me to pass through.

The only thought running through my head is that I should be meeting the Schedulers.

8. The circumstances do not seem to be in your favor

"What's his problem?" I whisper to Willow while she and I try to keep up with Jonathan through the maze of hallways.

"Shhhh," Willow hisses back.

I fire back in a fast whisper, "So the memories aren't sticking. What's the big deal? It's not like I'm going to be reuniting with that girl or anything. We've lost enough time that we may as well kiss our plan goodbye. Do you realize how ticked off the others are going to be?"

Willow's face turns red and her jawline flexes, but she says nothing. She has to take two steps to my one, so maybe she's trying to save her strength by ignoring me. Or maybe she just likes to keep things from me. The latter is probably more accurate.

"Willow, we missed it!" My volume prompts Jonathan to glance over his shoulder, but I don't care. I smack the face of my calimeter to silence the buzzing that signifies the end of break. I redirect my thoughts to Lawson and how I'm going to explain this to him.

Willow's flip flops seem loud in the empty corridors.

With Jonathan mute, her shoes are the only sound of our journey when we reach the lobby. When empty, the space between the gleaming walls and floor seem impossibly larger.

My stomach feels sick. We missed break, and likely our only opportunity to plead our case to the Schedulers.

"I would like the two of you to accompany me, please," is all Jonathan says.

Willow sucks in air when Jonathan cuts his path towards the Orders hall. When he reaches the end of the hallway, he bangs on the golden desk three times, prompting the marble panel to slide open like an airplane hangar door on a much fancier scale.

Willow stretches on her tip-toes to get closer to my ear. "He's taking us to the Schedulers," she whispers, even though Jonathan can probably still hear her.

I can't hide my excitement. "This is it, Willow. This is the break we need. We'll finally get to see them and plead our case. Do you think it will work without the others?"

In front of us, Jonathan clears his throat in a reprimanding way. I stare at the back of his head for a couple of seconds while we walk through the corridors similar to those we just came from. Turning my attention back to Willow, she gives me a warning look and shakes her head. I ignore her, but keep quiet as we move through the rest of the hallways because my mind is busy searching for the best way to approach the Schedulers.

Jonathan wastes no time pushing one of the mammoth, glass-paneled doors open. He says nothing, but doesn't close the door behind him. Willow and I take this as our cue to follow him. When we walk into the Colosseum-like setting, hundreds of eyes lift to look at us, each pair belonging to the people occupying the two-tiered circular desk.

Before anyone can say anything, Jonathan's voice booms through the open space.

"We discussed this, Landon! Have we not?"

At the center of the lower desk, Landon stands and pulls on the cuffs of his white button-up shirt to straighten his sleeves. The starched material is as stiff as his posture. "Whoa, Jonathan. Please dial down a notch."

Landon glances at Willow and me. The last time I saw him was when he was releasing me back to Meggie's assignment. He looks about as happy now as he did then.

"I will do no such thing!" Jonathan looks close to throwing a punch. Or, two.

Willow's hand grips my forearm. I look down at her and try to offer a look that says, "It's all right."

"Three times." Jonathan turns slowly to look at all of the Schedulers when he reaches the tiled sunburst design at the center of the desks. "Grant has been through Programming three times! His memories are gone."

"Calm down, Jon—"

"I warned you about this, Landon."

Willow clings so tightly to my arm that my hand begins to tingle.

Wynn, seated next to Landon, clears her throat. How stupid of me to assume she was only meeting with the Schedulers. She's one of them! I could have talked to her when I saw her during break!

All the color has drained from her face. "How could you do this to that poor boy?" she asks.

Boy?

Anger crackles inside of me, probably from my dad calling me *boy* when I screwed something up at work. The memories of those moments are so clear, they could have happened yesterday.

"I'm standing right here!"

My volume prompts Willow to release her hold on my arm.

"I'm standing right here," I repeat in a calmer tone now that I have everyone's attention, though my fingernails continue to bite into my palms. "Will someone please tell me what's going on?"

"Yes, Landon, do enlighten us about this new revelation." Jonathan scans his eyes around the double desk. "New to me, anyhow."

Landon weaves his fingers together. "I think you ought to be the one to enlighten us, friend, seeing as I am clueless about the stones you are casting."

Jonathan grins, but not one of those friendly-type smirks. "I disagree, *friend*. You threatened to keep his memories and now it has transpired. The circumstances do not seem to be in your favor."

"Keep my memories?" I blurt out.

Landon clears this throat and holds his hand up to stop my interruption from going any further. "It is rude to interrupt."

Willow has my arm again. I'm sure this is her silent way of telling me to play it cool, which is difficult, given the current situation.

"If you remember correctly, I merely proposed that Grant not be allowed to proceed with Programming."

Jonathan looks like he's going to tear out of his blue T-shirt like the Incredible Hulk.

Landon seems oblivious to Jonathan's foul mood and continues. "As you and I know from our history of memory harvesting, each memory has the capacity to be replayed only three times. Never have we been faced with sending a Satellite through Programming more than twice. Certainly you must be mistaken."

Jonathan's crimson color deepens. "Stating facts we both already know is not helpful, and there has been no mistake made."

Landon is silent for a few long moments. His expression is unreadable. "Well then, if you are certain Grant has really gone through three times then maybe…" he trails off and looks thoughtful as if considering something.

"Landon?" an impatient Jonathan asks.

"Well, maybe, this is his destiny."

"This is not his destiny! This is a problem!"

Landon shrugs. "Maybe. Maybe not."

Jonathan exhales a deep breath that forces his shoulders to lower a bit. "This is not part of his path, as you and I both know from his book."

Landon pushes his chest out and leans forward. "I *wrote* his book."

"Rewriting a future is not something that should be taken lightly." Wynn's the only person besides me with the gonads to speak during this two-person conversation. I'd think some of the other Schedulers would want to put in their two cents. Everyone else around this place does.

Landon remains calm. "The boy has only lost his blocking ability. I'm sure finding a place for him in eternity won't be overly difficult."

Again with the *boy*?

"Excuse me!"

Oh, good. Someone else is willing to jump into the conversation.

Willow steps in front of me. "Sorry Jonathan, but I'm calling B.S. on this!"

Jonathan steps back in agreement, seemingly relieved to let Willow take over, maybe so that he can regain his composure.

"What about Tate's life? Are you going to rewrite hers as well? You're the ones who changed their futures! It's not his fault that his memories didn't disappear like they should have. You were the ones willing to risk the unknown to keep him as one of your superstar Satellites, were you not? And now you're going to tell me you actually have the nerve to write him off? No! That's not fair."

"Wait a minute! This is my life you're all discussing like I'm not even here! Personally, I don't see the big deal in these lost memories."

Jonathan sucks in a whistling breath.

"I'm sorry Jonathan, but I don't. Missing a few pieces

of my life doesn't change who I am. My blocking ability is gone, so I'm worthless as a Satellite. I get that. Here's the thing, though: Satellites are amazing. Really, they are." I look at Willow. "And Elites…there's no words for the emotional strength that some of them have, but even with all the talent and all the training, Satellites are not as effective as a person's own loved ones. I've seen this firsthand."

"Grant—"

"No, Jonathan, let me finish." I scan the faces staring back at me until I find Sophie, far to my left, in the second tier of the desk. She looks frightened, like she's silently pleading for me to keep my mouth closed. I have no intentions of outing her, but I won't keep my mouth shut about this. I can't. It's too important.

"Grant—"

Why does Jonathan keep interrupting me? "They need to hear this!"

I can only look at Jonathan for a second because his scolding expression makes me feel worse. "The last thing I want to do is get anyone in trouble, but something has to be done. Do with me whatever you want. Put me in some boring position forever. I don't care. But please, *please,* consider what I am saying. You have the ability to change the way the entire afterlife works. Consider how this could impact not just the living, but the dead." I pause for a quick breath and force myself to slow down. Otherwise, the Schedulers may discard my words as mere rambling. This is too important. "Stop taking our memories. Instead, let us help where we can be truly helpful. It's a win-win for everyone. I'm not the only one who feels this way. There are others—"

The veins on Landon's neck strain against his white collar. "I should have known it was you behind this mess. Others were here earlier, spewing the same lies you speak now."

"They were here?" Love and appreciation for my friends boil over inside me. They came! They found their way without Willow and they really came!

Jonathan places his hand on my shoulder. I pull away from his squeezing grip and ignore Landon's scowl, becoming more animated by pacing in front of Jonathan and Willow. "I've seen it firsthand, a dead loved one helping a live family member. You need to know the truth about this. It works! Better than even the work an Elite can do. Blocking isn't necessary, just having the presence of a loved one is enough. It can't be just Meg—"

"Grant!"

Realizing my mistake, my mouth snaps shut. Maybe I should have let Jonathan stop me earlier.

"Please, continue." Landon presses. "Who is it you saw with Meggie?"

"Let's focus on the more pressing issue," Jonathan replies in a stern tone. "How are you keeping Grant's memories from him?"

I put myself between Jonathan and Landon. "Who cares about my damn memories! Don't you see the bigger issue here? Sophie! Please help me out!"

Landon's smirk raises bumps along my arms and the

silence that follows brings so much tension, the columns around us could crumble into dust from the invisible pressure. Jonathan looks down at his leather shoes and rubs his forehead. Willow's mouth is hanging open. Sophie's face has gone from pale to green as she is now the center of attention.

"Sophie, why don't you join the three on the floor?" Landon's voice is eerily calm.

Sophie looks horrified. Slowly, her chair scrapes across the marble. She stands and moves stiffly around the back of the circular desk and into the opening that leads to the sunburst center of the circle. She stops beside Willow and hugs herself like she's cold. This could be from Landon's icy stare.

"Sophie, is there a reason why Grant would be asking you for help?"

"Sophie, do not answer him." Jonathan begins walking towards Landon. "Find a way to return Grant's memories. They are rightfully his."

The desk is all that separates Landon and Jonathan. Both men lean forward like two bucks about to lock antlers.

Wynn stands and puts her arm across Landon's chest. I almost laugh. Wynn couldn't stop the two if she tried. The hostility is so prevalent, I'm not sure a concrete wall could stop them.

"Stop meddling in affairs that are not your concern, *friend.*"

Jonathan bangs his fist on the desk, making Wynn jump back. "Everything that goes on here is my concern," he replies to Landon through clenched teeth. "I suggest you find a way to return to Grant what is rightfully his."

After an intense staring contest, Jonathan removes his fist, but keeps his hand clenched and presses it against his mouth. He turns to Willow, Sophie, and me and jerks his head toward the door as our cue to leave.

"We are not done here!" Landon yells.

I stop behind Sophie when we're halfway to the door, ready to turn and plead my case. I've already caused plenty of trouble, but Meggie could have died that day in her kitchen. Getting the Schedulers to understand this is too important to ignore.

"Keep moving." Jonathan's low demand in my ear says now is not the time to push him, so I resume my path to the door.

Once outside, Jonathan's tone is urgent. "Get them to Grant's home. Now."

Stunned expressions always look strange on Willow. "You mean his room?"

"No. His *home*. Wait for me there. And Willow," Jonathan pauses, making sure he has Willow's full attention. "Do not stop for anyone."

Willow swallows and nods. "Come on, guys."

I look away from Sophie, worried she's going to cry, and follow her and Willow. Even with my mentor's short legs, I'm jogging to keep up.

When we exit the orders hall, Willow continues her quick pace through the empty lobby, leading us toward Programming.

Meggie and I follow behind Willow and jog through

the corridors of Programming. I'm appreciative when Willow finally slows her pace. Around the corner, I recognize the hallway from the shortcut Willow forced me to use last break when she tricked me into seeing Jonathan instead meeting my friends in Benson. The elevator shaft is invisible now, hidden behind the photo collage wall of my two Tragedies.

Sophie gasps and moves closer to the wall, tracing her finger along Meggie's face in the family photo. It's hard to believe Sophie was just a child such a short time ago. She moves her gaze across the life sized photos of Meggie.

"She's so happy." Sophie's whisper seems to be more to herself, so neither Willow or I reply.

Willow's attention has stopped on a picture of Ryder and Hannah. I wish she were able to see him grow up. If things had been different in Progression and we could watch over our own families, she would have had that chance. The guilt weighing on me about getting Sophie in trouble lessons, but not by much.

Willow grabs my hand and gives me a tug, pulling me to the end of the hallway. I stare dumbly at the square insert next to the door wondering why we would walk all the way here just to open the elevator shaft and go back down to the lobby.

Willow huffs out a loud breath of disapproval. I snap out of my frozen state, realizing Willow has no interest in the glass insert where I placed my hand earlier today. Instead, she grabs the door handle and turns it herself.

The cool air hits my face, then my bare arms, but that's not what raises the goosebumps on my skin.

"Come on, move!" Willow's push on my back is forceful enough that I step four paces down the dirt path cutting through the trees, leaving Sophie plenty of space to enter. Willow's head jerks through the doorway for a glance back into my hallway of photos before she slams the door closed.

I try to rub the raised bumps on my arms away. "Where are we?"

Willow walks past me. "That's your house. Do you recognize it?"

"I don't have—I don't understand." I stare at the single story house in the clearing at the end of the path. It's not huge, but the masonry work is impressive. I know the front elevation, but—it couldn't be. Could it? "I was going to build a house like this."

Willow pauses on the path and spins around. Her face is as bright as the vivid tie-dye of her shirt. "Yeah?"

"The plans were almost done, but then…"

"What?" Willow's tone sounds hopeful.

"I was diagnosed."

"No recollection, I guess, of who helped with those plans?"

"My old man, of course."

She doesn't turn around fast enough to hide her disappointment. "This is where you're going to live once you complete your Legacy obligations," she says over her shoulder. "Under normal circumstances, you'd be joined with a loved one. If it were a spouse, the two of you would live here together." Willow's volume drops. "Since that isn't the case…"

"I'm alone," I say to finish the sentence when she doesn't.

Willow continues down the path leading to the house.

The trees surrounding the house are like fire against the clear sky, boasting brilliant reds, yellows, and oranges. Fall. I should have known it would be perfect. The season—my favorite season—marks the beginning of deer hunting.

Sophie walks beside me, but I have a hard time looking at her because I feel so crummy about dragging her into this mess. Instead, I focus on the lake to the right of the house. The fire from the trees reflects like a mirror in the still water. "I'm really sorry for outing you back there."

An awkward minute of Sophie maintaining her silence and Willow pretending to ignore us goes by.

"Please say something."

"What am I supposed to say? You've put me in a terrible position." The wind has grabbed some of Sophie's hair and she pushes the blond section behind her ear.

"I know, and—"

"No, I don't think you do!" She plants her slip-on shoes into the path, the glittery material sparkling against the dirt, and puts her hands on her hips. If she's attempting to look tough, the action fails. Like her mom, she's too cute to be intimidating, especially in her pink, plaid cowgirl shirt.

I wish this conversation was happening anywhere but here because Willow has stopped to join in on the already uncomfortable talk. There's nothing I want more than to wipe Willow's "Go Sophie!" expression away. Of course she would side with Sophie on this.

"Do you realize what this means? I am not going to be able to see my parents anymore, all because you couldn't keep your mouth shut! We were really helping them! My mom was even—she was—" Sophie lowers her volume. "She smiled yesterday. She and my dad laughed together and she was eating!"

"See?" I make eye contact with Willow, but I'm so hyped up, I probably look like I'm on crack. "I told you they made her better!"

Willow rolls her eyes. "Settle down, kid. You're liable to give yourself a coronary."

Her response prompts a small giggle out of Sophie. On one hand, I want to thank Willow for softening Sophie's response. On the other hand, I want to scream at her for not backing me on this. Instead, I opt for middle ground. "Says the freak to the dead guy."

Willow finally gives me a tiny smile. "Did you come up with that yourself?"

"All me," I say as we begin our trek back down the path.

"I really am sorry," I say to Sophie as we follow Willow up the steps that lead us to the wrap around front porch. "Things should be different around here, and there are others who agree with me. Why shouldn't everyone be able to watch over their own families? You're proof that it works. No one will listen to us, though." I pause and look away from her while anger festers in my gut. "Why am I subjecting you to the painful replay? You just witnessed my lame attempt with the Schedulers."

"They won't listen. Not while Landon's running things, anyway. He's set in his ways and the vibe I get is everyone is too scared to stand up to him."

"Aren't you all like a team or something?"

"Not exactly, or at least not when Landon is around. I agree with you. What you're proposing is better. No one knows that more than me. The likelihood of anything changing around here, though…" Sophie shakes her head.

"I know." Willow uses a sympathetic voice. Her focus moves to the front door. "Let's check out the inside."

I turn the doorknob that's as familiar as many I've installed, except this one doesn't require a key. In fact, there's no key hole at all. When the solid oak door swings in, I step back to let Sophie and Willow enter first.

Though larger and visibly more expensive than one I ever could have afforded, the stone fireplace is easily recognizable. The placement of the foyer, living room, and hallway match the blueprints my dad and I had been working on.

I walk across the thick rug covering the hardwood and the girls follow me into the kitchen. My hand runs along the knotty, pine cabinets, also identical to those I had intended to install. Of course, I couldn't have installed quite this many on my meager carpenter's salary.

Willow hops herself up on the counter. "I like the material choice," she says, patting the granite. "This place has a scary-good way of nailing down our dream homes, doesn't it?"

Nothing should shock me anymore, but I find myself,

once again, surprised. Every detail of this place— *my* place— is perfect. The craftsmanship, as much as I hate to admit, is better than I could do myself.

"I wish I would have had the opportunity to build this." Not that I could have built a house to this scale, or with so many extra details. In my defense, I was working with a fixed budget. If money posed no limitations, however, I would have built my house exactly like this one.

In her usual way, Willow tries to keep the mood upbeat as she hops down from the countertop. "Let's check out the rest of this place." She crosses around the log kitchen table to the French doors. "You've got a stellar backyard."

Sophie and I follow Willow outside. The timber deck that wraps around the house is larger than any I've built. Between the sheer size, the details in the railings, and the views, my eyes hurt. I can't find a place to focus because each feature one-ups the last.

The surroundings remind me of the way my mom described Vegas. She struggled to find the words to justify the scale of the city, and the photos, she explained, weren't anything like being there. I was seventeen when my parents went on the only trip they had ever taken, aside from their honeymoon. I struggled to leave the house during those four days because the silence was so terrific. My paradise ended abruptly when my old man stepped through the front door. He didn't even have his shoes off and he was complaining about their flight, their room, the poor food service…the list went on and on. When my mom told me about the trip later that night after Dad fell asleep, her smile said everything. She said the vacation was like a fantasy. She had the gall to even say my dad was fun to be around. I knew she had to be lying, or drunk. Seeing as my mom never cared much for liquor, I was inclined to go with my first choice. I let it go, though, because I couldn't kill my mom's post-vacation buzz.

"You all right?" Willow asks.

I nod. "Just remembered another memory."

"Yeah? About who?"

"My parents."

Willow bites her lip. "Oh. Right."

My gaze travels to the left, where I finally find a place to rest my eyes.

"They really do think of everything, don't they?" I mumble to myself while Willow skips down the split staircase.

Sophie pulls down the sleeves of her cowgirl shirt and rests her elbows on the railing. "What do you mean?"

"That's where I go when I'm coding." The field is the same in every way. Even the deer stand is visible far in the distance. I look at the tree line, expecting a buck to stroll out. Instead, I get to watch Willow, in all her hippy clothing, check out my field up close.

"Do you code?" I ask Sophie, realizing she may not understand what I'm talking about.

She nods. "Of course."

"Sorry, that was probably a stupid question. It's just that I don't know much about your job."

She shakes her head. "Don't apologize. My mom always says there's no stupid questions."

Meggie. "I miss her."

Sophie's hand covers mine on the timber railing. She squeezes lightly and smiles, but then turns away before the pooling water in her eyes spills over.

Long moments pass in silence while Willow strolls across the backyard, stretching her arms as she walks.

"Do you think it's better to forget?"

"No," Sophie replies immediately. "Never."

"But—look how remembering has affected you."

"Sadness is an important emotion, as important as happiness, in my opinion." Sophie turns and looks out over the field. "That may sound crazy."

"Yep. Certifiably insane," I tease.

She picks at her fingernails. "If we never feel sadness, we take our good times for granted. You know?"

"I'm probably not the guy to be asking. When it comes to emotions, I've always subscribed to the 'hide 'em at all costs' theory." I guess I'm more like my old man than I thought.

"I've always subscribed to the 'for every action, there is an equal and opposite reaction' theory. Difficult times force us to grow, and good times fuel us to press on during the harder times. They work hand in hand, and both are necessary if we ever want to mature in this life, or any other." She takes a deep breath. "Anyway, our memories are ours. They're not property, they're our experiences. No one should be able to take those from us. Being sad is tough, but not remembering my parents at all would be worse. Trust me."

After an uncomfortable silence, I ask Sophie who sent her to see Meggie. Then, I mentally cross my fingers in hopes that she'll actually tell me.

When she stares back at me, her expression is unreadable. Finally she says, "Josh, Harper, and I received letters with instructions to report to Programming. My bother and sister were as surprised as I was to learn we were going to see our parents. Some guy I've never seen before took us through Programming. He never told us his name, and said if we asked questions or discussed the visits, we'd never see our parents again."

"Have you seen the guy around since?" I ask, hoping for more information.

She shakes her head and pushes a loose hair behind her ear. "I don't know who sent the letter. I doubt it was the guy who met us, though. I'd say he just was following orders because he was clearly nervous. I'm sorry."

Sophie stands up straight after a couple silent minutes and fidgets like she's uncomfortable. "I just received my first assignment as a Scheduler. It's a girl!" She throws both hands up, as if to say, "Surprise!"

"Congratulations?" I ask, not sure how to respond.

"Her name's Ellie. I'm in the process of reading the books of those who will be close to her through her life. When I'm done with that part, I get to visit and observe each of those people. I know where all their lives are heading and when they will end on Earth."

Sophie reads the obvious confusion on my face and continues. "Knowing what kind of influences she has in her life tells me a lot about who she'll become. Each will have an impact on her, both good and bad. I'm not going to lie; this life planning thing is a bit of an undertaking. I feel like I am studying for the biggest exam of my life." She pauses. "Why are you looking at me like that?"

"Sorry. Listening to you describe writing someone's life just sounds…"

"Interesting?"

"I was leaning a little more towards creepy, actually."

Sophie laughs like I'm kidding, but I'm not.

After watching Willow stroll around the outside of the detached building on the right, I look back at the plowed field. "I'm guessing you don't believe in free will?"

"Of course I do. I'm not writing this girl's entire life minute by minute, only her big events like relationships, having children, specific career choices, things of that sort. The stuff in the middle is all hers, from her favorite color and favorite food to her interests and her weekend plans."

"Would it be so wrong to just let people live their lives?"

"I can see why you're a Satellite."

My mouth drops open. "What's that supposed to mean?"

"For starters, with that kind of attitude, you would be a terrible Scheduler."

Her teasing delivery makes me grin. "I'm taking that as a compliment, so thank you."

Sophie slowly circles her gold ring around her index finger. "Don't you believe we all have a purpose in life?"

I shrug my shoulders.

"If there was no purpose, what would be the point of

living?"

I open my mouth, but then close it because I don't have an answer.

"You've gotta check out this garage, kid!" Willow yells in the distance.

Sophie smiles and tilts her head toward the detached building. I nod and follow her down the steps.

As we cross the lawn toward the brick building, Sophie continues the conversation. "Like it or not, everyone has a purpose. Our lives are like interconnected gears, grouped into a network of others: our family, friends, and all the other outside influences that affect us. When those gears move together as they should, beautiful things happen."

"How do you decide a person's purpose?"

"Oh, my job isn't to decide someone's purpose. I just draw the map to get them there."

"Willow said it was the Schedulers who decided my death."

"They decided the *time* of your death, which was based on how your gears were moving within your network."

"Then who decided I would die?"

"Grant, everyone dies." She says this with a laugh. As annoyed as I feel, a bigger part of me wants to laugh with her because the question did sound foolish.

We reach the detached building, which is almost as large as the house. Willow is busy flipping the remaining light switches along the wall. As each area illuminates, my eyes grow wider. The best wood shop in the afterworld stretches out before us, making those magazine and television show workshops look child-like.

"What do you think?" Willow asks.

"It's so…clean." This is the best I can come up. Saying the space is elaborate, or fantastic, or anything else for that matter, would just be stating the obvious.

Willow finds my description funny. "I'm sure you can fix that."

She's right. I can't wait to fill this place with sawdust!

Sophie follows me to the longest of the work benches on the far wall. I grab one of two dozen shiny hammers off the pegboard and weigh the tool in my hand.

"It's hard to remember the last time I've used one of these." How long has it been since I've even held one? Over a year, at least. My poison treatments, a.k.a. chemo, made me too weak to hold a hammer, let alone swing one, in the months prior to my death.

"I'm sure it's like riding a bike." Sophie scans the tools hanging on the wall and reaches for a wood chisel. "I don't know what half of these things do."

I grin, setting the hammer on the butcher-block counter.

Willow comes out of a room in the back corner and pulls the door closed behind her.

"What's back there?" My voice echoes through the vast space.

Willow ignores me.

What more could possibly be in this place? I jog to Willow.

"It's nothing," she says when I reach her.

"Get out of the way."

"Let's go back into the house and check out the other rooms."

"Come on, move! What's in there?" I try to skirt around Willow, but, as if she's dancing with me, she moves side to side and blocks my way.

"It's just a storage area. Let's go."

Grabbing her muscled shoulders, I push Willow to the side as gently as possible and open the door. My hand runs along the wall for the light switch.

"Wow," Sophie whispers behind me a few seconds after the room lights up. "You're a musician, too?"

Sophie sounds so impressed I almost answer yes.

"Maybe you will be." Willow's voice is unsteady.

"I don't play violin." Even if I did, I couldn't possibly use all of the variations of the same instrument hanging along the back wall, especially with so many woodworking tools holding my interest.

"Willow." My voice is hard, wanting an explanation.

After an intense staring contest, Willow finally replies. "Tate plays."

"Tate?"

Sophie's hand pauses on the string of one of at least two dozen bows hanging on the opposite wall and turns her attention to Willow and me.

"Christ almighty, I knew I was right," Willow mumbles. "Tate was meant to be here with you. Jonathan's known it all along."

"Hey! Wait up!" I jog out of the carpenter's paradise

after Willow.

Her flip flops pound up the steps and she's through the middle set of French doors when Sophie grabs my arm.

"What do you think that means?"

I turn and stare lamely back at Sophie.

"If you were really supposed to be here with Tate like Willow says, then the future is being altered." Sophie takes a slow breath. "Or already has been."

I shrug and give my best *not-sure-why-you're-telling-me-this* look.

"Come on! You don't have to be a Scheduler to realize this is a big deal."

"I don't see the issue."

"If you don't remember Tate, how will you be reunited?"

"Well, ah, I guess I'm hoping we won't be?" I wish my voice sounded more certain.

Sophie morphs from concerned to angry. "Don't you see what this means? If Tate's not here with you, then who will she be with when she dies?"

"Maybe she'll meet someone else."

"Yeah, maybe. And what happens when that someone else is destined for some other girl? Remember the gears, Grant? You can't just pick one up and move it into another configuration without affecting others. It's not that easy. *Willow!*"

I rush up the steps after Sophie and almost crash into her when I enter the living room.

"...I'm not sure if it will work, given the way things are

progressing," Jonathan is saying to Willow. His mouth snaps closed when he sees me.

"I'm not a musician!" I almost smack my forehead from the absurdity that just flew out of my mouth.

They ignore my idiotic statement.

"Grant, please come with me. We need to get to training."

"Training?" my voice croaks.

"It is imperative that we continue on as if nothing has changed."

"Everything has changed!" I argue. "We have to convince the Schedulers—"

"Now is not the time. Willow, please do as I instructed. Take Sophie to Wynn on your way."

"What am I—" Sophie starts to ask.

"Willow will explain what has happened and what you are to do," Jonathan tells Sophie.

Willow grabs Sophie's arm to nudge her to the door. Jonathan follows them, leaving me no choice but to do the same.

9. He seems like a real jerk

At the top of the path, just before the four of us exit my perfect, little world, I decide I have to get more information before my unsettled insides knot even more tightly. I need to find out why Jonathan won't back me on letting us protect our own loved ones. It's too important. "Jonathan—"

"Not now, Grant."

Sophie looks back at me and tries to smile when she steps through the doorway. I want to say something to her, but I stay quiet.

We walk at a brisk pace through the hallways. Willow and Sophie leave us with a rushed wave and mumbled goodbye. A few times I have to jog to keep pace with Jonathan. I try to open the vital conversation three more times, but he maintains his no talking stance all the way to the field. When he finally speaks to me, his only words are, "Chris is waiting for you."

Chris, alone on the bleachers, hops down to meet me. "About time you showed up," he spews.

My jaw is clenched in fury when I cross the field for training. Here I am playing Chris's cadaver as he sharpens his blocking skills. Meanwhile, there are bigger problems I should be dealing with. Like getting back to the Schedulers. I have to make them understand.

Chris forces me to go left. After the first few times, I give up the urge to fight his thoughts merely to spare myself the throbbing headache. I'm grateful Chris is nothing like Billy because my mind isn't where it should be.

The guy is good. I'd even go as far as to say he's a natural. A quick inventory of the others around us tells me Chris is the best newbie out here. When Jonathan blows his whistle and tells us to come back after next break, I'm certain the only direction my feet will move is to the left.

"I'll catch up in a minute," I tell Chris and head towards Jonathan for instructions on where I'm supposed to go.

"Grant, why don't you spend some time coding?" Jonathan says as I'm approaching him.

I don't know who's worse: Jonathan the mind reader, or Willow the information hoarder.

"I need to talk to you!" I demand.

Jonathan holds up his hand. "My apologies, but now is not the best time."

"No time is the best time!" *Calm down,* I tell myself, but my thoughts aren't convincing enough.

Jonathan points his back toward me and is in conversation with another Satellite pair before I can open my mouth.

My feet stomp across the field and I don't care about looking like a toddler in mid-tantrum. This place is making me crazy.

I'm across the lobby and at the elevator in the B hall

within minutes. Chris pushes off the wall he's been leaning against and stands beside me.

"Jonathan thinks I need to code, although I don't see the point. It's not like I need a break from an assignment or anything," I spout. "Sorry, I'm just frustrated. Where are you going?" I ask as I punch the elevator's *up* button.

"Up to my…uh, I mean, your room?" he says like a question.

With so much going on, the "my room/his room" argument seems infantile. "It's your room now. It's all right to call it what it is."

"It doesn't bother me to call it yours."

I grin, hating to admit the guy is growing on me even more. "It's not mine anymore." I think of my new house, specifically the workshop, in hopes of convincing my brain that a better place awaits.

I leave the door open and drop my bag on the floor as soon as I walk into Chris's room.

"I'll be back here for a little while," I say on my way down the hall.

"Have fun," he hollers back, followed by the sound of a coffee cup clinking on the counter.

After I plop down on the mat, my gaze freezes on my reflection. I've never questioned who am. I'm a Satellite, and a decent one. At least, I was. Now, I hardly recognize myself and wonder why. Probably because the only identity I know, or at least remember, is getting stripped away.

I force my eyes closed and count down from twenty. My body becomes heavier and my hunting spot replaces the coding room. I expect to see my new house on the far side of the leaf-covered field, but the thick tree line acts as a barrier.

The musty scent of the damp earth relaxes me. By the time the monster buck comes into the clearing, I'm jelly. I watch the deer, still amazed after all this time by his lean, broad body.

The buck jerks his massive antlers to the left and then startles. He twists, hops swiftly, and disappears into the dense trees. I stand up, wondering what's spooked him.

The wind rushes by and I lose my footing. Good thing the branch to my right catches me. Otherwise, I'd look like one of those stick figures with a snapped neck from the "no diving" pool warnings. Considering how my luck has been going, maybe that option wouldn't be so bad.

"Graaaaant," someone—or something—hisses.

I don't remember moving, but I've managed to climb down the ladder. When I jump to the ground, my name is hissed again in the wind and the forest turns black.

"Hello?" I yell in the eerie darkness.

"Come back to me," a voice whispers, barely audible because it's so far away.

I run towards the voice, hoping I don't hit anything with my face along the way. As if a blindfold was removed from my eyes, I squint at white light in the distance, like a hole punch in a black sheet of paper.

Getting closer, I shield my eyes with my forearm to block out the blinding speck that's grown into a large, rectangular doorway. To be cautious, I slow my pace, but the closer I get, the smaller the lighted rectangle becomes, like a portal about to close.

I begin sprinting as if I was trying to reach the end zone during a football game. When I jump into the illuminated space, I have to drop my head to fit through. My feet hit hard against an unyielding surface, sending a shivering pain up my legs.

When my vision adjusts, my focus moves from my work boots to the stone path under them. I scan down the sidewalk that seems to lead into the forest of memories from Programming.

Remaining frozen, I hold my breath and my ears strain from the silence. When my name is hissed again, I'm sprinting down the walkway.

"I need…" The words fade away.

I haphazardly skid to a stop just before a very solid wall kisses my face, and not in a good way. My hands slap against the rough bricks. Could this day get any worse?

The texture of the surface changes, becoming cool and smooth under my hands. I lift my eyes and a sweaty, pale face very much like my own cries out in pain.

Something pushes hard against me.

"Grant!" a deep voice shouts.

Restrained on the ground, I squirm in effort to break free.

"Grant, stop!" the voice demands.

Fighting to lift my head, I catch sight of what must be Chris's arms around me in the mirror. No one else I know would wear the two spiked cuffs. Well, except for Reed, but Chris seems to be the more reasonable guess.

"Let me go!" I demand.

"Promise you'll calm down?" he says in a strained voice.

I nod because my teeth are clenched too tightly to speak. When he releases me, I grab my throat and gasp for air. Chris jumps back like I might punch him, which is actually a very likely possibility.

I put my hand up when Chris approaches. I don't want or need his help; I can stand on my own. Kind of. Once I'm almost upright, I pull off my sweaty T-shirt and drop it on the hardwood floor.

"I'm fine," I say in hopes of smoothing the lines in Chris's forehead, even though I'm not feeling fine at all and I'm dying of thirst, bad pun intended.

"Is this a normal part of the process?" Chris's voice is tense as he follows me into the closet.

"I'm not sure," I answer.

"What's happening to you?"

I ignore him, too focused on my burning throat.

You've got to be kidding me! Seriously? This had to happen today?

I narrow my eyes on Chris like my closet transformation is his fault, even though my rational side knows it's not. Unfortunately for him, my rational side is currently being held under water by my psychotic side.

"You've taken over my closet!" I accuse.

He looks around like I've just set him free in Dracula's dream house. "No way!" His hand runs along a row of various spiked belts that are the same color as every other article in the closet.

No way is right! My closet's been ruined! I'm not sure why I care; I don't even like clothes.

I'm obviously losing my touch because the guy doesn't notice the amount of crazy boiling within me. I'm tempted to deck him just to make his wide eyes swell closed. Instead, I huff out a breath and grab one of the two hundred identical black T-shirts from a hanger.

Glancing to my left, I'm not sure what's worse: the reflection of my chest in the too-tight shirt, or the row of spiked collars beside the leather pants.

My shoulder bumps Chris's in my hurry to get out of the dungeon. I can't get to the kitchen fast enough, and I'm pouring a mug of water down my throat a minute later. I fill the cup again, drinking slowly enough to at least swallow this time around.

After pulling the mug away, I wipe my mouth with the back of my hand and fill the cup for the third time.

"I wondered when you'd finally come out of the closet," I mumble when Chris joins me across the counter.

"Funny."

I shrug and take another drink. "Want one?" I ask because he won't stop staring at me.

Chris barely shakes his head, but continues his gaping.

I walk around the counter to the sofa. "That's a heck of a grip you've got. I didn't realize you were that strong."

He sits in the chair beside the sofa. "There's a lot you don't know about me."

I rest my head on the back of the sofa and stare at the

ceiling. What the heck happened while I was coding?

"If you think it bothers me, you're wrong. People always stereotype me."

I drop my head to look at Chris, who's now in the chair beside the sofa. My gut tells me to take advantage of the fact that he's speaking to me, so I ask the only question I can think of. "How are you holding up in the memory department?"

He shakes his head.

"Still have any?" I ask.

He shrugs and slumps further into the chair.

"You cool with that?" I watch him, curious about his answer.

"Am I cool with that?" he mocks. "No, I'm not cool with that."

"Good, you're normal then," I say lightly and look from his feet to his neck. "Aside from the collar."

He ignores my comment. "Can they keep our memories forever?"

The way he's phrased his question is strange, but regardless, I'm the last person who should be answering this. "They're supposed to come back in Programming."

He sits up straighter. "Have yours?"

I almost laugh. Like insane, mental patient laugh. "Not exactly."

"That blows."

He has no idea.

"I went with Lawson and the others to see them."

He has my full attention. My elbows are on my knees

and I'm leaning closer to him. "The Schedulers?"

He nods.

"And?" Come on, give me something!

"They turned us away as fast as we filed into the room. Lawson and Billy tried to be persistent, but the head guy threatened us."

"How?"

"He said if we showed up there again he would never return our memories."

"He can't do that! They don't belong to him!"

"That's exactly what Billy said, but that guy didn't care."

Why wouldn't Sophie have told me this? "How many Schedulers were there?"

"Twelve. I was expecting more, given the size of those desks."

"Landon," I mumble.

"Yeah, that was the guy who did all the talking. He seems like a real jerk."

Even though I'm angry, the corners of my mouth twitch up. "That's one word for him." I pause. "Did anything else happen?"

Chris shakes his head. "Like I said, he turned us away as soon as we got in there."

"How'd you find the place?"

"Evidently, Morgan and Willow are a lot alike when it comes to memorization."

"But Morgan was in training. I saw her myself."

Chris nods. "She was upset that she couldn't go, but Lawson thought it was best, figuring Jonathan would be suspicious if she didn't show up to train. She told Lawson she wrote the directions down after our first trip and still had them in her pocket when she saw him. He wasn't going to take them at first because he figured Willow would take us back. Good thing he had them. Why'd you bail?"

"Jonathan made me go back through Programming again."

Chris, by no fault of his own, has no idea what I'm talking about.

"Programming is basically a series of movies. It's like watching home videos of your life. After watching them, the memories of what you watched feel real. Then, later, more memories centered around the movie clips come into your head."

"I know, it's weird," I say to agree with the look Chris is giving me. "Anyway, a few of the movies I watched never felt real, so I had to watch them again with Willow, and then once more with Jonathan. I would have rather been with you guys. Trust me."

"Was Lawson angry that I wasn't there?" I ask when Chris doesn't say anything.

He shakes his head. "I think he was more worried than anything. He kept asking if anyone had seen you or knew where you were. Clara said it wasn't like you to not show."

I need to see Lawson and explain my disappearance. Hopefully he's not assuming something happened with Meggie. I'd hate to give him more stress than necessary, especially after all the help he's been in getting to the Schedulers. I can't believe they were turned away so quickly.

It sounds almost as if Landon knew they were coming. I'm getting the feeling Landon is more dangerous than I originally thought.

After a couple minutes of silence, Chris asks, "So, knowing you won't be doing this anymore is tough?"

I'm not sure how to answer. What's tough is knowing nothing around this place is changing. What's worse is knowing how much better things could be for both Tragedies and Satellites if we could protect our own loved ones.

"I feel like my life was ripped out from under me, too," he whispers. "You've got to be excited about what's waiting for you, at least."

"Surely you've heard? There's nothing waiting for me or the other Elites. We were pulled because our ability is gone. Oh, and while we're on the subject of things that suck, apparently my memories haven't all returned."

A crease forms between Chris's eyebrows. "Lawson said the Schedulers can't take our memories, even though that guy said they could."

"I'm not sure what they can and can't do. Jonathan seems to think they've taken mine."

Chris's eyes widen, probably in fear of permanently losing his memories, too. "Do you believe him?"

"I don't know. Honestly, I can't seem to buy into it. He and Willow insist that I should remember this girl, Tate, but I can't find any evidence that she was ever a part of my life."

"Liam and Elliott would disagree."

I nod. "It's not like Willow to lie." As much as I give her crap about it, I know she loves me. Sure, she's withheld information—lots of information—but she's the last person I would expect to lie. Not just to me, but to anyone.

My eyes move away from Chris's and focus on the floor. "I feel like everyone is telling me who I'm supposed to be." I swallow. "I just don't feel anything. That probably sounds crazy."

"It sounds sad."

"I don't need your pity."

"I'm not giving you my pity. I'm sad about the situation. Liam said you and Tate had something pretty good."

"He's quite a bloody romantic, isn't he?" My English accent is lacking big time, but Chris finds humor in my bad impression of Liam.

"How did you lose your blocking ability?"

After circling around it for a couple of laps, I decide to fill him in on the story. The one I've been told, at least. Chris is a decent listener. Not only does he not interrupt the story that makes zero sense, he doesn't question the parts about Tate either. I appreciate this because I wouldn't have an answer if he asked.

The rehash makes me antsy and I decide I want to find Willow. I need to tell her what the Schedulers told the others. Maybe we can find Jonathan and talk to him. "You mind if I cut out for a while?"

Chris shakes his head, so I push myself up from the sofa and grab my bag at the door.

"Is there something I should be doing in the meantime?"

"Think you can track down Lawson during break and

explain to him why I missed our meeting?"

"I'll try."

"If you do find him, will you also thank him for me?"

Chris nods.

I cinch my book bag straps tighter, and my hand freezes on the doorknob. "Chris?"

He turns in the chair to look at me.

"Underneath all that black stuff, you're an all right guy. I'm glad I'm your Legacy."

He's still chuckling and shaking his head when I close the door.

———

"I figured you'd show up here," Willow says as she moves aside to let me through her door. "Nice shirt. A little more snug than your usual threads."

I consider commenting about the green tank, corduroy pants, and combat boots that have replaced her previous hippy attire, but since I have more urgent matters needing attention, I ignore her remark. "Any idea where Jonathan is?"

She shakes her head and moves to the coffee pot. "Want one?"

"Nah, I'm good. Chris told me he was with the others when they went to see the Schedulers."

Willow freezes mid-sip and then lowers her mug. "Yeah?"

"Landon threatened to steal their memories if they didn't drop the subject."

Willow's mug hits the counter with a hard thump and coffee splashes out. "They can't do that!"

That seems to be the consensus. "Do you think they could have stolen mine? Is it possible?"

"Tate is real," Willow says point-blank and locks her eyes on mine for a handful of uncomfortable seconds. Her face softens, but then her forehead creases. "You two are meant to be together, as much as Troy and me. You have to face the fact that she's real or you won't have anything to fight for."

"I have plenty to fight for. This isn't about me, anyway. This is about being able to protect our own loved ones for the sake of all Tragedies."

Willow picks up her mug and I see that the coffee spots have already vanished from the countertop. "How do you protect what you can't remember?" she asks.

"Exactly my point!"

"No! How do *you* protect what you can't remember?"

Jeez, woman! "This isn't about me."

"It's all about you! Landon has proven he's capable of stealing memories. I'm certain now that he stole yours. What happens when he decides to do that to all of us, to take away our free will? Then they can control us, and that's not what this place is about."

"Have we ever had free will?" I mumble.

"Did you ever not want to protect your Tragedies?"

I pace from the makeshift kitchen to the sofa, thinking about Ryder and Meggie. Of course I wanted to protect them. "I get your point, but by losing our memories in the first place, doesn't that sway our choice? I mean, if I hadn't forgotten my parents, I can't honestly say that I would want to protect someone else instead of them."

Willow stays quiet for an unusually long time. She looks sad after taking a drink from her mug. "All this time I believed it was me who killed your memories of Tate."

"You weren't alone, remember?"

"I felt alone," she whispers.

I get the feeling Willow is using the excuse of putting her mug away as a diversion tactic, hiding her face from me. "I've never felt more alone," she says to the sink.

I was right. When she crosses the room, her eyes are glassy. "I'm so sorry this is happening to you."

"Willow," I mumble into her dreads while she maintains her bone-crushing squeeze around my chest. "It's not your fault."

She releases her hold and looks more like herself again. "We should find Jonathan."

As soon as her words are out, the door bangs open, making both her and I jump at the intrusion.

"Well, that's certainly convenient." No use hiding my sarcasm anymore.

"Willow, it is urgent that I speak with you." Jonathan is so far from his usual cool and collected self, I hardly recognize him.

Willow turns from Jonathan to gawk at me, as if silently saying, *See, he really is a mind reader!*

I nod in agreement with her unspoken statement.

She huffs out a mentally-unstable sounding laugh and

follows Jonathan into the hallway.

"Alone," Jonathan says sternly because I've followed them.

"Good talk," I say to the closed door.

Alone in Willow's room, after a failed attempt to listen through the door and then pacing in front of the barricade for a few minutes, I decide to take advantage of Willow's earlier offer. I help myself to a mug and am about halfway through my coffee—black, straight-up—when the secret hallway meeting is adjourned.

Willow presses her hand against the doorframe. Her eyes are hard to read, but her face is pale against her green shirt.

"She's here," Willow whispers.

Jonathan moves around Willow. "Grant, under very difficult circumstances, I have made arrangements for which I could be reprimanded greatly for if anyone were to find out."

My stomach feels sour. "Who's here?"

"Tate," Jonathan answers flatly.

The rhythm of my heartbeat triples. "But—she's alive."

Willow won't look at me. Her sight is locked, instead, on the hardwood floor.

"Please, follow me," Jonathan says.

"She's dead?" I whisper.

"Not exactly," he answers.

"Then, how is she here?"

I only follow Jonathan because I want an answer. Every step makes my heart thunder harder against my breastbone.

I'm glad Willow is close behind me because her presence brings safety. Still, my fear continues to bubble and is dangerously close to spilling over.

"Not dead, exactly," Jonathan says over his shoulder while we walk. "She's dreaming. Or I should say, she thinks she's dreaming."

"She's really here?" I'm not sure why I'm questioning this. If Jonathan says she is, then she is. It also means she's real. And, likely, our relationship was real as well if Jonathan has gone to all this trouble.

"I am hopeful that seeing her in person may retrieve your lost memories. It is of extreme importance that your memories return."

"They were stolen, Jonathan!" Willow belts out from behind me.

"Maybe. Maybe not."

"But I just told you a few minutes ago about Landon threatening to steal the others' memories. Now we have proof that he can do it!"

Jonathan continues walking, but his pace slows.

Willow continues. "Chris told Grant about it. Tell him, Grant!"

I replay the conversation I had with Chris to Jonathan. When I've finished, Jonathan remains quiet and turns to face us.

When Willow stops, she's fidgeting like a kid who needs to pee. "They can't do that!"

Jonathan leans closer to us and his volume lowers. "Landon is known for being zealous and I have no doubt he would threaten such a thing. I've been examining the logistics, however, and I believe that to expedite something so profound is beyond even Landon's ability." He nods, turns, and continues walking.

"So you *don't* think he stole Grant's memories?"

"Those were not my words, exactly."

"So then how—" Willow looks like she wants to say something, but pops her mouth closed instead. Her hand clamps around my upper arm while we walk behind Jonathan. As her grip tightens, my nerves spike. She's uneasy. So much so that she's practically vibrating against me.

Jonathan turns down one of the corridors on our right. Willow must be new to this hall as well, because she appears as enthralled as I am by the single, emerald door awaiting us at the end. The door is not just emerald in color, it appears to be made from a solid, emerald slab. Behind the thick door, a lighter yellowish-green color moves alongside dark green shadows. The effect is like looking into an outdoor aquarium made of green, obscured glass.

When we reach the end of the hall, Jonathan moves to the side, leaving me face-to-face with the brilliant, emerald stone.

"Here we are, then." He says as if he's just presented me with a sandwich, not a door that has the ability to change everything I know to be true.

10. Do you believe in fate

My hand twitches like a magnetic force is pulling me toward the smooth door. I swallow and push my palm against the cool surface. I glance over my shoulder and immediately regret my decision. Willow looks terrified. Jonathan, on the other hand, is smiling like a proud, yet reluctant parent sending me off to school.

I grit my teeth together and press both hands against the glass-like surface since there's no doorknob. The door swings in easily, too fast, in fact, causing me to panic. I'm not prepared for what may or may not happen in the room that awaits.

When I step over the threshold, bright light blinds me, making me disoriented. The sound of Willow arguing with Jonathan about Landon begins but then halts, letting me know the door has swung closed completely. I'm on my own.

I squint in effort to bring the blurry silhouette into focus. The afternoon sun is too bright beyond the glass wall, even with my hand shading my eyes. I turn away from the light and my free hand rests on the cool door. I consider pushing against the emerald slab to make my escape, but I take the moment to let my eyes adjust, instead.

Maybe hoping for my vision to return was a bad idea.

Anger quickly burns off my residual panic once I've turned around and brought the world back into focus.

There's no way this girl was ever my fiancée. She contrasts so much with the wheat field beyond the windows, not due to the sun, but the black clothing that covers her from the neck down. With her back to me, I can only imagine her make-up choice. Ten bucks says her eyeliner matches Chris's. Maybe Jonathan meant for me to bring Chris to meet this girl. Certainly, the guy makes a mistake every once in a while.

I wish it were true that all of this was one giant mix up, but my gut knows better. Jonathan doesn't make mistakes.

I'm grateful for the two leather chairs serving as a divider between us, though a part of me can't help but wish for a concrete wall, instead.

The room is so silent, I'm afraid to step away from the door in fear of making a sound. Certainly she heard Willow's voice while the door was open, but she looks out over the golden field like she has no idea I'm standing here. Honestly, I prefer to keep it that way. Maybe I can stand here for five minutes or so and then sneak out. I can tell Jonathan everything went fine and then be on my way.

I wish.

I can't deny that the girl, at least from behind, looks like the one from my make-believe flashbacks in Programming, even with the all-black getup. She's thinner, though, in an unhealthy way. Her frame is much too small to support such a large amount of hair. The streaming sun makes the ends of her curls glow like fire.

Her hands are the first thing to prove she's not just a

mannequin when they rub down her hips and thighs. She reaches up to her hair and manages to collect it all within a rubber band. After messing with a few curls at the top, she pulls the band out and sets the fire free again.

Deciding I may as well face the unknown, I clear my throat to announce my arrival.

Her hands freeze in her hair and then drop to her side as she turns. "Grant?" she says in a gasp.

As the sun lowers into the wheat field, my eyes are forced to readjust again. When the girl steps forward, features become more predominant, especially her heart-shaped lips. She's the one from my flashbacks. No question about it.

"Grant!"

I'm focused on her glossy lips, but she's moving too fast. I want to jump back as she maneuvers around the chairs, darn near leaping over them, but my boots might as well be nailed to the floor. She solves this problem when she crashes into me. The force pushes me back, sandwiching me between her body and the unyielding glass door.

"Grant!" Her words muffle against my shoulder and her warm breath passes through Chris's too-tight shirt. "I can't believe it!"

I lift my chin higher to escape her coconut-scented, tickling curls. Her fingers pressing into my back are not painful, but stronger than I would have guessed considering her size.

"You're here! You're really here! He said you were, but I didn't believe him!" Her rapid heartbeat drums against my ribcage and her breathing is ragged. "Grant!"

Grabbing her shoulders, I try to push her away gently, but I'm forced to use more strength than I prefer.

Not seeming to understand that I want more than just a step between us, she keeps her hands on my upper arms. Her watery, hazel eyes move over my body the same way Willow looks me over when she's making sure I'm still in one piece.

"Look at you!" The girl traps my jaw with both hands and holds my face still. The she trails her hands down my neck, over my shoulders, and across my chest. "You look amazing! I mean…Wow! You look really good." She pauses and looks up at me. "Baby, say something."

I swallow and shake my head. "I don't know you."

Her expression makes me wish I could take the words back, but I don't want to lie to her.

"Of course you do." Her curls bounce when she nods. "It's me, baby."

I manage to keep my composure, even though my brain is rebelling against my heart. My brain wants to scream obscenities at Jonathan through the emerald door. I'm already envisioning my word choice, similar to what Meggie used during childbirth. With a lot of effort, I side with my heart. There's no reason this girl should have to suffer just because everyone has been lying to me. There's not a cell in my body that knows this girl. This is just a ploy to push someone's agenda on me. But why?

"You don't remember me?"

I grab her hands and direct them from my chest into her own space. She hesitates, but then steps back.

I can't believe someone would go through so much trouble to make me believe this lie; and not just me, but this stranger as well. I feel terrible that this poor girl was sucked into this demented game as a pawn. Unless—

She's in on it, too.

Unable to think clearly with her in my view, I force myself to look over her bony shoulder at the wheat field beyond the window. The crop has become a darker brown, swaying fluidly like ripples in a lake.

"Grant?"

Maybe she's not even real, just some holographic image or something. Stranger things have happened around here. I can't convince myself of this hopeful theory. Her body was too warm against mine.

"Please, say something."

My attention shifts back to the actress. Her confusion makes my anger build like a forgotten tea kettle on a hot stovetop. "Why would I remember you?"

All the air leaves Tate's body—if that's even her real name—and she recoils like a snapped rubber band. The chair stops her when her calves hit the seat cushion. "Is there someone else?"

Are you kidding me? Of all the things wrong with this situation, this is her concern?

Water collects in her eyes. I push my back and palms on the emerald door, hoping it will budge when her tears spill over and run down her cheeks.

Her quiet sobs make me decrease the pressure I'm putting against the door. She's so much more beautiful when her hands aren't covering her face.

No! She's just an actress. A really good one.

Before my conscience makes me doubt myself, I spin around and use my full force against the door. My sweaty hands slide down the surface and leave smudge marks in their place.

The room begins to shrink, or maybe it's an illusion. Either way, I have to struggle for breath and my pushing turns to pounding. I wish I could break through the precious stone, but the six-inch thickness would never allow it.

"Jonathan, let me out!" I yell, banging on the unforgiving door.

"This isn't right," Willow's voice muffles on the other side. "We need to get him out of there!"

I stop banging and put my ear against the smudged emerald.

"This isn't working. He doesn't remember her!" Willow's voice muffles so softly that only her tone proves she's yelling.

My calimeter buzzes and my fist slams against the watch face. I wish the calimeter glass would crack, but that's about as likely as breaking through this door.

After a minute, the noise in the room and in my head lessens. With my forehead still pressed against the glass, I turn just enough to glance at the girl in the chair, hopeful that she is going to fess up to her acting role in this fictional story.

The way she's hugging her shivering body, I have to wonder: what if she's not acting?

Feeling like I'm suffocating, I suck in a breath and then

pound against the door once more.

"Do you love her?" the stranger's shaky voice says from behind me.

I press my cheek against the cool emerald. "Please, Jonathan," I plead, ignoring the question.

"There's someone else. I get it," she says and tries to keep her sobs under control. "I just need to know: do you love her?"

There's a heated conversation happening on the other side of the door, but their voices are too morphed to decipher.

"Why are you doing this to me?"

"Shhh," I hiss, trying to listen to what Jonathan is saying. I'd swear a third voice was just added.

A quick glance at the stranger, bent over in the chair and holding her stomach like she's in pain, is all I need to turn my focus back to the conversation taking place in the hallway. The voices are even softer now, not from lowering their volume, but from moving away.

"I know people change—" the girl is saying.

They can't leave me here! I'll lose my mind! "Jonathan!" I yell out in panic against the glass.

"—I can't believe…I never thought—"

"Never thought what? You don't even know me!"

A deep line forms between her eyebrows. "Of course I know you! You're my fiancée! I was there with you through all of it, the cancer—"

"Yeah, I know." I regret my mocking tone when she winces.

Why am I being so sour with this poor girl? Nobody can act this well. I'm certain of that based on her devastated reaction. She has clearly been brainwashed like everyone else about this fairy tale.

"I'm sorry you got pulled into this mess. I'm not sure why Jonathan felt the need to screw you up, too. Look, this whole thing—you and me—it's not real."

She looks at me like I'm crazy, like *I'm* crazy! I've got to be the only sane person around this place.

"Do you believe in fate?" she whispers.

"No." There. I said it, and as gently as possible.

The girl exhales sharply and then vanishes into the floor like she's just displaced. I reach out to her, regretting my answer, but she's already gone.

I sink into a chair and rub the prickling sensation from the scars on my chest and knee. I hate that the last word I said to the girl was a lie.

"I'm sorry," I whisper to the empty room.

———

"Can I come in?"

When I raise my head, Willow steps through the doorway and sits in the chair beside me.

After a five-minute staring contest with the rug, Willow says, "By the banging on the door, I'm guessing your meeting didn't go well?"

Willow accepts my silence as an answer.

"A few of my memories of Troy didn't surface until I

saw him in the flesh," she says. "I had a shred of hope that maybe yours would be the same. I should have known they wouldn't. Maybe it really wasn't Landon. What we did—"

"Stop it!" I force myself to lower my voice. "Please, Willow, just stop talking about what was done."

For the next ten minutes or so, we disappear into our own heads. The silence between us is in no way awkward. In fact, I feel more at ease and centered by the time my calimeter beeps.

"Break's over, kid." Willow's voice is flat, almost dead sounding, which is beyond out of character for her. "You'd better get to training. Chris will be waiting for you."

I deflate. Training is the last thing I want to deal with, but I follow Willow anyway.

"I prefer the other route," I say when we turn down my Hall-O-Tragedies.

"I figured, but this is faster. Do I need to push you again?" she tries to joke.

I want to hold my palms up like I'm surrendering to her crazy nature, but I'm feeling too deflated. "I'm good."

"I'm really sorry, kid."

On the square insert, the blue light glows around my hand and the wall panel slides into the floor.

After a quick hug, Willow's down the hall before I think to ask when I'll see her next. Mental sigh.

I fist my hands around my backpack straps and close my eyes. Holding my breath, I step over the ledge. The claustrophobia is not quite as awful as I remember, mostly because three seconds later, the golden panel is sliding up to set me free in the B hallway.

In the courtyard, Chris is already seated on the lowest bleacher along with the others. I squeeze myself in next to him.

"What's up BFF?" I whisper in effort to lighten my mood.

Chris presses his lips together to keep from smiling.

Jonathan begins his rambling and I turn my attention in his direction. Watching him talk, my fury towards him multiplies. How could he lock me in that room? What did he actually think was going to happen? I would finally succumb to the brainwashing like a fool and be all happy about the situation? And what about her—

"...Grant and Chris. Thank you," Jonathan says, but I have no idea what he said before that.

The others start filing down the bleachers and disperse on the field.

"What are we supposed to be doing?" I whisper to Chris.

He rolls his eyes and hops up. I follow him over to Jonathan like I have a clue what's going on.

"Thank you for joining me," Jonathan says. "Grant, how are you feeling?"

Really? He's going to lock me in a room and allow me to ruin some girl's day and then ask me how I'm feeling? I refuse to answer him. He counters my silence the way he counters everything. What I wouldn't give to make this guy frown.

"Just a heads ups," I say to Chris, "Programming is a

crock of—"

"Grant! That is quite enough."

Yes, victory! Jonathan's grin is gone, but only for a short three seconds. "Chris has the good fortune of following in his Legacy's footsteps. He has been cleared from training and I'd like you to displace with him today. A trip to Meggie's will aid him in acclimating to Earth."

"We need to talk about what happened! That girl, Tate, she was really upset. What happened to her?"

"As much as I would love to continue with this conversation, now is not the time. I will see you soon."

"It's never the right time!" My annoyance is wasted because Jonathan has already started toward the field.

Chris allows me to pout and stare at Jonathan for entirely too long. I finally dig into my bag and grab the tocket at the bottom corner.

I click the locket open and my thumb and index finger cover one of the two tarnished hearts. I extend the free side to Chris. "Here. Take this."

"What?"

I shake the open locket in front of his back-lined eyes. "I need you to hold the other side."

"There is no other side."

I want to laugh, but instead I push the locket closer to his face.

He caves and reaches out.

"Better hang on." Maybe this will help raise my spirits. "Displace."

The grass drops out from under our feet and Chris

screams. And screams. And screams. By the time our feet hit solid ground, my ears are ringing.

"Cool, huh?" I say from the four foot by four foot sloping front porch. Yes, it helped lift my attitude, even if only a little bit.

Chris leans over and yacks up his last meal on my boots before I can jump out of the way. He looks up at me and wipes his mouth with the back of his hand. "Yeah. Cool," he croaks.

The vomit disappears from my work boots around the time that the color returns to Chris's face. Huh. By the way the kid drove, I would have thought traveling would be easier for him.

"You deserved that," he says.

I'm just glad the vomit didn't stain my boots, considering I have no idea where my clothes have relocated. "Fair enough. Come on."

I walk through the door. This is the first time I've ever displaced so far from my Tragedy. I wonder why I didn't land in the living room with Meggie, but figure it has something to do with the tagalong, who's *still* outside.

I push my head through the door and look up and down the street. "There's nothing happening out here." I jerk my head to the right as a nonverbal way of saying, "get in here."

Chris looks at the front door like it might capture him midway through. "How?"

I'm back onto the porch. "Easy, just walk through it." I give him another example and wait against the wall in the foyer that's barely big enough for the coat rack.

Chris's head comes through first like he's popped through a doggie door. Add in his spiked collar, and he's even more canine-like. I decide against making a joke since he looks like he's going to hurl again.

I leap out of the line of fire just to be safe. "Weird, huh?"

Once all the way through, he shivers and looks back at the door. "I didn't like that."

"Don't sweat it, no one really does. This is Meggie," I say to direct his attention somewhere other than the door.

He walks into the room and stares at the woman on the faded, pink and yellow plaid sofa. Behind him, Brody comes from the kitchen and walks halfway through Chris. I cover my mouth to keep my grin hidden.

"Uhhhhh!" Chris flails his arms like a bad dancer.

"I know," I'm all-out laughing now. Yes, I needed this diversion. "Objects are one thing, people are even worse."

I ignore Chris's glare and turn back to Meggie and Brody who are now both on the sofa with their attention on an action movie playing on the television. I didn't realize how much I missed Meggie. She looks better than the last time I saw her, but she's still much too thin. Her shoulders are pointy under her pink scrubs. She smiles when Brody reaches for her hand. By their agreeable dispositions, I'd say they are both keeping up on their meds.

"These two weren't nearly so boring a few months ago."

"What do you mean?"

"They had a lot of...*passion* for each other." The thought of Brody chasing Meggie through this same room and the bottle nearly smashing Meggie's head turns my stomach. The wall now sports a fresh coat of paint. I wish I had been here to see that happen. I hate being away from them.

As if orchestrated, a loud explosion immediately changes the vibe in the room. Meggie jerks forward and grabs the television remote. The room is silent a second later.

Brody's pulls Meggie close to him and whispers reassurances to her that it was just a movie; that the explosion on the screen didn't create a real fire like the one that killed their babies and her mom.

That last part is added by me, but that's no doubt what she is thinking.

Out of instinct, I pull my filter in when Meggie's lip twitches. I fail, of course, because I can't block anymore.

"It's OK, Mom. I'm here," a soft voice says from behind me. I spin around in time to see Harper, Sophie's identical sister with longer hair who also happens to be one of Meggie's dead daughters, coming from the kitchen. She brushes by Chris and me without acknowledging either one of us.

"Shhh," she repeats.

Meggie calms down more quickly than I could ever achieve with my blocking ability, even back in the day when I was actually decent at my job.

"Harper?"

The blond haired girl doesn't answer me until she's

certain that Meggie is under control.

"I heard you got my sister in trouble." Harper is clearly not a fan of mine. Chris catches this, too, and his smirk tells me if he has to choose a side, it won't be for Team Grant.

"I didn't mean to pull her into this mess. Honestly. I was trying to convince the Schedulers that we should be watching over our own loved ones. I was caught in the moment and blurted out things I shouldn't have."

"Well, thanks to your big mouth, Sophie can't come back here anymore because she's being watched."

This news nauseates me. Meggie needs her daughters with her. "I swear that's not what I wanted to happen."

The three of us look back at Meggie when the television noise fills the room again. Meggie wastes no time in switching the channel to a family-friendly sitcom.

"What about Josh? Is he still able to visit?"

"For now. We have to be extra cautious so he and I are alternating visits."

My hand massages my neck, wishing some of the tension would magically disappear like the trays of food in Progression. "Harper, do you have any idea who sent you here?"

Her eyes get big, not in the shocked way, but in the 'you've got a lot of nerve' way. "I'm not telling you anything."

Can't anyone ever just play nice with me? I pace in hopes of working out some of my frustration. "What about other Satellites? Who's watching your parents when you're not here?" I look around the room even though I already know my answer. There's no one else here.

"As long as we can keep our visits hidden, my parents don't need anyone else." Harper squints her eyes at me before turning her attention to Chris. "I hope your lips aren't as loose as his."

"I'm nothing like him. Trust me."

Jeez. The two of them make me sound like I'm a murderer or something. Instead of pouting, I keep my thoughts to myself. It is my fault that Sophie can't be here, after all.

"What happened to your parents?" Chris's voice is gentle, something I have yet to master myself.

"Me, my brother and sister, and my grandma were killed in a fire."

"Ouch." Chris looks over at Meggie and Brody. After a long silence, he says, "Do you think I'll be able to visit my family again?"

Harper sighs and looks at me.

My feet stop moving and I'm unsure how to respond. "That seems to be the ultimate goal, doesn't it?" is the best I can do.

"Why are the Schedulers so against the idea?" Chris asks.

Harper leans her hip against the side of the sofa, close to Meggie. "Sophie thinks it's a power thing. The Schedulers love what they do."

Chris shoehorns his hands into the back pockets of his leather pants. "It's not like they wouldn't have a job anymore. They will still need to direct people towards their purpose regardless of who's watching over them, right?"

Harper shifts her attention to her parents. "Sophie says if we watch over our own families, a lot of the planning work will be eliminated."

"That's a good thing, though. Why would they want to make their jobs more difficult?"

Harper barely shakes her head in a way that says she can't understand why things have to be the way the are. I couldn't agree more.

"Wouldn't the Schedulers want to protect their own families, too?" Chis adds.

Harper shrugs.

"Not if they don't remember them," I mumble. The image of the girl in black pops into head, and my attempt to drive Tate out of my thoughts is futile.

"Based on what Sophie's said, I have a theory," Harper fidgets with the cuff of her red sweater. "I think the Schedulers are only following Landon because that's what they've always done. There's nothing safer than routine, right?" Harper continues without giving Chris or me a chance to answer. "I think Landon is afraid of having to protect his own family."

"Who would be afraid of that?" I question.

Chris clears his throat. "Someone who doesn't remember his life."

I open my mouth to argue because his statement seems to be directed at me, but I'm not sure what to say.

Chris continues as if he hasn't noticed my unhinged jaw. "If we all stopped losing our memories, though, there'd be no issue at all!" For the first time, Chris's enthusiasm—and concern—on the subject is apparent, most likely because his own memories are on their way out.

Harper shifts her weight to her other hip. "One would think, but we can't change the natural part of the process."

"You remember," I remind Harper.

"I went through Programming."

I glare at my boots as if they're the cause of my aggravation. "There has to be something that is making us lose our memories."

"Well, when you figure it out, let me know," Harper says with zero trace of optimism in her voice.

Meggie rests her head on Brody's shoulder. The audience in the sitcom laughs in the background, though by Meggie and Brody's expression, you'd never know anything was comical. Harper's eyes are sad when she watches her parents. Maybe she's wondering the same thing I am: whether the two of them will ever laugh again.

Knowing I can do nothing more to help Meggie, my shoulders fall and I turn to Chris. "Our bodies move and react differently here. Want to practice getting around?"

Chris looks away from the couple, seeming happy for a diversion. "Why not?"

Looking at Harper, I say, "It's good to see you here." I take a cue from Chris by using what I think is my nice voice, hopeful that maybe someday we can be friends. "I'm glad your parents have you watching over them." God knows I wasn't much help.

Harper's goodbye wave is hard to read, but if I had to guess, she likely still hates me. She wishes Chris luck before my trainee and I walk through the back wall.

When Chris is next to me on the patio, I nod towards the dilapidated shed in the far corner of the dusty and dry back yard. "Meet me up there."

He looks at me for more direction and then back at the shed. I step past him and leap with just enough force to clear the length of the backyard to land gracefully on the metal roof.

Chris walks over the brown grass that would crunch if he had any real weight to him. When he reaches the side of the rusted shed, he looks up at me.

"Come on," I urge. "Jump."

He bites his bottom lip and studies the roof line. Bending at the knee, he leaps off the grass. I can't deny I'm impressed by his strength. My pride, however, dissipates as soon as he starts screaming. I shake my head and fly after his glowing yellow contrail.

I catch him by the ankle about a hundred feet up and yank my arm down. He blurs below me. Landing gracefully is something he'll need to work on.

I drop lightly beside him. "Sorry about that."

Chris serves up his best evil glare while he does a push-up to get his chest off the ground. Standing, he brushes off his black clothes like they could actually get dusty here. "You're strong now. I realize that's an adjustment for you." I can't help but grin.

He glances at my too-tight black shirt. "Kind of like wearing something decent must be an adjustment for you."

He's looking back at the shed while I muffle a laugh.

Swallowing, he tries again. Another inch and he would have overshot, but he catches his balance and sticks his chest out like he's Neil Armstrong about to plant a flag into the peak of the metal shed. I admire his perseverance.

"Not bad," I say.

With the sun behind him, the black clothes and makeup get lost in his shadow. He looks almost normal.

I cross my arms, looking up at him from the dead lawn. "Ready to head back?"

"Are you kidding?" he replies and his feet push off the roof.

I shade my eyes and look into the sky until he becomes nothing but a yellow speck.

Something hits the back of my head, prompting me to spin around. As I'm ruffling my hair in search of the object that struck me like a target, I expect to see Harper. Instead, an eerie laugh echoes around me and then fades away. I bend down and focus my energy around the possible culprit, but I'm even more confused. Focusing my energy around the popcorn kernel, I try to pick it up, but my filter is too weak.

"Look out!" a voice yells above me.

I jump back a half second too late. Chris clips my shoulder and takes me down with him. "Watch what you're doing!"

Chris's apologetic expression morphs into giddiness. "That was sick!"

I push myself up to refocus on the popcorn kernel, but it's no longer there. Instead a small pile of black ash sits on the concrete like a tiny ant hill. I focus my energy until my head hurts and trail my finger through the burnt remains. The black ash doesn't move.

Chris kneels beside me.

"Would you do something to humor me?" I ask.

When he shrugs, I remind him that he just landed on me even though he probably would have agreed without the extra persuasion. "Pull your energy in like you're blocking and focus it as tightly as possible around that." I point to the ash pile. "Then, swipe your finger through it."

I expect him to argue, or at the very least ask for an explanation, but Chris surprises me and moves his finger along the concrete. A black smudged line trails behind his index finger on the concrete.

Chris turns his hand to study the tip of his index finger, probably looking surprised because the pad is not blackened. "That's tight, man! How'd I do that?"

I explain the phenomenon of moving things here on earth. Chris looks as excited as I was when Willow explained this same thing to me. His enthusiasm worries me a bit, much like I'm sure mine worried Willow.

A gust of wind pushes through both of us and blows the ash away.

Chris gives me a questioning look.

Dumbfounded because there's no longer a trace of black on the concrete, I can only shrug. Standing, I try to let the mystery go, but the strange event roots itself in my uneasy gut. "We should head back."

"Hold on." Chris jogs over to the shed.

I squeeze the bridge of my nose. "What are you

doing?"

He bends his knees, focuses on where the metal meets the grass, and shoves his fingers under the base of the rusty sheeting. The shed starts to lift with a loud pop of metal.

"No!" I yell.

When he drops the decrepit shed, the metal pops again. The structure shifts to the left and stills.

"Really?" I say when I'm certain the structure has settled. "You've given them the Leaning Tower of Pisa."

Chris's boyish grin fades and he mumbles an apology.

"I suggest being a bit more inconspicuous with that little trick." I point my eyes to the sky. "The powers that be don't seem overly thrilled by us making our presence known down here."

I look back at the shed and can't help but feel a bit of pride towards the kid. His blocking power is stronger than mine. When I could actually block, that is.

"You should start some kind of rebellion here on earth to get back at the Schedulers."

My eyes move from the leaning shed to Chris. He looks as though he's second-guessing himself for opening his mouth.

When I don't answer, he mumbles, "That's probably a dumb idea."

"Actually, no. Jackson mentioned a similar idea." I walk two steps to the edge of the patio and look out at the patches of dirt and dried up grass. "The thing is, what would we do?"

Chris stands beside me. "We could move stuff. Big stuff!" He stares across the lawn at the Leaning Tower of Pisa.

"Like the shed," I state.

Chris grins wider. "Like the shed!"

"I have no doubt that would get the Schedulers attention. I'm not sure it would be a convincing way to change their minds, though. The problem is, I have no idea what will."

"I'll keep trying to think of something, if you want."

"I appreciate that." I pull the straps of my backpack down so it hugs tighter against my body and look back at Meggie's house one last time, hoping she will be OK. A part of me wishes I could stay here with her.

A long breath escapes from my lungs in preparation of the next step. I refuse to look at Chris when I say, "Grab my hand." Fifty bucks says someone up there is laughing at us right now.

"No way," he argues.

"Look, I'm not keen on the idea either."

From my sideways glance, the guy's face is as sour as I feel about this whole thing.

"Hurry up so we can get this over with," I say.

"No way."

"Now!" My tone is even less happy than before.

His hand wraps around mine and every muscle in me revolts.

Then, he has the nerve to say, "If I were to go that way, you would be my last—"

"Displace!" I shout.

11. You can't spy on someone like him

In my history of flights up to Progression, this one is the longest. I try eight times to yank my hand free from Chris's while we soar upward, but his fingers won't budge.

As soon as we land, I slide my sweaty hand from his. Then, as if synchronized, we both squirm. He rubs his palms on his black leather pants and I rub mine on my worn out jeans.

"We need to head back to the field," I tell Chris when he disappears into the closet. Man, I wish my clothes were still in there. "I'm not hanging around while you play dress-up."

Chris catches up with me just before the elevator doors close. On the way down, he straps on another bracelet because, apparently, he wasn't wearing enough of them already.

I give up on my fit when GPS Jeanette bids us farewell. "Sorry about that," I mumble. "I knew this transition was going to suck, but I didn't realize how much it would actually bother me. I miss Meggie more than I realized."

"I get it. I hope Harper can stay with her." Chris adjust his new wrist accessory. "It's a real shame knowing all those fashionable work boots were hauled off to die somewhere."

I can't help but smile because the kid has a decent sense of humor and an impressive ability to lighten the mood. The rest of our walk through the vacant lobby and hallway to the courtyard is quiet.

Seeing Jonathan on the edge of the field, my anger crackles like volatile embers. Knowing Jonathan, Wynn's joined him so the guy can take off as soon as I open my mouth. That seems to be the norm for him when I ask a question these days.

Because Jonathan and Wynn appear to be discussing something important by the way they're leaning into each other, I raise a finger to motion Chris to stay put for a minute. I divert my approach a bit to the left to get behind them. I do my best to keep my boots quiet and I stop near enough to eavesdrop on their conversation without being noticed.

"…could stop adding Landon's powder. That would at least take care of the new arrivals."

"The timing is still premature. We cannot risk being discovered."

"Now is the time." Wynn's whisper is laced with urgency. "The fewer requiring Programming, the better. The task is daunting enough already. It's not like we're closing Benson, we're just not altering what's there. Landon won't know."

Programing? They have to be talking about our memories! But what does Benson have to do with it?

"Landon seems to be more in the loop than we've given him credit for." Jonathan's voice mimics Wynn's low volume. "He knew about Meggie's kids before our meeting.

Grant's misstep merely allowed him the ability to win over more Schedulers by playing on their fears. His cunningness is increasing."

"You have to say something. He's already convinced so many. He's becoming dangerous," Wynn hisses.

"The timing is not yet right."

I lean closer as their voices lower even more.

"I still don't understand. If you didn't send Meggie's kids, then who—"

Thump. Oh no.

When I look back at Chris, I want to tighten his collar about five notches. He reaches down and picks his bag up off the ground. His apologetic look is wasted.

Turning back around, I see that Jonathan and Wynn are staring at me.

Wynn's eyes move to Jonathan. If she were a cursing girl, I can guess what word she'd choose by the look on her face. She remains quiet, though.

Jonathan, on the other hand, is...well, Jonathan. The guy's dentist must love how much he shows off his bright teeth. "You're both looking well. Tell me, how was displacing?"

"He did fine," I say dryly, wanting nothing more than to elbow Chris in the ribs.

"It was awesome." Chris's voice behind me is shaky. Clearly, he knows how I feel about him right now.

"Excellent." Jonathan continues like he doesn't know I was eavesdropping. I'm not buying it. The guy knows everything. "Your journey sounds like a successful one.

Grant, sometime before next break, please oversee Chris while he displaces to his Tragedy. You will find instructions in your bag."

I've had enough of Jonathan evading the discussion. The crackling embers within me ignite. "Harper was at Brody and Meggie's house."

Jonathan turns away like he's deaf.

"I know you heard me!" I yell to his back as he walks away.

Like Jonathan, Chris is ignoring me and appears much too excited. He may as well be skipping beside me when we leave the field.

I slow my pace and fume because Chris's carelessness with his bag made me miss the rest of Jonathan and Wynn's conversation. "You realize what's about to happen, right?"

Chris has traded his excitement for a blank expression.

I grab his shoulder. "Someone's life is about to change, and not in a good way."

"I know, but—"

My fingers squeeze into his dense muscle. "Remember Meggie? We're not talking a little sad here. Your Tragedy is about to experience something devastating. Training is one thing, but this is serious. You'd better be emotionally prepared."

I release my hold when Chris finally looks more like he should. I don't feel any better, though. If there's one part I hate about our job, this is it: knowing and understanding how a traumatic situation will change someone forever. I glance at Chris and wonder if he realizes how the upcoming events are going to change his life forever as well.

"Tell me about your memories," I say when we're passing Alogan. I glance at the pews and church-like alter, remembering Jonathan's welcoming speech when I arrived. At the moment, I can easily say I liked him better then. "What do you remember about your life?"

I slow my pace and glance through the middle doorway and up at the scarlet tanagers. An anxious feeling makes me increase my stride like I need to get past this room.

Chris keeps up easily. "I remember my parents. I think my dad was sick. I have a sister and we got along well. My whole family was decent. In this day and age, that's unusual right?"

I think about Chris's family dynamic as I witnessed it. "More like lucky, I'd say."

My next question lingers in my brain like an unwanted odor. I'm unsure if I want to hear the answer, but when we're in the elevator, I ask, "What about Liv?"

He's caught off guard and then looks angry, or maybe confused. I'm crossing my fingers for anger from prying into his personal life.

"Who?"

The air escapes from my lungs. He doesn't remember her.

"She was your girlfriend."

"I didn't have a girlfriend," Chris says when the elevator doors open.

He follows me into the hallway. Could he possibly know nothing about her? If so, where does that leave me?

I saw Liv myself. I know she's real. But that would mean that Tate could be—

Focused on my—I mean, Chris's—door, my peripheral vision blurs. Chris's voice has a strange echo to it. "You look really pale."

Chris is kneeling in front of me. How did I get down here?

"Should I get someone?" The morphed drawl in his voice begins to shift back to normal.

I force myself to stand up. "I need to go to Programming. I'll catch up with you later." No wonder Willow's so mental. This Legacy business sucks.

I snake through the hallways back to Programming. A few people look at me strangely along the way; a fair reaction since I'm out of breath from running.

"Anyone seen Willow?" I ask a crowd of people gathered in one of the circular rooms.

"I think she's with her man," one of the guys answers.

"Any idea how I can find her?"

He shakes his head. "Sorry."

"She's at home," a girl's voice says.

I turn to look at the sofa that's been shoved into the hallway branching off the round room. The blond-haired girl has taken a time-out from her magazine and stares back at me as if saying, *"What?"*

"Do you know how I can get there?"

"It's in your book," she says and then shoves her face back into the celebrity tabloid. "On the map," she adds over the pages.

I shake my head and dig through my bag while the crowd goes back to their conversation. I flip through the pages until I get to the map and look the blueprint over. "I've already seen—"

"You need to unfold it."

I look up at the girl who is still consumed in her gossip column. My fingers feel along the binding. Bingo! I unfold the accordion paper…and unfold…and unfold. Obviously the magic of Progression had a hand in keeping the main map as thin as the other pages. By the time I reach the end, the paper runs halfway down the hall. Thirty-seven pages seems excessive, but who am I to question anything? My opinion has never mattered here before.

My eyes go to work, scanning the outer hallways. Tiny names are written on each passageway, so small that I have to hold the paper up to my nose and squint to read them. After more than ten minutes of searching, I find Willow's name among the thousands of others.

I look around for something to mark Willow's hall. After a few seconds, I end up digging through my bag, coming up with Ryder's granite stone. I drop it on the paper and walk back to the center of the book where the binding lays open.

"Do you happen to know where we are right now?" I ask the girl on the sofa.

She seems annoyed when she closes her magazine, but she stands and walks toward the map. After scanning the middle area for a few seconds, she leans down and points. "Here."

Thanks!" I yell after her because she's headed down the hall with her magazine rolled under her arm, likely in search of a quieter reading place.

Kneeling, my finger runs through the hallways. Like a maze, I occasionally have to backtrack when I reach a dead end.

When I've got the route embedded in my brain, I refold the pages and return the book and the rock to my bag.

Right, right, second left, third left, right, second right, forth left, first right…out of breath and out of memory, I finally reach her hallway. According to the map, anyway. It's not until I recognize a photo of Hope on the wallpaper in the hallway that I know for sure I'm in the correct place. Hope looks just like she did when Willow took me to her during my own displacement training

I walk down the hall, scanning over the wallpaper of photographs that extend along the ceiling. Near the end of the hallway, my hand presses against one of the photos of Tate. I stare, wondering what my life would have been like with a girl like her. The fairy tale is impossible to imagine. Obviously she's real; I've seen her myself, but why are the others trying so hard to convince me that we were a couple?

Willow wouldn't lie to me. Deep in my gut, I know this. My brain, however, continues searching for something—anything—that would prove our relationship actually happened.

To relieve my frustrated head, I ignore the glowing purple square on the wall and turn my focus to the golden door. My knuckles barely make a sound when they hit the gilded metal. Déjà vu overwhelms me as I remember knocking on Willow's door for the first time. I had no idea what or who to expect. One thing's for certain, I wasn't ready for her. Heck, half the time, I'm still not.

After a couple of minutes of pounding with no answer, I turn the knob and the door swings inward. Warm air hits my skin and my nose wrinkles from the potent sulfur smell.

"Willow?" I yell from the doorway, immediately feeling like invading her privacy is a bad idea.

Her laughter carries up the slight hill from behind a modest stone cabin. A faded, red barn is just visible behind the house.

"Willow?" I yell again, taking a few steps down the sparkly, granite path.

She laughs louder, so I step onto the grass for a better view around the house.

"Willow?"

Her laughter stops.

When I'm closer, I can see her standing in the wide opening of a deteriorating barn. Behind her, a hanging light in the shoddy red building does little to illuminate the inside.

"Grant?" She jogs up the granite sidewalk. "What are you doing here?"

"I'm sorry, I shouldn't have come."

"You're always welcome at my home. I'll give you the grand tour. I'm not gonna lie, it's a magnificent place." She looks over her shoulder. "Troy, Grant's here!" she yells towards the barn. "What's going on? You okay?"

"Yeah. No." I pause and look in her eyes. "I don't know."

"Come on," she says and pulls me towards the barn just as Troy is coming out.

"Hey Grant. Sorry I can't shake." Troy lifts his greasy hands as he wipes them with a shop towel. "How are you?"

"Sit," Willow demands before I can answer and points to a dirty stool just inside the barn.

Troy looks around the dimly lit barn. Dozens of tools lay on the dirt floor close to the open hood of a vintage, mint green Chevy truck. I'd love to hear that thing run. "Willow, maybe Grant would rather go in the house."

"Please, the kid doesn't mind a little dirt." Willow answers for me.

I grin. "This is good." I actually feel more comfortable here than anywhere else in Progression.

"See." Willow turns to Troy and sticks her tongue out like a child.

Troy grins. "Endearing as ever, my wife."

"He loves my quirkiness," Willow replies. "What's up, kid?"

I mull over my thoughts, not really sure how to begin. Deciding the secret conversation between Jonathan and Wynn is the most important, I explain to Willow what I overheard.

She mulls it over for almost a minute before saying anything. "What is Landon up to?" she says to herself.

"He didn't send Meggie's kids. I swore it was him, but it wasn't. Who else would have done that?"

Willow shakes her head slowly enough that her dreads barely move.

"What about Programming and Benson? They have to be connected somehow."

Willow's combat boots leave footprints in the loose dirt when she paces. "This doesn't make any sense."

"There has to be a connection, right?"

"It certainly seems that way."

"We need to find out more. Do you know where Jonathan is? Maybe we could spy on him again."

Willow's feet stop and she looks over at me. "Please tell me you're kidding?"

Ugh, this girl makes me crazy. "Of course I'm not kidding."

"This is Jonathan we're talking about, kid. You can't spy on someone like him."

"Sure you can! I just did."

"Please tell me you don't really believe he didn't know you were listening."

"He didn't know I was there until Chris dropped his bag!" I'd like to blame Willow for my raised voice, but I know my intensity has more to do with Jonathan's lack of communication. He couldn't have known I was standing there. Could he?

I glare at Willow, hating that she could be right. The tension between us is misdirected, I know. Jonathan is whom I should be angry with, but I was really hoping Willow would have some answers.

Jealousy fills me when the top half of Troy's body

disappears under the Chevy's hood because I wish I had someplace to divert my attention.

"I'm sorry," I finally say to Willow. "I wish I knew what was going on around here. I'm so worried about Meggie. She doesn't have a Satellite anymore, which is good, I guess." I'm not sure if I add this for Willow's sake or my own. "I saw her today during displacement training with Chris. Harper was there and said she and Josh are alternating visits. What happens if her kids aren't able to see her anymore?" I swallow to force my panic down my throat.

Willow steps over to the truck and leans her hip against the shiny fender. "Look, kid, I know this is frustrating, and I wish I had some answers. I'll keep thinking on this and I'll talk to the others if I see them. They're a bright group. They may have some ideas."

"Thanks," I mumble, deflated because I'm not any better off than I was before I got here. Still, I'm grateful for Willow's help.

I should probably excuse myself and give Willow and Troy back their privacy, but I like the safety I feel when I'm with Willow. She feels like I'm home. I'd never tell her this, of course, for fear that her head would grow even larger under all that dark hair.

"What's really bothering you?"

"I just told you."

"Come on, kid, I know you better than that. Spill."

After enduring Willow's glare for a full minute, I finally say, "Sparky doesn't remember his girlfriend." In an effort to downplay my concern, I cross the dusty barn floor and shift my attention to Troy's work under the Chevy's hood.

"Who's Sparky?" Troy asks in a strained voice while he's tightening a nut on the engine block.

"Chris." Willow stands straighter against the fender and looks at me. "His name is Chris."

"He wears a dog collar," I explain to Troy.

Troy's eyes raise to Willow and he starts to laugh, but she cuts him off with *the look*; the one every woman possesses and that makes every man shut up.

"You came all the way here because Chris forgot his girlfriend? How'd you find my place, anyhow?" Willow asks.

"It's on the map, and I came here to talk to you about Jonathan. He doesn't remember her at all," I continue without pause, running the two topics together to prove Willow's right once again. "He doesn't even know her name."

Willow's even expression remains unchanged. "And?"

My finger traces around the smooth edge of the fender. "Well, I guess it's kind of like that with me. I mean with…you know, that girl."

"Tate! Her name is Tate! Holy Hail Mary, what is it with you and names today?" Willow's boots are back to pacing again.

"Fine, whatever. Taaaaaate," I drawl for effect. "Is that better?"

Willow crosses her arms and leans against the old barn wood wall. "A bit. Go on."

Troy runs the greasy towel between his hands and looks at me with sympathy, probably because I have to put up with his wife as much as he does lately.

I kick my boot in the dirt and watch the dust form a small cloud. "There may be a small part of me that wonders if my memory is like his."

When my eyes raise, Willow throws both hands in the air. "Are you kidding me? That's what we've all been trying to tell you! *Good night,* you're draining, you know that?"

"There's a much larger part of me that thinks you're all lying!" I argue.

"Christ," Troy says. "Now you've done it."

"What?" I ask.

"I. Am. Not. A. Liar!" Willow barks and then turns to Troy, "Language!"

I raise my eyebrow. "Language?"

Willow's glare blazes even hotter. "We don't use the *C* word in vain."

"A moment, my dear." Troy grabs Willow by the elbow, forcing her away and giving me an apologetic smile. They disappear into the back corner of the barn.

I grab a wrench. The weight and the feeling of the cool metal makes me realize how much I've missed working with my hands.

"He called me a liar!"

I juggle the wrench and shake my head from Willow's raised voice.

Troy says something back in a much calmer tone.

When they return, Willow looks, frankly, like she's trying very hard to keep her cool.

"I'm not a liar," she says in an *I'm going to play nice* tone.

I shouldn't push, but—oh heck, why not? "Then brainwashed, maybe?"

"You should be committed." Willow looks over at Troy when he clears his throat. "I'm sorry, but he should!"

Troy appears to be silently urging Willow to drop her volume back to normal. Normal, of course, for her, is a decibel louder than the rest of the world. His focus returns to the innards of the truck.

Willow's shoulders drop and she looks back at me. "And who, exactly, do you think would brainwash me, or us? Because I'm assuming all of your friends have been brainwashed as well?"

I shrug. "The Schedulers."

Willow stares at me for a long time like she's trying to work something out in her head. "I was there. I've already told you all this. I saw you with her. Nobody put that in my head. Do you understand me? Something that real cannot be planted. That's not the way Progression works and you know it."

"Do I?"

"The Schedulers don't work like that. Becoming a Satellite takes away memories, but then puts them back. They gain nothing by conjuring a story of this magnitude involving so many players. I've been through this, Grant. I get it. I was confused, too, until I remembered my life with Troy. You'll see."

My hand grips the wrench tighter. "Will I? You told me the story of how you and the others wiped my memories. Assuming what you said is true—"

"Which it is," she interrupts.

I hope my expression tells her how annoying she is. "*Assuming* what you said is true, what happens if my memories never return? Don't say that doesn't worry you. Honestly, you're more concerned about it than I am. If they don't return, then what?"

Willow turns to Troy like she needs to be rescued.

Troy catches her plea from his sideways glance. He trades the chrome head gasket for a shop towel. "You both have to have faith that things will turn out the way they were intended."

Willow looks back at me.

I reply by kicking the dirt floor.

"What did you say to her?" Willow asks in a quiet voice.

I shake my head without looking up. "Not a lot."

"How was she?"

"I don't really know. All I wanted to do was get out of there."

"Oh, poor Tate. She must be a mess."

"Poor Tate? What about me?"

"Stop making this all about you! Consider what Tate must be going through."

"But I feel nothing for her. What do you expect from me, to put on some big production? I'm not a great actor."

Willow shakes her head. "Have a little empathy, kid."

"You say that like it's easy."

"It is. You empathize with your Tragedies, don't you?"

I think of Meggie and Ryder. "That's different."

"How?"

"I've seen what they've been through. I've experienced their loss with them."

"You know what Tate has been through. I'm not the only one who has told you. Why can't you sympathize just a bit with her?"

"Because she's not real! Not to me, anyway!" I return the wrench and my thigh accidentally bumps the stool over in my escape from the barn. I don't bother picking it up before stomping away. I realize I'm being as futile as a child in full tantrum mode, but I'm too escalated to care.

Willow finally keeps her mouth shut, at least from what I can hear. Who am I kidding? If Willow had something more to say, I'd know it.

Feeling more embarrassed than angry now, my feet can't carry me fast enough up the granite pathway.

"Hey man, wait up!" Troy yells behind me.

At the top of the path, my hand freezes on the door knob.

"Grant, listen. This is killing her." Troy points his stare towards the barn. "I've heard the stories about you and Tate more times than I can count. I don't understand what you're going through, but I do know how Willow has explained the memory loss. She said it's terrifying to know that you feel nothing about a person who played such an integral role in your life."

Troy grabs my arm and his eyes lock on mine. "Whether or not you shut out the idea of Tate, please don't shut out my wife. You're like a son to her. She didn't get to have that in life. I'm begging you, please don't take that away from her."

When he releases my arm, I only nod because I can't bring myself to lie to him.

———

After checking the map three times, I find my way back to a familiar place in Programming. I take the long way to my room instead of the creepy elevator shaft, hoping to sort through my conflicting feelings. Willow brought up points that are hard to argue with, but my head still won't embrace the idea. How am I supposed to trick my brain into believing this girl meant something to me?

"What's up?" I say to Chris with zero enthusiasm as I drop my bag at the door.

From the sofa, he silently looks back at me.

I cross the room and sit in the chair next to him.

"What's wrong?"

He remains quiet while his fingernails penetrate the hard cover of the book he's holding.

Crap! I didn't even ask him about his assignment. I mentally punch myself in the face. "Are you done?"

He looks down at the red book and nods.

"Sorry, man. I should have told you about that part and what to expect."

Chris shrugs. "Clara's been keeping me up to speed."

I owe that girl big-time. I should ask her for some pointers on patience.

Chris flips the book in his hand. "Why does everyone call it reading? It's not reading at all. It's like being in a movie."

"I always thought that was strange, myself. Par for the course, I guess. Think you're ready to displace?"

His top teeth scrape across his black lower lip. "Why not?"

I play the drums for a minute on my thighs, not sure where his tocket is, but remembering Jonathan saying the instructions were in my bag.

"You want coffee or something before you go?" I ask on my way over to the door.

"No. Thanks, though."

Kneeling, I unzip my bag to make the contents inside more easily viewable. I grab the only thing I don't recognize, untie the string, and then unroll and flatten the scroll of paper.

"Check the cabinet?" I mumble after reading the heavy, black script. That's it? Jonathan couldn't have just told me that on the field?

I cross to the kitchen. Upon opening the first three cabinets, my nerves spike because all I've found so far are rows of familiar coffee cups. Lucky number four saves my skin. I grab the peacock feather hair tie and spin it around my index finger.

Back at the sofa, I flick the band at Chris. He's fast enough to catch the thing before it snaps him between his black-lined eyes. I have no intentions of hurting the guy because he has kind of grown on me, but a red mark would have at least expanded his color palette.

"It's a tocket," I say when he turns the feathered circle over in his hand. "This belonged to your Tragedy at one time, but now it's yours. Holding it will take you to your person. That's your lifeline to your Tragedy so don't lose it."

He holds the band close to his face and studies it like it's going to talk to him or something.

"You ready?"

His hand stays frozen at eye level, but he looks over the hair tie at me. "Now?"

Sigh. "No, tomorrow."

His shoulders relax.

"Yes, now." I feel bad about screwing with him. How dare Willow say I have no empathy. "You're not starting your assignment yet, you're just acclimating to the travel and the environment, and becoming familiar with your Tragedy." There. I can be nice.

He takes a long breath, puts the assignment book in his bag, and stumbles to his feet.

"Getting there and back is simple. Hold your tocket and say displace to get there. Hold nothing and say displace and you'll be brought back. Not getting sick is going to be your challenge, as you've proven to my boots. Don't move too quickly. When you land, let your body adjust."

The fear in Chris's black lined eyes is apparent. Terrified is more on par than the stoked attitude he had earlier. Despite the challenge and gratification, the dark undercurrent of why we are needed will always taint this life. If nothing else, as Satellites, we need to respect our Tragedies and the sadness they are about to face.

"Ready?"

Chris keeps his voice low. "Am I?"

I look him in the eye and try to ignore his makeup. "You are." He is.

Feathers poke out of Chris's clenched fist like he's just killed a bird. He looks at me for a few more seconds, says the magic word, and is sucked into the floor in a blurry streak of black.

I stare at the place he was for a while, wondering how he is doing. To prove that I've turned soft, I wish I was there to make sure he is all right.

As the minutes pass, the tension in my muscles worsens. If this keeps up, my limbs are going to snap by the time Chris returns. On my way to the kitchen, the end of the hall catches my attention and I choose coding over coffee.

For the first time, this room no longer feels like mine. The thought of giving my place up turns my stomach, but at the same time, an invisible force seems to be pulling me away.

I try to clear Chris from my head and begin counting down from twenty. Before reaching fifteen, I'm in my tree stand staring down at the dead leaves below. Breathing in the damp air, I relax even more. I wait for the monster buck to come like he always does, but the forest remains quiet. So quiet, in fact, the squirrels aren't even snapping the tree branches around me.

My body tenses from the silence. A voice in my head screams that something is wrong and I'm climbing down the ladder rungs a minute later.

Other than my feet rustling the leaves, the forest

remains too still.

A hiss cuts through the silence and my head jerks to the right. My feet follow and, without thinking, I'm jogging towards the sound. Something whispers my name so quietly that I'm questioning whether or not it was real when everything turns black.

I moan in frustration. I can't even code right anymore! My life is unravelling too fast. My arms flail around for something to grip in the darkness.

"Pleassssssse," the voice hisses.

A pinprick of light appears and I sprint towards the beacon. The tiny spot grows into a rectangular doorway and I cross the threshold, stopping on the stone path while my eyes adjust.

"Graaaaaaaant," the voice whispers from down the path.

Running towards the sound, my speed gets the best of me and I can't stop in time. The brick wall takes care of this, using my face as the emergency brake.

When my vision returns, the hardwood floor of the coding room greets me. Gasping for air, I manage to raise my head, but not much else. What's happening to me?

12. We'll kick it old school, then

I'm still guzzling water when Chris materializes by the sofa. I pull my head from the faucet and use the back of my hand to wipe my chin.

"How'd you do?" I ask and then go back for another drink.

His bag hits the hardwood with a light thud and he moves towards me. "What's with you?" His black makeup accentuates his pasty skin.

"Forget about me. You're really pale." I turn the faucet off. "You OK?"

He looks like he's going to lose his lunch. His black lips form a thin, tight line, but he remains mute. Finally, he nods and looks more stable before moving around the sofa and plopping himself in the chair.

He pulls on the silver hoop in his ear. "This whole thing, it's really messed up. I just need a few minutes to process it all."

Nope, I can't deny I'm beginning to care about him.

While I resume my position at the counter and swallow more water under the faucet, I recall my first time displacing to Ryder. I still can't believe I was assigned to Willow's son. Willow, of all people!

My head lifts and, peeking over the counter, I stare at Chris. Could he be watching over someone I know, someone from my mortal life?

No way.

Regardless, I remember how grateful I was when Willow left me alone to absorb the reality of my new life.

"I've gotta step out for a bit, unless you want to talk about anything."

In a bit of a daze, he shakes his head.

"Or, if you have any questions." My tone is so nice, Willow would be beaming at my manners.

"I'm good," he mumbles from the chair.

With that, I grab my bag and make my way to the elevator.

GPS Jeannette bids me farewell and I step out of the gold box, noting that nothing about this day is, quote, *fabulous.*

I glance across the vacant lobby towards Benson and change my direction. Seeing as I have no one to visit and nowhere to be, my pace is slower than normal through the courtyard hallway and into Programming. I only pass a handful of Satellites as I snake through the halls. I stop in one of the empty circular rooms and park myself on a sofa to kill time. The thought of so many stagnant memories beyond the surrounding doors makes my head hurt. I lie back on the sofa and close my eyes, wondering why our memories can't stay inside us where they belong.

When I've finally managed to settle all the swarming thoughts in my head, an unwelcome voice above me says,

"Hey, Princess."

I open one eye to see Billy staring over me.

I sigh and open my other eye before pushing myself into a sitting position. "Hey," I answer and run my hand through my tangled hair.

Billy pushes his blue sleeves over his forearms. "You a gamer?"

I shrug, realizing my R and R is over. "Not really."

He disappears around the corner. When he returns, his eye gear is strapped to his forehead and he's carrying two large gaming chairs like they're bags of feathers. "I'll go easy on you, then."

The chairs thud loudly against the marble floor. Billy unstraps the extra goggles from his upper arm and chucks them at me.

I force myself onto one of the chairs and strap on the headgear that morphs the world into a strange virtual reality.

"You want to play yourself?" Billy asks, scrolling until he stops on Elite Force Seven. "You're awful pretty, Princess."

"I remember when your comments use to bother me. Man, that seems like years ago. Have any other games?"

"So they did bother you?" Billy is obviously happy about this revelation.

I don't answer.

"All right. We'll kick it old school, then."

The graphic on the screen resumes scrolling through titles. Billy stops on a game called Memory Lapse. How fitting.

"You'll like this one," Billy says. "Use your hands to

select the glowing lights and a tocket will appear. You're trying to match pairs."

"Isn't this a kid's game?"

"Same concept, but this one is more difficult. Trust me."

Billy goes first and selects one of at least a hundred glowing orange orbs. A 3D diamond ring appears and spins. He selects another orb and a gold key rotates. Both objects puff back into orbs and then all of the glowing balls begin spinning in all directions.

"You've got to be kidding?" I mumble.

Billy laughs. "Told you."

I select a toy car and a gold winged airline pin. "I'm glad you're enjoying yourself."

The orbs move around, faster this time, and Billy completes his next turn.

When I make my first pick, the gold key spins and Billy mumbles, "Oh man."

I move my finger between four orbs, trying to remember which one held the other key. I almost touch one, change my mind at the last second, and choose the one to the right instead. Jackpot!

Both gold keys come towards my face and then join as one before landing on the bottom of the screen.

"Beginner's luck," Billy says.

"We'll see," I reply.

After about twenty more rounds, I'm up one on Billy with six tockets on my board.

"Grant, can I have a moment?" a voice says, just as I'm

selecting the match to a red bouncy ball. When the object is added to my collection, I pull off the goggles.

Wynn greets me with a smile. "Jonathan asked that I come see you about Chris. Did he displace successfully?"

I nod. "He seems to be doing well." Even I can't deny that.

Wynn nods in approval. "I'm sure his success has a great deal to do with his Legacy."

Ha! More like Clara.

"Will you please bring Chris to the Orders hall following next break? Jonathan would like to see the two of you."

"Sure thing." I'd like to see Jonathan anyway. The guy is going to have to talk to me eventually.

Wynn's silence tells me she's done delivering her message, so I ask: "Can I talk to you in private for a minute?"

Panic flashes across Wynn's face, but her kind expression returns a second later. This woman must take pointers from Jonathan. "I'd love to chat, but I really have to be going." Her thin legs move fast as she makes her exit.

Sigh.

I reach for the binoculars.

"Have you remembered any more from your past?" Wynn's distance voice carries to me.

I push the headgear back up to free my eyes. After I shake my head, Wynn spins around and continues her path down the hall. I don't particularly like the troubled look on her face.

"Not bad," Billy says.

"I'm only up by two," I point out.

"I was talking about with Chris. That was quick training."

"I didn't have anything else to do," I mutter.

"Yeah, I hear ya," Billy answers, reminding me that he and I are going through the same turmoil. We're both being pushed out of this life too soon.

"I overhead a conversation between her and Jonathan earlier."

Billy sets his binoculars beside his curved, leather chair. "Yeah?"

I explain the cryptic message to Billy. He's as perplexed as Willow, bringing me no further in figuring out the conundrum than I had been.

⸻

After getting beaten by Billy—only by one tocket, I remind myself—I decide to go collect Chris when my calimeter signals break. I figure the two of us can chill in Benson before meeting Jonathan after break. The thought of voluntarily spending time with Chris doesn't repulse me, which proves that I'm getting soft. Plus, spending some time in Benson may be helpful in sparking any ideas about how the place could be related to our memory loss.

At the seating area just outside of Programming, Trina is in one of the chairs with her nose in a book. Although it's only been a couple months since I've seen her, it seems like years. Her wild curls are tamer today, with half of them being held back in a loose braid. I glance at her lips, remembering the handful of intense kisses we shared when she was still an Elite.

She doesn't see me approach, so I sneak up behind her and put my hands over her eyes. "Guess who?"

She pulls on my hands and turns her head. "Hey, stranger!"

"Hey, yourself. What are you doing out here?"

"This is my favorite reading place. I discovered it when I was going through Programming. Tell no one, but this chair is the bomb! If that gets out, I'm coming after you." Trina closes her book as I move around the furniture. When she stands, she pulls me into a tight hug. "It's great to see you."

"You, too. How's your brother?"

"He's fantastic, thanks for asking. It's the strangest thing, though. It's as if no time has passed between us; like a hole I didn't know existed has been filled. You know what I mean?"

I wish. I shake my head, not wanting to rehash my missing memories because the topic has already exhausted itself.

"You've been through Programming, right?"

"Yeah."

"Then you get it. Having your memories back and all."

I nod so I don't have to lie out loud. Maybe it's not really a lie. I do remember my loved ones, just not the one

Willow assures me should be there. In any event, I hope my nonverbal answer is enough to pacify Trina.

"I was thinking about heading to Benson." She fans her face with her book. "I haven't been there in a while. Want to join me?"

"I was headed there myself. I have to get my Satellite, Chris, first. I can meet you there, unless you want to walk with me."

"I'd love to. How's the food been? Anything new worth trying?"

My feet stop moving at the courtyard doors. Could it be? "What'd you say?"

Trina is obvious confused and rightfully so. "How's the food been?" she questions.

That's it! "Trina, you're a genius!" I grab her hand and pull her along with me.

"I am?"

"I promise I'll explain in Benson," I say to defend my odd behavior. I'll catch her up while the others are there so I don't have to repeat the story about Jonathan and Wynn again.

The food! Why hadn't I realized this earlier? The food is making us lose our memories!

Still connected to Trina's hand, I'm practically bouncing across the lobby. We pass a group of three girls who apparently find Trina and me interesting.

One of the girls whispers to the others and they all laugh. Trina winks at them and they giggle even louder.

"What was that about?" I ask when we're almost

through the lobby.

Trina looks over her shoulder and uses a softer voice. "You know us girls and our jealous tendencies."

"Why would they be jealous?"

Surprise covers her face. "You're kidding, right?"

I shake my head. "Why are you looking at me like that?"

"They're jealous because you're unbelievably gorgeous," she says matter-of-factly, making my cheeks get hot. "Doing that only makes it worse."

"Doing what?"

"Pretending that you're oblivious to how hot you are. Tate's a lucky girl."

I flinch at the sound of her name. I may as well mark Trina down as another one who's on board with trying to make me remember my relationship with the girl.

When we're in the B hallway, Trina asks, "Have your memories of Tate come back?"

I scowl at the black marble floor, putting the food revelation aside for a moment.

"I take that as a no," she mumbles.

Feeling as if I owe her an explanation, I pull my hand from hers and begin my rant. "I don't believe she's real. I mean, I know she's real—I've met her— but if we really *had something*," I mock quotes, "wouldn't my memories have come back by now? That's the way it works, right? Your memories came back!" I don't realize how much my volume has risen until Trina takes a step back. So much for the rehash.

She grabs my arm, stopping me when we're at the elevator. "You met her?"

I nod.

Trina's mouth drops open. "Is she dead?"

"No. Somehow Jonathan arranged it. Don't ask me how because I have no idea."

We stare at each other and I notice how small the space between us has become.

"Everything will work out," Trina says.

I step forward, close enough that our noses almost touch. "She means nothing to me."

When Trina gives me that awful, pitying look I hate so much, I pull her roughly against me and put my lips on hers. She doesn't respond.

What am I doing?

I pull back, but then Trina's fingers lace into my hair and she jerks me close again, extending our aggressive, make-out session. I can't help but feel like I'm trying to prove something to myself. What that something is, I'm not sure. What I do know is that I don't like it, and my conflicting emotions spoil the moment. This makes me force my body to go along even more. Trina's hot. What's wrong with me? My head wants this, but her body feels unnatural against mine.

Now furious, I move one hand to her lower back with my other hand tangled in her braid. Her body doesn't seem to be having the same difficulty as mine.

The sound of clapping brings me back in check. Remembering where I am, and at the same time remembering my feelings regarding PDA, I pull away from Trina. I'd be lying if I said I wasn't embarrassed even though our audience consists of just one person. One is enough.

Liam continues to clap slowly, but loudly enough to draw the attention of a few others who have wandered into the hall.

Trina wipes her lower lip with the side of her index finger and puts more space between our bodies.

Liam's grin is not sincere. "Nice display, lover boy."

I want to crush his hands. Enough with the clapping. "What's your problem?"

Liam doesn't answer at first. When he does begin talking, however, the guy can't seem to stop. "You have this amazing, beautiful girl waiting for you—who's way too good for you, by the way—and you do this. You have no idea, no bloody idea, how lucky you are—"

"Lucky?" I yell. "Lucky! I remember nothing about that girl! Do you understand me? NOTHING!" I roar. Yes, I've lost my cool, but I feel like I'm entitled to do so. Nothing has gone as planned for me. "I can't even block anymore! I don't have a choice in any of this!"

"Oh, that's right, poor Grant doesn't have his superpowers anymore," Liam mocks.

I move towards him, but Trina puts herself between us and pushes on my chest. No way could she hold me back, but I force myself to simmer because the last thing I want to do is hurt her in my raging state. I take a deep breath and step backwards.

"That's enough," I say sternly to Liam.

"No, it's not enough! Nothing is ever enough for you. You've crushed Tate and you have no freaking idea. What's worse is you don't even care! She's one of the best people I've ever known. She'd do anything for you, *anything!* And this is how you choose to spend your time," Liam shoots his glare at Trina.

"Hey!" Trina argues.

"Walk away, Liam," I growl in her defense.

"Bloody right I'll walk away."

When Liam reaches into his pocket, my muscles tense unnecessarily. It's not like the guy is going to throw a knife, seeing as I'm already dead.

Liam flicks something from his index finger with his thumb. "You sicken me," he says as the object flies through the air.

Light shines on the silver and I catch the ring before it nails me between the eyes. The metal burns into my hand and pain radiates from my chest and knee. My fist is frozen closed when I try to grasp my head to keep my pounding brain inside. Trina's blurry face fills my vision and her voice is a slow echo.

Clenching my teeth against the pain, a white light blinds me and Trina's voice fades away.

13. You're on first by default

"Grant!" a breathless voice hisses.

I wrap my weak fingers around the wrist of the hand that keeps slapping my face because my voice won't work. My throat feels like I've just taken the cinnamon challenge as I struggle for air.

"We need to move him. Back up!"

I manage to squint my eyes open, knowing that couldn't have been Jonathan; there was too much urgency in the voice to be his. Through my blurred vision, I groan at all the faces I'm being bounced past as I'm haphazardly carried. Whoever is in charge of my top half is nearly dropping me while each of their fingernails bite into my underarms.

"Hurry," the strained voice at my feet says. "Move out of the way!" The voice *does* belong to Jonathan, but why is he so frantic?

My eyelids pop open when screaming rings through my ears. I search the unfocused collection of faces staring down at me for the source. Good God, somebody make it stop!

"Grant! Grant! Look at me!"

My eyes darts upward. Willow, upside down from this angle, is the one carrying me. *Christ,* as Troy would say. Why

241

the heck would she take my top half?

"Stop screaming!" Willow shouts over the shrieking.

Yes, please stop screaming! I think, but can't form the words.

My head falls to the side, and I can see my partial reflection in the shiny black marble wall. That's when the realization hits: I'm the person wailing. My brain is about to wallpaper the hallway, but the pounding is nothing compared to what's happening to my chest and knee. They're both being ripped open by a searing blade.

"Oh no, not on my watch, kid! You stay awake! You hear me? You..." Willow's distorted voice fades away.

———

"Are you sure he's okay up there?"

"He's fine. Look at him, the kid's in his glory!" I shout while my hand shades my eyes from the afternoon sun.

"But he's so small!" Tate yells back over the skid loader's rumbling engine.

"You need to loosen up!" I give Fischer a thumbs up when he lowers the bucket. Grabbing Tate's hand, I pull her with me. "Better move before he buries us!"

We jog ten yards to the right before Fischer drops a load of dirt in the place we were standing just seconds ago. When the dust cloud reaches us, I laugh at Tate's dramatic cough and lean close to her ear. "The air's not that bad."

"Honestly, I don't know how you breathe this in every day."

Tate tenses when I wrap my arms around her waist, but before she can argue, I throw her over my shoulder. She complains by pounding on my back until I carefully set her on my truck's tailgate. My arm is assaulted a few times by her playful fists when I sit beside her.

Fischer has our full attention while he circles the vacant job site, digging holes with the skid loader to make the ground look like a life-sized game of whack-a-mole. My truck's distance from the machine gives our ears a reprieve from the reverberating engine.

One by one, short denim threads float to the gravel below our dangling feet. "He's fine," I say in hopes of sparing the surviving frayed ends of Tate's cutoff shorts.

"Thank you for doing this."

I hope she's impressed. God knows the effort it took to get her here. I'm amazed she even agreed to see me again after my blunder on our first date. Debacle is a more appropriate word to describe that night at Juju's Arcade with her and Fischer.

"Does this buy me a ticket to first base?" I plan the statement as a joke, but the actual delivery doesn't come out so well.

She leans up and kisses my cheek. "We'll call that a walk."

The heat in my face has certainly turned my tan skin red, and my arm bumps against hers. "I'll take it."

Tate keeps her eyes locked on Fischer. "You're on first by default. Don't think that's going to move you to second any sooner."

"I happen to like first base. Besides, there are eight innings left and I intend to get to first a few more times on my own."

Tate raises her eyebrows. "Is that right?"

In a bold move against my better judgement, my fingers slowly weave into her curls and I pull her heart-shaped mouth to mine. I figure I'll deal with the consequences after our lips separate. Whatever retaliation she chooses—which I realize could be a fist to my face—will be worth scoring another kiss from her.

Tate looks back at Fischer when I pull away. Her teeth bite into her lip, but her smile makes a tiny appearance despite her attempt to stop her lips from curving upward. I don't think I've ever been this happy.

I can't breathe!

Gasping for air, I try to sit up, but my muscles revolt. My eyes want to focus on the blue, cloudless sky, but the birds are nothing but blurry shadows as they dart overhead.

I need air!

My hand searches for my chest while I wonder if I can pull my lungs out to give them direct oxygen. My hand touches a wet, gauzy material. Clara yells something over me as I raise my arm enough to see my distorted, blood-covered fingers. I want to tell Clara I'm all right so she won't look so terrified, but a woman I've never seen declares the space between Clara and me as her own. Something bites into my knee and a stinging fire spreads from the spot of impact throughout my body.

The sky turns black.

———

"Get out!" Tate says and pushes me until I'm clear of the door. When the particle board panel slams closed and the lock slides over, I return to the stiff chair at the end of the dressing room.

Bored, my thumbs have officially run a mile around each other when the white door opens. Tate notices my breath hitch and she turns red all the way down to the extra low V at her chest.

"I really like that one." I swallow to keep my hormones in check. "A lot."

"I can tell." Tate walks past the abandoned clothes rack. "I don't know, I think I like the green dress better," she says over her shoulder and then spins in front of the trifold mirror.

I force myself to stay seated for the sake of the dress remaining in one piece.

"You've got to get that," I demand, wondering if I'm actually panting.

"It's so…black," Tate says. "You know I don't like black."

"You're hot in that! I mean, you're always hot, but," I shake my head and grunt like a caveman, "you could kill me wearing that, and believe me when I say I'd die a happy man."

Tate walks slowly towards me. Yes, the black dress could kill me, but that crooked smile would make me claw my way back from Hell.

"So you like this one?" she whispers and sits on my lap.

My hands slide down her bare back until they touch the slippery material. If the fabric hugs her body any more, I'll explode. She leans into me and brushes her smile against my lips.

While we kiss, I manage to mumble, "My vote," she is so hot, "is for black and clingy," she really is killing me, "like this one."

She pulls away from my lips so I move her hair to get to her neck. She squirms when my teeth scrape on her shoulder.

"Fine, I'll get this one," she hisses. "Now let me go so I can get out of the thing. I hate dresses. I want my jeans back."

When she stands, I grab her hands and stand, too, bringing her back to me. "I'll help," I whisper.

She frees her hands and pushes my chest, making me fall back into the chair. "Sit." She points her finger at me. "Stay."

I dig my hands into my hair and watch her until she disappears into the fitting room. I'm the luckiest man alive.

───

My eyes won't open, but I can hear Willow in the far distance. "When will he…?"

Her voice fades away.

"Where were you!" I blurt out, holding the doorway for support.

"Baby, what's wrong?" Tate remains calm while my heart is about to bust out of my chest.

I cross to her bed in such a hurry, I'm surprised I don't trip on the mound of clothes in the middle of her floor. Shoving the textbook aside, I bury her in my arms.

"Can't. Breathe," she muffles into my shoulder.

I ease off, but not much. "I was so scared."

"Hey." She struggles out of my grasp and slides her hand down my face. "It's okay. I'm right here." She presses her head against my chest. "I'm right here."

Tears build in my eyes. No! Do *not* cry, you sissy!

"Babe, I'm here. I'm right here."

"When I heard the news on the radio—" I stop before my voice betrays me. Men do not cry!

"It wasn't a big deal."

"Not a big deal? There was a bomb threat on campus! That's a big deal!"

"My drawing class wasn't even near Hickman Hall, and according to FOX news, the whole thing was a false alarm, anyhow. I'm fine, Grant. Everyone's fine. The evacuation wasn't even necessary."

"I tried to call and you didn't answer. I texted you at least twenty times!"

"You know my crappy phone, the battery's dead again. Wait—you don't even know how to text."

I pull her tighter into my arms because she can't possibly be any more perfect. "I can't ever lose you," I whisper into her curly ponytail.

"I'm here, baby. I'll always be here."

She lets me hold her for a long time until I finally get control over my emotions. Her hand rubbing up and down my back is comforting.

"Aren't you supposed to be at work?" she muffles into my shoulder.

When I don't answer, Tate leans back and smacks my arm. "Your dad is going to kill you!"

"Now that you mention it, he didn't look very happy when I tore out of there."

She pulls away and tries to shove me off the bed, but having only half my strength, her efforts are comical. "Go back to work!" she says in a strained voice because she's using all of her energy to push against my chest. "Your dad doesn't need another excuse to hate me!"

"He loves you," I argue and, with zero effort, remain seated to drive her crazy.

"Right."

"I swear. He loves you more than he loves his own son."

Her hands drop an inch and relax against my ribs. "You're being ridiculous."

"I'm not. He says hi to you all the time. Sometimes he even smiles."

"That's all he ever says," Tate argues.

"That's more than I've gotten in the past five years." She

actually thinks I'm kidding.

"Go!" She resumes her attempt to force me off the bed when I try to spark a make-out session.

"Grant!"

Willow's face blurs in front of me.

"Sorry, kid, I didn't mean to yell," she whispers. "I'm elated to finally see your eyes. You've been out for so…"

Willow disappears.

A peanut shell hits my arm and Tate tells me to sit down.

I grin wider. "Hey, batta, batta, batta. Sa-wing batta!" I yell from left field.

Tate turns two shades darker, making her skin almost match her red tank top. "You're annoying everyone around us."

I plop into the plastic stadium chair, throw my arm over her shoulder, and use my free hand to reach into the peanut bag on Tate's lap. "I love embarrassing you. Don't roll your eyes at me, either. It's your fault."

"How do you figure?"

"You make it so easy."

"Whatever." Tate shoves a peanut into my mouth. "Maybe that will shut you up for a minute."

I spit the salty shell on the concrete and reach for my drink, but my hand freezes when the unmistakable crack of the bat meeting the baseball spreads through the stadium.

A voice yells over the roaring cheers and applause, "Heads up!"

My eyes catch sight of the white blur and I curse and dive to block Tate. The next thing I know, my extended hand stings so bad I'm convinced there's been blood shed.

I manage to get myself halfway back in my folding seat. "Are you all right?" my panicked voice rings out.

Tate's stares open-mouthed at me without answering. I'll take that expression any day over how she could have looked; if I had been a mere second later, her face wouldn't be so pretty.

After a couple of deep breaths to stifle my adrenaline, I work my hand into a fist to dull the stinging.

"Are you OK?" Tate asks after a dozen strangers, who, at a Cards game are considered best friends, have slapped my shoulder and praised my catch.

The home run fireworks blaze above us and I smile through the pain still radiating through my palm. "I got you a souvenir."

When I toss the ball to her, she tosses it right back. I want to wince in pain, but refuse to let her see my weakness.

"No way, that was your catch!" she says over the last booming firework.

"This thing almost ruined your face. It's rightfully yours." I grip the ball with three fingers and my thumb like a pitcher, mostly to keep the leather from touching my sore palm. I hold it in her line of sight so she can't ignore my request.

Tate eventually gives in, taking it from my grasp. "Your stubbornness drives me crazy." She says this like she's mad, but then she makes herself comfortable under my arm.

———

"Jonathan!" Willow yells over me.

I must be dreaming. Why is she squishing my cheeks between her hands? More importantly, why is her nose almost touching mine?

"Stay with me. Please, Grant, stay…"

———

The crickets are loud in the still night. Tate stares up at the sky, telling me about the constellations and trying to point them all out.

"Are you even paying attention?"

My head comes back to the present. Thoughts of how lucky I am always consume me when Tate and I spend time like this in the bed of my truck. I smile to lessen her annoyance at me. She hates when I don't pay full attention to her, especially when she's sharing her knowledge.

"I love you." I know it's not fair to fight dirty, but this statement has a success rate even greater than owning both the Park Place and Boardwalk properties in a game of Monopoly.

Her face softens, making me glad I said them.

"What I was saying is, you're buying me a dog."

I grin because this is her response whenever she catches me not listening.

"No dogs," I counter, like always, to our inside joke even though I'm not against the idea. In fact, the thought of having a dog sounds fun as long as I get to do it with Tate. I can't help but mess with her, though. She's adorable when she pouts.

Knowing she could make me buy a rabid coon for a pet if she really wanted, she turns from her back to her side and kisses me for a long time. There's nothing better in the world than tasting her. Yes, I am so lucky.

Tate pulls away and her eyes lower to my chest. Before they do, though, I catch the sadness in them.

My muscles tense and I push up so I'm resting on the back of my elbows. I grab her chin and lift her face towards me. "What's up?"

Panic washes over me. Did I do something wrong?

"I'll die if I ever lose you." When she blinks, a single tear rolls over a peach-shaped freckle and down her cheek. She kisses me more urgently than before.

I love her so much it hurts.

My eyes begin to open in the quiet room, but I have to squint from the brightness and turn my head to the left. The slight movement sends a shooting pain down my neck.

"Tate," I try to say, but the fire in my throat keeps any noise from actually coming out. Willow's blurry backside is maybe three feet away. Even unfocused, I know it's her from her short stature and medusa-like dreads.

"Tate." My second attempt at speaking is as unsuccessful as my first, but the energy it takes to try puts me back in the dark.

—⁓—

Down on one knee, my hands soak Tate's with sweat and my heartbeat quickens at her silence.

"Tate?" I ask when she doesn't answer. I just made an ass of myself. As if that weren't bad enough, she's probably realizing she's too good for me. The kind of life she could have—the kind of life she deserves—is more than I could ever give her on a carpenter's salary.

She laughs at me through her tears. "What was the question?"

"You're impossible! Marry me!"

"Yes! Yes! I'll marry you!" Tate squeals.

Elliott takes a few steps back from the table because his sister is bouncing erratically up and down.

Fischer doesn't seem to know what to make of this. Overall, he looks as happy as Elliott, but maybe just a bit confused by his sister's reaction.

I grab Tate when she's on a down bounce and pull her tight against me. "Thank you, babe. Thank you," I whisper in her ear. "You've just made me the happiest man on Earth."

Tate said yes! To me! This is the best moment of my entire life.

———

My body hates me when I take a deep breath. "Where…?" Only the first word of my question croaks out.

Jonathan's face appears over me. "Welcome back, Grant. You're in the Mending wing."

To avoid the pain of speaking, I shake my head to tell him I don't understand.

His eyes move down toward my body and a flash of shock, or maybe fear, crosses his face. "Wynn!" he yells and pushes on my chest, forcing my back to dig into the hard bed.

I try to scream and flail so he'll stop, but I'm paralyzed.

A second later, a glimpse of a long needle flashes in my vision before a sharp sting bites into my knee.

———

"Say something."

Tate swallows. If she doesn't talk soon I'm going to drag her down to the ER.

"This isn't happening," Tate whispers, still looking at my chest instead of my face.

"We'll figure this out." I try to sound optimistic in the hospital hallway, but I'm certain my voice falters like the dimming florescent light above us. "I can beat this." I'll say anything to bring a semblance of life to her dead expression.

Her breath quickens and she pulls at the collar of her faded green T-shirt. "I can't breathe," Tate chokes. "I can't breathe!"

I crush her against me. "We'll get through this," I repeat and rub my hand hard along her spine. "I promise I won't leave you. I won't ever leave you." I pull back and make her look at me. "Do you hear me? I won't ever leave you."

She kisses me with so much intensity I'm thrown back against the hospital wall. The harder she kisses me, the more terrified I become. She knows I'm not going to survive.

———

"Willow?" Relief overwhelms me because my voice works even though my throat hurts like hell.

"Easy," Willow says and holds a cup in front of my face. "Jonathan said you woke up a few days ago. Don't try to talk. I'd like for you to stay awake longer than five seconds."

I suck on the straw, wondering who this person is in front of me. She certainly looks like Willow, but she's being unusually friendly.

"Congratulations, kid, you're the first Satellite to ever need a doctor. Go figure."

Ah, there's the freak I know and love.

The water brings some relief to my throat. I want to check out my surroundings when Willow's eyes circle around the room, but I'm too weak to lift my head.

"They'll probably end up naming this place after you," Willow adds.

I try to ignore the banging drum in my head to work on remembering how I got here, wherever *here* is.

"Our memories…" The fire in my throat halts my words.

Willow puts the straw back in my mouth and I'm grateful for the sip of water that helps extinguish the flames.

"Food," I croak out.

Willow's laughter trills around me, making my head hurt worse. "You're hungry?" Her rejoicing continues. "It's good to have you back, kid!"

I reach up to grab her hand by my side, but my focus is off, so I miss. My weak arm drops limply back to the bed. I manage to shake my head and Willow's cheerfulness melts away.

Panic takes over because I have to tell her how the Satellites have been losing their memories, but I also need to tell her about Tate. I reach to my chest in hopes of soothing the burning pain centralizing there. My head is cloudy and the ache throbbing through my brain makes the jolt of blocking seem like a day at the spa—not that I would know the first thing about a spa.

"Tate." My voice is quiet and hoarse, but I know Willow heard me.

Something warm and wet spreads across my chest, quickly soaking my hand.

Tate's laugh bounces through my truck and the sun

makes her bare feet resting on the side mirror almost glow. In slow motion, her curls blow in the wind. She looks over at me and ruffles my hair, a gesture that won't be possible in a month. We're so in tune with each other, I know the moment she realizes this. Her eyes lower and she looks back out the window.

———

"He asked about her." Willow sounds like she's directly over me.

I try to open my eyes, but my body is useless.

"You can't ignore what's happening. He started bleeding when he said her name."

———

"He's got nothing on you." Tate's soft, breathy voice tickles my ear like a feather. She brushes her lips down my jaw and lightly kisses my neck.

I feel sick, but not in the same way the cancer has annihilated me. This feeling is worse.

I force my eyes off the guy with a body like the one I used to have and turn myself back around. Tate straightens and continues wheeling my chair to the hospital cafeteria.

———

"Tate!" My body kicks up into a sitting position.

"Grant, please lie down!" Jonathan sounds far away.

Despite my swelling brain pressing against my skull, I manage to focus. Jonathan runs across the vacant marble room, but he's not looking at my face.

My eyes dart down to see what has his attention. A red stain is spreading through the bandage on my bare chest. I look past the red jogging shorts that appear to fit me but are certainly not my own. The same crimson color is growing through the gauze wrapped around my knee.

"I need to see her." Dear God, am I really crying? "Please," I beg.

Something warm drips down my abs.

An arm kicks across my shoulders, throwing me back, and what feels like a rubber band snap stings my knee.

"Go. Please. I don't want you to see me like this," I plead from my hunched position on the bathroom tile.

Tate wrings out the washcloth in the sink. "I'm not leaving you."

I try to argue, but my stomach has other plans, forcing me to turn my head back to the toilet. As if losing my own life wasn't bad enough, I'm taking her down with me.

"It's just one more time. Come on, you've done it before," Willow is saying.

"I should not have done such a foolish thing, and I certainly will not allow it again. Liam is still dealing with the backlash of my mistaken judgment."

I keep my eyes closed because past experience has proven that when my presence is known, conversations tend to come to a halt.

"You didn't have a problem destroying their connection! Now you decide to have a conscience?"

"Willow, with all due respect--"

"Respect? Are you kidding me?"

"That is enough! She could eradicate him!"

The silence lasts a long time and I'm glad neither of them know I'm listening.

"I apologize for raising my voice," Jonathan says. "Please try to understand the severity of this situation. You've seen what the mere mention of Tate's name does to him, and thus far, the only way to stop the bleeding is through sedation."

"Honestly, what's the worst that can happen? The kid's already dead. Bringing Tate back has to be worth a try."

Yes! I need Tate! My body tenses and I have to focus on not opening my eyes.

Jonathan continues in a voice so low, my ears strain to hear him. "His wounds are expanding at an uncontrollable rate. If they continue at this pace, they will tear his body in half and his soul will have nowhere to reside. He will be physically destroyed, Willow. He will become a lost soul." The room falls silent for a couple seconds. "For eternity."

"How is that even possible? We're already dead! Our

bodies heal themselves when they've been damaged."

"Grant's body is not regenerating as it should. I've only witnessed a phenomenon such as this one other time. I am certain if we don't find a solution to reverse the damage, Grant will not survive."

"But—" Willow's voice stops abruptly, leaving the room silent.

"Bringing Tate here will guarantee this devastating outcome. Our only hope is to gain control of his wounds until the Menders find a cure."

"And what if they don't?" Willow's more angry than before.

I need Tate. She is the only one who can fix me. Every cell in my body knows this!

I open my mouth to plead my argument, but warmth spreads out over my chest and down my leg. The wetness comes so fast, my arms can feel the warm liquid pooling on my sides.

I reach for my knee, but paralysis holds me hostage. Why don't they understand?

Not being with Tate is what's destroying me!

Tate's body pushes harder into my side. I'm so thin the both of us don't fill my twin hospital bed.

"Fight, damn it! Fight for me! Don't let this take you away," Tate cries into my shoulder.

"Good to see those eyes open."

A blurry Jonathan leans over me.

"I—water?"

I take a few sips with Jonathan's assistance and he returns the cup to the bedside table.

"How are you feeling?" he asks.

"Jonathan. Please. Listen. To me," I beg in a slow voice. "I must see her. You don't understand—"

Jonathan squeezes my arm and the light pressure calms my adrenaline a little. "Please be still."

"I remember all of it, my life with Tate, my scars." I look down at my bandaged chest. Already, the bright red spot is the size of a grapefruit and growing. "She gave them to me, she can heal them."

I lie back in exhaustion while the moisture creeps across my chest.

Jonathan does a "come here" motion with his hand. A second later, something pinches my knee before I can argue.

"Wait!" Willow's echoing shout is far away.

Please don't leave me," Tate pleads while she sobs. "I can't do this without you. I can't survive without you."

"I'm so sorry, kid," Willow's whisper bounces through my head before my eyes have opened completely. "I agree with you about Tate; I think she can heal you. I tried to get her here, I really did, but Jonathan won't listen to me."

When I try to sit, Willow pushes me down. "Relax."

"You were right about her. I'm the one that's sorry. I should've believed you." Usually I hate admitting Willow's right, but in this case I would hug her if she'd just let me up.

"Turns out you're more like Superman than I thought."

The croaking sound that comes out when I clear my throat prompts Willow to reach for the cup.

After Willow helps me take a few sips of water, she reaches in her pocket. Her hand returns with a silver ring. "You've got your very own kryptonite, it seems. This little bastard nearly killed you."

"Language," I try to use the same disapproving tone she would use, but my attempt at drama fails. I use what little strength I have left to reach for the ring.

Willow swats my hand away. "Nuh uh, you're not out of the woods yet. Heck, you're not even on the dirt path. We can't take any chances."

"Just let me hold it." I need to feel something of Tate's, no matter how small because the emptiness within me is too vast. I feel like a hollow shell.

"Oh no, it's happening again!" Willow grabs a roll of gauze from the table and clumsily unwraps it.

When she presses on my chest, darkness swallows me.

I struggle to inhale. "We'll always be together," I whisper to Tate, though I'm not sure my words are audible. I'm not even sure if my lips move.

Even in this state, sobbing and exhausted, Tate is beautiful. What will become of her? I can't leave her. I'm not ready! Please, God, please let me stay!

"Be good," I hear my mom say through her own sobs as I take my last, shallow breath.

"Come on, kid, wake up! We don't have a lot of time! Wake up!"

A frantic Willow comes into focus. Her eyes dart to the right and then back to me. When I try to speak, she presses her hand against my mouth.

I try to push myself up to get out from under her restraining hand and, more importantly, breathe, but I fail.

"Listen, kid." Willow, now above me, lets me have some oxygen by catching my face between her hands. "Focus on me for a second. This is important. You're weak, but I need you to try and stay with me here."

When she sees my obedience, she continues talking low and fast. "A lot has happened while you've been out. Things around Progression are different."

"The food," I manage to say when she breaks for air.

She sits up straighter and pulls the bottom hem of her purple tank top to cover the sliver of exposed skin above her cargo pants. "Your riddle took a while, but Morgan finally put it all together. We got the word out to some of the newbies through their Legacies. You've saved a lot of Satellites from losing their memories. We may have even gotten to Chris in time. He still remembers some things about his family."

Maybe, but Chris doesn't remember his girlfriend, Liv. I decide not to mention this because Willow seems like she's having a tough time maintaining her optimism.

"Someone was able to close Benson for a few weeks, so that helped, too."

"Who?" Pain shoots through my head, making me regret my hasty reply.

"Stop talking! You're weak, remember?"

Not only do I hate the fact that Willow's so bossy, I wish she'd stop calling me weak. I don't need the reminder.

"Most people initially thought it was the Schedulers. Our group knew it wasn't, though, seeing as Landon is the one who's so insistent about losing our memories in the first place. That guy would prefer we gorge on our forgetful food all day long." Willow pauses. "Our group thinks Jonathan was behind it, but we can't be sure."

"*Our* group?" I manage. "So you're in?" My attempt to smile fails.

Willow rubs her bare arms like she's cold. "I started to realize you were right once Landon threatened the others. You wouldn't believe the number of Satellites on our side now. A lot of the Schedulers are against Landon, too."

"Sophie's been keeping me updated," Willow says as if I've asked for an explanation.

"Landon's powerful, though, and he's not backing

down. We aren't allowed to congregate during breaks anymore," Willow looks toward the doorway before she continues at an impossibly faster pace. "The Satellites are required to stay in their rooms. None of them have, of course. We've been holding secret meetings in Evelynn's old room to try and sort out this mess."

On the side of the bed, Willow shifts her weight and folds her left leg underneath her. "Programming did that girl some good. You wouldn't believe how modest her clothes have been. I haven't seen her girls make an appearance in months."

"Months?" my voice croaks out.

Willow turns away from me and doesn't say anything for a few seconds. "You've been out of commission for over two months."

Willow glances at my chest and murmurs, "Oh, crud."

She pulls something from her pocket and appears to be having a mental feud with herself, looking from her open hand to me.

She leans in when she talks, which is good because her voice is so quiet, I wouldn't hear her otherwise. "I could take a big risk here, but I'm not sure if it would even work. There's a chance it could destroy you."

She closes her hand and straightens her back, putting space between us. "I'm sorry. I can't."

I use all my strength to grab her wrist before she stands.

"I trust you," I say when her watery eyes meet mine.

Impatient for an explanation, I have to force my mouth

closed to allow her the time she needs to take a deep breath in hopes it will erase the fear in her eyes.

She removes my hand from her wrist, sandwiches a cold metal ring between our palms, and whispers, "Displace."

14. This is quite a world you have created

Confusion instantly replaces panic after Willow and I drop through the floor. The clouds are so thick, I can't see her face even though her fingers are pressing into my forearm.

"Willow!" I yell into the white fog.

"I'm sorry, kid," she yells back. "It was the only thing I could think of."

Five seconds later, we've landed.

"Please tell me you're all right."

I turn my head to the left. Willow's face is so close, I flinch. Only now do I realize we're both laying on our backs.

"Hell of a landing," I manage to say.

"Hail Mary, full of grace!" Willow belts out. "Thank goodness you're OK."

I push myself up on my elbows. When I feel a little steadier, I sit up.

"Easy. Don't try to get up yet."

Still dizzy, I opt to heed Willow's advice and take a second to focus on the trees that show the first signs of Autumn.

Willow's eyes fall to my chest. Her wrinkled forehead causes me to look in the same direction. If the red stain on the gauze wasn't creeping outward, I'd probably be embarrassed about being shirtless and in gym shorts. Instead, I share Willow's worry.

"Let's get moving, kid." Willow hoists me up by my biceps muscle. "Can you walk?"

When I shift my weight to lean away from Willow, I stumble like I'm intoxicated. My bare feet don't disturb the damp leaves on the sagging deck, though.

"Stop," Willow orders, likely nervous about me toppling over. "New plan. Grab my hand."

My fingers entwine with hers and a second later she's pulling me up the side of the house like she's Peter Pan.

"Other things have changed around Progression, too," she's saying as we pass through the wall. "Jonathan hasn't been around. The only time I've seen him is when he's been checking in on you. Even then, he's been disappearing as quickly as he comes. He dodges all my questions. Frankly, it's been quite frustrating."

Under different circumstances, I'd probably laugh at Willow's nonchalance. Under these circumstances, however, I find it disturbing, as if this is the least of her worries.

I lean on Willow as we pass through the small bathroom. Tate's bathroom. I'd been so focused on Willow and not falling over, this fact escaped me.

"I hope this works." She drags me through the closed door. A second later we're in Tate's room.

Heat fills my chest and a warm trail rolls down my abs, stopping at the waistband of my shorts. When I reach for the gauze, the material feels more like a sponge than a bandage.

My shorts stick to my leg where they hit just above my

knee cap, reiterating the fact I already knew. The scars are the same in every way, just as they've always been; their shape, their size, and even how they now bleed and refuse to heal. Of course they're the same. They're both from Tate. I can't believe there was a time not long ago when I had no idea how I got these scars. My stomach lurches at the thought of forgetting Tate—

Tate!

I turn my head and glimpse Willow, staring open-mouthed at me. My breath hitches and I'm frozen in place. The only movement is the trail dripping heavily down my stomach and leg.

Tate.

"Tate," I whisper, and at the same time, fall over.

"Tate," I say again, though I'm not sure if my voice works.

She's sideways in my view, coming closer. Her caring expression, her full bottom lip, her curvy body, her curls sprouting out from her ponytail—she's exactly as I remember. She's beautiful. She's perfect. She's Tate. My Tate.

I'm smiling as she approaches because that's the only reaction my strength will allow. Tate moves closer and then kneels beside me.

I try to focus on the pear shaped freckle on her left cheek, but my sight is hazy. I'm positive no sound comes out when I say her name this time.

Her angelic, blurry, heart-shaped face begins to darken like her black clothes.

"No. No, no, no..." Willow's voice echoes. "Grant,

come back!"

Blindness overtakes my vision, but I'm not afraid. A comforting warmth surrounds me like bathwater. Though I can't see Tate, I can feel her.

A pin prick of white, like a spec of glitter, breaks through the darkness. The small dot morphs into a larger ball of light as it gets closer. A minute later I'm squinting from the brightness.

When my eyes are able to refocus, a black curvy figure grows in the distance. The silhouette quickly becomes familiar.

"Tate," I breathe. This time my voice works.

When she reaches me, Tate grabs my hands to pull me up.

I counter the movement, forgetting how fatigued I am, but manage to bring Tate down to my level. As we make the musty forest floor our bed, I barely feel her weight on top of me. My arms lock her body against mine. I'm never letting her go.

While my face is buried in Tate's dark curls, a faint sound behind me grows louder. Running water, a stream maybe? Then a single chirp of a bird seems to summon others. I don't loosen my grip, but I turn my head.

I swear I can see my buck far in the distance beyond the trees, and could that really be my hunting stand along the wood line? More importantly, how did I get here?

"Grant. Can't. Breathe."

I loosen my arms enough for Tate to sit up. Her legs straddle around my waist while my fingers trial along the slippery, black material covering her thighs. "I love this dress," I whisper. My eyes linger on the low V-cut neck. Yes, this one is my favorite.

Tate's forehead wrinkles. "You're hurt."

"I'm fine," I lie, ignoring the wetness that is dripping down my sides. "Funny thing, though. I think your tears did this to me." My attempt to smile fails, which is unfortunate because now Tate looks even more distraught. So much so, that tears well in her eyes.

"I'm so sorry," Tate whispers. "What have I done to you?"

"Please don't cry. I'm not sure if my body can handle any more lesions."

Like always, her face shows disappointment in my coping mechanism of making jokes at inappropriate times. This time could be the worst. Even more so than at the funeral visitation when I said Grandpa looked like a mannequin that had been stored in a closet too long. Honestly, though, what did Tate expect? It was either I say that, or fall to the ground and sob like a child. I like my choice better.

Tate's tears begin to roll down her face, becoming steady enough that a single stream forms a path of least resistance on each cheek. I focus on her chin, watching the water collect like heavy rain drops before falling on my chest. The gentle patter of them hitting the gauze is audible because someone hit the mute button on our surroundings. The next sound is Tate's breath catching.

Her wide eyes are more than enough to build my

curiosity, so I switch my focus to my chest. Glancing back to Tate, I see that her amazement is as great as mine. We silently watch her tears dissolve the blood that is staining the gauze.

"Babe, you're crying peroxide." OK, again, probably inappropriate timing, but I've got nothing else.

This time, Tate half smirks and rubs her hands along the now-pinkish gauze.

"Can you sit?"

"I think so." I push on her thighs when she attempts to swing her right leg over me. "Stay." My voice cracks, but Tate complies as I pull my upper body up until I'm in a sitting position with her still straddled around my legs.

She scoots back a couple of inches, redistributing her weight on my lower thighs, but I don't mind. Her fingers search along my chest. She finds the end of the gauze and begins to unwind the bandage, grabbing the material with her other hand when she reaches around my back.

Around and around she goes. The gauze seems to stretch on forever. I have no complaints. The longer Tate takes, the longer she stays on my lap. Eventually, the last bit loosens and falls to my stomach. Unwilling to leave any job incomplete, Tate does one final circle around my torso.

"Wow," I whisper when I look down. The tear-shaped scar is back to its original pea size. "Wow." Willow would be displeased by my vocabulary, but that's the only word I've got.

Tate takes advantage of my shock, using the distraction to hop her right leg off me so she's kneeling at my side. Just when I'm about to argue because I preferred her on my lap, she moves her head towards my lower body.

Tate hovers over my mid-section, looking back at me with a grin, even though her eyes are still watering.

She shakes her head, as if to say she knows what I'm thinking. She continues moving down my body, stopping just over my right knee. Her head drops until it's almost touching the center of the twelve-inch red stain.

Again, like an illusionist, her tears fall on my knee and magically change the color of the bandage. In only three drips, the gauze is tinted light pink.

Tate sits at my side and brushes her cheeks with the backside of her hand. I move her hand away to dry her face with my thumb. Her tears, though still collecting in her eyes, take longer to spill over until none are falling at all. All the while, we're both silently staring at each other.

"Thank you," I finally say to break the silence.

"I caused those horrific wounds," she says lightly. "I'm grateful I could heal them."

"No, not for that. Although it is nice to have my strength back and not leave a blood trail wherever I go—"

Oh, her smile. I'd crack jokes all day to see her smile, but my tone becomes serious. "Thank you for loving me."

The waterworks are back in play as Tate wraps her arms around me.

"Thank you for being so easy to love," she muffles into my shoulder.

Now it's my face that's wet. I cling tightly to the slippery material covering her lower back for fear that she'll pull away and see me crying. For the first time, I feel worthy of her and her love. This makes the tears come faster. I've never felt like I deserved love. I've blamed my dad all these years, but it was me who's caused all my problems. I've never allowed myself to feel worthy of anything. It's my fault, not his.

Sobbing now, Tate holds me tighter. She doesn't talk. She just holds me and lets me sob.

Tate and I are both sniffling when our grips finally loosen.

"You can't judge me for this," I joke as I dry my face with my hands.

"You're kidding, right? You've never opened up like this before. I like this side of you."

"I'm not planning on making a habit of it." My discomfort from all this feeling talk makes me grin.

"Are you better?"

I juggle her question in my head.

Unbelievably and unquestionably, yes.

Yes.

A lightness I've never felt before fills me, making me think of those metaphors about chains being removed and whatnot. I used to internally roll my eyes at that sort of thing, but I think I finally understand.

Unsure how to put this into words without sounding like a cliché, I choose a simple nod as my answer.

A loud rustle from across the field steals our attention.

Tate tries to stand, but I pull her back down until she's on my lap.

"Grant, we have to go."

"Where?" I ask, tightening my grip.

"Back."

"Back where?"

"Come on, baby. We need to go now!"

I look over my shoulder at the distant field. "No, we can stay. It's just a deer."

"We can't." Tate wiggles, trying to break free.

"Yes we can. Don't you see? We can finally be together again."

Tate struggles with me until I loosen my grip for fear of hurting her. The peace I felt moments ago is replaced with panic when Tate steps away from me. Her heels make her stumble when she runs towards the tree line opposite where the deer moved. She slows her pace enough to remove her black shoes, drop them in the field, and then sprint away from me.

"Come back," I plead. "Tate! Where are you going?"

I have no option but to chase her. I can't lose her again.

"Tate!" The fear in my voice bounces off the trees. How did the forest become so dense so quickly?

Her hair swings across her bare, exposed back as she runs. I reach for her arm and push my legs to move faster, but Tate maintains her six-inch lead. The trees surround us like giants as we sprint through the narrow pathways between them. In contrast to the way the elements never physically affected me when running after a Tragedy on Earth, the sticks and rocks stab into my bare feet and my lungs tighten in need of air.

I reach again and again for Tate's arm, but every grasp comes up empty. The trees thicken even more and their limbs are like arms, blocking me while Tate bends easily around them.

I'm struck in the face with a branch and stumble backwards from the blow. "Tate! Tate, stop!"

"Come back to me." Tate's voice is far away. She couldn't have taken that much of a lead. I was right behind her.

"Tate!" I sprint toward her voice, ignoring the pain biting into my arms and bare chest from the tree limbs. "Tate!"

"Grant!"

Her pleading voice keep my legs moving, but my lungs eventually give in. Hunched over, I try to catch my breath. "Tate," I say with each exhale.

"I need you." Tate's eerie whisper blows past me like the wind.

I force my fatigued body to move toward the light that is cutting through the trees about fifty yards ahead. Every muscle rebels. I collapse when I reach an open field.

From my knees, a shadow covers the grass like a solar eclipse, followed by a flash of light. I shade my eyes to keep the white light from burning my retinas. A blurry, dark rectangle where the horizon should be is all that breaks up the light. Certainly it's a doorway. It has to be. That's where Tate is. I just need to get there. Unfortunately, in my condition, crawling is my only option in achieving my goal.

It feels like decades when I reach what is, in fact, a door. The brightness has dimmed, changing the black rectangle to gold metal. The handle seems to be smiling down at me, as if welcoming me, proving my exhaustion has made me delusional.

When my hand touches the handle, a zing of electricity cycles through me, making my chest and knee throb again. I pull down on the handle and push with my last bit of strength. The door creaks open. My head hits the ground; my eyes look through the doorway.

Heaven.

The real Heaven.

Finally.

Sitting cross-legged with a few books fanned out in front of her, Tate smiles down at me from her bed. I don't know how she changed clothes so quickly, but I'm not complaining. She looks as amazing in faded jeans and my navy blue hoodie as she did in her black dress.

"Finally," I breathe.

"Don't!" a ragged, winded voice yells from behind me.

"Grant, stop! It's a trap!"

I can't look away from Tate, even as the familiar voice gets closer, pleading me to stop.

Anger, sadness, and fear swirl through me. I just want to be with Tate. I need to be with her.

I push myself forward.

"Grant, no! That's not Tate. It's an illusion. If you cross over that threshold, your body will be destroyed." Jonathan, now directly behind me, sounds like he's just run a marathon. "He takes a few quick breaths. "Your soul will have nowhere to live."

Jonathan sits on the ground beside me. "This is all

Landon's doing. I am deeply sorry I could not stop this earlier."

Tate, though blurry now from the water pooling in my eyes, smiles as if nothing is happening.

With Jonathan's help, I'm able to get into a sitting position. "I don't understand. What does Landon gain by any of this?"

"You and your friends, along with all the other Satellites that have come and gone through the years, have done so because of Landon's vision. He formed the entire Satellite program, with the help of many others, of course."

"But you…" I look away from Tate, trying to grasp what Jonathan is saying. "You went along with all of it. You were our trainer!"

"I never disagreed with Landon's plan. In fact, I quite favored the idea in the beginning. It seemed to simplify the process of protecting those on Earth."

Jonathan pauses and looks at Tate. "Until recently, I never witnessed such commitment as Landon had for his wife, Grace. When Landon arrived in Progression, he faced difficulty letting go of his past. Landon's love for Grace nearly destroyed him. It was his idea that the Satellites be stripped of their memories. Landon believed the only possible way he could maintain his sanity in Progression was by forgetting Grace. I carried a deep sympathy for him and the loss he endured. I realized if we didn't change the program, his self-destruction was imminent. Landon is a gifted Scheduler. One of our best, in fact."

Jonathan gazes at me until I turn my head back to Tate.

"His entire program is threatened by you wanting the Satellites to remember their lives. I believe Landon cannot fathom how anyone could function while carrying such a heavy loss. Please know his intentions are noble, though his delivery may seem a bit insensitive."

"But it isn't a loss," I argue.

Tate maintains her oblivious state, chewing on the sweatshirt hood's drawstring while scribbling something in her notebook.

"We may disagree if our true loves were to find happiness with someone new. I imagine protecting someone you feel shunned by could be emotionally taxing." Jonathan inhales a long breath. "Sometimes knowing a loved one is moving on is comforting. Other times, witnessing the blossoming of new relationship filled with hope and promise can be purgatory."

I swallow, thinking of how I would react if I was forced to watch Tate replace me.

Maybe forgetting her would be the better option.

No! No.

Stealing our memories is wrong.

My eyes sting from my mixed emotions, so I turn away from both Tate and Jonathan. How could I have denied knowing Tate for so long? I honestly believed she didn't exist. The truth is, for a time, I didn't want her to exist. This makes me feel like a monster.

"Landon believes his life is unraveling, and this scares him. To counter his fear, he is trying to control Progression, which is not a practical solution, nor an overtly productive option."

Jonathan's eyes lower to my knee. "My apologies for shifting gears; however, my curiosity about your lesions has gotten the better of me. Your healing is remarkable. May I ask how this happened?"

"Willow—" I stop myself. Willow, with all her quirks, is one of the best friends I have ever had. The last thing I want to do is get her in trouble. I owe her so much for bringing me to Tate.

I try my best to sound convincing, which makes it impossible to look at Jonathan. "Willow had, um, Tate's ring so I stole it and displaced to see her. Tate's tears healed me, which, now that I think of it, is kind of ironic considering that they caused the wounds to begin with."

I try to silence the voice in my head screaming that Jonathan knows the truth. The guy knows everything.

"Anyway, that's what happened. Willow doesn't know I'm here." I shrug as if to say, *See, no big deal.* "Where are we, by the way?" Hopefully, a subject change will save Willow's tail.

When Jonathan looks at Tate through the doorway, my stomach sours. I want so badly to cross over that threshold.

He scans the surrounding forest. "That is the question, isn't it? This is quite a world you have created."

"Are you saying none of this is real?"

"On the contrary." Jonathan must sense my confusion, because he goes on. "I've always been captivated by our thought processes as humans. Our minds are not utilized to their fullest potential in our earthly bodies. How unfortunate for those that cannot believe in anything beyond their own world." Jonathan pauses. "Why do we limit ourselves, I wonder."

I'm fairly certain there wasn't an actual answer to my question anywhere in Jonathan's statement. "So this is real?" I ask again.

Jonathan nods and gives me one of his famous, kind smiles. "I imagine Willow told you—before you stole Tate's ring from her, of course—about the changes happening around Progression?"

"Not in great detail, but yes. Was it you who shut down Benson?"

Jonathan turns to Tate. "Much to Landon's disapproval, I spared the latest Satellite arrivals."

"So it *is* the food that makes us forget?"

"Two for two." Jonathan leans over and holds his hand up, leaving it there until I give him a high five. The guy is actually pretty funny when he wants to be.

"As I've always said, I do not believe in coincidence. Each Satellite being comforted by their favorite food in Progression is no exception. In addition to being a talented life planner, Landon is also responsible for the invention of the perfect mind eraser."

"The guy deserves a Noble Peace Prize for all his accomplishments."

Jonathan doesn't find the humor in this, even when I smile extra wide.

He clears his throat. "After much testing, his concoction was found to work only when mixed with an individual's favorite food. We believe this is related to the emotional connections to the foods we love. Landon's development also ensures that memories can be regained through Programming."

Tate stands and walks toward us. In the doorway, she's just a foot away from me. Focusing on Jonathan is not easy when he goes on to explain how the degree of the mind-erasing is a combined result of each individual's tolerance and the amount of food consumed. I'm sure he says a few other things, but I'm too captivated by Tate to notice or care.

"She has to be real," I murmur to myself.

Jonathan grabs my hand as it extends to Tate and returns my arm to my side. "Landon will continue to fight against us, so we must stay alert. I do hope we can convince him to join our side quickly."

In the doorway, Tate does a graceful spin and skips back to the bed.

"The good news is, most of Progression has come to agree with your idea. I knew they'd come around over time."

I draw in a long breath and turn to Jonathan in effort to give him my attention. "You were against us."

"I was not against you, but we had not reached the opportune time; therefore, a bit of stalling was necessary."

"What about Rigby?" Not wanting to hear confirmation of Rigby's dislike for me, I pick at my toenail, wishing I was wearing my boots.

"Ah, Rigby. He took some convincing. His skepticism had very little to do with your friendship and more to do with me, I'm afraid."

"You?"

"Not all memories are good memories. Hardships are sometimes useful starting points for moving forward with the evolution process; however, this does not make facing those memories any easier."

Jonathan continues before I can ask what any of that has to do with Rigby. "Were you aware that Rigby was in the Army?"

I shake my head, but can easily pair Rigby's crew cut with Army fatigues.

"He can deactivate one of the world's most complex bombs in under thirty seconds," Jonathan says like a proud father. "Of course, the one that took his life was designed in such a way that deactivation was impossible. Joining the Army was Rigby's only way of escaping his abusive father. He suffered many unnecessary beatings throughout his life." Looking bewildered for a few seconds, Jonathan clears his throat and pops back to the present.

Thinking of my own dad, guilt settles in my gut like a chemistry experiment gone bad. I had it easy.

"I knew Rigby's heart well enough to expect the emotional turmoil he would endure upon being reintroduced to his past. Thousands of others have faced unfortunate circumstances such as his. I had to collect proof that those particular subjects would be able to watch over their own loved ones, despite their histories."

"Why didn't anyone stop Rigby's dad?"

Jonathan's confused expression prompts me to continue. "Couldn't you have sent a Satellite to change his dad's thoughts, or a Guardian like Josh to change the direction of his fist? I mean, there's got to be something you could have done."

"Oh, Grant, please don't misunderstand. Progression does not condone stealing anyone's free will. The tasks performed throughout Progression are merely to keep people on course. Not just Tragedies, but all of humankind. Take the Menders, for example. If the life of someone is threatened, such as Ryder's when he experienced that eventful car accident—"

I flinch as the memory of Ryder's Shelby wrapped around the tree inhabits my mind. "I'm so sorry! I really messed up."

Jonathan squeezes my shoulder. "Mistakes are unavoidable. They are, in fact, the reason Progression was created. We cannot diminish hardships, though I wish we could. We merely assist in allowing humans the timeframe necessary to live the life they were meant for."

Jonathan smooths the stubble above his upper lip with his palm. "It seems we have careened a bit off course. Let me explain a bit more about Rigby. I sent him through Programming around the time you were trying to recruit Satellites. We had just finished a Programming session, in fact, the day you and your friends visited me in my office while you were searching for the Schedulers."

He continues, even though I look away. "Despite what he may have told you, Rigby did maintain a few memories following his arrival. When he learned about the program, he realized this was the fresh start he had been praying for, so he independently blocked out his past life, even the parts he had not forgotten."

As angry as I should be with Rigby for lying to me about his memories, I can understand why he did so. "Has he been watching over his father?"

Jonathan nods. "Rigby had forgotten about his younger brother until he completed Programming. Watching over his brother has now become Rigby's purpose. We've also found his father's temperament has greatly improved from Rigby's presence. I do feel badly about having to conduct this experiment; however, the doubts I've held over the last centuries in regard to the Satellite program have been validated."

Jonathan rubs his hands along his dark jeans. "Please understand I was not against you, nor was Rigby. A proper amount of time to assess Rigby's case was required to present proof to the Schedulers so they may see our proposal as the right thing to do."

I try to bury my next question, but I have to know the answer. "Are you sure having a loved one there is better in every instance?" I look at Tate, not caring that this won't help the tears already stinging my eyes. "I made her worse."

"Actually, no, you didn't."

A tear spills over and rolls down my cheek. "I was there, Jonathan. I did."

"Tate's behavior appeared so, yes. However, I promise you that Tate's condition was rapidly decreasing. She would have been a Rebellion regardless of your presence."

I turn to Jonathan. "You don't really expect me to

believe that?"

Jonathan places his hand on my knee. "You are welcome to believe whatever you choose."

"I saw her. Liam confirmed it!" A deep breath brings my adrenaline down a bit, but not as much as I'd like.

The look on his face exasperates me. How can he actually think he can argue this one? "Every time I was there, she veered off course from her book."

"The book in Liam's possession was a decoy."

I glare at Jonathan in disbelief, unsure of what question to even ask. I wish I could slap the sympathetic smile off his face.

"The Schedulers write everyone's life, this is true, and they perform their jobs extremely well. What you may not be aware of is that every book passes through me."

"You don't expect me to believe you've read everyone's book."

Come on, enough with the staring!

My voice raises. "That's impossible. I mean…" I pause, not sure how to proceed. "Between training and passing out assignments and everything else you do around Progression, how would you ever have time for that?"

"Time is merely an Earthly invention."

I shake my head. "That doesn't make sense."

"My position has its perks." Jonathan acts as if this is an acceptable explanation. "Not only do I read everyone's book, I occasionally make revisions as well. Between you and me, there have even been a few I've rewritten."

Jonathan refuses to answer when I ask whose books

he's referring to. I know him well enough to save my energy instead of trying to convince him to tell me.

The silence that follows is not uncomfortable. Jonathan's like that. He has a way of calming even stubborn people like myself.

Tate looks up from her notebook as if she can see me. As she chews on her full lower lip, I have to summon every ounce of self-control to force myself to stay on this side of the door. Having Jonathan here helps because I know he'd stop me if I tried.

"Grant, there is something you must understand," Jonathan says a few minutes later. "As with all the other programs in Progression, the Satellite program will not be ending."

Jonathan holds up his hand before my mouth has a chance to spew its objections.

"The Satellite program will indeed decrease in numbers; however, not every person needing assistance has a loved one who can watch over them. In some situations, a single death may result in widespread bereavement. Demographically, this is an impossible undertaking for one person. We will be utilizing Satellites for events such as this."

Jonathan glances at Tate. "That being said, all of the departments in Progression will receive full memory recovery. In addition, every department will have ample opportunity to visit their loved ones, but will continue to be tasked with their normal duties, whether that be protecting, mending, tocket-hunting, and the like. Going forward, the Schedulers must make the necessary alterations in their subjects books, and I must begin notifying the departments of the upcoming changes. Getting Landon's prompt approval is imperative."

"Aren't you in charge around here? Just tell him, 'this is how it is.'"

"I would prefer not to use my authority in such a way." Jonathan sighs. "I had hoped he would have come around by now."

After a few minutes of silence, Jonathan leans back and takes a deep breath through his nose as if he's walked into a donut shop at five in the morning. "The point of your mortal life and the experience gained from the programs that follow in Progression is to evolve." He shifts his weight, leaning his arm on his left leg. "To fully prepare for what awaits in eternity, one must master cooperation, kindness, and humility. It is only then that mankind can exist peacefully."

Jonathan turns his attention back to Tate. "I hope you understand this is why each person's purpose, both in life and in Progression, is so important. We are merely a team assisting each other so we can evolve in preparation for what's to come."

Like Jonathan, I watch Tate twirl the hood's string around her finger while she reads. "And all this time, I thought you were just trying to screw up my life." My tone is jocular, but I realize I actually believed this.

"On the contrary, though you are certainly not the first to think so. You see, Grant, Programming is as much for you as it is for those on Earth."

I let the information settle in my system for a minute. "I get what you're saying, I think. One time, though, Owen mentioned something about people being Satellites forever. I forget what he called them, but he seemed to think they were lucky."

"Ah, the infamous Lifers. I didn't realize this false information was continuing to circulate. A handful of Satellites have taken over a century to complete the program as their evolution process has been a bit prolonged."

"A bit?"

My sarcasm puts a grin on Jonathan's face. When he stands, he offers his hand and helps me up. My legs are steady, but my head spins like I've had too much to drink.

"We should be on our way. Please do not fault Landon for his actions. Change is difficult for some, especially when a livelihood depends on business as usual."

Jonathan and I watch Tate flip through her book.

"It's not a terrible compromise, is it?" Jonathan asks a minute later.

"No. I guess not."

"As you can imagine, this transition will take some time. Between our departments, there are hundreds of thousands that will undertake the memory recovery process."

I nod, trying to fathom the endeavor.

Tate closes a book and opens another.

Jonathan squeezes my shoulder. "We must go. There is much preparation to be done."

Tate raises her head from her textbook and locks eyes with me. When she grins, I know she sees me. Jonathan's wrong. There's no way Landon could have made such a trap. Seeing as I can't block anymore, I'm worthless in Progression. Why can't I stay here with Tate forever?

Still grinning, Tate chews on the fingernail of her index finger. When she lowers her hand from her mouth, the same finger motions for me to come to her.

If it is a trap, I'd rather be destroyed than live another moment without her.

"I'm sorry, Jonathan," I whisper.

My right foot is the first part of me to cross the threshold.

"Grant! Don't…" Jonathan is saying, but his words are warped and muffled.

The sting from my chest and knee are unbearable and I instantly regret looking downward. Tate's room and everything in it circles around me while the image of my blackened and hollow, gaping chest nauseates me. I can't focus, nor can I close my eyes. My vision is stuck between two hells until I lose consciousness.

15. If it isn't your fearless leader himself

A loud bang jerks me awake, though I'm unsure if my body actually moves in reaction. My eyes are like a dead camera. No matter how many times I blink, the view finder remains black.

"I was expecting you."

My ears, unlike my eyes, are not completely broken. I wouldn't consider them one hundred percent operable, though, because the man's deep voice vibrates in my head.

"Landon! What've you done?" Chris's voice, though echoing, is recognizable.

"I believe it was by his own choice that he came to be here. I have, in fact, done nothing."

"You trapped him!"

"His choice."

"You've destroyed him!" Chris's voice is louder, both from anger and possibly a closer proximity.

"This boy destroyed me!"

I fail at moving my head and when I call out to Chris nothing happens. Worse than being imprisoned by my own body, though, is having my thoughts intact. The heat escalating in my chest and knee seems to coincide with my increasing panic.

"He didn't destroy you. You have to fix him!"

Landon's laughter bounces around in my brain.

"You used me!"

"Come now. You didn't even like him."

"Of course I liked him!"

"You have a funny way of showing it, don't you? As I recall, it was you feeding me all the information regarding his whereabouts. It was you who kept me informed about his plans to ruin me and all I've created."

Chris? My own Satellite sold me out!

"You made me tell you!"

"I did no such thing."

A wresting noise follows. Something rolls against my body and pushes me to the left, but is gone a second later. This happens two more times, along with some low grunts.

A far away rumbling grows louder, making me wonder if the noise is my brain about to explode.

"What's going on?"

"Who is that?"

"Billy, help me separate them!"

Lawson?

"Who did this?"

I don't recognize the other voices, in part because my head is vibrating even more.

"Grant!" This voice I know. Willow. "Oh no. No, no, no!"

Something nudges me, shifting my limp body. I try to speak, but nothing works.

"There's so much blood!"

"What's going on?"

"Does Jonathan know?"

The task of keeping up with all the different people talking at once is difficult.

"Clara, back up. You shouldn't see this."

"Stop...struggling."

"How did this happen?"

"Where's Jonathan?" Willow shouts over the others.

"Sophie went to find him!" a girl answers.

"Chris," Willow's voice becomes muffled in my groggy head. "What happened?"

"I'm sorry, Willow! Really, I am!"

"Let him go," Willow says. "Billy, it's fine. Chris isn't the problem here."

"Landon said if I didn't keep him informed about Grant's whereabouts and plans, he would hurt my dad!"

"I never mentioned your father specifically," Landon says.

A loud shuffling is mixed with a few deep groans.

"Settle down," Billy's strained voice echoes.

"I'm...sorry...I didn't...realize he...would...do this to...Grant!" Chris's heavy breaths cause him to pause between words.

Laying here in a heap of whatever I am now, I still can't believe my own Satellite sold me out!

"Why didn't you just tell Jonathan that Landon was threatening you? I mean, he could have helped you. That's what he does, right guys?" Even muffled, this one is easy. Jackson.

"Landon said he was the one running this place, not Jonathan, and that Jonathan was going to destroy us so he could be in charge. He said Grant was in on it, too. That's why he made me watch him."

"You didn't honestly believe him?" British accent equals Liam. I'm getting better at this game.

"How was I supposed to know?" Chris shoots back. Even groggy, I can hear the panic in his voice.

"It's not Chris's fault! He didn't know!" Clara's higher pitch is no good for my headache. "He's new here! Grant had a lot on his mind. He wasn't able to explain everything that goes on around here like he should have."

"Landon was the one who sent Grant's Tragedy's kids back!"

"Whoa! What?" Lawson's baritone voice fires back at Chris.

Chris has to be lying. What he says doesn't make any sense. Landon couldn't have sent Meggie's kids. He acted too surprised when I outed Sophie in front of the Schedulers.

"He wanted to prove that we can protect our own loved ones. He thought we should keep our memories. He said it was Jonathan who was against the idea!"

A throat clears. "Is that so?"

Jonathan!

The footsteps clicking toward me may as well be screaming in the silent room.

"Well, well, well. If it isn't your fearless leader himself." Judging from the groan, someone didn't appreciate Landon's reply. I can't deny being hopeful that Billy is the one punching him.

"That's enough!" Jonathan's voice is stern. "You tricked him. You've killed him!"

Wait. No. "I'm not dead!" my voice shouts in my head, but nowhere else. I mean, yes, obviously I'm dead, but—ugh, this is bad.

"You of all people have no right saying this is my fault! I sent Meggie and Brody's kids back to prove your terrible idea would never work. Just look at the mess it has caused. You've dismantled the way my entire program runs!" Landon's voice is winded.

"*Our* program. I do hope you have not forgotten the efforts and talents of the others that have made the Satellite program possible. I knew you weren't happy about this decision and I knew you wouldn't take it lightly. I expected some pushback, but this, Landon." Jonathan's voice stops for a long time. "This is incomprehensible. You've destroyed one of our own!"

"He got what he deserved. He could never follow the rules. Never! He was nothing but a thorn, and yet you carried on about him like he was some golden boy."

Why am I being referred to in the past tense?

"You've had Beaman watching him, and you turned your head every time he did something wrong! You know, Jonathan, now that I think of it, maybe you should be the one laying there."

Someone sucks in a sharp breath.

"Landon," Jonathan growls. At least I think that was Jonathan. "You've crossed the line."

"Yeah? Whose line?"

"My line!"

What sounds like a struggle ensues, though I can't imagine Jonathan actually fighting. I wish I could see.

Come on! my head screams when I try to open my eyes.

The room fills with the noise of grunts and groans.

"Jonathan!" Willow's voice morphs. "Lawson, help him!"

Come on eyes! Work, darn it!

I gather every bit of strength I have, but the blackness wins.

After some shuffling, Willow's panicked voice rings out again. "Lawson! Help him!"

Confusion swims through my brain as I try to make sense of the sounds of a struggle to my left. I'd swear my head is breaking in half.

"Hold him!" Willow's voice yells from my left. "Billy!"

"Let me go, Billy," Lawson's strained baritone voice says.

"No," Jonathan's voice is laced with gurgling sound.

"If you won't fight back, I will," Lawson responds.

I think Jonathan repeats the word, "No," but I can't be sure.

Someone groans.

"Lawson, please let me handle this." Jonathan's voice is strained. "Please, Landon, I beg of you, go through Programming like we discussed. If you still want to destroy me after you've seen your life, then so be it."

"No Jonathan!" Willow shouts.

"Still a fool after all these years." Landon's tone is condescending.

"No, Liam." Jonathan says firmly followed by a slew of groans.

"Billy!" Willow's voice seems to prompt an overload of shuffling and shouting, but the voices all morph together.

Come on eyes! Work, damn it!

I gather every bit of strength I can and the blackness begins to shift to dark blue.

Focus, Grant, focus! I think to myself.

The blue morphs to a brighter sapphire color and begins to retract. In the meantime, I'm certain my skull is splitting in two.

Open! Please open! I internally scream to my eyes.

A perfect, sapphire sphere begins to form and floats slowly through the blackness. My eyelids begin to flutter.

Come on!

Yes!

I can see again! The dark paneled wall is blurry, sideways, and covered in my blue filter. Still, seeing this way is better than being in the dark.

My eyelids feel like they're being pulled down by hundred pound weights. I'm too weak to hold them up for more than a few seconds, but it's enough time to find Jonathan because he's laying just a few feet from me. His eyelids flutter, or at least I think they do. Since he's blue from my filter and my head is being tortured by the freight train that's taken up residence, I could be delusional.

"Block him."

"Block him," Jonathan's voice repeats, so quiet I'm not convinced I really heard what I think I did. Unfortunately, I have no way of questioning him because (a) every part of me except the train station in my skull is broken, and (b) Jonathan's eyes just rolled to the back of his head.

Block him? I can't block! Jonathan knows that!

I regret moving my eyes upward. The way Landon is coming at Jonathan is pure evil. There's no other way to describe the look on his face.

"Haze!" I murmur. The word boards the train in my head, bouncing through the vacant cabins.

Think, Grant, think!

"Grace loved you," is the thought that forms. Instead of wondering what orifice I pulled the words from, the freight train crashes and the claws of blackness sink into me.

Block. My severing command is a mere whisper in my head. I wonder if my body has just been destroyed. If so, things could be worse because the train whistle has halted, along with the pain.

My vision flickers in and out like a strobe light. Landon's eyes are locked on mine and he looks...peaceful?

"Out of my way!" a distant voice yells.

The strobe effect stops, but leaves a bright white tracer behind like I've been blinded with a flashlight. Its diamond-shape is the size of a walnut. I move my eyes, expecting the light to move with them, but the diamond remains on Landon's chest and increases in both size and lumens, splitting him down the middle.

A second later, Jackson sprints into my small range of vision, and, man, is he mad. "Argggghhhhh!"

The brightness from Landon's chest forces my eyes closed as Jackson's volume increases.

A wet, gurgling sound follows. I'm not sure if I can open my eyes, but I'm terrified to check.

The silence solidifies my earlier assessment. Panicked, I try to move my eyelids in hopes that I haven't actually been destroyed. Though blurry, I'm sure I'm hallucinating when I force myself to look.

A fiery iron wall sconce has pierced Landon's abdomen, pinning him against the wall. On the other end of the make-shift weapon, Jackson is speechless. I'm not sure which is more unbelievable.

Jackson's hands fall open and he takes a step back, putting space between himself and the wall's new flaming decor. The diamond-shaped light spreads until the flames are concealed, and proceeds to expand until only the top of Landon's head is visible. When his hair disappears, the brightness flashes and pops like a burned out lightbulb and dissipates just as rapidly.

I'd blink if I had the strength to be sure my eyes were properly functioning. The trail of smoke that has replaced Landon's body moves like a snake, but can't be emerging from the flames that have engulfed the wood paneling. No fire would emit such a bright green smoke.

My eyelids give in when the snaking trail swims beyond the ceilingless room and into the dark sky.

It's hot. Why is it so hot?

"We have to move!" Willow shouts.

I'm jostled a few seconds later and then my worthless body is being haphazardly dragged.

"He's not moving," someone shouts behind me. I can only assume they're talking about Jonathan, seeing as I'm pretty sure I haven't moved for some time—on my own, at least.

16. I'm afraid my time here this evening is brief

Feeling groggy, my eyes are slow to open. When they do, the brightness makes focusing more difficult.

What the—?

I sit up to bring the sideways world upright.

Childhood memories of this same street come flooding back to me. After a few deep breaths, I start towards the front porch of the home I know so well from my past.

"Hello?" I holler from the small foyer after letting myself in the house.

A guy in a yellow button up shirt and dark blue jeans comes around the corner. We stare at each in silence for what seems like almost a full minute.

"Well, I'll be darned! How the heck are ya, son? Annie, get in here! Quick!"

Could it really be? The voice is the same, and there is some resemblance...

"Grandpa?"

He no older than I am. Is this even possible? The guy does a little skip and then extends his hands like a performer. "In the flesh!" He flexes his arm. "Can you believe it? I

301

couldn't myself, I tell ya. I mean, look at this muscle!"

A brown lab rounds the corner and jumps on me, full force.

I rub the dog behind his ear. "Tucker?"

Grandpa chuckles. "You remember!"

Of course I remember Tucker. I had some great times playing with him as a kid.

My youthful grandpa takes two steps forward and embraces me. It takes me a couple of seconds to fully register what's happening so my return hug is a bit delayed.

"What is it, Clyde?"

Looking over my Grandpa's shoulder, a beautiful, brunette woman in her mid-twenties approaches, dressed like she's just stepped out of a 1950's advertisement, floral gardening apron and all.

When Grandpa lets go, he stands back and examines me. "Annie, look at him! Doesn't he look like just like Jack?"

The woman stands behind my Grandpa, clearly in shock.

"It's Grant!"

"I figured that, you old lug. Well move over and let me see for myself!"

Grandma's hands are trembling when she grabs mine. "Oh my, you do look just like your father! I've been waiting to meet you for years, although it certainly doesn't seem that long." She hugs me almost as tightly as Grandpa did. "I didn't expect to meet you quite so soon. Your father must be a mess. Your mom, too. Oh, how is Mary? When did you arrive?"

"One question at a time, sweetheart. You're going to overwhelm him."

I smile to tell her the line of questioning is fine. "I've been here awhile, actually. Well, not here, but in Progression. I was a Satellite."

Grandma releases me, but keeps hold of my hands. "A Satellite! Oh, how marvelous. A Satellite, Clyde! Can you believe it? Our grandson is a Satellite. Well that is something. Wait until I tell Carol and Jeanne."

I cock my head to the side. "You've heard of Satellites?"

"Oh yes, dear! I spent my time as a Mender until your Grandfather joined me."

"You're kidding!"

She shakes her head and unties her apron. "Where are my manners? Come in, come in." Grandma places the folded apron on the counter when she reaches the kitchen.

"You look fantastic, son. How do you feel?"

I shrug at Grandpa. "Physically, I've got no complaints."

"I can certainly see why."

I cross my arms when I realize my feet and chest are bare and I'm still wearing gym shorts. At least my scars are back to the way they should be: small and not ripping in half.

"Well, come in, come in! Make yourself comfortable. Would you like a shirt?" Grandma acts as though she sees nothing wrong with the fact that I've just shown up half naked on her door step.

"A shirt would be great." I hope she doesn't see my embarrassment.

Grandma disappears down the hall. Tucker thunks

down under the table.

"Sit. Sit."

I do as Grandpa says and he plants himself in the seat beside me. The kitchen is exactly as I remember it, orange paisley wallpaper and all.

"How are ya', son?"

"Do you know Jonathan? I mean…sorry, Grandpa. I'm fine, thanks." Calling him Grandpa feels odd because he's my age. "Do you know Jonathan?"

"Of course we know Jonathan!" Grandma is back in the kitchen with a green shirt, jeans, and a pair of boots in tow. "These should fit you nicely."

"Thank you." I want to ask how she managed to get my exact pair of work boots, scuffs and all, but I'm more concerned about Jonathan. I excuse myself and step around the corner into the living room to change out of my jogging shorts. "Have you heard from him?" I ask as I pull the T-shirt over my head on my way back into the kitchen.

"Is everything OK?"

Sitting at the table, I lean over and pull the rolled pair of socks out of the boots. "I'm not sure." Probably better not to share the events I witnessed with Landon and Jonathan. For all I know the whole thing was some strange dream. Although, I haven't dreamed since being here, aside from my flashbacks-o-Tate. But even those were memories, not dreams. The sour pit in my stomach grows with worry.

Grandma taps her red fingernails on the vintage table. "Jonathan visited us a few weeks ago. When did you see him last?"

Oh, you know, just a few minutes ago, before I blacked out and showed up here. He was lying in a heap on the floor because Landon beat the hell out of him. Um, no. Going with the truth is a terrible idea.

"I'm sure he's fine." God, I hope he's fine. "Do I smell a chocolate cake?" I ask to change the subject.

Grandma goes to the oven and opens the door. "You have excellent timing. It's almost done."

"She makes the best chocolate cake in the afterworld."

I can't help but smile, even though seeing them together is strange, especially with Grandpa appearing to be so young. It's easier with Grandma, as most of the photographs I've seen are similar to how she looks now.

"You used to tell me that all the time when I spent the night." I half laugh and look at Grandma. "He was always bragging on you. Where are we, by the way?"

Grandpa looks over at the vintage appliances across the kitchen. Even the refrigerator magnets advertising the local Weldon Spring businesses are the same. "You don't recognize it?" His tone is filled with worry.

"No, no. I recognize the house, of course."

Grandpa's shoulders relax.

Grandma leans forward on the small table and places both her hands over mine. "Jonathan didn't tell you?"

As I shake my head, I think back to the last thing I remember. I flinch at the image of Jonathan's eyes rolling upward. Arriving at Grandpa's house was never on my radar as an option of where I might turn up. Honestly, I thought for sure I'd be dead. Well, deader anyway.

"Are you sure you're all right? Would you like some water?"

"Water would be great. Thanks, Grandma."

While Grandma gets a glass from the cabinet, Grandpa points his finger on the table. "This is Viscal, son."

"Viscal? I don't understand."

"Certainly you know, Viscal!"

"Clyde, where are your manners?" Grandma's look is kind when she turns to me. "When you're on active duty in a program, such as yourself, you spend twice a year in Viscal with your deceased loved ones. If you're not in a program, such as in your Grandfather's case, Viscal is the place you arrive following your death."

My memories of Willow explaining Viscal surface. She left me shortly after my arrival to Progression and I spent some of that time with Anna and Rigby. The rest of the time I was secretly coding to see Tate.

"Oh, I'll never forget the first time I visited my folks. I was so nervous. Of course, those nerves faded as soon as I saw my mom." Grandma's eyes crease when she smiles. "Certainly Jonathan explained Viscal, this being your first trip and all."

I shift in my seat at the mention of Jonathan and the sickly feeling in my gut reemerges. "What's out there?" I ask as a subject change, nodding to the sliding door behind Grandpa.

"Oh, that's my favorite part!" Grandpa pushes the lace curtain aside. "Have you ever seen such colors?"

Mirrored on the smooth lake, the trees appear to be on

fire.

"I spend most days fishing," Grandpa says as he looks out the back door.

"I can see why." Grandpa's yard on Earth was nowhere near large enough to house what must be a ten acre lake, let alone a floating dock with three shiny fishing boats. And the garden, which I take to be Grandma's project judging from the pink gardening tools, is grand enough to compare with the landscaping of the courtyard. I don't recognize half of the colorful, blooming flowers.

"Viscal is truly a remarkable place; magical enough that sometimes it doesn't feel like a place at all." Grandma sets a glass in front of me and returns to the stove. The smell of chocolate fills the air when she pulls the oven door open.

Grandpa, though young, still has that amazing deep chuckle of his. "You remember my neighbor, Joe?"

"Of course." Joe and my Grandpa, both widows for as long as I can remember, had been inseparable when I was growing up. When they weren't fishing, they were goofing off over a couple beers and reminiscing about their military days. I'd always wished my dad had been more easy going like his old man.

"See that house on the hill way in the distance there?"

Way in the distance is an understatement. The house looks smaller than a Lego from here.

"That's Carol and Joe's place. Their lake is just as impressive as ours." Grandpa gets up and walks around the table. "How was your father when you saw him last?"

"Oh, you know, same old Dad. Full of complaints and

too manly to show any emotion."

Grandpa retrieves three plates from the cabinet above Grandma. "You're a lot like him, you know."

"I'm nothing like him," I counter.

"You've never been one to complain, I'll give you that, but you've always been one of the hardest workers I know, just like your dad. And in the emotional department, well," Grandpa chuckles, "you two are cut from the same cloth."

"That's not true."

Grandpa laughs again. "Jack wasn't always such a difficult man, you know. He used to have a lot of fun, believe it or not."

"Dad had fun?"

"Oh, yeah."

Grandma smiles. "I can't tell you how many times I had to visit the principal. Your father was a spirited boy, always getting into mischief. Mostly, his shenanigans involved being the class clown. How he loved to make people laugh."

My Dad? There's no way.

Grandpa grabs two plates, now filled with warm cake, and delivers them to the table, sliding one in front of me. "I wish you could have known him before your grandmother's death. He was never quite the same after that. Got more and more closed off from the world. You mother—what a saint that woman is—could always see the good in him, though. If only he'd learned how to deal with loss in a healthier way. Lack of faith, that's always been his problem."

Grandma joins us at the table and straightens the bottom of her green dress over her knees. "Now Clyde."

"He wanted to believe me when I told him he'd see your Grandma again, I could tell, but his doubt always got the better of him. That stubbornness came from me, I'm afraid."

"One day he'll understand," Grandma says.

Grandpa sighs. "Until then, I do worry about him, and your mother, as well. All she ever wanted was a child. I've never witnessed her as happy as the day you came along." Grandpa cuts off a piece of his cake with his fork. "Well, go on, eat up before it gets cold. I'll take you out on the boat when we're done and we'll throw in a line or two. You've never seen bass so large, I tell ya."

Grandpa, true to his word, spends the next couple hours giving me a boat tour of the lake. I'd be lying if I said I didn't love feeling like a child again. I forgot how to relax and have a little fun.

Not only is Grandpa right about the size of the bass, his stories about Grandma's cooking are also true. The supper Grandma has prepared when we return in the afternoon is equal to the quality of food in Benson, with the added bonus of not being laced with forgetful sauce.

I study my mashed potatoes and sliced turkey for a few seconds and then look up at Grandma. When she smiles at me over her forkful of sweet corn, I mentally slap myself for even considering that Grandma would lace my food with such poison.

I help clean up the kitchen after we eat, even though Grandma says not to bother. She says cleaning up after ourselves is not necessary in Viscal, but she continues to do so because she's always taken pride in such things.

The three of us talk around the table after the meal. The cool breeze coming through the open patio door smells faintly like a bonfire. Grandma and Grandpa share a bunch of stories about my parents. Some I've heard before from Grandpa when I was younger, but I don't interrupt because he's a rock star storyteller. No one is more animated than Grandpa.

There are some new tales about my dad that Grandpa probably thought I was too young to hear before he passed away. If Dad was here now, I'd give him grief about the police busting up his high school party while Grandma and Grandpa were in Tennessee for the weekend. My dad's lucky I didn't cause him trouble like that in school. Grandpa didn't handle the situation with much grace, probably because the chief of police was Grandpa's high school football rival. Still, my dad would have done way worse than ground me for a month.

I love listening to Grandma's stories, too. Typically, I wouldn't care about wedding decorations and cake, but being able to visualize my parent's wedding turns out to be a cool thing. The part about my mom and dad being crazy about each other, well, that's a bit more difficult to visualize. Clearly, Grandpa didn't exaggerate about Grandma. She is as amazing as he made her out to be. I wish my dad had talked to me more about her.

Grandma stirs her coffee. "Oh, I can't wait to see your father again."

Grandpa's teeth shine when he smiles. "I expect it'll be any day now," he says, more to himself.

My heart drops into my stomach. I swallow down extra saliva, the warning that Grandma's meal could resurface at any moment. "Dad's coming here?" What about my mom? How will she bear losing both of us?

"Heavens, no!" Grandma places her hand over mine. "We get to visit them on Earth. I was certain it would be awhile before I saw your folks again. What a delightful surprise from Jonathan."

"Jonathan?"

"That's why he visited a few weeks ago." Grandma's brown eyebrows raise along with her voice. "I can't wait to see the look on your grandfather's face when he displaces for the first time! Oh, the surge of adrenaline from free-falling was one of my favorite things about being a Mender, aside from healing people, of course."

Thinking of Grandma as a dare-devil is comical, but a more pressing issue keeps my head preoccupied "Is there a way I can get in touch with Jonathan?"

Grandpa reaches for the fancy sugar bowl with the hand-painted roses. "Ready to get back to work so soon?"

"No. Nothing like that." More like, I need to check if Jonathan is still alive. I try to keep my expression level to avoid an unnecessary freak out by both my grandparents and me.

Grandpa's spoon clinks against his coffee cup. "Maybe

you can join us when we visit."

"Visit?"

"Your parents, son. Are you feeling all right?"

"Yeah, fine." Could I really join them and see my mom and dad again? Maybe I could drop in on Tate while we're there. Anticipation mixes with my worst fears about Jonathan's well-being, making my insides feel even more uneasy.

Grandpa slurps his coffee. "Never would have thought I'd see Earth again, especially at my own discretion. Jonathan says we'll be able to visit any time we'd like." Grandpa looks at Grandma. "I'm afraid we may never return."

Grandma's eyes crease from laughing at Grandpa's joke. "Now Clyde, you know you'll want to come back occasionally for a home cooked meal. Plus, you know Jack and Mary will need some private time."

Blech! I know exactly what Grandma is referring to, and I prefer to pretend that my parents were only intimate once, about nine months before I was born.

Grandpa scratches Tucker's ear, prompting the dog to put his head in Grandpa's lap. "Your Grandma's right. Saying I wouldn't come back is a lie. There's no greater place than this. I've never felt such wholeness in all my years."

Though the sun has almost disappeared, a faint glow shines on the water, making the ripples illuminate as they extend on the lake from the leaping fish. I can't help but agree with Grandpa, despite my worries about Jonathan. This place is beautiful.

"Hello?"

The deep voice that carries into the kitchen has me standing as fast as Grandpa. Seeing him spring up so quickly in his younger body is still strange to watch. Who am I kidding? This entire situation is strange.

"This is a surprise! Would you like some coffee?" Grandpa says.

"As great as that sounds, Clyde, I'd better decline. Thank you, though. Annie, you're looking wonderful as always."

"Jonathan?" I finally say when I hinge my jaw back in place. My eyes do a quick pass over his body. His jeans and brown sweater could be masking some damage, but he doesn't appear to be in any pain.

While Jonathan returns Grandma's hug, he speaks over her shoulder. "Good to see you, Grant. Viscal appears to be suiting you well." I can't help but notice Jonathan looking over my body the same way I just scanned his.

"What are you doing here?"

He releases Grandma and takes a step back. "Would you mind joining me out front?"

Grandma's smile to me is warm and genuine. "Don't worry about us. Go on."

Jonathan waits for me to lead.

"Annie and Clyde, please accept my apologies for this unexpected visit. I hope I have not interrupted anything."

"Don't be ridiculous," Grandpa says. "You're always welcome in our home."

"I appreciate that a great deal. How I wish I could stay and chat. It's always a pleasure to see you both."

Grandma hugs Jonathan again and then pats his shoulder. "You stop by anytime. Anytime at all."

Jonathan pulls back and takes Grandma's hands. "I will visit again soon. I promise. In the meantime, someone should be here tomorrow with instructions about that other visit we discussed."

Jonathan leans down and whispers something to Grandma. I wish I could tell if her creased forehead, along with the tears now rolling down her cheeks, are from joy or sadness.

Grandma puts her hand on Jonathan's cheek. "Thank you for giving me the opportunity to meet my grandson."

"Grandma?"

"Go on, honey. I'm sure Jonathan has important business."

I'm reluctant to turn away from her, but I force myself out the front door.

"What did you say to my grandma?"

Jonathan remains calm and kind as usual. "I realize this is your grandparent's version of Viscal, but what do you think about this place so far?"

I shake my head, aggravated that he's avoiding my question. "It's perfect. What happened to you? I wasn't sure I'd ever see you alive again. Or myself either for that matter."

"Your grandparents are exceptional hosts and the stories your grandpa can tell...I could listen to that man for hours."

"Jonathan! Stop! You have to tell me what happened."

Jonathan pulls a long drag of the autumn air through

his mouth like he's smoking a cigarette. "It seems Landon has departed the afterlife."

"You can't actually be upset about that?"

"One of our own has perished. This saddens me a great deal, yes."

After our long staring contest, I wish he'd look back up at the sky.

"He tried to kill you!" I look over Jonathan's shoulder at the porch and lower my voice. "I mean—he tried to kill you," I hiss.

"I healed as I knew I would. The situation did not have to end in this way. I grieve for Landon and for the hate that rooted in his heart." Jonathan covers his face with both hands and massages his forehead like he's trying to rub a headache away. "Hate is such a useless emotion that has caused many problems in our history, but has yet to resolve a single one."

"So he's really dead? Like eternally?"

Jonathan sighs and lowers his hands. "Our souls are made of energy, and as you may know, energy cannot be created or destroyed. Landon's soul is floating out in an abyss somewhere. If you're asking if he will ever live in a human form like ours, sadly no. We could have come to an agreeable solution, I'm sure of it."

"Landon was a bad man." I hope reminding Jonathan of this will lift his sunken attitude.

"He was a good man who did a bad thing."

I clear my throat. "He did more than one bad thing."

"Please remember, Grant, it is right and just to forgive our enemies. Otherwise, we risk our own hearts darkening as well." He looks up at the sky. "I'm afraid my time here this evening is brief. We'd better get to it."

Aside from the orange glow left behind by the sun, the darkening violet sky is clear. I look back to Jonathan, but his attention stays focused upward.

Awkward is the only word to describe the next minute of silence. It's not until I see the green streak that my thumbs stop racing around each other. When the orange, pink, and teal lines become wider, almost a dozen more streaks in varying colors follow close behind like a rainbow of shooting stars.

17. The kid with two first names

A few seconds later, Rigby, Whitfield, Anna, Owen, Liam, Clara, Jackson, Reed, Evelynn, Trina, Lawson, Billy, Elliott, and Chris are standing around me. It's the last streak, the beautiful purple one, that makes my tears spill over. I mean, my crying is so obvious, I could potentially drown a water lily. The last time I saw them all, I thought for sure I was a goner.

Jonathan clears his throat. "It seems I've experienced some difficulty coming to terms with the fact that you were never able to bid a proper goodbye to your friends."

"Goodbye?"

Jonathan squeezes my shoulder.

But I don't want to say goodbye. "I'll still see them all the time." Panic causes my words to come out quick.

Jonathan leans down and whispers, "We don't have a lot of time, Grant." His second firm squeeze tells me that I can either accept this small time frame and use the opportunity to my advantage, or I can let it pass by.

In effort to focus better, I press my palms against my eyes to wipe some of the moisture away. "You have no idea how great it is to see you all." They've surrounded me so I turn in a circle. "Honestly, I thought I was dead. You know what I mean."

While my friends laugh, I look back at Jonathan, still confused. "Goodbye? Really?"

Jonathan's lips stay tight.

My tone becomes more serious. "If you haven't figured out by now, humor and sarcasm are my coping mechanisms." My eyes lock with Chris's for a couple seconds. "I know I've come off harsh at times. If I've ever offended you, I'm genuinely sorry. I have so much respect for all of you."

I spend the next several minutes going around the circle, briefly addressing each of them.

Remembering Rigby as the Toothpick Guy, witnessing his first of many advances made toward Whitfield, and our notorious fist fight in Benson, I end this monologue the same way our relationship began: with a simple handshake. When we shake, he thanks me for being a part of getting his memories back. He also tells me not to blow things with Tate because from what he's heard, she's way too good for me. I couldn't agree more.

While Whitfield fidgets with her fire-red hair, I thank her for being a much-needed light during Meggie's darkest days. She hugs me and whispers her thanks for the hook up with Rigby.

Soft spoken, sweet Anna; how we laughed until we cried as we stood in line on that confusing day. I tell her she'll always be the sister I've never had. She cries and throws her arms around me.

How could I ever forget Owen the bulldog, his concrete hair, and his effortless knack of irritating Clara?

I close with a handshake and a quick reminder of how I will hurt him if he dares hurt my sister. Anna openly approves of this last bit.

Liam, to whom I owe my life because he watched over Tate, was adamant about her existence, and most importantly, gave Tate back to me through my memories, whether intentional or not. I can't imagine where I would be if not for Liam tossing me Tate's ring. He calls me a pansy when we shake.

Next is the beautiful, artistic Clara who made me face my biggest regret of not marrying Tate, though she may not have known it. She saved my skin by being there for Chris when I wasn't. I'm sure to tell her she's a hundred times more amazing than she thinks she is. We close with a hug and I'm fairly certain she leaves a few tears on my shoulder.

Small, but mighty Jackson always played fair in training. He has more words, enthusiasm, and passion than anyone I've ever met. When I mention him singlehandedly taking down Landon, Jonathan diminishes the cheers from the others with a simple clearing of his throat. I thank Jackson for standing by me when so many others wouldn't. He throws his arms around me and then apologizes profusely, certain that he's almost knocked me over.

After I gently push Jackson back and he finally stops talking, I extend my gratitude to Reed for keeping my coding problem a secret, for giving Willow the advice that allowed me to code correctly, and for trying his best to not laugh at me in training when Billy turned me into a ballerina. We part with a handshake.

I address the always persistent Evelynn, reiterate that declining her advances was nothing personal, and mention that she's stunning in her turtleneck and jeans. She clings to me in true Evelynn style until I peel her off, making the others laugh.

I thank Trina for being a great friend, for listening to my problems, and for understanding that Tate is my true love. Her hug is more appropriate than Evelynn's. I kiss her forehead when she tells me Tate is a lucky woman.

To Lawson I could say so many things, but instead I use only the words, "for Meggie and Brody," and nod. His Chocolate Hulk bear hug tells me he understands how much his friendship means to me.

When I get to Billy, my somberness is replaced with laughter. The others agree when I tell him he's the worst person in the world to train with. I add that he should have been chosen much sooner to be an Elite. Like our first encounter, he ignores my hand at first. Instead of crushing it this time, though, he uses it to pull me against him. He slaps my back and is sure to call me Princess one last time.

Elliott is a tough one. So many things run through my head about Tate, Fischer, and his parents. Before I can say anything, Elliott pulls me into a hug. I tell him I wish we could have been real brothers-in-law. He says that wedding or not, I'll always be his brother. After the manliest, "I love you," we can manage, we separate. Billy doesn't have a single snide remark, so we must have done all right.

I apologize to Chris for my disservice as his Legacy, for making him sit with the suits in Benson, and for the horrid sofa I left behind. Willow, of course, vocalizes Chris's good fortune on his furniture score. When we hug, I tell him he and his family are wonderful people and I apologize again for not being the Legacy I should have been. I even go so far as to put on the spiked bracelet he gives me.

When I reach Willow, I become too choked up to talk. She merely nods in acceptance of my silence, joining me in my waterworks session. We hug for a long time. I don't want to let her go. It's not until Jonathan clears his throat and the others begin to heckle that we separate. "The kid with two first names," she whispers before pulling back.

I feel like I should say something more when Jonathan says it's time for my friends to go, but I'm too preoccupied keeping my tears in check.

They say goodbye and, one by one, rocket into the air, leaving a rainbow of colors in their path.

Jonathan turns away from the sky and claps his hands together. "I'll admit, there was a great amount of fear that we might lose you forever. Your scars have proven to be quite bothersome in Progression." Jonathan places his hand on my chest for a couple seconds, covering the spot of one said bothersome scar. "Those lesions seem to be faring well here in Viscal. I, along with so many others, am thrilled to see that you've remained in one piece."

Jonathan's eyes are focused on the grass in front of his leather loafers. "Jackson has been quite a hero around Progression. I will have to share the truth with him in time, but for now, I believe I will allow him to be celebrated in the way he has always deserved to be."

Jonathan folds his hands together and grins at me, but this grin is one that doesn't hide his sadness. "Did you see the light illuminating from Landon's chest just before Jackson stabbed him?"

I nod.

"I've mentioned Landon's and Grace's connection, but what I did not tell you was that Landon, himself, broke a few rules long ago. Despite his duties in Progression, he couldn't stay away from Grace, as with someone else I know."

I get it. Jeez, man, you can put your eyebrow down.

"Their connection went far beyond the heartbreak we've come to expect from loss. He couldn't let her go. I watched him try multiple times. Grace was the same. Landon could not physically adapt to his new life."

Jonathan rubs his chin for a moment. "Landon visited me following one of his unauthorized visits to Grace with a lesion on his stomach. He promised to discontinue his visits to her, but every time Grace entered his mind, his lesion expanded, coming dangerously close to splitting him in half."

I want to use Jonathan's pause as an opportunity to question him, but I have no idea what to even ask.

"It was I who suggested we take away his memories. Landon fought against me. Eventually, he realized he had no choice if he wanted any chance of survival. The suffering he endured in letting Grace go was unlike any I'd ever seen."

"Why not just erase his memories? You didn't have to take everyone's away."

"Landon was in unfathomable emotional pain. He did not want anyone to suffer as he had. He truly believed we could alleviate unnecessary heartache, allowing others to work more efficiently within their programs." Jonathan's eyes are glassy when he stares at me. "Landon's intentions were purely out of love for others. I would have never agreed to put his proposal up to vote otherwise."

He squeezes my shoulder. "The two of you have much in common. It seems your words to him were enough to return his memories of Grace. The light protruding from Landon was his lesion tearing apart. In the end, it was Grace that destroyed him."

But how— "Jonathan, how did I even block him?"

"It seems a bit of your ability has remained within you."

I shake my head. I tried so hard to block Meggie. Certainly blocking would have worked then. "The words I said—I don't know where they came from."

Oh, now the guy grins. When he glances up at the sky, I can sense he's about to leave.

A game of twenty questions takes the place of Landon in my head. Is this where I'm supposed to stay? What about my own Viscal? Will I see my friends again soon? Will I be able to go to Progression again? Do I get to visit my parents now? What happens to Tate? Do I get to see her? Will she be OK?

I'm unsure what to ask first. Feeling like I've just finished packing a load of lumber, I try to catch my breath. "What happens now?"

I bite into my tongue, waiting for Jonathan's answer. For a guy that seems to have a million places to be, he's certainly taking his time to reply.

Jonathan gives my arm a light squeeze. "That, my friend, is up to you."

I stare blankly back at him, having no idea what he means. He lets out a small breath and the sides of his mouth curve upward, though his eyes look sad. "You are so talented, so much more than you'll ever realize. Within that hardened exterior, you are a genuinely kind and wonderful man. I wish you all my best."

"You think I'm wonderful? Wait until you meet my father," I joke because this is feeling an awful lot like goodbye when he shakes my hand.

Before I can say a proper thank you, or ask Jonathan what I'm supposed to do now, he winks and morphs into a golden streak against the darkened sky.

After staring into the sky for five minutes, I jump from the surprise of the hand on my shoulder.

"Everything all right, son?"

My eyes remain fixed on the stars that are beginning to punch through the sky.

"I'm not sure."

Grandpa keeps his hand on my shoulder and moves to my side. With his arm around me, he directs me back toward the house. The porch light is like a beacon in the darkness and gives me a new respect for moths. The warm glow certainly has an undeniable pull.

"I'm not sure what I'm supposed to do now," I whisper as we walk up the steps to the front door where Grandma is waiting.

"I imagine, like us, you're going to see your parents soon."

Even with the wholeness I feel, there's a part of me that fractures when Grandpa says this. I'm relieved to know I'll see my parents again, and maybe even Tate. I'm comforted knowing that when they die, I'll see them in a real way and we'll be able to actually communicate. Selfishly, though, I wish I was living out the remainder of Tate's life with her. To be honest, I don't know how I'll handle seeing her with another man, if I am, in fact, able to visit her. She's too young, too beautiful, inside and out, to live her life solo. She has so much to offer someone. My insides twist together wishing her someone could be me.

"You're going to have the best of both worlds, son." Grandpa says when we're in the kitchen. His arm falls from my shoulder and he takes the coffee cups from Grandma to put them in the sink. "What do you say, Annie, should we turn in for a bit?"

Grandma stops before she reaches the counter to deposit the sugar bowl. "Maybe Grant would prefer to stay up awhile longer." The lid of the china bowl clinks lightly.

Grandpa has the bowl out of Grandma's hands a second later. "It's been a long day. It's time we let Grant sleep."

I stand up straighter, concerned about Grandma. "Sleep?"

"Of course." Grandpa sets the bowl on the far side of the counter.

"But I've never slept before. I mean, after I died. I've only coded to relax."

Grandpa chuckles. "You don't need to sleep to relax. I'm fairly certain if you note how your body feels, you should be fairing quite well in the relaxation department."

Grandpa is right. I couldn't possible feel more relaxed than I do right now.

"Come on in here and lay on the couch. Sleep isn't necessary, but it is a comfort of our earthly life that I happen to enjoy. An occasional dream here and there is good for the soul."

I follow Grandpa and, as instructed, lay on the floral printed sofa I remember from my childhood. Tucker spins in a circle and plops himself down on the floor beside me.

Grandma covers me with a blue and green afghan that I'm certain was in my mom's hope chest before I died.

I grab her hands. "Why are you shaking?"

"Oh, honey, don't you worry about me. Now you go on and rest. I look forward to hearing about your dreams." Grandma squeezes my cheeks between her hands. "My handsome grandson. I am so happy to have finally met you."

As strange as it sounds, I feel like I've known her my whole life. "Me too, Grandma."

"Sweet dreams." Grandma kisses my forehead and walks out of the room. The kitchen light clicks off, leaving just a small glow at the doorway, probably from the smaller light over the stove.

Grandpa, now just a silhouette in the darkened room, squeezes my shoulder and then takes a step back.

"I'm glad I'm here. It's the closest feeling to home I've had since my death." I pause. "Is Grandma all right?"

"It's been a big day for all of us. Get some sleep. There's nothing like a good dream to reset our spirits. It's so great to see you, son."

When he's gone, I mull over the whole sleeping thing, certain I will be unable to nap after all this time. My mind begins to spin though everything that has happened here and my conversations with my grandparents.

I know Grandpa is right about having the best of both worlds. My feelings towards Viscal are warmer and more connected than how I feel about Progression.

Thinking about Progression makes me think about Ryder and Meggie. Looking out for them, Meggie in particular, was a grueling task. Maybe grueling is the wrong word. Looking out for her was difficult, no doubt, but it was experiencing the loss of her mom and kids that was the grueling part. I'd take the physical pain of my cancer a hundred times over before I would ever want to experience the pain again with Meggie. Still, helping Meggie and Ryder gave me a real purpose. I have no purpose now.

What am I saying? I fought to get here so the others could connect with their loved ones. The others fought so hard as well. Harder actually. Living an existence without purpose isn't an unreasonable price to pay if it means everyone is able maintain a connection to their human lives after their death.

My eyes grow heavier with each thought until, eventually, they give in and my mind shuts off.

18. A decision will need to be made soon

Beep.

Beep.

Beep.

"Grandma?" My attempt to speak fails. My aching head must be too fuzzy to make my mouth work. I'm not sure if my lips even moved.

I don't recall feeling this groggy after a nap. Maybe this is what happens when a person doesn't get real sleep for a while. I move my hand to find the afghan, but feel the texture of a sheet instead. The heavier blanket must have fallen off. Or maybe Grandma switched it out for something lighter while I slept. I want it back now, though, because the chill is making me uncomfortable.

Why won't that rhythmic beeping noise in my head stop?

My eyes open less than a millimeter, allowing just enough light to illuminate a sliver of blurriness before they fall closed again. I have zero luck trying to force my eyelids to cooperate. Even my attempt to pry them open with my fingers is a loss. My hand barely flinches when I try to move it across the thin sheet.

Heaviness presses against me. I try to fight it, but the

urge to submit is stronger. Then, the beeping stops.

I'm not unhappy about the last part. It's the new setting that has me worried.

"Dad?" I yell because his truck is here. Other than that, the job site is empty. The walls are still in the framework stage, so I can easily see my old man isn't on the main floor. If he's here, the basement is the only place he could be.

"Dad?" My voice is distorted. Maybe I'm just hearing it wrong.

"Hello?" Nope, definitely distorted. Not only that, but my body feels disconnected, as if I'm floating. Not in the same way as when I visited earth for my assignments. This is different, like I've taken too much sinus medicine.

I hang on to the makeshift two by four handrail in order to avoid rolling down the basement steps.

"Hey, kid. Grab that chalk box for me, will ya?" Downstairs, my dad is partially hidden behind the circular saw. Before I can say anything, the scream of the powerful blade fills the basement.

I get closer to him. "Dad? Can you kill the saw for a minute?"

Part of a two by four hits the ground and silence follows, but my dad doesn't look up.

"Dad?"

"Damn it, where is that kid?"

"I'm right here."

My dad walks straight through me, making me lose my balance, even though I don't actually feel him.

Thump, thump, thump, thump…

What the—

Those are my boots coming down the steps.

My breath rushes out in a whoosh.

Not just my boots. That's me.

My dad stalks past the *other* me. "Where were you?"

"I just met Tate at the neighborhood entrance. She left her jacket in my truck last night."

A piece of wood hits the concrete, which as I can attest to, is my dad's way of showing his disapproval.

"Calm down, I was gone for less than five minutes. What's your problem with her, anyway?" the other me asks.

"What's my problem? Well, let's see. A girl I barely know is keeping you from work. In the rare occasions when you are here, your head is somewhere else. You get distracted in a job like this and it's game over. This isn't like school. You mess up here, you get a hell of a lot more than a detention. You could lose a finger, a hand, or your whole damn life. Do you understand what I'm saying to you?"

The other me gets right in my old man's face. Long gone are the days when he was bigger than me. "Yeah, I understand. You don't want me to have a life. It kills you to see something finally making me happy, doesn't it?"

The shock on my dad's face is gone almost as soon as it came. I'm not sure if the other me even noticed.

My dad stands straighter and broadens his shoulders. "Yeah." He nods to make his point, though he appears to be nodding to convince himself, not the other me.

Even closer to my dad now, the other me talks through his teeth. "Don't make me choose between her or this job, because you won't like my choice."

My dad's left standing alone when the other me stomps back up the steps. A minute later, his shoulders jump from the slam of the truck door.

"Dear God," my dad whispers. "Please help my boy see that I'm only looking out for his best interest."

Curiosity draws me closer to my dad to hear him better.

"I can't lose him." His eyes fill with water. My *dad!* Crying! And praying?

"He's all we have. Please protect him."

All those years went by, and I never saw my dad as anything more than a cold, emotionless wall. He was the enemy.

I was blinded by anger. I was no better than him.

I watch my dad work for a while, simmering in regret for misjudging him. He's a skilled carpenter, there's no denying that, and the lack of incessant cursing is a welcomed change.

A grogginess grows heavy, though, despite my efforts to stay alert. Blackness fills my vision like billowing smoke until I'm surrounded by nothing but darkness.

Beep.
Beep.
Beep.
Again with the beeping?

"Nothing new to report," a woman's voice says. "Brain activity is the same as it's been for the past two months. We're reaching that point, Mr. Bradley. A decision will need to be made soon."

Someone inhales and exhales slowly and loudly. I flinch from the touch on my hand, but my body doesn't react like it should. It does nothing, in fact.

The sounds of footprints grow softer, followed by the clicking sound of the door closing.

Someone squeezes my hand. I like the warm touch, mostly because I'm so cold. How my body is not shivering is beyond me.

"Son."

"Dad?" My voice doesn't work. "Dad, is that you?" Instead of coming out as a yell like it should, the words bounce around in my head like an echo. Why won't my body cooperate?

"Dad, say something else!" Still nothing.

What feels like hours pass. My dad's still holding my hand, and occasionally squeezes, but he doesn't say anything. I wish he'd talk. I never thought I would wish such a thing. Ever.

Maybe if I focus on something less complex than talking I'll have better luck. I think about squeezing my dad's hand. I don't let another thought in. Just this one small gesture. Certainly I can give a quick return squeeze.

Come on!

Nothing.

OK, I'll just move a finger. That's all. One tiny

movement.

Come. On.

Come on!

Inside my head, I'm now screaming and thrashing in anger. On the outside, my body may as well be a worthless shell housing nothing. It's as if someone unhooked my brain from my body, but forgot to turn the power switch off. If I could talk, I'd beg someone to either rewire my brain to my body or pull the plug. I'd take either because my current state is going to push me into the realm of insanity.

"I brought you some coffee."

Mom?

Mom! I'm here!

Mom!

Mom!

Mom! The yelling in my head keeps time with the rhythmic beeping.

Mom! Please, Mom!

"Baby, I need you. Please wake up. You have to wake up! They're going to disconnect the machines soon. Come back to me!"

Her perfect voice echoes in my head.

Tate. I'm here.

"I can't give up. I can't let you go."

Baby, don't cry.

"Please." More sobbing. "Please come back."

Warmth streaks down my forearm starting at my wrist. The trail turns cold as moisture collects in the crook of my elbow and rolls down to the sheet.

"Fischer wanted to visit, but mom wouldn't let him miss soccer practice again."

Tate.

Her voice is raspier than usual, but so comforting, like a favorite song that's been unplayed for years. She's home to me. There's nowhere else I belong.

She holds my hand between both of hers and I can feel her breath on my wrist. "I told him you'd understand." She half laughs. "His team's doing well. They're four and oh in their division. Fischer thinks being on a winning team is cool. Personally, I think he likes the extra time Dad's been spending with him kicking the ball around. He's playing goalie at this weekend's game. He's excited about that."

Beep.

Beep.

Beep.

"I swear he's grown a foot since you've seen him."

Beep.

"He misses you."

Beep.

Beep.

"We all miss you."

Beep.

"Of course you know that. I tell you just about every day. If you'd just come back…"

Beep.

Beep.

Beep.

Tate sighs.

After four more beeps, I will all of my energy and strength to my hand. Just a small movement, that's all I need to do. Come on man, wiggle a finger. Something! Anything!

Beep.

Beep.

Beep. Beep.

Beep. Beep.

Beep. Beep.

My finger hasn't moved, but as I strain, I know the beeping picked up. I know it!

"Grant?"

The warm breath on my skin disappears and my hand lowers to the sheet.

She heard it, too!

Yes, Tate! It's me! I'm here!

The sound of light footsteps move away from me.

No, Tate! Come back.

"Jenny, his heart rate just increased. I swear!"

My panicked brain relaxes when my hand is back inside Tate's.

"All right. Just calm down."

"Check the monitor. I swear, Jenny!"

Beep.

Beep.

Beep.

My hand is dropped and falls to the bed, leaving me feeling cold again. "Mr. and Mrs. Bradley! Thank God you're here! Grant's heartbeat just increased. I heard it!"

"What?" My dad's voice is close.

"Hang on before we go blowing this out of proportion," the nurse says. "We don't know anything for sure yet."

"Of course we do!" Tate says. "I heard it myself! Mr. Bradley, you have to believe me!"

"You know I would never doubt you, kid."

Dad called her kid? That was his voice all right, though he's never used a tone so kind when he's referred to me as 'kid.' Instead of bothering me, an overwhelming feeling of love for my dad swells up in my chest. If my body was capable of reacting, I'd be crying right now. Sure, it was only one sentence, but I could hear everything in those few words. My dad finally knows her. He took the time to get to know Tate, which is as good as taking the time to get to know me.

"Jenny, what does this mean?" My mom asks.

Beep.

Beep.

"I'm sorry," the nurse says slowly. "There's still no sign of brain activity. I'll have the doctor take a look to be sure if you'd like, but the computer readings are pretty clear."

Are you kidding? No brain activity? My brain is the

ONLY thing working right now!

I can do it again. Yes. I'll focus again to increase my heart rate. I did it once. Certainly, I can do it again.

Like before, I focus all my energy on moving one of my fingers. I mentally strain, wishing this would work more like blocking. Being able to see my blue filter would at least let me know I'm making some progress.

Beep.

Beep.

Beep.

Beep.

Damn it!

I try again, but am beginning to feel myself tire. It's more difficult this time for my brain to stay focused.

Beep.

Beep.

Beep.

The inside me is deflating from exhaustion, while the outside me remains stone still.

"I swear I heard it." Tate's voice, now down by my feet, is soft.

My right hand is scooped up and someone rubs my arm. It has to be Mom. I know Tate's touch and I also know my dad's hands aren't that soft.

"What are you thinking?" my mom says.

"I think we should wait another week," my dad answers on my left and puts his hand on my shoulder.

Tate lets out a breath as if she'd been holding it and thanks my dad.

I try again to make my presence known. This time, my brain aligns with the rest of me, but not in the way I'd like. Instead, my vision and hearing goes as dead as my useless body.

———

I'm elated when brightness fills my vision. Anything is better than darkness, but this is an extreme change. The blinding white fades a little. What began as warped noise   has morphed into orchestra music. I recognize the song. Tate's played this before.

As my vision focuses, I have the same strange floating feeling I had when I saw my dad in the basement, so seeing another me standing to my left is less of a shock this time. What's more shocking is the way I'm dressed. For a carpenter, I have to admit, I clean up pretty well. The suit is more formal than I'd prefer, but my body looks more like it did in Progression and less like it did in my cancer-ridden days.

A shuffling turns my attention forward.

My God!

Tate's more stunning than I've ever seen. So much so, I'm certain my twin's tears are about to spill over.

Tate's dad nods to her and then steps forward, bringing her with him through the two open doors at the end of the long aisle.

I don't take my eyes off her, but my peripheral vision expands a bit, showing that the large audience is equally entranced by Tate. Like me, they can't turn away from her. Row by row, their heads swivel like they're doing the wave when she walks past each pew.

The way she's looking at the other me through her own tears makes me wonder how the hell I became this lucky.

My twin accepts Tate's hand from her father and says thank you, though thank you doesn't come close to expressing my gratitude for such a gift.

Tate and my twin turn to face the altar, putting Tate face to face with the ghost me.

She looks into my eyes as if she can see me and whispers, "Thank you for coming back to me."

———————

"…two more days. How am I going to say goodbye? I know you haven't really been here these past months, but you're still here, you know?"

Beep.

Beep.

"My parents and Fischer will be stopping by tomorrow. Fischer—" Quiet sobbing replaces Tate's voice.

"Don't. Please baby, don't cry. Please. Can you hear me?" I plead, but only inside my head.

Beep.

Beep.

I've got to break through. There has to be a way.

"I knew this part was going to be tough for you to grasp." Willow's voice chimes inside my head, taking me by surprise. "It's like this: you possess an energy that's in constant motion throughout your body. You need to focus this energy, because you will be transferring your thoughts through it."

But I've already tried this.

Willow's voice pops into my head again. "Once your energy is tightened, give the order 'haze.'"

That doesn't make sense. Tate isn't my Tragedy, and I don't have my blocking ability anymore.

"Just concentrate, will you?"

I can't help but appreciate the annoyed yet humored tone I've come to expect from Willow. I'd trust her with my life, so I decide to try her advice, however unlikely it seems.

Instead of concentrating on my body, this time I focus on my blue filter. At first there's nothing. Slowly, though, the familiar faint blue forms behind my eyelids. When it glows brighter, replacing the darkness, I open my eyes.

Tate! I can see Tate! She and everything else is covered in the sapphire filter, but she's here. Right in front of me! I wish she'd lift her head from my chest so I can see her face.

"Tate," I try to say, but my mouth still won't work.

Willow's voice repeats, "Once your energy is tightened, give the order 'haze.'"

I concentrate on pulling my blue filter in as I've done so many times before. It retracts slowly, but then pulls in faster, until the translucent ball is floating between me and Tate.

In my head, I shout, "Haze!"

The word bounces like an echo through my brain. The magnitude of pain it brings is unlike anything I've experienced from past blocks. I expect my body to be flailing as if I'm being shocked with paddles, but it remains lifeless. Even if the pain is one hundred percent mental, just as Lawson described it on that first day with Meggie, I need it to stop!

Tate, the blue ball, and the small room are replaced by blackness.

"Oh no, not on my watch, kid! You stay awake! You hear me?" Willow's voice is far away.

"Block," I mumble.

The torture subsides—*Halleluiah!*—but I continue to be trapped in darkness. There's no sound. Nothing. Even the beeping has stopped. And I'm cold again. Not just cold, frigid.

"No, baby, no!" Tate's voice is far away. "No!"

Open your eyes, I tell myself.

It won't work, the part of me that has had enough failure argues.

Try.

My eyelids flutter. It's a small victory, but they're moving. Come on. Come on!

Tate is in my vision. I can see her! And—whoa—she's losing her mind!

My body lightly bounces each time her fist pounds on my chest.

Come on, body, I need you to work!

My hand moves quicker than I expect, and I grab Tate's wrist.

Beep.

Tate freezes with her eyes on my chest.

Beep.

She turns her head to see my face.

Beep.

If I was, in fact, dead, getting to see Tate's expression right now isn't such a terrible consolation prize.

Beep.

"Baby!" Her fist opens. She puts her warm palm on my cheek and brings her face close to mine. "Oh my God, Grant!" She says through her sobbing. "Can you hear me?"

I swallow, but something blocks my dry throat, making me choke.

"Nurse! Someone help!" Tate is yelling.

Panic from not being able to breath on my own forces me to close my eyes.

"Help! Someone help!"

My arms jump, trying to reach whatever is constricting my airway. A minute later, someone is holding both my hands at my side, so my chest flails up and down while I try to breathe. A terrible noise fills my head. When I realize it's my own choking gargle, my body becomes too heavy for me to control. The heaviness wins and blackness surrounds me.

19. With everything that's happened, crazy is my new normal

Beep.

Beep.

Beep.

Tate.

Her head shares my pillow, making her eyes level with mine, but they are closed.

My lips move without producing any sound. I try again, forcing a croak out. Luckily, whatever was painfully blocking my throat is no longer there.

Tate opens her eyes and sees mine, but she doesn't react. If I had to bet, she probably thinks she's dreaming.

I try four times to speak, before my voice croaks out, "Marry me."

Tate bolts into a sitting position beside me. "Grant?"

She's going to make me speak again, I can tell. Already, she's a pain in my butt and I just woke up. God, I love her.

She's sobbing now. "Baby? Can you hear me?"

"Is that a yes?" I manage to say.

A second later, the weight of her chest is on mine and my neck is wet from her tears.

After laying still for a considerable amount of time in a claustrophobic tunnel, Dr. Adamack and I are back in my room with my parents and Tate.

"The test results we're seeing at this time are promising. We'll know more when I review Grant's MRI and the final pathology report from the lab tomorrow. I'm also conferring with Dr. Lassleman from Washington who worked on a similar case last year."

The doctor circles his fingers on either side of my neck after blinding each of my eyes with his flashlight. "Based on the initial blood work, I'm certain chemotherapy will need to be resumed, though we won't be able to proceed until Grant gains some strength back." The doc places his clipboard under his arm and shakes my hand. "Grant, I'd say you're a lucky man."

Tate swipes two fingers under her left eye to dry her tears and smiles at me. Dr. Adamack has no idea how truly lucky I am.

"Thank you, doctor. Thank you so much." My dad's chipper attitude as he pumps the doctor's hand up and down doesn't deliver the shock it did yesterday. In fact, I'm enjoying the new and improved man he appears to have become. Granted, I haven't had to work with him yet. If that should ever happen, being on the job with my old man will be the true test for whether my recovery really did alter him for the better.

While my mom keeps Dr. Adamack talking by

questioning about what my future recovery looks like, my brain is elsewhere.

Tate's breath tickles my ear when she whispers, "What's on your mind?"

God love her, she hasn't left my side since I woke up. She spent the night curled against me. I should have tried to sleep, but I was afraid if I closed my eyes, they may not open again. After the anxiety attack from having to be separated from Tate for my procedures this morning, the exhaustion is taking its toll. I know I'm going to have to submit, but I still don't trust that I'll wake up. Until then, I plan to fight for every second I have with Tate. This could be it, after all.

"What's going on in that head of yours?" Tate's voice remains quiet as to not disturb the conversation happening at the foot of my hospital bed.

I look into Tate's hazel eyes. Would she even believe me if I tried to explain things?

I don't know if I even believe it. Could Progression have been real? Just like my coma recovery, I'm having difficulty accepting such an absurd idea. When I think of all the people I met, Willow especially, my gut flutters with fear like I'm about to jump into a dark hole of the unknown. What if she wasn't real? I want so badly for her to be real.

Some things line up, though. After the initial shock of finding out I had been in a coma for almost a year, I tried to do the math in my head. It seems like that's about how long I would have spent in Progression. A few months on Ryder's assignment, a little longer than that with Meggie, and then the time it took to fight the Schedulers in between my conscious and unconscious state…it could be possible.

"Grant?" Tate's voice brings me back to the present.

I wish there was a way to verify the story without actually sharing the story. My throat still hurts and the amount of talking I'd have to do, along with the questions that would surely follow are more than my exhausted mind can take right now. There's something more that's keeping me quiet, though. What if they don't believe me? Would they forever look at me like I'm crazy? I'm not sure I could handle seeing that in Tate's eyes for the rest of my life, assuming I have a life ahead of me.

"Sorry, babe, I'm just tired." My rough voice has enough of an impact that Tate doesn't question me. Instead, she rubs her hand up and down my arm, tells me I have to get some sleep whether I like it or not, and hums in my ear.

She's not doing much to help me fight off my exhaustion. I try to find something from my experience that would prove Progression happened, or didn't.

I force my heavy eyes open. When I say Tate's name, she stops humming and lifts her head.

My eyes almost close before I get the question out, but I manage to stay awake. "Where's Elliott?"

Tate looks away quickly. Aside from the monitor that's been turned down a few notches, the room becomes quiet. The conversation between Dr. Adamack and my parents has abruptly stopped. Tate doesn't look at me, but the three of them do. No one needs to answer the question. I can see it in their faces.

I try to speak, but my body fails me, sending me into

the black hole I hate so much.

"Good morning, sleepyhead. About time you woke up. It's almost noon." Tate keeps her hand on my arm, but shifts over to give me some extra room on the bed. "My parents are here. They just went to get drinks from the vending machine. They'll be back in a minute."

I swallow and try to push myself into a sitting position.

"No, lay back down. You're still weak."

I lightly push Tate's arm to the side and am more successful in my attempt to sit up on the bed. Or, at least, I'm propped up a little higher than before.

"Elliott?"

"Look at me," I say when Tate turns toward the door.

"Where's Elliott?"

"You need to lay down. The doctor said we need to keep you relaxed and—"

I grab Tate's hand so she'll stop fidgeting with my pillow and straightening my bedsheets. Focused on her eyes, I wait because I know I don't need to say anything else.

Tate looks toward the door so I squeeze her hand. When she turns back to me, I wish I could erase the tears streaming down her cheeks, or, more specifically, the pain behind them.

I pull her until she falls against me, adjusting my body to get more slack in my IV tubing. Tate says nothing more. The warm moisture rolling down my neck is answer enough.

It was real. It had to be.

"Rock climbing."

Whispering these two words prompts her shoulders to stop bouncing. She lifts her head. I wipe her cheeks with my thumbs.

"How did you know?"

"I saw him."

One by one, her thoughts paint her face: confusion, disbelief, more confusion, and finally, curiosity.

"I think I was dead."

Tate doesn't appear to want to make a run for it. So far, so good.

I shake my head. "I know it sounds crazy."

Tate's glassy eyes show how broken she is. "With everything that's happened, crazy is my new normal." She reaches for my cheek. "Where did you go?"

"Grant!"

Our attention is forced toward the door. Tate quickly wipes her eyes and sits up straight beside me. "Hey, Fish, not too much excitement, all right? The doctor says—"

"Doc, smock!" Fischer bumps Tate out of the way. "I can't believe you're awake. Finally!"

I nod when he asks if hugging me is all right. Not only has he gotten taller, he's stronger, too. Strong enough that the beeping monitor increases when he crushes his arms around me. I lock eyes with Tate and try to telepathically tell her that I'd rather continue the conversation another time.

She half smiles. I hope she understood.

"Fischer, let the man breathe!" Mr. Jacoby says from

the other side of the bed. When Fischer releases me, I shake Tate's dad's hand, but he comes in for a hug. His hug, along with Mrs. Jacoby's, is less assaulting, but equally appreciated.

When my parents arrive a few minutes later, our moms exchange hellos and our dads exchange handshakes. Seeing my dad play nice with Tate's parents is something I never would have expected.

My parents stay toward the end of the bed since my sides are crowded at the moment. Fischer reminds me of Owen when his attention shifts to the three pizza boxes my dad set on the rolling table. My mom tells him to grab some lunch and he wastes no time.

It's when Tate joins Fischer that I realize just how much Fischer has grown. He's got an inch on his older sister now, though he's still thin. His soccer uniform being a size too big doesn't help his stature, but I can't fault him for that. I remember wearing larger clothes myself when I was an early teen. Now, more than ever, I can't understand why I wanted to grow up so quickly. Tate is busy separating paper plates and passing out slices of pizza, offering me the first piece. I thank her and inhale the pepperoni and cheese too quickly.

"Hot," I mumble through my mouthful of food. The roof of my mouth stings from the burn. I'm not going to lie, fast healing is one thing I'll miss about Progression.

The next hour is filled with small talk about Mr. Jacoby's new job as a plant supervisor for Stevenson Pharmaceuticals, my dad's heavy work load this month, and the scorching heat over the summer. I'd take some of that heat in this room right now. I've been cold since I woke up.

I've got to pack some weight on soon.

"September is shaping up to be a good one for us." My dad looks over to me. "I hope to have some extra help soon."

"My mom leans forward on the mini vinyl sofa. "We discussed this. We're not pushing him into anything too soon."

"We should be going," Mrs. Jacoby says.

"No, no," my dad says. I can count on one hand how many times I've heard him chuckle like this. I'm grateful that his reaction lessens the heaviness in the room.

I grin at my old man, "I'll be back soon."

"Only when you're ready," is his reply. No mumbling, no cursing, no nothing. This agreeable version of my dad is going to take some getting used to.

"What if Grant decides he'd like a different career?" my mom challenges as if she's trying to tick him off.

"Mom—"

"Honey, listen, your father and I discussed this and," she pauses and looks at my dad, "we both agree that you might like to do something different with your life. We understand—"

"Mom," I interrupt. "I want to work for Dad."

"You do?" they both reply, making me and Tate laugh.

I nod. "Assuming everything still works." When I make a fist, my hand isn't as strong as I'd like, but I shouldn't complain. I'm awake, after all. "I'd like to work with dad."

"You would?" My mom can't hide the shock in her tone.

"You sound surprised."

"Well, yes. I am. Your father and you—"

I stop her. "I think things will be different."

I have to look away from my old man when his eyes fill. He stands and excuses himself, saying he needs to check on one of his crews.

The Jacobys head out shortly after my dad, with my mom insisting she walk them out.

"We have a lot to talk about," Tate says when it's just us.

Before we can go any further, the nurse interrupts us to remove my IV. She tells me the doctor is expecting my test results by the afternoon and I could be released as early as this evening.

"Oh, that reminds me." Tate jumps up as the nurse covers the IV site with a bandaid. "Your mom brought in some clothes for you last night."

She retrieves a bag from the window ledge beside her purse and brings it to the bed while the nurse is busy messing with something on the monitoring equipment.

My hand runs along the blue canvas fabric of the familiar bag. "Where'd you get this?"

"Your mom brought it." Tate pauses and looks concerned. "I just said that."

I turn the backpack over. The frayed edge along the zipper confirms it's the same one. Maybe I was wrong about Progression after all. Maybe I overheard Tate talking about Elliott while I was in a coma. That could explain how I knew his cause of death.

Tate takes the backpack from me. "These'll probably be loose on you," she says as she retrieves a pair of jeans from the bag, "but they've got to be better than those threads, right?"

I give my hospital gown a disapproving look. "Anything's better than this thing. Speaking of clothes," I pull at the hem of her black T-shirt, "what's with this?"

Tate casts her eyes downward as if in embarrassment. I pull her chin up and lean close to her ear. "You're just as beautiful in black, but color makes you look happier."

With the nurse in the room preventing us from talking more, I decide now is as good a time as any to change clothes. After kissing Tate's forehead, I excuse myself.

Whoa!

In the bathroom, I stumble backward and my hip smacks hard into the shower handrail. The blow makes me drop my backpack.

"Everything OK?" Tate's muffled voice asks from the other side of the door.

I rub my hip. "You should have warned me about how pale I am!"

"Fair warning. You're really pale."

"Thanks a lot," I holler back.

Before I allow myself to be traumatized even more from my sickly reflection, I focus on getting dressed. I can't help but feel like Fischer. Everything is too big, just as Tate said. Even the thick, navy blue hoodie can't completely conceal my pointy shoulders, though it does a better job than my T-shirt alone. Plus, it's warm and helps with the chill I can't shake.

"Your mom said she threw your wallet and a belt in there, too," Tate says from the other side of the door.

I open the bag's main compartment expecting to see a locket, a rock, and a handbook, but find nothing until I hit the front zipper pouch. There, I discover a belt that proves to be the most useful item of the bunch. Without it, I'd never be able to carry my wallet without losing my pants.

A minute later I'm sitting on the toilet lid staring at my driver's license. I squeeze the bridge of my nose, which also feels thinner than usual. Will I ever look healthy again like I did in that photograph?

I spread the inside of my wallet open, wondering if I had any cash to my name before I fell off the grid. It's not the money that catches my eye. I open the wallet wider and slide my hand inside. Fortunately, I'm no longer hooked up to the monitors because my heart rate would likely alert the staff.

"Your patient is crashing," I mumble to myself, glad to still be sitting down.

I hold the silver ring up, turning it to get a better look. Not that I need one. Like my backpack, it's the same.

"Liam?" I whisper.

Irritated, I stand and shove my wallet into my back pocket. The ring clicks against the porcelain when I set it on the sink. I spend the next few minutes splashing warm water on my face.

Progression had to be real. What's with all my stuff returning, though?

When I've calmed down, I grab my empty bag.

"Good news," I say to Tate, glad the nurse is gone.

"Yeah?"

"I've got eighty bucks to take you to dinner. You're

going to have to drive, though, because it appears my license expired while I was sleeping."

"That's sad." Tate keeps our playful banter going as she uncrosses her legs and dangles them off the side of the hospital bed.

"Oh, and another thing."

"What's that?"

I get down on my knee in front of her, ignoring the awkward space between us because the hospital bed is taller than a regular chair.

"What are you doing?"

I smile. "If you'd give me a chance…" I slide the ring from my pinky knuckle. "I noticed you weren't wearing your ring—"

"Baby, I can explain—"

"You threw it off the bridge. I know."

Tate's jaw falls open, rightfully so, and I draw in a breath of relief. Another small clue that perhaps Progression was real and that maybe, just maybe, I'm not a lunatic.

I take her left hand and push the ring onto her finger. "I'll get you a better one, I promise."

Tate spins the ring around her finger a couple times. "No, this one's perfect."

I flip her hand over and I'm certain Tate misreads my sharp breath as shock from discovering her scar. She has no idea that my reaction has to do with getting more proof that my experience may have been real.

A very unmanly tear runs down my face as the magnitude of having Tate back hits me. Pulling her into a hug,

I've never felt so complete. My happily-ever-after with her is really happening! Suddenly, I don't care about the past, or whether it was real or not. None of that matters anymore. Tate and I are together again. Finally, we're really together again.

"I missed you so much," I say, gripping her tighter, feeling her sob against my chest.

After a couple minutes, Tate pulls back. My thumbs slowly slide across her cheeks, wiping her tears. She angles her head and when we kiss, I realize I missed her taste so much more than I thought was even possible. A strange feeling overwhelms me, like I'm homesick despite having everything I've ever wanted. Doubt whispers in my head, telling me this will all end like before.

We're breathless when we pull away, but this does nothing to stop us from going another round. And then another. If this turns out to be short-lived, I plan to take advantage of every minute. Tate's lips work in perfect unison with mine and I pretend, for a few minutes, that we've never been apart.

After an intense, overdue make-out session, we end up on the hospital bed. I hold on to Tate, unwilling to let her go, knowing that even forever won't be long enough.

20. *I wish I had an explanation for you*

"Mind if I interrupt?"

Tate sits up, but I keep a firm grip on her torso. "Not at all, Mr. Bradley. I was just about to grab a couple drinks."

"No you weren't." I argue, but Tate pushes my hand away and hops off the bed. She gives me a quick kiss and tells me she'll be back in a little while.

My dad steps closer, wringing his hands together. "How are you feeling?"

I shrug. "It's weird, right? How I just...woke up?"

My dad takes up most of the vinyl sofa when he sits. Fidgeting with his hands, I can tell he's as uncomfortable as I am. "It's a miracle," he says quietly.

"Come on, you don't believe in that stuff."

"This past year has been—"

When my dad pauses, I look away in fear of seeing him cry.

"Well," he says after almost a minute. "Believe it or not, this experience has changed your old man."

"Me, too." I sit up straighter on the bed, thinking of my flashbacks from Programming, the way my dad was so involved when I was little. Really, he was never *not* there, he just got more vocal over the years. "I know how you feel about me, if that's what this is about." I take a slow breath in effort to keep my eyes dry. "You'd disappear in the hospital hallway when my cancer treatments started tearing me down. You tried so hard to hide your epic sobbing fits from Mom and me," I joke, trying to keep things light.

My dad puts his man-face back on. "I wasn't *sobbing.*"

I stare back at him.

"What? I wasn't!" He's trying hard to redeem himself, which makes me smile. "Yes, I was a bit upset! My only son was dying!" My dad pauses and then lowers his volume. "I wanted to fix you so badly, but I couldn't. I've never felt so helpless. I'm your father. I'm suppose to protect you."

My smile dissipates and water prickles in my eyes. I blink, hoping to stop the tears. No dice. Niagara Falls opens up.

What in the world is going on?

"Dad. Can't. Breathe," I manage, but I hug my dad back anyway.

We're hugging? We both know Bradley men don't hug, at least these two don't!

When my dad pulls away, I use the back of my hand to dry my eyes. "I love you, old man." I clap my hand on his upper arm. There, that's better. I'm feeling more masculine already.

"I love you, too, kid."

"I saw Grandpa." Did that really just fly from my mouth? I look down from embarrassment. My dad is the last person I want to discuss this with. If anyone will doubt my story, it's him.

I glance up since my dad is silent. His expression surprises me. Leaning forward on the sofa, he actually looks interested in hearing this.

"I mean, I'm sure it was just a dream."

"How can you be sure?" Dad asks.

"Well…I can't."

"Tell me about him."

"You really want to hear this?"

"Are you kidding? Yes."

I inhale, wondering if this is really the best idea.

"Look who I found outside," my mom's voice interrupts.

"Come in, come in," my dad says in a rush, pulling two more chairs close to the small sofa.

My mom and Tate take a seat while I squeeze the bridge of my nose. Continuing this conversation is a terrible idea. I'm about to be released from this place. If my story gets out, however, I'll probably be locked up in a hospital much worse than this one. "Maybe another time would be better—"

"Now's the perfect time. I'm sure the ladies would like to hear this, too."

My mom shoots my dad a suspicious look. "Hear what?"

"Grant saw Dad."

I flinch from my old man's blunt reply. Certainly, him of all people, would be my number one skeptic. Heck, I'm not even sure I believe myself, and I experienced the entire thing.

My mom's face is easy to read when she looks back at

me. She doesn't believe my dad, and, clearly—and by all rights—, she's worried about my sanity. "You saw Grandpa?"

I swallow, considering my options. I could lie and tell them I'm beat and I'd really like to sleep for a while. All three of them would honor my request, I know, but I also know they'd be ready to hear my story as soon as nap time ended. I could buy myself some time, but I'm actually not tired at all. I'm ready to sever ties with this hospital bed once and for all, so the thought of having to pretend to sleep for even an hour sounds terrible.

Tate glances nervously from me to my parents, probably enjoying the tension as much as I am. "I got you a drink."

I accept the can from Tate, wishing it was something stronger than Coke. A little liquid courage would certainly help right now. I pop the tab and the hiss of the can rings through the room.

Gulp, gulp, gulp.

They know I'm stalling, but they wait in silence. The vinyl creaks when my dad leans back in the sofa. He acts as if he's settling in for a good story.

When I start talking, I keep my focus on the Coke can turning slowly in my hand. "You have to understand, what I'm about to tell you—I'm not even sure if it really happened. The more I think about it, the more impossible it all seems. You saw me lying here for almost a year, so to say I was physically somewhere else sounds absurd. This story is more likely just that, a story. Something I made up in my head. Maybe the drugs they pumped through me messed my brain up. I don't know."

"Grant?"

I look from the can to Tate.

"We're not here to judge you, we just want to know what happened, or at least what you remember. Does it really matter if it was real or not?"

I don't answer. Does it matter? For my sanity, yes.

No, not for my sanity. It matters because I want the people I met to be real. I respect them. More than that, I consider them my friends. It feels good to be part of something bigger than myself. It signifies that life has a purpose and that the mundane things we go through day to day are part of a master plan, even if we don't see or understand it.

I chew on my bottom lip while I conjure up as much courage as possible.

"Be honest," Jonathan's voice says in my head.

All right. Fine.

"I saw Grandpa." I look from my dad to Tate. "And Elliott, too."

When Tate gets up and walks around the bed, I move over. The tension in my shoulders lessons when she sits beside me and takes my hand in hers.

"I thought I was dead." As I start at the beginning, explaining Progression and my reason for being there as Jonathan explained to me on that first day. I tell them about Rigby and Anna. When I get to Willow, Tate happens to be mid-sip in her soda and almost spits Sprite all over my parents.

"Sorry," she says after swallowing.

I laugh. "I had the same reaction to her. Trust me. The girl is a nut."

Tate sets her soda can on the bedside table. "She sounds cool. My reaction is from your reaction. If you could see your face..."

My dad smirks.

My mom lets out a laugh. "Tate's right. The sour face makes you look so much like your father."

My dad sits up straighter, but his smile remains. "I'm not sure what that's supposed to mean."

The comment about being like my dad doesn't sting like it used to. In fact, it doesn't bother me at all.

I continue with the story and explain my purpose in Progression. I get caught up in details about the place. I would usually skip over such things, but somehow, elaborating on specifics such as the buffet and the building itself gives me a tiny bit of hope that maybe I didn't imagine it all.

I can't remember the last time I talked so much. My parents and Tate allow me to go on and on, occasionally interrupting with a question here and there.

My dad's the most curious about the architecture, specifically the floating lights in Benson. I tell him they boggled me, too.

When I explain the age thing as my friends explained it to me, I can tell my mom has a soft spot for Willow. She verbalizes her disapproval of my reaction to Willow's stretch marks. I agree that I should have been more tactful.

In my defense, I wasn't expecting to see her stomach. Heck, I never expected most things Willow did. I wish I could apologize to her for my childish reaction. I know why she loved those scars. After getting to know Ryder and Mya, I would love them, too, if I were her.

When I mention seeing my mom in my room and witnessing her breakdown on my bed, my mom begins to cry. She confirms having a lot of days like this, which is not helpful in determining the likelihood of what I experienced being real. How, though, could my imagination conjure up something that actually took place?

On the other hand, Tate's demeanor changes when I explain the times I visited her. I can't help but wonder if she seems more withdrawn because she never felt the connection I am describing. I want to ask, but because she seems so uncomfortable, now doesn't feel like the right time.

Over two hours later, the Dr. Adamack interrupts when I'm telling them about Meggie and the awful day she had to bury her mom and kids.

"Your brain scan shows no signs of permanent damage." Dr. Adamack grins, but appears perplexed. "Your blood work has confirmed your cancer is not in remission, however, your cell counts aren't nearly as elevated as they were before the coma. We'll need to biopsy a few more lymph nodes and do some scans, but I'd like to wait a few days. Let's see how quickly your strength resumes. For now, I see no reason to keep you here any longer. I wish I had an explanation for you. After speaking with Dr. Lassleman this morning, we may have to chalk this one up to a medical miracle. Last year, his patient woke from a coma after eight months with no explanation and, I'm happy to report, has made a full recovery. I'm hopeful your recovery will be the same."

My dad claps his hands together. "That's great news, Doc!"

I've never seen my old man so animated.

My mom grabs a tissue from the box in the window sill. After dabbing her eyes, she stands and wraps her arms around Dr. Adamack. "Thank you so much."

"I wish I could take the credit, Mrs. Bradley." He squeezes her shoulder when she pulls away. "I'm nearly as ecstatic as all of you. I never thought we'd have the privilege of seeing Grant with his eyes open again. We still have his cancer to contend with, but the results I'm seeing thus far are promising."

Dr. Adamack smiles while his pen scribbles on his clipboard. He removes the top sheet, passes me a signed paper, and shakes my hand. "Here's my direct line. If you should need anything, don't hesitate to call. If you're feeling light headed or nauseous, I want to know about it immediately. I'll have someone from my office call you tomorrow to check in and schedule an appointment. I'd like to see you in three days to discuss our next steps. Until then, you're free to go."

Tate hops off the bed and gives him a hug. "Thank you for giving us the extra time we needed. If we'd unhooked the machines last month, I…" Tate doesn't finish her sentence, but pulls away and swipes her fingers across her eyes.

"It's been a pleasure getting to know all of you over the past months. I do wish the circumstances had been different, but things have turned out very well, I'd say."

"How about some dinner?" my dad asks when Dr. Adamack has left. "I'd like to hear the rest of the story."

My mom collects the three small plants on the window sill and puts them in a box on the counter. "Me, too."

My dad picks up my backpack and puts his arm around me when I stand. "I never thought we'd be walking out of here together. This is a good day, kid."

On our way out, my parents and Tate exchange hugs with a few nurses. The nurses hug me as well, which is a tad awkward. They've seen me in a vegetative state over the past year, yet I barely know them.

"Do you mind if I ride with Tate?" I ask my mom in the parking garage.

She's hesitant at first, but agrees after a tight embrace. "Let's meet at Dominic's for pizza. Be good."

I missed my mom so much.

"I have to tell you something," I say when we're in Tate's Jeep and out of the garage.

Tate turns the radio down, even though the volume was already low. "Yeah?"

"Do you believe what I told you?"

She glances over at me and then looks back at the road. "I do."

The Jeep slows to a stop behind my parents at the red light.

"I kissed someone."

She doesn't reply, nor does she look at me.

The light turns green. "Tate?"

"Who was she?"

Gulp. "There were two girls actually. No, three. The third doesn't really count, though. I mean, that one kissed me. I didn't kiss her back."

Tate jerks her car to the right and pulls into the grocery store parking lot, stopping sideways between two parking spaces.

"Three?"

Maybe I should have waited to tell her. No, I have to be honest. This conversation wouldn't be any easier a week from now.

"The first was the girl Clara I told you about."

Tate sucks in a breath. "The artist?"

"Yeah."

"The second was another Elite."

Tate puts the Jeep in park. "Trina?"

"You were paying attention to my story."

Tate looks insulted. "Of course I was!"

"How'd you know it was Trina?"

"Well, I certainly wouldn't have expected you to say Evelynn."

"Evelynn was actually the second, but she kissed me. I swear. I pulled away as soon as she did."

"You didn't pull away with the other girls?"

My eyes move to the glove box. "Not as quickly as I should have."

When I look back, Tate's eyes are glassy.

"Did you love them?"

"No. I swear. I've never loved anyone the way I love you."

A tear rolls down her cheek.

"I'm so sorry. I never wanted to hurt you." I wipe my thumb under her eye. "This is crazy. I don't even know if it was real."

"When you talked about the times you visited me...I remember those days. I destroyed lots of things that reminded me of you. I thought you would never wake up. I didn't know how I was going to get through life without you."

My stomach tightens. "When I was in a coma, did you ever visit me and talk about those days?"

Tate swallows and then shakes her head. "What would I have said? Hi Grant, I tore up a few more of our pictures today?"

She's so cute when she's being sarcastic. Still, I find this interesting. I knew about Elliott, seeing my mom in my room certainly seems to have really happened, and now Tate is confirming her bouts of destruction.

A knock on my window makes me jump.

"Is everything all right?" my anxious mom asks when I lower the window.

"Sorry, Mom. We're fine. We're just having a quick conversation. We'll be at Dominic's in a few minutes."

The worry leaves her face. "OK, take your time. We'll see you when you get there."

"I kissed someone, too."

My hand stops before I roll the window up the rest of the way. "The goth guy?" I had left that guy out of my story earlier on purpose. I wanted everything to be real, except him.

Tate doesn't miss the aggression in my voice. "You don't get to be mad about this! You kissed three different girls!"

I turn my body to face her. "Not three! My situation was different!"

Tate crosses her arms. "How do you figure?"

"I thought I was dead, for one thing! You, however, were very much alive."

Tate can shed as many tears as she wants. I'm not budging on this.

Tate looks away and I have to lean in to hear her. "You were pronounced brain dead the week before."

"Well, I'm not!"

"You were!" she fires back.

I lean away from her in my seat and look out at the Hill Grove Grocery sign, forcing myself to calm down.

"He almost raped you."

When Tate doesn't reply, I glance toward the driver's seat.

Fine. She wins. I can't keep up my tough guy front. I push on the button to release her seatbelt and pull her into my arms. "I don't want to fight."

She sobs into my shoulder.

I kiss the top of her head. "I'm sorry. It's been an emotional day. We can talk about this another time."

She pulls back and wipes her eyes. "You have this story about all these amazing things that happened to you. The crazy part is, a lot of what you say could very well be true. You had lots of distractions." She leans over and opens the glove box. Her hand returns with a napkin she uses to wipe her nose. "I was stuck here, day after day, with a comatose fiancée, who by all rights, may as well have been dead. There was never any good news. Nothing. And then, Elliott…" Tate's tears start rolling again, but she pulls away when I reach to wipe her eyes. "Elliott goes and dies on me when I needed him! He was the only one I could talk to about you. He was the only one who would listen. He would just let me talk. Everyone else was always trying to fix me."

I reach for Tate's hand and push the sleeve of her sweatshirt over her elbow. I lean down and kiss her exposed scar. There's so many things I wish I could change. There are so many things I want to say to her. "I missed you so much," is the best I can do. I press her wrist to my mouth again and cry. I cry with such force that I'm afraid I may never stop. Tate cries with me.

Eventually, whether by exhaustion or dehydration, we both begin to calm down.

"You're a mess, you know that?"

I look up at Tate, noting the red blotchy eyes that are never my favorite look on her. "You're not much better."

This makes her laugh, and eventually, I'm laughing the same way I laughed along with Anna all those months ago. Being with Tate, though, feels so much better than how I felt that day with Anna. I feel whole again.

Tate kisses me in my favorite way, deep and intense. She leans back sooner than I'd prefer despite my pulling her towards me again. "Your parents are waiting. We have plenty of time to catch up." Her heart-shaped lips curve upward. "The rest of our lives, it seems."

I put my hand over Tate's when she puts the Jeep in drive. "We have forever."

"Sorry we're late," I say when Tate and I sit across from my parents in the red booth.

My mom leans forward, certainly noticing our blotchy eyes. "Is everything all right?"

I nod.

My dad, keeping with his natural aversion to emotional stuff, tops off his beer. He points the pitcher at me in offering.

"I think I'll stick with Coke tonight."

He nods.

My mom reaches for Tate's hand. "What's this?"

I can feel the heat on my cheeks, embarrassed by my subpar ring choice. "It was all I had. I'm getting a better one."

"I'm not accepting another one. This is perfect."

My mom smiles. "I agree."

"The wedding is back on," I explain to my old man to ward off his confused expression.

"I didn't know the wedding was ever off."

"Well, seeing as I was almost dead, I guess I wanted to

be sure we were all on the same page."

"You were never almost dead to me, son."

I look down at the pizza pictured on the inside of the menu and smile.

My dad takes a sip of his beer. "So, let's hear the rest of that story."

21. This guy's a stalker

The keys dig into my hand, nervous about how this may go.

"You ready?"

"I can't believe we're here." I look at the small home. "You're amazing, by the way."

Tate gives me the well-known, "Whatever," look, but my favorite shade of pink reaches her cheeks to prove she's flattered.

"It's true. How many wives would spend their honeymoon with complete strangers just to prove her husband isn't mental?"

"Oh, you're mental all right. Don't go thinking this will prove otherwise."

I become more serious. "Thank you. I would have never found the information to get us here."

"Are you kidding? With the internet and social media, you can find anyone these days."

"No, *you* can find anyone. I barely know how to turn on a computer."

Tate and I both stare at the house. She knows I need a minute.

I take a deep breath and the truck door creaks open in

the still, summer day.

Tate keeps hold of my arm as we cross the lawn. She stands patiently beside me on the front porch.

Part of me wants to walk through Ryder's front door. I'm grateful the smarter part of me remembers this is impossible. Funny how certain parts of the afterlife have stuck with me. I hope to never give into this particular urge, as walking into a wall would be embarrassing.

"What if he's not home?"

Tate doesn't answer. Her level of calm is not helping my anxiety.

What if he is home? Maybe it would be better to come back tomorrow. Tate and I can check into the hotel and I can collect my nerves. After nearly twenty-two hours on the road, we could both use the rest. Maybe tomorrow I'll feel less disheveled.

No, I have to do this now. I nod to Tate before I change my mind.

She leans forward and pushes her finger on the doorbell.

"Moment of truth," I mumble under my breath while my nerves make my heart work overtime.

Tate squeezes my hand. "You're gonna do great."

"Can I help you?"

I'm thankful when my breath hitches because I almost call Hannah by her name. You'd think going over the script in my head twenty dozen times or so, I'd feel more prepared than I do right now.

"Hello."

Tate notices the hitch in my voice and, God love her, saves my life. "Hi. I'm Tate and this is my husband, Grant. Does Ryder Beckmann live here?"

When Tate calls me her husband, my breathing levels out. I'll never get tired of hearing her saying those words.

"Ryder, someone's here for you," Hannah yells towards the kitchen. If she knew how familiar I am with this house, she'd probably sneak upstairs to call the police.

"Coming!"

Ryder's voice sends my heart rate back into overdrive. Tate squeezes my hand again. When she nods to me, her eyes say everything is going to be OK. I hope she's right.

Breathe, Grant, breathe. I'm trying so hard, but with Ryder right here in the door way, my thoughts begin to spiral. So much for reciting my lines.

Ryder stops flipping the pen through his fingers and places it behind his ear. "Yeah?"

Deep breath. Extend hand. Keep it simple, stupid. "I'm Grant Bradley. This is my wife, Tate."

Ryder accepts my handshake and then shakes Tate's hand.

"You don't know me, but I knew your mom. Do you mind if we come in?"

Ryder's eyes move to Hannah. Without an answer to offer, Hannah can only return his questioning look with one of her own. After a couple seconds of resistance, Ryder steps to the side.

I wish I was able to be more discreet about the sigh of relief rushing out of my lungs. "Thank you."

I allow Tate to go in first. We follow Hannah to the kitchen with Ryder behind us.

"The kitchen looks great. You've done a lot work to the place."

Ryder closes his two textbooks and slides them and his notebook to the far side of the table. "Have you been here before?"

Mental head slap. I'm not supposed to know the brown walls were once yellow, nor should I know anything about the new tile flooring. "Uh, yeah. A long time ago."

Thankfully Ryder's confusion doesn't last. Tate and I accept his nonverbal offer to have a seat.

Ryder and Hannah sit close together and stare at Tate and me.

I rub the sweat from my palms on my jeans. "I guess the best way to handle this is to get right to it. I promise what I'm about to tell you is going to make me sound like I need to be committed."

Unlike Hannah, Ryder doesn't look worried. His reaction is even less favorable. The doubt on his face says what I'm about to tell him will probably be accepted as easily as a fox would accept a rabbit as its own.

"Please." I maintain eye contact with Ryder. "Just hear me out."

Ryder leans forward with his elbows on the table. "How'd you know my mom?"

"I swear I'm not here to cause you worry."

Ryder and Hannah stare back at me and I can tell if I don't start talking, he's going to kick me out.

"I met your mom—" I pause for a couple seconds. "Let me back up. I was diagnosed with cancer a couple years ago. When I was at my worst, I flatlined. At that point, the doctors put me in a drug induced coma."

OK. So far, so good.

"Now for the crazy stuff. Please, just listen before you say anything."

Ryder stares blankly back at me.

"When I flatlined, I was, by all rights, dead. But I wasn't. I woke up in another world." I grin, not out of happiness, but because I know all this sounds unbelievable. "I met your mom there."

"You saw Heaven?" Hannah asks.

"It was never referred to as such, but all the elements were there. So, yes, you could call it Heaven."

I look back at Ryder. "Your mom was my mentor. She trained me to be a Satell—" I stop myself and choose the route Tate suggested for the purpose of clarity, even though calling myself an angel of any sort is laughable. "To be a guardian angel."

Ryder pushes himself back into his chair, crosses his arms, and smirks.

"I know this sounds ridiculous, but hang on, because this wild story gets even better. During my short stint as a guardian angel, I was sent here," I point to the tile floor, "to watch over you."

Ryder's humored reaction causes me sit up straighter. "I got here when your dad died." My voice comes out harsher than it should.

Ryder's chair scoots across the floor and he's in my face a second later. I don't even remember standing up.

Hannah grabs Ryder by the elbow and Tate grabs my forearm.

"It's true." Tate's voice is calm, but I doubt her nerves share the same feeling.

"You and Hannah were snowmobiling when you got the call. She drove you to the hospital," I clear my voice. "Well, she drove after you almost wrecked your car."

Ryder comes loose of Hannah's grip and he's in my face. "Get out!"

"Honey, calm down," Hannah says.

"No way! This guy's a stalker."

Sheesh. He sounds just like Tate when I was trying to convince her to go out with me. I'm not a stalker!

"It's nothing like that, man. I swear." I tick through other examples in my head, hoping for something more effective.

"You visited your mom's grave on her birthday."

"If you value your teeth, you better move towards the door."

"You left her a granite rock. That was her thing. She loves granite."

Granite. That's it.

I talk faster, hoping that Ryder will relax his fist. "You had a dog growing up. Granite. You had to put him down because of a blockage."

Ryder's eyes narrow. "How'd you know that?"

"I told you. I watched over you."

"You said from when my dad died, not from when I was a kid."

"I saw your life in flashbacks." Ugh. This is so much more difficult to explain than I imagined. "I know you think I'm crazy, but this is all true. You punched holes right here," I point to the smooth drywall. "You did a great job patching that up, by the way."

Ryder takes a step back and then another. He keeps his eyes on me, though, like I'm a child about to steal something.

I let out a breath, not realizing I'd been holding it. When Ryder sits, Hannah and Tate calculate the risk of Ryder blowing again before taking a seat themselves. I'm the last to park my butt on a kitchen chair, grateful the tension has cooled.

I begin telling the story from the beginning. I give the CliffsNotes version of my cancer days, getting more detailed from the time I arrived at Progression. I tell Ryder as much as I can about Willow. I'm honest with him about my feelings when I first met her. Halfway through my story, Hannah goes to the fridge and returns with four bottles of water, giving one to both Tate and me. I take this, and the fact that they haven't kicked us out yet, as a good sign that Ryder and Hannah may actually believe me.

By the time my story reaches the present, over an hour has passed. I apologize for taking up so much of their day.

"Why did you come here?" Ryder asks when I've finished.

"Honestly?" I pause. "I needed proof myself."

"You mean you didn't believe what happened?"

I shrug. "What I experienced…well, you've heard it. It's an outrageous story. I'd considered so many explanations. Maybe it was just a dream, or a side effect from the drugs, or my comatose imagination running wild." I smirk. "Your mom would be shaking her head at my cynicism if she were here."

"But to drive halfway across the country? No offense, but I probably would have written the whole thing off as a dream."

Tate leans forward. "Trust me, he tried."

"You could have just called."

"I thought about it, but I had to see for myself. Besides, how long would I have kept your interest before you hung up on me?"

Ryder nods because he knows I'm right.

"The vividness is what got me. Every detail is still so clear to me. My dreams are different. They usually have more holes and a kind of grogginess to them."

I scoot my chair back and stand. "There's this other thing, too." I lift my shirt to reveal the perfect, tear-shaped scar on my chest.

Hannah sucks in a breath. Ryder's reaction is less audible, but his eyes are equally as wide because I briefly explained the scars to them during story time.

"The one on my knee is the same. Tate and the doctors tell me they're from my IV lines," I shake my head, "but, they're identical in every way."

Tate reaches up and rubs my arm. "When Grant was in a coma, he usually didn't move at all, but sometimes he would have these episodes."

I half laugh. "She calls them episodes. They sound more like wild fits to me."

"The first one happened the night after they induced the coma. He started flailing and jerking around on his bed. The nurse was in the room and gave him some medicine that calmed his body down pretty quickly. Another one happened the next day. His parents were there and got the doctor."

I lower my shirt and sit back down.

"The third time was more eventful. His parents had left about five minutes earlier for a coffee run. I tried to hold him down, but I wasn't doing much good, so I was going to call the nurse. Grant grabbed me as I was leaning back and he wouldn't let go. His body wouldn't stop bucking, either."

Tate squeezes my forearm. "By the time the nurses arrived from hearing the noise, Grant and I were on the floor, tangled in tubes. His chemo port had ripped out of his chest and left a pretty nasty wound, and ultimately, a tear-shaped scar. His IV came out, too, but luckily that was with much less force." Tate turns away from me when water pools in her eyes. She looks up at the ceiling for a few seconds. "Getting another IV in him wasn't easy. He had to be strapped down and his veins kept rolling and blowing. Five nurses, one doctor, and eighteen sticks later, Grant had a new port and a double dose of drugs running through his system. He only had two more episodes after that, but the IV stayed in place both times."

I roll my wedding band around my finger with my thumb. "One guess where they put the IV."

Ryder and Hannah stay silent.

"Going just above his knee was the doctor's idea. It worked until the infection came. It was a nasty one; took almost a month to stop oozing. Anyway, they moved the IV to his arm without any issues, and the episodes stopped. At that point, Grant had enough drugs running through him, his chest hardly moved when he breathed."

Ryder relaxes a little in his chair.

"How are you now?" Hannah asks me. "Your health, I mean."

I reach over and squeeze Tate's hand. "I'm in remission. After the coma, I had six rounds of chemo. It sucked…" my voice trails off as memories from those days creep in. The only other time I recall being so afraid was when I thought Tate had taken her life in the bathtub.

Tate's voice summons me back to the present. "The treatments after the coma were still physically tough, but they took more of an emotional toll on Grant than before."

"I was worried I wouldn't make it." I look over at Tate. "Losing her once nearly destroyed me. I'm in no rush to go through that again."

I pull my hand from Tate's and lean forward on my elbows. "Listen, Ryder, my reasons for coming here were selfish, but you should know your mom is an amazing woman. I know it tore her up that she wasn't around for you. Had it been her decision, things would have been different. You'll meet her someday and you'll see for yourself. There's no one like her. Not in this world, or any other world out there." My eyes sting with tears, prompting Tate to grab my hand.

Feeling less than manly, I excuse myself and ask to use

Ryder's restroom.

"Sure, just up the—"

"Stairs," I say. "Yeah, I know."

"Oh. That's disturbing."

I wipe my eyes and laugh a little. "You've got a point," I say over my shoulder as I climb the steps.

"Your mom sounds stunning. Grant really loves her and talks about her all the…" Tate's voice fades when I close the bathroom door.

The cold water is just what I needed to clear my tears. I splash my face a few more times just to be sure my emotions are in check. I pause while wiping the splattered water from the vanity to glance at my eyes in the mirror. They're a tad pink, but overall, not terrible.

To the right of my reflection, the mirror begins to fog. That's strange, I didn't have the hot water on. I hang the towel, but keep my focus on the mirror.

A spot appears, and then a straight line erases the fog.

A letter forms. And then another. And another.

Unbelievable. This is what I'm thinking, but I'm too dumbfounded to speak.

Thank you, kid.

"Willow?" I whisper.

No one answers, but I know it's her. My heart pounds as I look around the small room wishing I could see her.

"Stop spying on me, freak," I try to joke, but my voice comes out too serious.

Man, I miss her.

The mirror fogs again and a smiley face appears.

I shake my head and my eyes sting with tears once more. "Willow. I didn't think you'd--" I stop myself and a muffled laugh comes from my mouth. "I should have known you'd be here."

A lightness like I've never felt overcomes me, and, although I feel like shouting out in excitement, I keep my voice low. "It was real, Willow. It was all real."

More fog and another smiley face appears.

"I miss you so much. No matter how much of a freak you are," I pause, trying, but failing, to blink back my tears. "I love you," I whisper.

The mirror fogs once more and my tears roll down my cheek just as the heart shape closes at the bottom.

"Thank you for everything. You've got great kids. Stay close to them." There's no point in hiding it, so I don't bother to look down when I wipe my eyes. "Catch you on the other side."

On my way out of the bathroom, I smile almost as wide as when I finally got to call Tate Mrs. Bradley.

"I'm wiped out," I say to Tate when we're leaving Dewey's Pub. Lunch paired with a couple beers was exactly what I needed after my visit with Ryder. Tate had to sit in the parking lot with me for twenty minutes before we could even go in because I was shaking so badly. What a relief to finally silence my doubting voice of reason. My first words to Tate, when I was able to speak, were, "I feel sane again."

"Keys," Tate demands when we reach my truck. Not my company truck either. This one has a lot more options, including leather seats and an air conditioner that works.

"Not without a kiss first."

"A request I can't refuse." Tate plants her lips on mine.

I'm not sure if it's her or me that extends the kiss longer than should be allowed in a public parking lot. Either way, I'm grateful and, like always, I want more.

"Remember to look before you back up," I say as I buckle my seatbelt.

Tate shakes her head. "That one never gets old to you, does it?"

I grin and punch the next destination's address into my truck's navigation system.

"In a quarter mile, turn right on Portsmouth Avenue."

I cross my arms and sink down into my seat, comforted by GPS Jeanette's voice.

"Wake me if you need anything."

Tate agrees and switches the radio station. My head bobs up and down from dozing off and I'm too relaxed to complain about her music choice.

Three hours later, Tate wakes me up when we're pulling into at a gas station. She disappears inside to use the ladies room while I pump the fuel.

"It seems everything has worked out just as it was meant to be."

At the adjoining pump, Jonathan leans against a white Jeep, identical to Tate's. He straightens his ball cap and glances at the convenience store. "The past is always clearer when viewed from the future. Wouldn't you agree?"

It takes a few seconds for the shock to dissipate enough to allow my voice to work. "You say that like you knew this is how things would turn out."

Jonathan says nothing, staring back at me the same way my dad did on the job site the moment I realized he was proud of me.

He rubs the dark stubble on his chin. "Have you ever considered that your life unfolded exactly as planned?"

"That's ridiculous."

Jonathan lets out a low laugh and shoves his hands in his jean pockets.

"I sense there is something you'd like to ask me?"

This guy! I've had a question brewing in my head from the time I began processing my surreal experience. I'd assumed it was one that would never be answered. "You really are a mind reader, aren't you?"

"I can't give away all my secrets." He smirks. "I don't think that's the question you had in mind."

Boom! There! He is a mind reader. I knew it.

Jonathan laughs and the victory dance happening in my head halts. I'd be lying if I denied being a little weirded out.

"How is it that I was able to keep all of my memories, while the others didn't?"

Jonathan removes his hands from his pockets and folds them together. "Ah, yes. Although I did not share the culinary talents of Landon, I had connections in the food preparation department. Your venison stew was never mixed with Landon's mind eraser. Speaking of, your mom is a magnificent cook."

Maintaining my memories was not achieved by my own accord? I'm not sure why this bothers me. Maybe a part of me liked to think I was mentally stronger than others.

No. That's not it at all.

I turn away from Jonathan and watch Tate through the convenience store window while she waits in line for the restroom.

"Grant, excuse my ignorance. Did I say something to upset you?"

Unable to look at Jonathan, I direct my stare at the plane overhead. "It's just…this sounds stupid, but I had thought our bond was indestructible. Or, hoped, at least."

"Do not be fooled by your own doubts. The bond between you and Tate is remarkable, indeed. If you recall, the separation nearly destroyed you. Love is the most magical emotion we are blessed with. Never doubt for a moment that love cannot span worlds. Love will always be one of our most basic needs. It can lift us, and it can destroy us as well. There will never be anything more powerful."

Looking back at Jonathan, my only other question springs to mind like Jack coming out of his box.

"Typically, I would never allow such mind alteration. Your situation has never been typical, though." Jonathan winks. "Elliott's memory of your death and funeral was fabricated. Ironically, he was given a glimpse of his own funeral. In the altered memory, however, you mom and mother-in-law were reversed, and Elliott was placed in

Fischer's role alongside Tate." He unfolds his hands and puts them up likes he's surrendering. "OK, fine, I am a bit of a mind reader."

Well, that explains why my parents and Tate have zero recollection of my death and the aftermath that followed as Elliott explained to me.

"Elliott's memory has been corrected and he now knows the truth. He is a very understanding soul." When I finally smile, Jonathan continues. "I thought you'd be interested to learn the reason why blocking is so painful. Our brains build a metaphorical wall around themselves from the pain we experience in life. To penetrate that fortress in order to transfer our thoughts, a Satellite must accept their subject's pain as their own."

Jonathan puts his hands in his pockets again and rocks back on his heels. "I hadn't realized the extent of this phenomenon until recently. When your friends were preparing for the group block performed on Tate, I concluded the physical pain endured from blocking stemmed from the combination of both the blocker and blockee, so to speak."

I shake my head. "Sorry, you lost me. I thought blocking was a chromosome thing."

"The chromosomal make-up is necessary to penetrate the wall, yes. While you're blocking, your own protective wall is dropped as well. When the group block was performed, the emotional pain was not only from the subject and the Satellite, but from the additional Satellites as well. In essence, each Satellite involved took on not only their own pain and

Tate's, but that of each of their teammates as well. As you can imagine, the result was debilitating." Jonathan massages his forehead with his right hand as if he was trying to work out his expression lines. "I recently shared this with the Satellites and thought it was important for you to know as well."

Jonathan reaches out and squeezes my arm. "I have always found your ability to reject blocks as both remarkable and confounding. Upon my blocking revelation, I believe you to be—and please to do not take offense—one of the least vulnerable people I have yet to meet."

I flinch.

Jonathan releases my arm and holds his palm up. "Please, hear me out. This discovery has opened up the need for a new department in Progression. We are in the process of building a team called the Remedies. They will assist in breaking down the walls which house a person's emotional pain, thus making humans more inclined to naturally live out the lives they were meant for. It will be many years before our first members are in place; however, I am hopeful that this team will lessen the need for Satellites."

Jonathan glances at the side of my truck when the gas pump handle clicks off. "Please understand, the pain Satellites have endured over the years is not something I've ever taken lightly. I have spent many years searching for a better solution to keep humankind on course. Already, we have had a significant drop in the necessity for Satellites since individuals are helping their own loved ones here on Earth."

I think about Willow and her love of the program. "Have you mentioned this to the others?"

Jonathan nods. "They realize the evolution of human-kind is our upmost goal. Grant, I'm telling you this because you have no idea how much happiness life holds for you, but you will never feel the full extent unless you allow people in. Love may be what's most important, but vulnerability is what's needed to experience its full magnificence."

After a short pause, he says, "Be proud of the life you're building and the accomplishments you have achieved. Progression is filled with a new enthusiasm, unmatched to any I have ever seen. The change was necessary. Thank you." Jonathan looks into my eyes for a few seconds, proving his sincerity as if I would ever question it.

"I must be going," he says as he looks over my shoulder, "but I wanted to say a proper goodbye. Again, thank you for all you have done. I waited many years for your arrival so Progression could, once again, function as it was meant to. I look forward to our time together in the future."

I accept Jonathan's handshake, but consider the probability, or rather, impossibility, that he actually could have foreseen the events that took place. "I'm almost tempted to say you miraculously orchestrated all of this."

His grin reaches his eyes. "I am not especially proficient in the Orchestra. Miracles, however, I quite enjoy.

I smile because the guy is just so darn likeable. "You're really something."

"You think I'm something? Wait until you meet my father." Jonathan gives me a wink and steps toward the Jeep. "It's refreshing to see Tate doing so well. Between you and me, all of that black clothing never matched her personality. I do prefer seeing her in brighter colors."

"Thank you for giving me another chance with her."

Jonathan looks at me over his shoulder and waves. "Don't blow it."

I promise him that I won't.

"Hey babe, you'll never guess what kind of candy they had in there!"

I turn as the convenience store door swings closed behind Tate. She walks towards me, shaking two boxes of Lemon Heads. Jonathan's right. The pink sundress makes her look radiant.

Remembering Jonathan, I'm not shocked when I spin around to see that both he and the Jeep are gone.

Tate climbs into the driver's seat, leans over, and kisses me like she means it.

After the click of her seatbelt and the rumble of the truck's engine turning over, Tate says, "Maryland, here we come!"

Epilogue

"Oh, would you just look at them," Willow says, leaning her head on Troy's shoulder. "Of course they'd pick this lake."

Troy turns to Willow, making her head fall from its perch on him. "Wait, this is *the* lake?"

"One and the same."

"Huh." Troy rubs his chin and slowly scans the area. "Bet you never thought you'd be visiting them here like this."

"Not in a million years. She has his eyes."

"You say that every time you see her."

"Because it's true. I'm glad. His eyes have always been one of his best features. And paired with Tate's pouty lips, she is one beautiful little girl."

"Hurry, you've got one!" Grant yells to the two-year-old girl running towards him.

"She's coming as fast as she can." Tate jogs behind, nervously holding her arms on either side of the toddler.

"I think it's a big one!" Grant wrestles with the bent pole after pulling it from the orange pole holder staked in the ground.

"Honey! Wait a sec!" Tate says to the girl, and then to Grant, "Can't you see she's not very stable yet?"

Willow squeezes Troy's arm and leans into his ear. "This oughta be good."

"Babe. She's been walking for a year."

"I know, but she's wearing new shoes and this ground isn't level."

"And her mom's a bit overprotective," Grant says back, grinning.

Willow smiles. "The kid never disappoints."

"I am not!" Tate says when she and the toddler have almost reached him.

Kneeling down, Grant smiles up at Tate. "It's a big one!" he says to the little girl, helping her spin the handle on the reel.

Willow twirls one of the beads on her dreadlock. "Aren't they adorable?"

Troy squeezes Willow's arm. "That they are."

Beside the truck, Willow and Troy watch the family as the little girl pulls in a two pound bass.

"Oh my gosh! Look at that fish! Good job, honey!" Tate cheers.

Grant smacks a kiss on the girl's cheek. "That's my little fisherman!"

Tate pulls her phone from her pocket. "Look over here! Let me get a picture." She holds the phone out in front of her. "You're not helping!" she says to Grant while he makes fish faces at their catch.

Grant laughs. "OK, fine. Honey, look at mommy so she can take your thousandth photo this week!"

"Hey, you'll be glad for these pictures when she's older."

Willow nudges Troy. "He really will."

Tate waves an arm over her head while trying to steady the phone. "Over here! Willow, look at Mommy and say cheese!"

Troy squeezes Willow tighter.

Willow smiles up at him. "I gotta admit, the kid's got a great name. Let's just hope she's not as stubborn as her dad."

"Or, as stubborn as her namesake."

"Hey!" Willow's laughter echoes and then fades as the purple contrail cuts higher into the clear sky, chasing behind the neon green streak like a bottle rocket.

The End.

Acknowledgments

The Satellite series came to me during a time in my life when I really needed a positive diversion. I have no doubt God was doing some serious divine intervention. The real Heaven is surely bigger than my imagination, but I had a lot of fun daydreaming about Progression. I thank God for giving me this story when He did, and for proving He is always full of surprises if we listen.

To Dan, I'm am grateful that you always have my back when things get tough. You continue to cheer me on and I couldn't do this without you. Our boys are blessed with a dad who is not only present, but a faithful role model as well. I am so lucky to have you.

Alec, Ben, and Will, you guys are the reason I stayed the course on this venture. Aunt Dawn said you would read this story someday, and that really does mean the world to me. Always know that with hard work and dedication, you can do anything! I can't imagine this crazy life without the three of you.

To Mom, Dad, Heather, Linda, Mary, Lisa, Karen, Wendy, Sherry, Shelly, Dawn, Kelly, Candace, Brenda, and Angela Jo: thank you all for continuing to ask about Legacy. You've kept me in check by asking and I've been looking forward to the day I can answer, "It's available!" So, finally, "It's available!" Whew, that feels good! And to Russ, I owe you for the perfect gears.

Debi, my brilliant editor, I'm grateful you jumped on board again for Legacy. I value your opinion, which has been spot-on. You push me to be a better writer, and I appreciate you. Kelli, I've said it before: your knack for finding typos is scary-good. Scary, because you still manage to find errors after dozens of edits; and good, because you still manage to find errors after dozens of edits! I'm glad you and your eyes are on my team.

A HUGE shout out to the fans of this series! I'm shocked by the outpour of support I've been given. My sincere apologies for the delayed release of this final installment. I had no idea how much daily life would derail this adventure. I hope you enjoyed the story as much as I enjoyed writing it.

Thank you to each and every one of you reading this. Truly. I am blessed.

About the Author

Lee lives in Missouri with her husband and three sons. She received a BFA with a Graphic Design emphasis from Lindenwood University in 2000. She spends her days as a graphic designer for a billboard company that makes having a day job not so terrible. You can usually find Lee hanging out with her boys—preferably by a body of water, hidden behind her laptop, or conversing with her dog, Dixie. Satellite, Lee's first novel, was selected as a quarterfinalist in the 2012 Amazon Breakthrough Novel Award contest. Visit www.leedavidson.net for social media links, book updates, and more.

Made in the USA
Middletown, DE
20 September 2022

10756665R00246